BUFFOLE

'BUFF-OH-LEE'

Hells Lefse

America Star Books
Frederick, Maryland

Second printing

All characters in this book are fictitious, and any resemblance to real persons, living or dead, is coincidental.

America Star Books has allowed this work to remain exactly as the author intended, verbatim, without editorial input.

Softcover 9781627720830
PUBLISHED BY AMERICA STAR BOOKS, LLLP
www.americastarbooks.pub
Frederick, Maryland

DEDICATION

This book is dedicated to my canine partners Sven, Lena and Tesse whose love and inspiration are my life's savior. Never to be forgotten and always remembered is my other inspiration Einer and his human.

DISCLAIMER

To all or any of you who happen to read this book please take note that Hells Lefse does the proof reading. Any errors are either unintentional or intentional depending on the mood he is in. If you think that any fictional character in this book resembles you then that would mean that you are also fictional. If you find any spelling, grammar or fictional character mishaps please address your comments, complaints or praise directly to Hells.

OTHER BOOKS BY HELLS LEFSE
Dogpire
Dogoyles
SvenSagas
Zomdoggie
Drogons
Booger Fairy

CHAPTER 0

PUPPYLUDE. All good Norwegian Sagas need a special introduction. This Saga is no different. The puppy tails and human Sagas of Sven and Ole are now becoming legend. You need only to look back at the Sagas contained in the Hells Lefse books Dogpire, Dogoyles, SvenSagaS, Zomdoggie, Drogons and Booger Fairy.

This is a story of the Wild West. An American tradition. A place where myth and legend often combine to blur the truth between fact and fiction. It was a time when there were good men, bad men, strong women and loose women, heroes and villains and many, many who have been forgotten to history whose lives ended on lonesome prairies from starvation, Indians, animal attacks, desperadoes, bad luck and maybe even loneliness.

This story is told by me Sven the computer savvy, human communicating, good looking Shih Tzu dog. It has my long ago relatives Sven and Ole as the main characters. It seems all my relatives were named Sven and Ole so it makes telling these Sagas much easier.

You may want to call the family together and read this in front of a warm glowing fire place in the comfort of your home. Or better yet find a secluded site in the wilderness. Gather some dry leaves and very dry wood and make a smokeless fire that way you won't attract the attention of renegade Indians or desperados. You can make some 'smores if you want to add a little modernity to life. Better yet just heat up some strong black coffee grab a chunk of jerky and enjoy this book.

The story is called Buffole. Pronounced Buff-oh-lee. Make sure you read this right or nothing from this point on will make any sense. You are about to meet a Wild West Legend. There will be bloodshed, death and action galore. There is even a little romance tossed in for our women readers. You may want to skip the really bad parts if you are reading to young children. Our young ones have enough problems caused by today's politicians and lawyers without adding any other undue stress to their lives.

I am the keeper of the Sagas and Hells Lefse does the typing and editing. So if you find any errors he may claim they are intentional to keep you on your toes and give you something special to look for. In reality Hells Lefse is just human. So if you find errors or you think some character may resemble you, well you can go to Hells.

CHAPTER 1

The Civil War was over. Ole and Sven had been with the Minnesota Volunteers at Bull Run and also at Gettysburg. They had seen enough death and destruction to last a lifetime. Ole felt good to be back on the dairy farm his Norwegian grandfather had started when he first came to Minnesota from the old country. His grandfather had died when Ole was young but he remembered that the old man said Minnesota was the closest thing he could find to his native Norway. He loved it here and hoped that the dairy farm would be passed on from generation to generation. For Ole this was somewhat of a problem. His older brother would be next in line to inherit the property after their father passed away. This left Ole and his family in a position as the farm help in the family. That seemed fine for years until Ole went off to war. He had seen a lot of the country from the east coast to the southern states and it caused an itch in him to want to see more. The west was wide open for people wanting to start new lives. The railroads were heading that way to open the country to settlers. Ole, his wife and fifteen year old son would soon decide to join countless thousands who would take flight to a new unsettled promised land.

Ole and Sven could communicate with each other which is of course unusual for a dog and a human and after a long discussion they both decided a move to the west was a good idea. Ole approached his wife and son with the idea of moving west. It did not take long for them all to agree this would be in the best interest for all concerned. Ole's father and his brother and family could continue the tradition of passing down the farm to the eldest son.

The extended family ate all their meals together and it was at one of these meals that Ole brought up the move to the rest of the family. His father was reluctant to let one of his sons go on such a perilous and unknown journey. Ole's brother was of course in favor of the idea. Of course it would mean more work but in the long run his brother knew he would be better off with his younger sibling out of the way.

Dale the older brother mentioned that he heard about a small wagon train forming for a journey west. Dale liked to think of himself as a religious man except when it came to increasing his own personal fortunes. Helping his younger brother on his way west was certainly within the boundaries of being in his best interest. Dale encouraged his fellow parishioners to urge their more 'pagan' members of the community to join up on the western pilgrimage. What better way to eliminate the unbelievers from their ranks. Dale figured Ole and his family were prime candidates for his congregation to urge out of their midst.

Ole started to ask around town about the wagon train that was supposed to be forming for a western trek. He finally got a lead that the head scout for the journey was a frontiersmen by the name of Dancer. Dancer he was told was easily recognizable by an ever present cigar in his mouth. If he was not out hunting or trapping or just wandering he would most likely be at the Rapids Saloon next to the Mississippi river.

Ole made his way to the Saloon. It was situated on a rocky outcropping of granite which overlooked the swirling rapids of the river as they cascaded over the boulders and made their way to New Orleans. The building had a weather beaten look about it. Occasional spring floods had left their stain marks on the walls. The years of each flood were written in black letters on the stained water lines like a catastrophic history book. The louvered batwing doors were open to the suns warmth on this particular day. The heavy solid oak doors were latched open inside the saloon waiting for the day when fall and winter winds would require their use. The windows were open and a warm breeze circulated the normally stale smoke and liquor filled smell from the room.

Ole entered through the batwing doors and a few of the regulars at the bar looked his way. Another local man at a corner table was doing his best in an inebriated way to impress the local bar girl. It was mid-afternoon and the place was on the empty side as far as customers were concerned. Most of the regulars were working jobs or farming and would not show up until evening. One table caught Ole's eye. Sven was waiting outside and he peeked under the swinging doors to see how Ole was doing. Ole approached a table with five men sitting around having a drink and talking. A tell tale cigar in one man's mouth was an indication that this might just be the person Ole and I were looking for.

Ole walked over and introduced himself. "Good afternoon gentleman, my name's Ole, that little dog peeking under the doors over there is Sven. I was wondering if one of you might be a man named Dancer."

The man with the steely grey eyes and shoulder length dirty blonde hair looked hard at Ole before he spoke. "I'm Dancer, what do you and your dog want? The dog comment brought chuckles from everyone in the saloon. Ole and Sven were partners in the best sense of the word and the comment did not faze either one of them.

"I've heard you might be getting a wagon train organized for a westward trek. I would like to sign my family, Sven my dog and me up to go with you."

"Have a seat mister you've come at just the right time. Call Sven in here to join us."

The bartender looked over at the table as Sven trotted into the barroom and jumped up on an empty chair next to Ole. "No mangy mutts are allowed in this bar. Get that mutt out of here."

Dancer rested his hand on the handle of the large skinning knife that was in the sheath of his belt. He looked directly into the bartender's eyes as he spoke. "The dog was invited in here by me. He's a might better then the majority of your customers. If you know what's best you will let him stay. In fact I think maybe you should bring Ole and Sven a SvenBrew beer, make sure you put Sven's drink in a bowl for him. While you're at it you can fill up the rest of the table with drinks too."

The bartender saw Dancer's hand resting on the pommel of his knife. He knew from past experience in this very Saloon of his that Dancer was extremely proficient with his blade. Under the circumstances he felt it best to serve the men and the dog at the table and leave the matter of whether dogs belonged in a saloon or not to a different time.

Ole went to pull some money from his pocket but was stopped short when Dancer spoke. "Mr. Besser's buying the drinks tonight boys no need for us to spend our hard earned money. Ole and Sven you two arrived just in time. Our meeting was just about to start. Mr. Besser called these fine gentlemen together to arrange a wagon train to the west. This little pow-wow was set up by me as the hired scout of this expedition. Seeing none of you have been west before my job will be to keep you all alive until you reach your destinations. I ain't gonna make no promises about keeping ya all alive but I will do my darndest best to do so. I think it best you all introduce yourselves to each other. Mr. Besser as the founder of this train should probably start out telling us where he plans on going. He will be the captain of the wagon train, but hear me clear I am the leader as far as where we go, when we go, when we stop. You best listen to me or all of you might end up dead. Now Mr. Besser you can have the floor."

"For any of you who have not heard of me my name is Korn Besser and to my right is my son Lake. We have a ranch just east of here and we raise quarter horses for riding and more importantly to us for racing. I have got two Minnesota champions right now and I expect to take a lot more championships in the future. I decided to move some of my best stock to Texas. My wife, son and I will take a small herd of my best horses with us and start a new ranch when we arrive at our destination. I've got a few cowboys to ride herd on my stock. My son and I are both accomplished game hunters and Lake here can shot a bow and arrow better than any Indian. I hope to get at least five more wagons to join up so that we have a half dozen in our group plus my stock of horses. Dancer will lead the wagon train and do the scouting. I and my family will head south when Mr. Dancer advises us to. The rest of the train can come with us or keep heading west. I have arranged for Mr. Dancer to stay with whichever party has the most wagons when it comes time for us to split off. Mr. Kund would you like to tell us about your wagon and its occupants?"

"My wife and I are heading west to start a new life. I spent three years fighting for the Confederacy and the people here don't take to kindly to a rebel living in their midst. I figure the west is a place where a man can make a fresh start. I'll take care of me and my own just fine without asking for help from others."

The next man at the table picked up the conversation after Mr. Kund ended his introduction. "I'm Mr. Anderson, I'll be traveling with my wife and sixteen year old son Trapis. My boy has been in a little trouble with the military. They accused him of being a spy but he assures me it's a false accusation. Never the less I feel it best for us to leave the past and false accusations behind and start a new life in the west."

"I'm Henry Eichmann, my wife and I are expecting our first child in a few months. I know this is not the best time for us to take a trek like this. Both of us have an adventurous spirit and we have been honing our skills for many years in expectation of just such a journey. We have been camping, living off the land, rock climbing and canoeing to build ourselves into the best woods persons we feel we can be. We are prepared for this trip and we want to continue all the way to Oregon to start a new life for our family. My parents have already made the journey and they are expecting us so we will have a good start in the land we have chosen."

"My name is Casey. I will be traveling alone with a wagon full of store goods. I'm not sure how far I will be traveling. I hope to find an area I can set up shop and make a living. The west needs storekeepers, people to supply the goods for the settlers. I plan to be one of those people."

Dancer looked at Sven and Ole. "What's your reason for wanting to join our little wagon train?"

"Well it is sort of one of those age old stories. My father and his father's before him believe that any property and wealth should be handed down to the first born son. Being the second born son leaves me with nothing. If I stay with my family I become a slave to my brother. My brother already has a son and this means even if he should pass away his son would inherit everything. Once again I would be left with nothing. My only hope for my family is to leave all this behind and start a new life. A life where my children will be equal to receive whatever properties or fortune I may accumulate in my lifetime. Building a new life in the west seems to be my best hope. Sven and I would be grateful if all of you would accept us into your wagon train."

Besser asked Ole the next question. "So what skills can you offer us as a member of our party?"

"I'm dependable as my dog Sven. I have experience in defending this country from my time in the Minnesota first regiment. I have been in a number of battles during the Civil War most notably my service with my regiment at the Battle of Gettysburg. Sven was there with me and he served as company mascot. He was of great assistance after the battle in helping to track down and locate our surviving wounded soldiers. Loyalty and protecting those who I care about would be my strong points."

Dancer took a shot of whiskey and downed it with a beer chaser. He rubbed the stubble on his chin and sat back in his chair. "All of you sound like you have your own valid reasons for making this journey. I'm gonna tell ya something and you best all listen well. This trip ain't gonna be no picnic in the park. Some of you might not make it to where you want to go. Some of you may die of fever, be drowned in a swollen river, get hit by lighting, or lose your scalp to Indians. Even the white man who may look to be a Christian might rob and murder you just for the goods or money he thinks you might have. Besser you especially best think it over. Running prime horse stock in rugged country just invites Injun's and rustlers like a bear to honey. So all of you think hard before you sign on. I made my deal with Besser, he's my boss and he pays my wages till he cuts me loose. Here's a list of provisions for your wagons to be loaded with. He tossed a paper on the table listing food, flour, coffee, sugar, and dried fruit. Remember you can't have too much food with you. Water barrels will need to be filled every time we come to a water source. All the do-dads like furniture and fancy items ain't gonna help you survive when food runs low and animals to eat become scarce. Make sure you got a good rifle, a few handguns, lots of ammunition and some good hunting and skinning knives. If you all still want to go make your deal with Besser. We will be pulling out in five days. Oxen is best for pulling the wagons, mules is all right and both can be mighty tasty if we run low on meat. Horses may do in a pinch but they ain't good for long term wagon pulling especially when we hit the dry areas and the mountains." Dancer pushed his chair away from the table and walked away.

We finished making arrangements with Besser and Ole paid him the fee for our journey. Dancer left us a lot to think about and Ole knew he had to be truthful with his wife and son about the dangers that lie ahead of us. We were a family and everyone must agree that we try for a new life in the West.

CHAPTER 2

Ole told Kate his wife what had transpired at the saloon. He had shook hands with Besser and the bargain was struck. Kate was very happy at the prospect of starting a new life and getting out from under the yoke of Ole's older brother. Their son Zebulon was sad that he would have to leave his friends. Ole explained to them what a grand adventure they would be having and that seemed to help. I also heard Zebulon tell his friends that there were no schools where he was going so he figured he was heading out for a grand life without books and teachers. Little did he know that his mother was very well educated and she would be stocking the wagon with educational materials to make sure young Zeb would grow to be a learned man.

The next day Ole and I went shopping for a wagon. The local blacksmith had a beautiful Conestoga wagon for sale at his shop. He had partnered with a Mr. Hammerbeck who did all the wood work on the wagon and Mr. Alexander the blacksmith made all the iron fittings and wheels. The wagon was almost a work of art. Mr. Alexander also had a good choice of Oxen to pick from and I could see we were in for a long day of dickering over the price. I finally lay down in the shade and took a nap while Ole and the blacksmith made their deal. I heard Ole call my name and I awoke to see him sitting on the wagon with two huge oxen yoked and ready to go. Tied behind the wagon were two more oxen and an extra yoke for the wagon was slashed to the underside of the wagons bottom. It was too high to jump up so Mr. Alexander picked me up and tossed me to Ole. "Well Sven here we go. I bought two oxen for the lead and two extras for when the going gets rough. The day will be ending soon best we take our rig home and show the family. Tomorrow we'll buy supplies."

When morning came Ole hitched up the buckboard and Kate, Zeb and I all got on board for the trip to town. Our town was quite progressive once you hit the main street. It had cobblestone roads and even a horse drawn trolley that consisted of five full miles of track. Ole, Zeb and I made our way to the town grocer for salt, flour, coffee, dried fruits and even some sugar. We were buying goods by the sack full and of course it drew the attention of the town gossips. You could hear the old ladies and even a few of the men whispering to each other.

"Well I guess Ole is finally getting kicked out by his brother."

"I bet Ole's old man cut him off, you know he went off to war and left the family shorthanded."

"Bet their pulling out, that wife of his always was rather domineering, I'm sure the family will be well shed of her,"

"Ole and his wife and kid never really did fit in to the church. They always had that idea that God loves 'em all and ya all don't need organized religion as long as you believe. Good riddance to that family."

Ole and Zeb ignored the snide comments that were made just loud enough for us to hear. As for me I snarled at a few of the town gossips as we left the store. The owner wheeled out our purchases on a two wheel handcart and deposited them on the wooden side walk. Ole and Zeb loaded our goods into the wagon as I kept a wary eye on the busy body townsfolk.

We had just finished loading when Kate showed up with baskets full of cloth and sewing goods. She told Ole that he and Zeb would need good strong clothes for the trip. She even had new boots for both the guys. The baskets contained nice white cloth to make bandages plus some bottles of laudanum and herbs for injuries or sickness that may occur. Of course none of us wanted to think about the bad things that could happen to any of us. Once the buckboard was loaded Ole suggested the family should take time for a celebration treat. It might be a long time before any of us would get a chance at a store bought meal.

There was a new store in town that some fella from out east had just opened. It served sandwiches and for desert it offered a delicacy called ice cream. None of us had ever tasted ice cream and Ole felt the family deserved this special treat. Ole told the proprietor that even though I was a dog I was part of the family and I went wherever they went so if he wanted the business from Ole's family well then I was part of the family and would dine with the family. The place was empty except for us and the proprietor had enough business sense to let us have a table and serve us our lunch. The ice cream was smooth and cold sort of like frozen milk in a pail but much creamier, we all liked it. Ole paid our bill and we took a leisurely wagon ride home. Ole pointed out all the sights that seemed so familiar yet would soon be just a distant memory as we left our home and headed west.

The next few days Kate, Ole, Zeb and I spent packing the Conestoga wagon. Everything had to be fitted and made secure in the least amount of space. Kate wanted to bring a fancy wood writing desk that was her mothers and Ole had a German free swinger pendulum clock that his parents had given them for a wedding gift. Other than those two frivolous items our packing was kept to the essentials. Of course Zeb did not feel that the trunk full of books was needed yet Kate insisted as these would be the only learning materials available for a long time. Ole agreed with a hint of selfishness to himself as he was an avid reader. Many nights Ole would read out loud to the whole family and I must admit I rather enjoyed our book reading evenings together.

The day for us to leave was coming quickly. Zeb went to see all of his friends as did Kate. Ole and I were sort of loners so we only had a few close friends to bid farewell to. Most of our goodbyes went to a tinkerer named Kilroy. We spent a half day with him and he showed us some of the mechanical marvels he was inventing or working on. It was a nice day for us and after a few SvenBrew beers Ole gave his old buddy a bear hug and I gave Kilroy a lick on the cheek. Tomorrow we would be on the road for our westward adventure.

We spent the evening with Ole's parents and his brother along with his family. Kate's parents and brothers and sisters plus a gaggle of kids were also present. It was like a thanksgiving feast. Some of those in attendance I am sure were giving thanks that we were leaving. Ole's father gave a toast to our departing. "To my youngest son and his wife Kate and of course my grandson Zebulon I pray that God be with you in your endeavors." I of course felt a bit slighted that he did not mention me in his toast, but I guess he meant well and after all he is getting on in years and might be a little senile which would tend to let me forgive him for not mentioning me.

After our meal the family got together and mingled and visited. It was nearing bed time and the guests had left for the night while a few of our far away visitors bedded down in the barn. Ole's father pulled him aside and led him to his workshop in the farms blacksmith shop. He pulled a fancy wooden box from a high shelf and handed it to Ole. "Son, I have had this in my possession for a few years now. I bought it for protection when I first settled the farm here. The country was still wild and Indians occasionally came to our door for handouts, and sometimes just to see if we were afraid of them. I learned from the old timers not to show fear to an Indian or he would think you were weak. Next thing you know he might just kill you and take whatever he wanted. So in those early days I carried this to protect my family. Now that you are heading out on your own it may come in handy. This land is settled now and I no longer have a need for it. God bless you boy." He said. Ole was now the proud owner of a six shot revolving barrel pepper box handgun. The family coat of arms was carved on each side of the walnut grip. It was a Viking ship with a horse riding Cossack on its sail. The Cossack had his arm raised and was wielding a sword as his cape seemed to flow with the wind. The leather belt and holster were dark brown and made as a shoulder strap to conceal the gun under your coat. The holster itself had the same scene as the gun handle etched onto its side. It was it little outdated for the times but still a very impressive and most likely a very useful gift for our journey.

I asked Ole before we went off to bed just what he planned to use for protection on the trail. He took me to the sitting room of our house and he walked over to the fireplace. Getting down on his knees he removed a large stone from the back corner of the fireplace. The stone slid out onto the floor as he pulled on it. Behind the stone was a box in a cubby hole which contained our emergency savings for our trip west and also another box and a canvas bundle. Ole unrolled the canvas to show me a hand tooled brown leather gun belt he had saved from his time in the Union army. Next he opened the box and carefully unwrapped from the cloth cover inside a very unusual handgun which I sort of remembered seeing when we were traveling with Ole's Minnesota regiment.

Ole took the gun out and held it in both palms of his hands so I could see it. "Sven I never told you this as things got a little hectic at times when we were in the war. I got it from a Confederate Officer that surrendered to me during the battle of Gettysburg. I treated him well and guaranteed his safety as a prisoner of war even though some of the Union boys wanted to string him up for leading a charge that killed so many of our men. He told me we had beaten him and his men fair and square and he just hated to see his handgun got tossed into a pile of confiscated weapons. He gave it to me as a gift as long as I promised not to use it against any Confederate troops. I gave him my word and I packed it away with my traveling kit. After I came home I put it in here and sort of forgot all about it until now."

This just so happens to be a late model Le Mat Confederate pistol. The first models were not as useful as they used .41 caliber bullets which were hard to find so most of the time the men that had these had to make their own ammunition. This one was upgraded to use standard .45 caliber ammunition which I can buy almost anywhere. One of the advantages to this gun is it is a nine shot instead of the standard six shot like most revolvers are. Now for the kicker you see that bigger barrel there." He held the gun so I could get a good look at it. "That big barrel is for a .20 gauge slug or a load of buckshot. It acts as a small version of a shot gun. This was not a weapon you wanted to come up against when you were in battle with the Confederates. Luckily for the Union army only a couple thousand made it from France where most of them were made through the union blockades. The early ones were not real reliable but the latter ones like this had to go through the United Kingdom and be checked before they were sent here. See this little stamp on the gun it's from the Birmingham Proof House which did the quality check before it was shipped to the

Confederate States. I think if we need a sidearm out west this will give us ample fire power. What do you think partner."

"Very impressive." Was all I could say.

The morning brought sunshine and heat. It had been unseasonably hot for the last week. Temperatures soared into the eighty's and nineties everyday and the rains had been scarce. Kate and Ole finished loading the wagon while Zeb and I supervised. This was to be our last day at the old farm and tomorrow we would be joining the wagon train west.

Four in the morning and it was stifling hot and the humidity was so high that Ole was sweating so profusely that his eyes burned from the salty drops of perspiration that ran down off his forehead. As for me I finally laid in the shade of the wagon and panted to my heart's content. Ole was busy hooking up the ox team to the front of the wagon and Zeb was tying the extra oxen and two riding horses to the back of the wagon. Kate was double checking everything to make sure we had not forgotten anything. Being the last to sign on for the trip we would start out as the last wagon in our group. Each day the wagons would rotate so that everyone would change position. Being last meant putting up with the dust from the lead wagons and was by far the least desirable position to be in.

The oxen were hitched up and we were ready to leave the home we were so accustomed to. Ole's father and mother were there to send us off. Handshakes, hugs and kisses goodbye were passed around. At the last minute Ole's brother, and his wife and children appeared. I figured they were glad to be shed of us and didn't really care what happed from this point on. Ole's brother had a tear in his eye and he and Ole hugged goodbye. I was near enough to see Ole's brother slip five hundred dollars into Ole's hand to help us along the way. It was a nice gesture, yet in my own mind is not love and family more important than money? Kate and her sister-in-law hugged and cried. Zeb shook hands with his two male cousins and acted every bit the grown up as he wished them goodbye. Ole and Kate mounted the wagon and sat on the hard wooden seat as Zeb and I peered out from between them. Ole's family gave us a God Bless and farewell. Ole urged the oxen on as we slowly went down the road.

We had one more stop to make. Kate's parents, brothers and sisters were up and waiting for us. Once again everyone made their farewells and Kate's mother pressed two hundred dollars into Kate's hand. For Kate's family that was a lot of money. They had never been well off and the gesture was much appreciated by all of us. Ole whispered to Kate that he would like to give them their money back. She said they would be offended if we did that so we left well enough alone.

We entered the street near an old saloon called Brickey's. This was a rather seedy side of town which was obvious by the small one room cabins that were located near Brickey's Saloon. Ole whispered to me that the soiled doves would take their clients there to satisfy their manly urges. In other words it was like a small city of miniature brothels.

This was where Dancer was assembling our wagon train. The Besser wagon was in the front, followed by Kund, Anderson, Eichmann, Casey and finally us. Besser's two horse wranglers were just out of town on some open fields waiting to fall in behind us with a dozen handpicked quarter horses. Dancer told us the small herd of horses would be following the end wagon until we moved out onto the prairies. The horse's then might be in the lead as they could move faster with Korn's wranglers and it would give the horse's a better chance to feed along the way. The wranglers figured to keep a few miles ahead of the wagon train which would also make the trail easier for us to follow when Dancer was out scouting ahead of us. A few cows had been mixed in with the horse stock to supply meat for the trip.

The sun was rising in the east and Dancer gave the standard 'wagons ho' shout as he waved his hat in the air to begin our journey. Just as the wagons began to move a late comer pulled up and joined us. Ole's and my old friend Kilroy had set himself up a nice wagon rig and pulled in behind us.

CHAPTER 3

We made good time as we crossed the Minnesota prairies. The wagon trains before us had made a well marked although rather bumpy trail for us to follow. The prairie grass was still green and proved to be good forage for the animals. The trail was rut filled and dusty in the dry heat. Being in the last wagon we soon came to appreciate why being the lead wagon would be advantageous.

The first day seemed almost exciting. We left civilization as we knew it and made our way on to the prairie grass. Lunch was eaten as we moved. Some jerky, bread and water were what would sustain us until supper time. When Dancer signaled for the wagon train to stop he had us pull the wagons into a circle with the livestock in the center. For our first try at circling wagons we did not do to badly. Yet Dancer barked out that we should be doing much better.

Dancer was giving orders and seemed to be everywhere at once. Tonight was just a practice for things to come. The wagons were circled for protection from Indians who might wish to sneak up on us. The livestock was to be kept inside the circle to protect it from Indians, thieves and animal predators. The first thing to be done after the wagons were circled was to unhitch the teams and groom and feed our livestock. The animal's good health and strength might mean life or death for all of us as the going became rougher. The women gathered wood and made a communal fire for cooking. The younger members gathered wood for the fire. Guns and ammo were to be checked and kept in good order every night. The dust and grime from traveling could wreck havoc on our weapons. Wagon loads, water barrels and wagons themselves were to be checked over every night. All of these things could mean the difference of life or death for any of us as we traveled into the dangers of the unknown west.

As the days passed the novelty of wagon train life quickly wore off. We had made our way to the Dakota territories and the seas of prairie grass flowed like the undulating waves of the ocean. Dancer was often out of sight and scouting a trail for us. Just crossing a small stream would sometimes take us miles out of our way. For what appeared to be a trickle of water would often have banks so high the wagons could not traverse them. Dancer told us that a sudden summer thunderstorm could turn a small stream into a raging torrent eroding the streams banks and tearing up brush and trees as it rushed it's way to the next big river and then on to the ocean. It seemed hard to believe that the water we saw would someday be the same water that a great sailing ship would be using to cross the worlds seas.

By now the nightly chores had become routine for all of us. Zeb and the Anderson's boy Trapis were becoming friends. They liked to pretend they were gunslingers protecting our wagon train from Indians and marauding outlaws. Each night all the members of our train sat around the campfire to discuss the next day's plans. Dancer was usually there to give us hints as to what to expect. Occasionally he had wandered far enough ahead of the train on his scouting missions that we would not see him until morning.

The journey ahead would be devoid of trees and Dancer had everyone hook canvas slings under their wagons. The humans who were not driving wagons or tending to stock had to walk along the wagon train and pick up dried buffalo chips which we would be using for fuel. Once there was a canvas sack full of chips it would be dumped into the sling under the wagon. I ran ahead of Kate and Zeb and smelled out the chips before they got to them to make their jobs of finding them easier. It sounds strange but those chips do burn very well. Being a dog I saw nothing wrong with food cooked over buffalo dung and dried grass. Most of the humans seemed all right with the arrangement. It was certainly better then not having a fire or hot food.

It was near noon when I noticed a speck on a far away hill that seemed to move along with our wagon train. I mentioned it to Ole and he pulled a pair of binoculars from the saddlebags that were behind him in the wagon. He handed the reins of the team to Kate and tried to shield his movements from Zeb who was walking ahead of us and helping to keep the oxen in line. Looking through the binoculars Ole could make out a lone figure on a horse. The man had long braided hair, buckskin pants and no shirt. The horse he rode was a paint pony with just a blanket on its back and no saddle. Ole had never seen a real live Indian, but he had seen pictures of Indians and this sure looked like an Indian.

He whispered to Kate his suspicions and told her not to tell Zeb. He figured it best not to get Zeb or anyone else in the wagon train upset just in case the Indian was friendly or maybe the Indian had not even seen the wagons. Ole made his way to one of our spare horses that was tied to the back of our wagon and saddled up. I wanted to go with him and having rather short legs Ole was prone to leave me behind. Of course I told him he would never have noticed the Indian if it was not for my keen eyesight. He grabbed me with one hand and deposited me in one of the saddlebags. I sat up with my two front legs hanging over the edge of the saddlebag with my head up and alert for any dangers we might encounter. Ole put his heels to the horse and we sped off to find Dancer.

Ole pulled our horse up along the lead wagon, Mr. Anderson was leading today and seemed content to just plod along on the trail Dancer had marked for us. Ole did his best to look calm and not worried. Mr. Anderson looked our way. "Ole I don't often see you on horseback. Are you getting bored of driving the wagon or just need some time away from the wife and kid?"

"None of that Mr. Anderson, I just wanted to give my horse a little bit of exercise, he's a good horse and he likes an occasional run, being tied to a wagon and prodding along day after day hurts his spirit. Thought maybe I'd ride on up ahead and see if I can find Dancer. I might just learn a thing or two about finding and reading trails. You have any idea how long he's been gone?

"I saw him an hour or two ago. You know how he is sort of the quiet type, don't say much. He just rode on ahead like he always does."

Well I think I'll let this old horse have his head and let 'em run for awhile. Maybe I'll run into Dancer and get me some good frontier training. You keep an eye out for anything unusual ya hear?"

Ole put his heels to the horse and we were off in a flash. I was on the Indian sighting side of the horse and I kept my eye on that brave as long as I could. It was about four or five miles before we caught sight of Dancer. He was off his horse and down on one knee. It seemed to Ole and I that he was examining something on the ground mighty closely.

Ole pulled up on the reins of the horse and stopped us a few yards from Dancer. For a moment Dancer just kept studying the ground before him. Finally he looked at us.

"I saw your dust coming mighty fast this way. You made enough commotion to wake up the entire Indian nation. Just what happens to be your reason for comin' out here and leaving your family and the wagon train short one man and one watch dog?"

"Sven, I mean I saw an Indian and he seemed to be shadowing the wagon train. There was only one so there should not be anything to worry about. Right?"

"Right. You said Right? Ole you got a lot to learn about Indians. They don't travel alone, if there's one there's more somewhere nearby. I was just studying their tracks. I'd venture to say we got us about a half dozen young bucks and there looking to score themselves some loot and maybe a scalp or two. The Sioux ain't none too happy about white men invading their territory. They been lied to and cheated by us whites to many times, best to figure they owe us our come up uns. We best hurry back to the wagons and warn the others to be prepared."

Dancer tore ahead of us as he raced his horse back towards the wagon train. Ole did his best to keep up but his horsemanship was not up to snuff with the well seasoned Dancer and his mount. The dust flowed behind us like billowing clouds and we made good time. Once the wagons were in sight Dancer slowed to a trot. Everything looked to be normal and if so he did not want to alarm anyone in the wagon train unnecessarily.

Dancer made a slow round of the wagons to make sure everything was secure and in place. All the while he kept an eye on the surrounding landscape for signs of a probable ambush. Ole and I returned to our wagon and tied our horse to the back, leaving its saddle on just in case we needed to have a mount ready for protection in case the Indians decided to attack us. Ole figured it would be better if he was on horseback with Dancer to ride interference so that the wagons would have time to gather into a defensive circle during an attack.

Dancer circled the wagons and casually mentioned to the men that we were in Indian country and it would be best to check their weapons and keep them at the ready. We kept going along at a steady pace. The Indian we had seen earlier in the day continued to shadow us.

The time came to make camp and Dancer made sure the wagons were in a tight circle and the live stock was tied and he even had Besser shackle his horse's legs to keep them from being stolen during the night.

Guards were posted throughout the camp and Dancer explained to everyone that Indians preferred not to attack during the night. It was unlikely as long as we were circled and prepared that we would see any action from the Indians. If anything was to happen it would be the attempted theft of livestock. Besser's horses had to look mighty attractive to the braves who were watching us. Ole and I took our turn at guard duty on the last shift before dawn. Tomorrow would be a long day with everyone now aware of the Indians and the men would be tired from doing guard duty during the night. We all knew we had to be alert to any possible attack that might come.

Everyone tried to act normal as we trundled across the prairie. The dust hung still in the calm air as we made our way over the tall dry grass. Dancer rode along the edges of the trail within our view ever alert to any danger. Ole rode the horse as Kate drove the wagon and Zeb sat at the back of the wagon with a rifle near him. Zeb had shot the rifle a few times but was certainly not proficient with it. Come to think of it Ole had some practice target shooting back home with a handgun and occasionally a rifle but the few times I saw him shoot was not a reassuring fact if it came down to protecting us from Indians or any other type of danger. Although I had to think he was a better shot than I might be aware of from our time in the Union army. I was usually left at the main camp when the soldiers went into battle but Ole always came back unscathed and a few times I heard some of the men remark on what a good marksman he was.

When it was time to stop the wagons were circled and the livestock was safe inside. The women of the group were preparing the evening meal. Korn Besser and his son Lake were showing the other men and boys in the group how to handle various weapons. If an attack came our lives would depend on the proficiency our group had in protecting themselves. Rifles, handguns and knives were to be standard accessories for the men folk for the reminder of our time on the trail. Lake had a bow and arrows along that he had designed himself. He showed the men the best way to use them. In an emergency of a jammed gun or rifle or lack of ammunition this training could be useful. A dead or injured Indians bow and arrow could be used against the other attackers. Dancer even showed the men how to throw knives and tomahawks. This training would be like a classroom every night from this point on Dancer told the men. As far as Ole throwing a knife or a tomahawk it seemed to be a futile exercise.

After we had eaten and things were stored away for the night Dancer took the women aside and did similar training with them in protecting themselves and their loved ones. Dancer explained that a western woman was just as important as any man. We were in a land that did not discriminate between good and evil, men and women, or race or religion. In this land everyone had to know how to take care of themselves. Death, disease, storms or accidents did not discriminate. Anyone could be separated from the others and left to their own wits to survive. Food and water were necessities and Dancer started telling us how to find the things we would need to survive. Then he gave a warning. Never trust any other human you see if you are alone and away from civilization. Sure some may be friendly and help you, just as many might look at you, smile and offer to help. Then in an instant they might rape a woman, kill a man or sell a child into slavery. The west could be as vicious as it was beautiful.

Humans call it the Badlands and I could see why. No water, and endless buttes, gullies and hotter than the fires of Hades. I heard Dancer tell the others it was actually given that name by the ancient Indian tribes. It was easy to see that they knew what they were talking about.

We did see a wonder that bewildered and scared me. At first it looked like a dark cloud moving eerily across the prairie. The sight seemed strange as this cloud was at ground level. The closer we came the stranger it seemed. The ground seemed to rumble beneath our feet and a growing mummer like low rolling thunder filled our ears. As we came over a small hill we were close enough to see what the cloud really was. Buffalo or as the Indians called them Tatanka. There must have been thousands of them. Their shaggy coats and beards made them look like four legged frontiersmen who had not seen civilization in years. A few looked our way but the majority took no notice of us. The wagon train stopped and everyone stared at this mighty herd of animals as if it was the most miraculous thing they had ever witnessed.

Dancer rode over by Ole. "Ole grab your rifle we'll kill us a couple of Buff. The meat is great and we can use the hides for blankets." I could see that Ole did not have it in him to just kill an animal as majestic as the buffalo. I think it had something to do with the big bull from the herd that Ole had made eye contact with. He and that bull almost seemed to have an understanding between them. Ole knew we could use the meat but he was more of a scavenger then a hunter. He finally answered Dancer. "Dancer I think I will pass this privilege on to one of the other members of the group." Dancer seemed to take it in stride and rode over to Lake Besser. "Well boy time to show me what you can do. Think you can down a couple of them critters with your bow and arrows. It would be better if we can do it that way. No noise from a gunshot and a lot less likely we might spook them and cause a stampede.

Ole knew we could use the fresh meat yet something in the eyes of the bull buffalo had mesmerized Ole's compassion for the magnificent beasts. The bull knew that humans felt they had a right to destroy other creatures to live. The buffalo on the other hand killed only to protect their young or themselves. Yet that bull buffalo understood that sometimes a few must die for the good of the herd. The weak and sick could not always keep up. That was when the predators would move in for the kill. Even the big bull knew it was better to have a quick death than to suffer a slow miserable death. So for this reason the bull pulled the healthy buffalo toward the center of the herd and left those to old and sick on the outskirts. Lake and Dancer approached the herd from downwind and Lake did what he does best. Two arrows and two dead buffalo. Quick painless deaths. The bull let the herd continue to graze and with a tear in his eye bid farewell to the two buffalo whose lives were sacrificed to save the strong and healthy.

Dancer and Lake skinned out the dead buffalo and cut the meat in to manageable pieces that could be loaded on to their horses. Ole looked on with sadness in his heart. Glancing towards the herd Ole's eyes once again made contact with the majestic bull buffalo. Somehow that buffalo told Ole what had happened was just a part of nature. The two dead buffalo had given their lives to sustain a group of humans. I could sense a connection between Ole and that buffalo much like the connection Ole and I shared. It was a rather spooky thing to witness.

Bubba and Tearhart volunteered to ride guard outside the camp so the rest of us could relax and have a good hot meal of fresh meat. Ole looked at the buffalo meat and the scavenger finally overtook his feelings of remorse for the animal. As for me, well I'm a dog and meat is meat, although I would draw the line at eating another dog that would just be cannibalism.

After our meal everyone helped to get the campsite cleaned up. Kund's wife brought out a guitar from their wagon. She sat on a wooden barrel and began to play and sing softly. As everyone gathered around the group soon had her strumming rhythms to dance to. Dancer even joined in on the action dancing with a few of the wives in the group. Nicole, pregnant as she was even decided to do a fairly fast jig with her husband Henry. Kilroy was more the shy type and he volunteered to take some of our leftover meal out to Bubba and Tearhart. It was the most pleasant night we had since being on the trail for so long.

During the night Nicole went into labor. Kund's wife Roxanne and Kate were in the wagon with Nicole and it looked like it would be a long and difficult birth. By morning the baby had not yet been born and Nicole was in very bad shape. Dancer knew of a town about a day's ride away on horseback, two days ride by wagon. Nicole was in no shape to ride a horse so Dancer had the men strip down the Eichmann's wagon until it resembled a simple buckboard with a small canvas top to keep Nicole safe from the elements. Nicole and Henry set off with Dancer for the town. With the buckboard type wagon and two quarter horses donated by Korn they could make better time and there might just be a chance to save Nichole and her baby. By this time Nicole was in and out of consciousness and all the rest of the group could do was to hope they would make it to the town in time for the mother and baby to survive.

Dancer and the Eichmann's left after dark so they would have a better chance of escaping on their own without the Indians seeing them. Korn took over as wagon master and leader of the group. The Eichmann's belongings that they had left behind were distributed amongst the other wagons so that the Indians would hopefully not notice anything unusual about the remaining group of travelers.

Bubba and Tearhart had gone ahead of us with Besser's horses so that the stock would get a chance to mosey along and feed on some of the fresh grass. The horses were also great indicators of water holes that we might miss. A horse had a sense of smell that could pick up a buffalo wallow filled with water that we humans would surely have missed. Keeping our livestock alive and healthy with food and water was almost as important as keeping ourselves alive. Both humans and livestock had to depend on each other in territory such as this.

Bubba and Tearhart were far enough ahead of us that we could no longer see them. We heard the sound of gunfire but that was all. After more than a dozen shots had been heard Korn made the move that any good wagon master would do. He ordered us all into a protective circle. Everyone took their assigned positions. The men and the boys were armed and ready. The women were ready to reload guns and had bandage dressings out for possible first aid if needed. Korn and Lake were anxious to leave and help out Bubba and Tearhart. Although to me I had to wonder if Korn was even more concerned about his horses.

Everyone was at the ready. The gunfire stopped. Far off in the distance we could hear some war cries coming from the Indians. Everyone in our group looked at each other and then quickly moved their eyes to a downcast position. It seemed the worst had happened to Bubba, Tearhart and the horses. Korn could be observed kicking at anything that was not stationary and blaming himself for not going to the aid of his wranglers.

The wagon train placed guards at strategic places and the rest of us waited until nightfall to see if anything new developed. The guards were rotated and Ole and I took watch. The moon and stars were bright and the night was clear. I heard the sounds of many horse's hoofs and told Ole to beware. Ole passed the word amongst the other members at their guard stations. Without the assistance of Dancer we had to fend for ourselves. Someone once told us that Indians prefer not to attack at night. It looked as if we would soon find out for ourselves.

Having better eyesight then humans I was the first to see the horses approaching. There were ten of them including two horses with riders. I could discern the identity of the two riders who were herding the horses towards us. I told Ole to shout out a warning to everyone to hold their fire. Then we all heard Bubba's voice. "Yo those in the train it's me Bubba and Tearhart. Open a path and let us in. Korn and Lake quickly pulled one of the wagon's tongues in and Bubba and Tearhart drove in eight of Korn's horses.

The boys quickly un-mounted their horses as Korn and Lake rounded up the eight quarter horses that Bubba and Tearhart had driven into our little stockade. Bubba was tired and out of breath. He sat down on the ground and stared blankly into space. Tearhart was as anxious to tell their story as the rest of us were to hear it. Korn of course noticed that two of his prize horses were missing and decided to hold his tongue until Tearhart told his story.

"Bubba and I were working the horses along the trail that Dancer had left for us. We knew we were far enough ahead of the wagon train that we could take our time. We moved slowly and let the horses stop and graze as we went along. Keeping a close watch for Indians we felt we had everything covered. Then out of a hidden buffalo wallow up pops this redskin. He came charging at me with a tomahawk so I pulled out my six shooter and nailed his bloody head right between the eyes. Suddenly another half dozen of the savages on horseback attacked us. Bubba already had his rifle out and was ready to shoot. I holstered my sidearm and jerked the rifle from my scabbard. Arrows were flying and we were shooting as fast as we could. One of the horses was hit by an arrow in the neck and it went down. What seemed like hours was probably less than a few minutes. The Indians scattered and ran off one of our herd. Two of the Indian's lay dead on the ground. The others rode off over a hill and out of sight. I rode over and checked out our wounded horse but it was too late for him and I took my rifle and with one shot I put the poor critter out of its misery. The herd had scattered some but Bubba and I managed to round up the remaining eight horses and then we skedaddled back here."

Korn seemed to be taking command now. He had his son Lake shackle their horses down to keep them from getting spooked and running off. The perimeter along the wagons was heavily guarded. Even the women and children were expected to help on guard duty. The Indians had our whole wagon train spooked and that even included Ole and me. Come morning with so many of us on guard duty we would all be too tired to pack up and keep going. Everyone in the camp knew by the next afternoon that sitting around and waiting for something to happen was not the answer. We would spend one more night and then it would be back on the trail. Korn relaxed the watch a little bit so we could all get some rest before continuing our journey. Ole told me that he had read stories about the Indians and this might just be one of their many tricks to wear us down and take us by surprise when we would start feeling safe again. The Indians seemed like they knew how to wear us down both physically and mentally. Tomorrow we would hit the trail and hope for the best.

CHAPTER 4

Morning came and the heat of day was beating down on our caravan as we made our way farther west. Bubba and Tearhart had been joined by Lake in keeping the remaining herd of horses in check. Ole and I were the lead wagon and the trail was marked well by the previous day's adventure that Bubba and Tearhart had left with the herd of horses that they had been leading up until the Indian attack. With guns at the ready we kept vigil on the surrounding prairie. If the Indians had planned on shredding our nerves in anticipation of what the day would bring they had done a very good job.

Pull Kund and his wife Roxanne were lagging farther and farther behind the rest of our group. Lake rode up to our wagon and told Ole that he was going to ride back and check on the Kund's. Korn as leader of our group made the decision that the train must keep moving. The Kund's would have to catch up when they could. Korn felt it best to keep the rest of the group together for protection. We moved on and eventually lost sight of Pull and his wife. We were making camp when Lake rode in and told us the Kund's wagon had a cracked wheel and it was limping along for a ways until it finally gave out. Lake offered to stay and help them repair it but Pull insisted he return to the wagon train for safety. Pull was a civil war veteran and insisted he could take care of Roxanne and himself until he got his wheel repaired. We made our camp for the night and a few of our more godly members said a prayer for the Kund's safety.

When morning arrived Ole and I were busy hitching up our teams for the day when Korn rode up on horseback. He stopped near us and pulled a set of binoculars from his saddlebag. Standing high in the stirrups he looked off into the distance behind us. "Black smoke, I don't like the look of that" he said.

We looked back and even without the help of binoculars we could see the tell tale signs of dark smoke punctuating the blue sky. Far in the distance we could see a shape taking form. At first just a black spot and it was moving towards us. Most of the occupants of our wagon train had now gathered and watched as the image we all saw slowly became larger and we could make out a rider and his horse. As he neared we saw it was Dancer. He had Easton's two quarter horses trailing behind him. The camp was overjoyed to see him. Slaps on the backs and handshakes from the men were the order of the day. The women whispered amongst themselves. Everyone felt safer knowing that Dancer was at hand to once again lead and guide us.

Dancer rode into the camp and he looked worn and tired. Even his horse looked as if it had been ridden hard. Some of the women folk ran and got hot coffee and food for our guide. Dancer was dead on his feet and Mr. Anderson helped him to a low wooden barrel so that Dancer could have a seat. Korn's wife Sindee pressed a cup of hot coffee into Dancer's hand and Kate set a plate of beans and bread down on the ground beside him. Dancer sipped the coffee and stared straight ahead. No one said a word as we all gathered around to hear the news of the Eichmann's. From the look of things we expected the worse. Easton of course had wandered over to his two quarter horse's to make sure they were all right.

Dancer finally seemed to come to his senses and started talking. "I suppose ya'll is wonderin' 'bout the Eichmann's? Well we traveled 'bout half a day and came upon a cabin with some settlers. Darn blessin' it was. The woman of the place used to be a midwife and the man had him some medical training from the war. Why they looked over Nicole and said there was only one thing to do and that was to cut the baby out of her stomach and sew her back up and hope for the best. I'll be damned if that ain't just what they did. The doc guy he slit Nicole open slick as a whistle and pulled him out a baby boy. I waited outside but heard all the details after it was done and finished. The doc and his wife sewed up Mrs. Eichmann and cleaned up her baby just as well as any big city doctor might have done. I stayed around for the next couple of days and by the Lord's mercy both Nicole and her baby which they named Oscar were doing just fine when I lit out to come back to find ya'll. I tell ya something that Henry Eichmann had to be the happiest fella I ever seen. I think he and I both figured neither Nicole nor that bay had a snowballs chance in hell of surviving. I ain't much of a God fearing man but I gotta say finding that cabin and two trained medical people in the middle of nowhere makes me think the Lord might just be watching over some of us."

"What I just told you folks is the good news. I'm sure you all wondered why I come in here all down and sad like. Well I got a heavy heart with bad news for everyone here. I figured I would intercept you folks on the trail and get back to work leading you on your journey. I picked up your trial and what I found was pretty disturbing. If any of you noticed the smoke in the distance you might have had an inkling of what it was from. I found Pull and his wife back there. The Indians got 'em both. Pull looked like he made a good showing of himself, both his rifle and pistol were empty and from the look of things at least three Indians died or were seriously hurt. I'm not positive 'cause the other braves took away the dead or wounded. Best I could tell Pull used the last bullet on his wife so that the Indians couldn't get her. He must have fought bravely right up to the end 'cause the Indian's didn't mutilate him or his misses. Just left 'em both laying dead for the buzzards. Old Pull must have had a dozen arrows in him before he gave it up. Brave man he was, we'll surely miss him on the trail. Like I said before I ain't a godly man but if any of you wishes to say a prayer for them I suspect they would appreciate it. I gave 'em a nice burial back by their wagon and marked their graves with their names."

Everyone was silent for quite some time. It was almost as if the good news about the Eichmann's had been eclipsed by the bad news about the Kund's. Yet we all knew the dangers we faced on an everyday basis. Illness or in the Eichmann's situation pregnancy, or death as in the case of the Kund's and danger that Bubba and Tearhart had so narrowly escaped from. Things had to continue on and soon we were back on the trail. It was nearing time for a decision to be made as to when Korn and his group would need to break off and head in a more south westerly direction to reach their destination.

Everyone who was not on lookout sat around the evenings fire and Korn announced that Sindee, Lake, Bubba and Tearhart would be braking off in the morning and heading towards Texas. Dancer took over the conversation almost immediately. "Casey and Kilroy you two have been sort of loners up to this time. We all appreciate the hard work you do for us and the help you give when we need guards and protection but with the Besser's leaving we need you to be more involved in our everyday travel. Either of you got any problems with that?" Casey and Kilroy looked at each other and gave answers in the affirmative that they would try to be more sociable and join in on any decisions that affected the wagon train.

With the Besser's, the Kund's and the Eichmann's all gone it left only four wagon's in our group. Dancer announced that even though Korn had hired him they both agreed that it was best for Dancer to stay with the larger group and keep guiding us to our destination. A vote was taken as to the new wagon master and Ole bowed out, he hated being the leader if he could avoid it. Mr. Anderson was elected and he seemed mighty proud of himself. I thought Kilroy or Casey would have been a better choice but what's done is done.

Mr. Anderson took on the job as wagon master with gusto. His son Trapis soon puffed himself up to be second only to his father in giving orders. Mrs. Anderson sat back and accepted things as they were. She felt some pride in their being the new leaders of the group but she was reserved in her vocal boasting which was totally unlike the two males in her family. Dancer continued to do his job and I'm not sure if he actually listened to Mr. Anderson's ideas or just continued to do things his own way as he had when Mr. Besser was wagon master. At least Korn Besser knew when to give a man his lead and he knew that Dancer knew his job and he let him do it. Mr. Anderson on the other hand was full of suggestions on how he thought things could go more smoothly or that some area off in another direction looked easier and better then the trails Dancer was picking out for us. Ole told me Dancer had the experience and it would be best for all to let his experience be our guide and not the let the opinion of some tenderfoot put us in danger.

It was a sad day as we watched the Besser's wagon and their horses head off into the distance. Ole, Kate, Zeb and I all made a special trip to their wagon the night before to wish them the best of luck. Ole mentioned to me that everyone in the Besser group seemed to be very proficient with weapons and if anyone could make it south on their own Korn and his group would do it. Indian or bandits had best beware if they decided to raid the Besser's.

It seemed strange as the next few days went along. It was a different atmosphere without Korn, his family or his wranglers and their horses. Dancer kept in sight of our wagons at all times. Although we did not see any Indians' Dancer told us there were plenty of signs to say that we were being watched. The country was becoming more rugged and water was scarce. It was telling on both the humans and the animals. Mr. Anderson was pushing everyone hard and he was the first to lose a horse to fatigue. Dancer ordered the horse butchered and the meat used for food. Nothing was to be wasted until we had crossed this area of our journey. Some days we only traveled a few miles due to deep gullies from infrequent flash floods or from breakdowns of the wagons now dried and worn parts.

It was early morning and the heat of the sun had not yet hit the earth. We started out with a cool breeze making our lives more comfortable. Ole and I were driving the lead wagon today. Casey and Kilroy were next in line with the Anderson's bringing up the rear. Dancer was ahead of us but within sight. He seemed agitated about something. We watched as Dancer and his horse would frequently stop and look at the ground. At the other times Dancer would have his binoculars out and was scanning the area around us. Ole and I had now been trail worn enough to sense some type of danger was nearby.

Suddenly like a freak thunderstorm the ground seemed to shake and the air was filled with noise. At first we saw nothing. Dancer and his horse raced past our wagon. His pistol was drawn and ready to use. He screamed as he went by. "Arm yourselves and take defensive action. Ole wheeled our wagon around to form a protective circle. In all the commotion I could see Casey and Kilroy doing the same.

Three wagons do not make much of a protective circle but it was better than nothing. Zeb took over unhitching our stock and getting it into the center of the circle. Kilroy was working with his stock and hollered over to Casey to grab his guns and Kilroy would get to Casey's team next. Kate was busy getting more ammo for the guns and I was helping to keep watch. Dancer could be seen off in the distance firing his gun at the marauding Indians. The Anderson's had fallen behind the rest of our little wagon train and none of us had really noticed. Although they were in sight they were well out of range of our guns. We had no one to spare to go to their aid and we could only hope that with Dancer's help they would survive. We could count at least two dozen of the red savages on horseback and many of them were armed with rifles.

The fight at the Anderson's wagon seemed to go on for a long time but in reality it was probably all over in fifteen minutes or less. The gunshots ceased and we could see Dancer astride his horse his rifle at the ready. He stayed a safe distance from the Indian's who were now swarming over the Anderson's wagon likes bees to honey. Two of the Indians remained on their horses facing Dancer, they also had rifles in their hands ready to use them at a moment's notice. Dancer finally raised his rifle into the air with one hand as if giving a salute to the Indians and then he turned and rode slowly back to our makeshift camp.

"What the hell is Dancer doing? He's not even going to check and see if the Anderson's are still alive?" Said Casey as he spit on the ground and walked away in disgust.

Dancer rode into camp and dismounted his horse. He knew we were all wondering just why he had abandoned the Anderson's. Casey strode up to Dancer and got in his face. "You coward, you left the Anderson's to die at the hands of those blood thirsty savages. You call yourself a man? You're lower then a rattlesnake's belly!"

Dancer looked Casey right in the eyes. "I don't answer to any man, especially a wet behind the ears greenhorn pup like you. For the sake of the others I'll tell you what happened. The Anderson's wagon looked like it broke a wheel and that's why they fell behind. Maybe one of us should have seen them drop back but none of us did. We all got a job to watch out for ourselves and then the others but we are human and we all make mistakes. So it ain't no one's fault that's standing here right now. The blame is this country it's harsh and unforgiving. By the time I got close enough to the Anderson's I could see the boy was already dead with a couple of arrows in him. Mr. Anderson was firing for all he was worth. Mrs. Anderson was cradling Trapis in her arms when she went down from a bullet. Mr. Anderson ran to her side and seeing both she and the boy were dead he kept fighting out of sure spite. I killed me two of the Indians from my horse but they were already upon Mr. Anderson. He was using his rifle as a club to take one of the Indians off his horse. Another Indian Brave came up from behind Mr. Anderson and split his skull with a tomahawk. There was no use in me dying for three already dead people. I raised my rifle in salute to them Indians. They understand a sign like that. The Anderson's went down bravely and the Indians respect that. They'll loot their wagon but they will leave the bodies alone. Indians don't mutilate a worthy foe. We'll stay here for the night and in the morning we can go back and bury them. For the time being we should be safe from attack. The Indians will be busy for some time with what they got from the Anderson's. If we're lucky they will return to their camp to brag of their conquest and show off their loot."

Dancer took over the camps security and using his best judgment we only had two guards posted for the night. With so few of us left even working in shifts would leave us all less alert during the day. Ole and I always took our shift together and working as a team we each got a little more shuteye then the others.

When morning came Dancer's horse was saddled and ready for burial detail. Everyone had breakfast together when Dancer made his surprise announcement. "Ya all know I could use one of you to help with burying the Anderson's I think the best choice would be for Casey to come along with me." Casey was still fuming about what he thought was Dancer's betrayal of the Andersons' but what could he say? Twenty minutes later we watched the two of them head off towards what was left of the now burned out Anderson wagon. The rest of us prepared our little wagon train to leave as soon as Dancer and Casey returned. Kilroy and Ole hitched up Casey's team for him and checked over his rig.

When Dancer and Casey rode up to join the wagon train Casey looked sick and pale. Kilroy asked him if he was all right. "As all right as I'll ever be after that experience. Dancer was at least right about one thing. The Indians had stripped the bodies but did not mutilate them. Although there were enough holes in two of them that you could darn near see through them. If this is how the west is I'm not so sure I want to be a part of it." Casey mounted his wagon and our small train pulled out for another days travel.

As the day wound down Dancer came up to the wagon train and told us we would be making camp early. A wagon would soon be joining us for the night. We circled our wagons as usual and set up camp for the evening. A short while later a wagon half full of buffalo hides appeared. There were three men with the wagon, the driver and a man riding shotgun next to him. The third man was on horseback. They had one extra horse tied to the back of their wagon. Dancer rode out and welcomed them to join us but he seemed apprehensive.

The three men left their wagon on the outskirts of our circle in front of the tongue of Kilroy's wagon. Kate had taken on the job of chief cook. Being the only woman left in camp she was treated like a queen by all of the other men, except of course Ole who treated her like his wife, which of course she was. I'm not saying that in a bad way but it seems when humans get married to each other they tend to take each other for granted. Once the strangers entered our camp Dancer told us they were buffalo hunters. Everyone thought it might be nice to get some news from outside our little circle of friends so we welcomed the men into our camp for supper.

It was hard to tell which one was dirtier and smeller then their companions. The men sat down on some firewood or wooden barrels around the campfire. Kate dished up some stew served with some sourdough bread she had been saving for a special occasion. Hot coffee rounded out the meal. Dancer seemed wary of the men and I noticed he had slipped the leather thong off the hammer of his pistol.

I mentioned it to Ole so that if we had trouble Ole and I would be ready. Ole was wearing his LeMat pistol as was his habit now days on the trail. Kilroy and Casey were also armed and even Zeb kept a rifle nearby him.

The three men were introduced by their leader a man named Bully who was about six foot tall with long shaggy dirty brown hair and a face that had not seen a razor in many a week, his clothes sort of matched his outfit, ragged and unkempt. Next there was a short squat fellow with a belly hanging over his belt and his pants legs were tucked into boots that were too big for him and came almost up to his knees. His name was Skinner and the dried blood on his outfit certainly matched his name. His job was skinning the buffalo hides for the group. Last of three and missing most of his teeth, those still in his mouth were rotted and yellow. His eyes seemed to almost bulge out of their sockets. They called him Popeye for good reason. Popeye was the main wagon driver and mule skinner for their party. Bully was the shooter. His job was to kill buffalos and not much else.

Bully started talking, "Ya folks headed west huh. Dangerous place the west. Mighty small wagon train considering all the Injuns and bandits we got out here. And you folks travelin' with a good lookin' woman besides." Popeye broke in to the conversation. "Ya she's a pretty one all right, not as pretty as some of them whores we had in Kansas City though."

Ole was losing his temper and I was getting worried. "If you gentleman don't mind that is my wife you're talking about and I would appreciate you keep a civil tongue in you mouths." Dancer had set down his plate of food and his gun hand was poised near his pistol.

"We're sorry if ya think we was bad mouthin' your woman ain't we boys. Didn't mean no harm we was just complitmentin' her. She's a mighty fine cook too. Me and the boys we just don't get to see a pretty face much in our line our work. Lookin' at buffalo all day just gets a fella a hankerin' for a little female company is all. Say you're sorry to the lady boys." Both Skinner and Popeye apologized and it seemed all most heartfelt but I doubt they really meant it.

Popeye took up the conversation next. "Where ya all destined for?"

Ole told them we were most likely going to settle in California or maybe Oregon. Once we found a good location with plenty of water and lots of grass for raising dairy cattle. Someplace near a big city where we could supply the restaurants and stores with fresh milk, cream, butter and cheese.

Kilroy and Casey had become good friends on our journey and were still undecided as to where they would settle down. They figured on teaming up and maybe starting a ranch. Casey was good enough with a horse that he figured he could round up some cattle and Kilroy was willing to learn to do the same. With Kilroy's skills as a tinker he could do blacksmith work to help them get by till they could establish themselves. Casey figured on selling his wagon load of store goods to raise enough money to buy some cattle and start a ranch.

Skinner set down his empty plate of food and took a bite of tobacco chaw from a plug he carried in his pocket. "I can figure Ole and his family for wantin' to settle down but you two fella's should be headin' for the mountains around Deadwood. They say there's so much gold in them mountains a man can make enough to buy drinks for the house in just one pan full from darn near any steam up there. Soon as us three make enough selling these buffalo hides for a grubstake that's where we're a going."

Kilroy and Casey looked at each other then Casey spoke up. "You know that don't sound like a bad idea. Kilroy, you and I could head up there make us a good grubstake and then buy us a ranch and some stock. It would be a lot less work finding gold and then buying what we need instead of rounding up stray cattle and working our tails to the bone." Kilroy did not take much convincing. The two of them wandered over to Casey's wagon and started making plans to head to Deadwood. Dancer just sat quietly by and said nothing.

The three buffalo hunters kept watching Kate and I could tell it was eating on Ole's nerves. Ole was no gunslinger and was not even much of a fighter unless he was riled. I kept telling him to ignore the buffalo hunters as once morning came around we should be shed of them. Dancer walked by us and told Ole and I to take first watch.

Kate and Zeb went to our wagon to get some sleep. The night went by peacefully without incidence.

When morning came and we were hitching up our teams Kilroy and Casey came over to our wagon. They had decided to head to Deadwood to make their fortunes. Dancer was listening to our discussion and he finally spoke up. "Boys there's lots of talk of easy pickin's in the mountains and steams of the Black Hills. All it is is talk. I've been there and seen me what they call the 'white elephant.' Dreams is all it is or maybe I should say a nightmare just like a white elephant. If it was so easy don't you think everyone in the Black Hills would be rich by now? But you boys do what you think is best. I'm going to stay on with Ole and his family till they get to where they want to be. If you've made up your minds to leave just be careful of Indians and outlaws. Best of luck to both of you." Well there was no talking Kilroy and Casey out of their mission. Their minds were made up. It was a sad farewell and we watched them head off into the distance. Only 5 of us were left now and only one wagon. Dancer, Kate, Zeb, Ole and I. Then the unexpected happened. The three buffalo hunters asked to join us. What could we say? We didn't trust them but three more guns and an extra wagon provided better security for all of us. Thus we started out on the trail for another day of travel. Ole drove the lead wagon and the buffalo hunters followed behind.

It was another hot dry day and our wagon kept the buffalo hunters in a cloud of dust for most of the day. No breeze and Ole kept wiping the sweat from his forehead out of his eyes. He told me it was hard to see with the salty drops of sweat clouding his vision. As for me I lay down on the wagon seat and panted for most of the trip. Kate and Zeb rode in the back of the wagon where it was shaded by our canvas top but even then the heat was stifling. Dancer rode up ahead checking trail and keeping a diligent eye out for Indians.

We could hear thunder up ahead yet there was not a cloud in the sky. The rolling hills we were crossing blocked our view of what lay ahead of us so we had to wonder just what or where the thunder was coming from. Ole told Kate and Zeb to tie down the canvas on the wagon just in case. A freak storm could wreck a lot of havoc on short notice. Looking behind us at the dust shrouded buffalo hunters we could just make out the fact that they seemed to be loading their guns. I told Ole to keep his Confederate LeMat pistol at the ready just in case.

Once again the shaking of the earth and the thunder had fooled us. We came over a rise and there they were. Thousands of buffalo as far as the eye could see. It was like a mighty ocean of brown furry beasts. Bellowing, shaking and rolling in the dust. The sight was almost unbelievable. Now we knew why the buffalo hunters were getting their rifles ready. Those men had heard the sounds before and they knew what to expect. For them the buffalo meant pay day. Every dead buffalo would put money in their pockets. For Ole and I it was heartbreaking to see these majestic animals about to be slain that had no enemy's on the prairie other than man. Even more heart rendering was the fact that these men did not kill the buffalo for food or survival as the Indians did, these men killed only for greed.

Bully and Popeye had saddled their horses and rode up beside our wagon. Bully gave us an order. "Hold up there Ole we got work to do. You might as well make camp right here for the night. Me and the boys got buffs to kill and we don't want you spookin' the buffalo with your wagon." Ole looked at me and told me we best do what the buffalo hunters said. We were outnumbered and outgunned. The safest thing to do was what we were told. Kate set up the area to do some cooking and Zeb went off to gather what wood or dried buffalo chips he could find for our campfire. Off in the distance I could see the silhouette of Dancer. He seemed to be watching the buffalo and was sitting perfectly still. Then again with Dancer you never knew. Maybe he was watching for Indians off in the distance or he might even of been keeping a watchful eye on us and the buffalo hunters.

As we made camp for the night we could hear the gunshots from the buffalo guns. The herd was off in the distance and we could see Bully and Popeye lying on a hill that over looked the buffalo. Both men were on their stomachs and had set up y shaped pieces of wood in which they rested the barrels of their guns as they took aim and fired. After each shot they took their time and methodically reloaded their rifles. They must have been far enough away that the report from their rifles did not spook the buffalo herd. Ole and I were standing on the seat of our wagon, Ole had his binoculars and I just have darn good eyesight. We watched in disgust as each shot from the hunters dropped another innocent buffalo in the herd. One big bull buffalo was standing off to the side of the herd and even from where Ole and I were it seemed his nostrils flared smoke and his eyes were blood red. I thought I recognized the big bull from the last herd of buffalo we had seen.

Sick to or stomachs we got down from the wagon and helped Kate and Zeb finish the chores of setting up camp. Kate looked over at Ole and started talking. "Those men are bad I can see it in their eyes. The way they look at me makes me shiver. Ole can't you order them away from us?"

Ole could see fear in Kate's eyes but he was not sure what to do. "Kate I really don't know what you expect me to do? There are three of them and they all seem pretty proficient with guns and knives. It would be sure folly for me to take them on by myself. I can ask them to go but that's about all I can do."

Ole and I mounted the wagon again and scanned the horizon for any signs of Dancer. We figured with Dancer here and Zeb holding a gun maybe we could convince our unwanted guests to leave once they returned from their buffalo hunt. By this time the shooting had stopped and in the distance we could see the buffalo hunters loading their wagon with buffalo hides and most likely getting ready to return to camp. I finally saw Dancer's horse not too far from the buffalo hunters but Dancer was not on it. The distance was too far to make out the dark shape that lay near Dancer's horse but I was afraid it might just be Dancer and he might be injured. Ole and I discussed the matter and we felt it would be best for us to mount up and go and check on Dancer. The sooner all of us were back at camp the better. If things went well we could locate Dancer and be back here before the buffalo hunters returned.

Ole plopped me into my saddlebag and off we rode in the direction we had seen Dancer's horse. The closer we got to Dancer's horse the better we could see that our worst fears for Dancer had been realized. Dancer lay on the ground and he was not moving. His horse was off about a hundred yards away spooked by the smell of blood.

Ole dismounted as quickly as he could and grabbed me from the saddlebag and put me on the ground. We both went to Dancer and started to check him over. He was on his side with one hand clutching his stomach and there was dried blood discoloring his fingers and the ground. His other hand clutched his handgun which was still cocked but had not been fired.

Ole rolled Dancer onto his back and pulled Dancer's hand away from his stomach. Dancer groaned and opened his eyes. "Ole, it's you. Bushwhacking buffalo hunting bastards shot me at long range. I was watching them from a distance and all of a sudden two of them aimed their rifles at me and shot. I pulled my gun to fire back but I knew they were out of range. Gut shot me they did. Not a chance in hell I can survive. Get a dying man some water will you?"

I sat by Dancer as he softly petted my fur. Ole returned and helped Dancer to take a drink from the canteen. "Ole, pull me over to the shade of those rocks." Ole did as he was asked. Dancer had Ole unsaddle his horse and bring the saddle over to Dancer so he could rest his head on it. Ole ripped some cloth from his shirt and did his best to stop the bleeding from Dancer's stomach. "Ole listen up to me now. I ain't got long to live. Being gut shot has no fixin' so my insides will bleed to death sooner or later. Let my horse roam the range free he'll be better off that way. As for you, take care of your wife and kid. Take my rifle with you and the clothes in my bedroll. Those clothes will serve you better out here in the wilderness then them store bought dudes you're wearing now. A few words of advice. Don't back down to any man or Indian out here they take it as a sign of weakness and will most likely kill you for it. Keep a gun handy at all times and clean and check over your guns every night, a little dirt, water or dust can cause your weapon to malfunction and it only has to happen once to be the death of you. Sven you watch over this tenderfoot for me now that I ain't going to be here to protect him. Now hand me my pistol just in case any Indians show up. Now leave me here to die in peace and get back to your family before them murdering buffalo hunters get back to your wagon. One more thing Ole. Kill them murdering bastards for me. Give Zeb and Kate a gun and ambush them when they return. Don't give them a chance to defend themselves for sure as buffalo droppings they plan to kill you and take Zeb and your wife. When they finish with Kate they'll sell her and Zeb to the Indians. Now go. Git!"

Ole looked back as we rode off from Dancer. Both of us had to wonder if as a frontiersman was it our job to have shot him and end his suffering? Yet we did as he told us and high tailed it back to Kate and Zeb.

Ole and I had our horse at full gallop as we headed back to our wagon. As we got closer we could see the buffalo hunter's wagon was already at our camp and their team had been unhitched. Ole pulled up on the reins and almost flew off his horse grabbing me in one hand and tossing me on the ground. Luckily I was ready and hit the ground running. We heard Kate scream as we came around the wagon. Ole had his LeMat pistol drawn cocked and ready. We both saw Zeb with his hands tied to the wheel of our wagon and he was bruised and bloody. Kate was being held down on the ground by Bully and Skinner as Popeye was tearing open her blouse. Ole was not very proficient with a hand gun and decided to order the men to stop and put their hands up. He felt it was safer then shooting at them during the struggle for he might miss and hit Kate.

Popeye who wore his gun tied down knew how to use it. He drew and shot Ole in his gun arm before Ole could fire. Skinner ran over and grabbed Zeb by the hair and held his buffalo skinning knife to Zeb's throat. Kate crawled backwards against a wooden barrel and was curled into a fetal position with her clothes torn and dirty. Ole went to his knees to get his gun when Popeye fired again hitting Ole's gun and sending it out of Ole's reach. Bully stood there staring at Ole and did the talking. "Ole you're just in time. I suppose you found Dancer, shot him dead we did. Your turn is coming soon. Skinner get rid of that snot nosed kid he's been more trouble then he's worth." With that command Skinner slit Zeb's throat from ear to ear. He let go of the boy and let him crumble in a bloody heap onto the ground. Ole screamed in pain and agony as he knelt on the ground with blood running down his arm. Kate seemed to be in shock and stared wild eyed at what was happening. I slowly made my way to Ole's gun which was now behind some camp supplies and picked it up in my mouth. I had to get it back to Ole.

As I made my way under cover over to Ole I was startled by the biggest meanest bull buffalo I had ever seen. Then I realized it was the same bull that was keeping eye on the herd that the buffalo hunters were killing off. The big bull stood at the edge of our camp and I could have sworn there was fire coming from his nostrils.

Popeye made his way over to Kate and grabbed her by the hair. "Bully keep a gun on Ole I want him to see this. Ole you ruined our little fun and games with your wife here so now you leave us no choice. Killed that boy of yours and now I can't afford to leave any witnesses." Popeye holstered his gun and pulled out his skinning knife. With the skill of a butcher he gave Kate the same treatment as they had given to Zeb, slitting her throat from ear to ear. I could hear Ole scream out in the most unbearable pain I have ever heard.

I rushed to Ole's side and almost forced the gun into his hand. Bully's attention was drawn to Popeye as he left the body of Kate crumple to the ground choking on her own blood. Skinner was still by the wagon standing over Zeb's dead body. Bully had not noticed the gun I had given Ole and as if by pure animal instinct Ole lifted the gun and quick as lightening he squeezed off four shots into Bully. I saw the slugs as they hit, the first one caught Bully in the gun hand and shattered his wrist, the next two were gut shots and the final bullet entered Bully's forehead and came screaming out of the back of his head like a spit watermelon seed.

Skinner sheathed his knife and pulled out his six shooter then fired at Ole. The bullet hit Ole and spun him around as he hit the ground. Like a flash of lightening the big bull buffalo charged into our camp with his head down and nostrils flared with what looked like blood red flame as the buffalo rammed into Skinner and crushed him between his massive buffalo skull and our wagon. I saw Popeye sprint for Ole's still saddled horse. He hit the stirrup of the saddle at a run and once in the saddle he was off and running.

I ran to Ole and looked him over. Skinner's bullet had entered Ole's right side but I noticed it exited at an angle away from Ole's vital organs. I licked Ole's face to revive him and slowly his eyes fluttered open. "Shot me twice they did, Sven." I told him that both wounds were flesh wounds and with a little doctoring he should be all right. Then I said "listen up Ole. You're my partner in this world and it looks like you and I are the only two left from our family. You need to get well and we'll track down Popeye and make him pay for what he and his men did." Ole propped himself up on his good arm and said. "Where are those murderer's?" I quickly answered him to keep him calmed down. "You shot Bully dead." I looked over at the big bull buffalo and he was using his massive front hoof to crack open and scatter what was left of Skinners crushed body. "Skinner's dead too, we got us some rather unexpected help at the very last moment."

The big bull buffalo was looking at Ole and me. I could feel a shiver run through Ole's body as I am sure he figured we were next on the buffalo's revenge list. Then the buffalo talked to me. It's a good thing that animals can communicate. In this case Ole could not understand the buffalo like he could me, but I understand the big bull just fine.

"I came here to help you and your human. I could no longer protect my herd from the onslaught of humans and their thunder sticks as the Indians call them. They come and they kill my cows from a distance and I am not able to fight back. Your human and you fight the same men as I do. I left my herd because I failed to save them from these killers, your human and you are now the same as me. You two also failed to protect your herd. We have all lost our family to these ruthless humans. The three of us should band together, become our own family and seek revenge on those who kill for no reason. I understand when an Indian kills an animal so that he can survive. Just as a buffalo may kill a wolf to save its herd, we all must do what is needed to protect those we care about and to survive. Those who kill for sport we must eliminate. I heard you talk to your human. Please communicate what I have said and see if he agrees. Tell him my name is Shag past king of the Tanaka.

CHAPTER 5

I helped Ole crawl to the wagon and got him inside. He collapsed on some blankets on the bed of the wagon. Ole's right arm and right side both had bullet wounds but he was lucky that in both cases the bullet passed through his flesh and no bones or vital arteries were damaged. I did the best I could with my paws and my teeth to pack clean bandages from our first aid kit into Ole's wounds. I even poured some whisky on them to cleanse them of germs as best I could. The whisky must have been painful for Ole passed out right after the pain shot through him.

I could hear what sounded to be a rolling thunder outside our wagon. I jumped down and off to the side of our campsite Shag was rooting and pawing the ground in a frenzy of movements which was creating a small dust storm. I carefully made my way to within his sight and asked him what he was doing. "Your human is resting from his injures is he not?

"He's sleeping comfortably for the time being." Was my answer.

"He is in no shape to dig a grave for his loved ones so it is up to you and me. I have dug hundreds of buffalo wallows as the humans call them and a grave is not much different. Before your human awakes it would be best for us to do this job for him. As for the dead buffalo hunters we will leave them out in the open for the buzzards to feed on."

Shag could tell it would be awful hard for me to bury my human family so he sent me to the buffalo hunter's wagon and told me to pull some buffalo hides over by the grave. While I was doing this Shag somehow move Kate and Zeb's body into the hole he had dug. The two of us continued to cover up the bodies with the buffalo hides until the hunter's wagon was empty. Using my paws and Shag with his mighty head and hooves we finally filled the grave with soil. Once we were finished Shag looked at me as he spoke. "Sven I know how hard this is for you. It is hard for me too. The hides of those buffalo in that grave were from my family and I am glad that we can share a bond of having our loved ones rest in peace together. Is there anything you would like to say about your people?"

I had never delivered a eulogy before and it left me at a loss for words. I knew Ole would want to hear something nice but he was resting in the wagon. I finally muttered a few words as Shag stood by. "Kate you were a good wife to Ole and Zeb a man could not have asked for a better son. Both of you treated me like family and understood the bond between Ole and I. You two never knew that Ole and I could communicate so I'll tell you now. We will miss you both and I'll do my very best to take care of Ole now that you two are gone. Amen." I wasn't so sure why I said amen, maybe my words were like a prayer at least I hope God was listening and takes care of the humans and buffalo's that Shag and I just buried.

Shag volunteered to stand guard at our wagon while I spent the night with Ole. He was restless most of the night. Between the pain and the hurt of losing the ones he loved I could understand why he couldn't sleep. Being a dog has some disadvantages and I felt bad that I could not get Ole the nourishment he needed. I did my best and kept a canteen full of water and some bread and jerky within his reach as he slowly started to recover. Shag mentioned he had seen a few Indians watching the camp but for some reason they shied away from us.

It took two days for Ole to get strong enough to get up and about. He was limping badly and his arm was stiff and hurting. He had enough strength to get us a fire started and we had our first hot meal since our run in with the buffalo hunters. Hot beans and soft bread may not sound like much but it sure tasted like a fancy meal to us. Shag was grazing nearby and I told Ole that he was our friend and wanted to stay with us. Ole kept looking at Shag and wondering if he could trust the big old bison. I assured him that the three of us would make a great team. Although Ole could not communicate with Shag I could so I soon became the interpreter for the two of them.

Shag and Ole kept a wary eye on each other. It takes time to build trust. Ole kept exercising his wounded arm to get it back to normal. One day he strapped on his gun belt and tried to practice drawing his gun like he had read the cowboys in the dime novels did. Shag and I watched Ole as sometimes that Confederate LeMat came smoothly from its holster. Other times the gun was jerked from the leather and sometimes Ole slipped and the weapon fell to earth. Everyday Ole's arm seemed to limber up some. Up until now Ole looked over at the big grave that held his wife, son and some buffalo's, he never said anything about it. He just stared at it. One day as I sat by Ole tending our fire we heard a cracking and breaking noise coming from the buffalo hunter's wagon. We looked over and saw Shag destroying what he considered an evil conveyance. When Shag was done he picked up a large flat board and brought it over to Ole. Shag stood looking at Ole and then dropped the board from his mouth at Ole's side. I looked at Shag and was sort of puzzled by his behavior. Shag looked at me and then with big sad eyes he looked right at Ole. "Sven tell Ole this board is for him to make a grave marker for his wife and child. It is time for us to leave this place. The Indians think we are possessed by spirits and don't dare come near us. A human, a dog and a buffalo are not something the Indians have ever seen working together. We may be evil or we may be big medicine in their eyes. If we stay to long they may want to test our strength. Tomorrow we leave here. Today Ole must say goodbye to his wife and child. When the marker is finished and planted tell Ole to cut one of the horses saddles and add some extra leather to the center. When it's done Ole will be riding me. The three of us are now family."

Ole looked at me and then at Shag. "Seems you two know when a man should stop feeling sorry for himself and move on. I'll start carving a marker for that grave right now. In the morning we'll say our goodbyes to the loved ones we lost and then we can move on. What are you two planning for Bully and Skinner? You just going to let them lie there and rot? I looked at Shag and gave the answer to

Ole from the both of us. "Yes Ole we are going to let them lie and rot. They deserve no better. Shag and I talked it over when we buried our loved ones. We figure the least those two varmints can do is to supply some food for the buzzards."

"Sounds like darn good reasoning to me." Answered Ole.

When night came I left Ole still carving on the grave marker. Shag was lying in some soft grass just off from our wagon. I jumped in the wagon and thought about the future. I said a prayer for Ole hoping he would be all right. When morning comes the three of us will start our lives over. Popeye was now a wanted man and we would hunt him down. Shag told me that he wanted to eliminate every buffalo hunter we could find. I had yet to break that news to Ole. Somehow with lots of thoughts running through my head about the past and the present I finally drifted off to sleep.

I must have slept soundly for when I awoke Ole was next to me and was snoring like an old bulldog. I quietly got up and went outside to do my morning duties. I saw that Ole had finished carving the words on to the grave marker and it was placed at the head of the grave. It had a line dividing the words and it had now become two separate markers. One side read. 'Kate & Zeb, beloved wife and child.' The other side read. 'Buffalo's lie here in rest beloved creatures of God.' Noting fancy but the words sure made an important statement. I noticed Shag standing looking at the marker. "Ole did a fine job with his words. We can be proud to call him family."

Once Ole was up and around we all talked over our plans. Ole and I of course wanted to go after Popeye. Killing him would be a pleasure. Shag was more than willing to join us as Popeye had killed more buffalo then any of us cared to count. Revenge can be a sticky thing to deal with. There were a lot of cold blooded killers and buffalo hunters out there. The three of us needed a purpose to unite and drive us. Our destiny might just turn out a whole lot different than any of us had ever planned.

It was time for us to leave and I saw Ole look over at the grave. "Ole you want to say something over Kate and Zeb before we go?"

"No Sven I said my peace last night while you and Shag were sleeping. Best now to leave our past behind us."

Ole was none too sure about saddling up and riding Shag but Shag insisted. Ole's first few tries of putting his foot in the stirrup and hiking himself up on Shag's back were not to successful. The first two times Ole slipped and fell on the ground. The third time he almost got up and then he slid back to earth. His bad leg and bad arm were just not strong enough yet to pull himself up. "Listen Shag I think it might be best if I switch over to a horse I'll have a better chance with my injuries of mounting up," said Ole.

Shag snorted and shook his head no and I interrupted for him. "Ole I let the horse's go last night. They agreed that they would be fine running free and grazing on their own. I told them about a herd of wild horse's just a few miles from here and they left to join them. I'll move over by the wagon and you can get on my back from there. Be sure to put Sven in his saddlebag so you don't have to get up and down again. We can always find a rock or old tree for you to use for saddling up until you get your strength back."

We rode away from our camp and none of us looked back. I thought the ride in the saddlebag on Shag was actually more comfortable than being on a horse. I could see Ole was not used to being on an animal of such width, or maybe it was his bum leg that was giving him trouble. After a few hours Ole suggested we stop and rest. Shag found us a place in a rocky area where a small basin of water had gathered. The shade of some rock overhangs kept the small pool from evaporating. There were enough rocks around us that Shag stopped near one so Ole could easily dismount. After all of us had our fill of water we decided to take a nap and rest up.

Shag was awake before Ole and I and we heard him lapping up some more water. "Sven ask Shag if he is comfortable with you and I riding on his back."

Shag gave me a lengthy but good answer to Ole's question. "No problem at all. I could carry half a dozen humans at full gallop and never even break a sweat. There is not any horse that could do that. Anyway if we are going to be traveling incognito so that no one knows who or why we are moving about this will be the best way. Anyone who sees a man, a dog and a buffalo traveling together will figure the human is crazy or else real dangerous, or both. Sven tell Ole that if we are going to pull this off he has to shed those city slicker type clothes he's wearing and change into something more practical. He may be dressed all right for a wagon train but now we need to make him into real westerner."

I relayed what Shag said to Ole and got an answer back right away. In fact it seems that Shag could understand Ole all right Ole just did not understand buffalo talk. At least it kept me from having to interrupt for both of them.

"Sven just what does Shag expect me to wear?"

Shag already knew the answer and told me to relay it to Ole. "Sven told me your friend Dancer gave you his things when he lay dying out on the prairie. Open up the bed roll and let's see what you have."

Ole laid out the contents of Dancer's bedroll and saddle bags so that Shag could see what he had to work with. Shag had been on the prairie all his life and he had observed enough humans over the years to know what kind of outfit a man would need to survive in this country.

Next thing you know we had Ole stripped down to his under clothes. Shag relayed the information to me and I passed it on to Ole. A pair of tan jeans with a leather belt. Some well worn down at the heel boots would make for comfortable walking and the heels were still good enough to keep a good hold on a saddle stirrup. A long sleeve dark brown buckskin shirt with a bib crossover could be buttoned or left open depending on the weather. A dark blue bandanna around his neck for help with everything from sweating to dusty dry days. A Stetson cowboy hat topped off the outfit. Ole's LeMat pistol and dark brown gun belt fit nicely with the rest of the outfit. The buckle on the gun belt was sterling silver with black hills gold and rose gold inlaid and it pictured a Viking ship with full sail and what looked like a Bohemian Cossack on horseback with his cape flying and his saber held high on the ships sail. One of the rifles left behind by the buffalo hunters was a Winchester model 1866 .44 caliber and Shag added that to Ole's arsenal for protection. A good knife with a six inch blade and an oak handle was sheathed at Ole's side. I remember Dancer telling the boys from our wagon train that he got the knife on a trade with some Cherokee Indians a few years back. The brave that traded it told him it had taken many scalps and was a fine weapon. Dancer said it best be a good knife for he gave up two store bought blankets for it and his spare coffee pot. Shag added one more important thing to Ole's new look. A name befitting a westerner was needed. Ole was a name that would not bring any fear into a man's heart. So from this day on my Ole was to be known as Buffole. The correct pronunciation would be Buff-oh-lee. We really knew of no meaning for the word so we picked, 'hunter of the bad, protector of the innocent.' It could also mean Ole the Norwegian riding a buffalo.

We decided to make camp for the night. Ole walked away from our campsite to get a little exercise for his leg and to break in his new duds. It was not long before we heard some pistol shots ring out. Shag and I rushed in the direction Ole had taken. We found him practicing at fast drawing his gun and doing some target practice. Ole said he knew that a quick draw from the holster was not as important as being steady and hitting what you aimed at. He had read enough dime novels on the west to realize that. Yet if he could have a fairly quick draw and an accurate aim he would have the advantage over most men he would go into battle with. We all walked back to camp and turned in for the night.

CHAPTER 6

Next morning the three of us had a pow wow around the campfire and then we saddled up on Shag and headed off. Shag knew the area well for he had been roaming this territory since he was a calf. One other thing Shag was good at was tracking. He had picked up the tracks from Popeye's horse as soon as we left our original camp. It had been a few days and Popeye had a good lead on us but with Shag's sense of smell and tracking ability we all felt we would catch up with Popeye sooner or later and justice would be served.

Ole was still pretty sore and we made frequent stops so he could walk around and limber up his arm and leg. After a few days on the trail Ole was walking almost normal, maybe a slight limp but that was about it. Shag announced that we would start running into a few homesteaders by tomorrow. Most likely they would be small ranchers and farmers trying their best to make a living in this wild and unforgiving country. Ole told us around the night's campfire that although he really enjoyed our company it would be nice to converse with a human again. Shag and I understood and we hoped to find someone for Ole to talk to in the near future.

It was nearing sundown and we could see a curl of smoke just over the next rise. Shag remembered that there was a small cabin there with a family of pilgrims as he called them from the east. He had watched them when his herd moved through the area. There was a man who seemed to be more interested in laying out a horse training track than he was in farming the land. He also remembered seeing a slim dark haired lady and a teenage girl. It might be a nice place for us to stop and get acquainted. Ole could then get himself a little human companionship before we moved on.

We came over the rise and just as Shag said, there was the cabin. It was a well built log home with a stone chimney on the side. The place was not very large, maybe two or three rooms inside. Off to the right was a small stable and corral. A stream flowed off to the right of the place so plenty of water was available. The land was rich with grass and a nearby forest would supply wood and game for the settlers. A small garden had been planted behind the house and it looked to be supplying an abundance of vegetables. It was a well chosen place to make a home for a man and his family.

There was a man out by the corral and he looked to be mending a fence post. While we were taking stock of things the man fell to the ground like a rock. He hit the dirt before we heard the report of a gunshot. Shag told us to look over to the edge of the forest tree line. A tell tale whiff of smoke showed where the shot originated. We were too far away to return fire and it would take us a good half hour to cover the ground to give help. Shag took off at a gallop and we wound our way in a zigzag pattern down the steep slope we had been observing from. Whatever had just happened could only be a bad thing. Ole and Shag kept track of where we were going so as not to make any misssteps and lose our footing. I kept an eye on the ranch.

I saw the young girl race from the house towards the fallen man and a woman was just coming out of the door when she stopped and rushed back into the cabin. The girl was bending over the man and even at this distance, with my dog ears, I could hear her screams of agony. The woman reappeared from the cabin carrying a rifle and rushed to the girl's side. The woman knelt by the man and turned him from his side to his back. She put her ear to his chest and then quickly stood up and grabbed the girl by the hand and started pulling her back towards the cabin.

As we were nearing the cabin, I was better able see what was taking place. A man stepped from behind the stable and had his six gun out. He stepped in front of the woman and the girl as they tried to get to the cabin. His gun was pointing at the girl. The woman stopped, and letting go of the girls hand she leveled her rifle at the stranger. I could sense that the man was threatening to shoot the girl unless the woman dropped her rifle. Sure enough, she lowered the rifle barrel and tossed the gun off to the side. A small puff of dust rose in the air as the rifle thudded to the ground. I shouted. "Ole! Shag! We have to hurry the man looks to be dead and the women appear to be in danger." Our path was steep and filled with obstacles of rocks, fallen trees, branches and loose shale. It would take us at least another twenty minutes to get to the ranch. "Shag you have to do better or we might be too late. I'm not sure but I think the stranger down there might be Popeye." With my words ringing in their ears, Shag gave all he had. Ole held on and moved his body to help Shag make his turns even quicker. The big buffalo could really move when he needed to. Ole was proving to be a better rider than even I could have hoped for. If only we could get there in time to stop any more bloodshed. If it was Popeye, things worse than death could be awaiting the two women.

We were almost with in shooting range when we heard one of the women scream "Get out!" we had seen now that the man was indeed Popeye. The man's voice swore in anger at the top of his lungs. Popeye came stumbling out of the cabin with his hands over his face. Ole saw Popeye rounding the corner near the stables. Ole couldn't wait any longer or he might miss his chance. Ole pulled the LeMat from his holster and took aim as best he could. He squeezed off two shots at the running man. One shot hit the dust at Popeye's feet, the other shot went somewhere, but it certainly did not hit its target. We all had a quick lesson in shooting. Trying to hit a target from a moving, bouncing buffalo by a man with a still healing wounded arm did not produce very good results. Ole reined up on Shag and he hit the dirt on both feet. He stumbled on his bad leg but managed to get his balance and ran towards the cabin. Shag and I saw Popeye riding off into the forest at full speed. I jumped down from my saddle bag and ran to see if I could help out in the cabin. The women were our first concern. Popeye would have to wait. Sooner or later we would track him down and take care of business.

Ole was already in the cabin when I came barreling through the door. To my surprise Ole was standing with his hands in the air, his right hand holding his gun. The woman had a bead on Ole with what looked to be a Volcanic lever action Navy pistol. Her gun looked mighty old and mighty unsafe to me. Then I saw a small white female Shih Tzu dog cowering in the corner and of course, I went to the dog's aid. I figured Ole could handle the human female on his own. The young girl was standing over by the stove and held a cast iron skillet in her hand as a weapon to back up the woman I presumed was her mother.

I gave a nose sniff to the little white Shih Tzu and she did the same for me. I asked if she was all right. "I guess so, the man that came in kicked me when I tried to protect my humans. I was dazed for some time and I'm just now coming back around. My name is Lena, who are you?"

"I'm Sven and that fella with his hands in the air belongs to me, his name is Buffole. We're here to help you, can you tell your human to relax and put down her gun?"

"What are you talking about? I can't talk to my human, can you talk to yours?"

"Ole, I mean Buffole, you're on your own with the lady there. Lena here says she can't communicate with her humans."

"Ma'am my name's Buffole and me and my dog heard shooting coming from here. We were a ways off and came as fast as we could to see if we could be of any help. How about I put my gun down on the table so that you know I mean no harm."

Ole had introduced himself to a human as Buffole. I had used his Buffole name to tell Lena who he was so as of this point in time throughout the west 'Ole' was now to be known as Buffole.

The woman had fear in her eyes, not just for herself but also for her daughter. "All right. Take the gun from your right hand with just two fingers on its butt. With your left hand put it down slowly on the table in front of me." Buffole did as he was told.

"You going to shoot me now ma'am? If so maybe you wouldn't mind telling me your name first. I'd hate to be shot dead by a complete stranger."

"I could see the woman was doing her best not to smile. "You can call me Krystal and this here is my daughter Jo. My husband is the dead man out in the yard. I ain't saying he was the best man in the world but he was my husband. He told me only this morning that he was going to leave Jo and me here to go off and find himself. What the hell that mean's I have no idea. I was almost thinking of shooting him myself but Jo needs a daddy and I had to hope he would come back 'cause it ain't fittin' to leave a woman and child out here in the wilderness to fend for themselves. Now that he's gone for good I guess I'm strong enough to make it on my own. Jo and I will get along just fine. It's against my better judgment but I'll let you go, just turn around and ride on out of here. You can leave your gun on the table it might come in handy for me and Jo in case any other hombre's like you show up."

Jo finally spoke up. "Mama you shouldn't be telling some stranger our problems. You're upset. Just quite talking and let him be on his way."

Ole smiled at Krystal and started talking. "Ma'am, I mean Krystal, by the way that's a mighty pretty name, I hope you don't take offense but I noticed the gun you're pointing at me, and by the way it's awful hard not to notice it with your hand shaking and the barrel aimed at my chest, have you fired that thing much in the past?"

"I've fired it at least a hundred times. My pa left it to me and he used it to fight Indians. Now you better get if you know what's good for you."

"I've just got one question for you ma'am. Kind of got my curiosity up. That gun you're pointing at me looks to be mighty old. I don't know if I've seen one quite like it. It's no ordinary gun because there's no cylinder for putting in the bullets. Would you mind telling me how you load it and what caliber ammunition does it take?"

"Not that it's any of your concern but just so you know I mean business I'll tell you. It takes a forty caliber bullet and I put it butt end down the barrel, then I lift the gun in the air and bullet slides down to where the hammer is. Whoops, I forgot to pull the hammer back." She quickly cocked the hammer while trying to keep the gun steadily aimed at Buffole.

Buffole pulled a chair away from the table and turned it so that its back faced Krystal. He straddled the chair and placed his elbows on the back of the chair. "Ma'am I hate to contradict your knowledge about that gun but it darn sure is a muzzle loader. It just ain't going to shoot that forty caliber bullet you dropped down the barrel. You need a lead ball, a wad of powder and a flint to shoot that thing. Like I said from the very start I'm here to help out and not to harm you. How about you put that thing away and we talk about what happened."

Krystal looked over at Jo. Jo slowly shook her head yes. "All right we'll trust you for now. Jo you get us some coffee if you would." Krystal sat down at the table and looked at Buffole's gun sitting there.

"Ma'am if you want to change your mind and hold me at gunpoint or shoot me you can use my gun. It's loaded right and proper but make sure you pull the hammer back if you're going to shoot me or maybe you want to shoot my partner Sven over there?" I looked at Buffole and said. "Hey don't give her any ideas. She's a woman and a human woman at that. They can be unpredictable as a jumping frog."

Krystal looked at Buffole and a smile crossed her face. "No you can have your gun back. I see my dog Lena has accepted Sven and she is a good judge of character. If Sven is all right then so are you.

Jo had sat down with Krystal and Buffole by this time. "Momma's right about Lena. She never did like my poppa much and it took a few years for us to see that he was heading in a bad direction. He was going to up and leave us to fend for ourselves. Told my momma he just got tired of her and wanted to go off and see the country on his own. Never mind that he was dumping me. Told me he still loved me and someday he would send for me. Well if he ain't sending for Mamma too, I sure wasn't gonna go and be with him. Now he's dead. I don't know if I should hate him for wanting to leave or forgive him. He was my Poppa and I loved him but what he was doing was wrong and he hurt Mamma awful bad."

Krystal's eyes had turned red and welled up some since the excitement over holding a gun on Buffole had died down. Her words were now sort of choked and hard to get out. "Jo you hush up about your daddy. He was a good man for many years. I think it was just some sickness got into him as of late. We have no call to tell our troubles to a complete stranger. In fact we best go out and take care of him." Krystal was about to break down and she got up from her chair and covered her face with a hanky to hide the tears that had began to flow. Jo got up and rushed after her mother as they both went into a room that was only separated from the rest of the cabin by a blanket that hung from the ceiling and served as a room divider. Buffole saw Krystal collapse on the bed and decided it was best for Sven and him to head back outside. Lena made an apology to Sven. "Sven I would like to stay and visit but I have to go and comfort my humans, I hope you and Buffole stay around for awhile and help us get through this terrible tragedy." Buffole and I both had to wonder if the tragedy was that the man of the house was leaving or that he was now dead.

Once we were outside Shag told me to tell Buffole to hurry up and unsaddle him for we had work to do. We were a team and not much else had to be said between us to get the job done that needed doing. Shag walked over to a large shade tree not too far from the ranch and started working up a buffalo wallow to serve as a grave. Buffole and I went over and prepared the dead man's body as best we could. There was some old canvas in the stable that was most likely left over from the Conestoga wagon that was out back. Buffole wrapped up the dead man in the canvas and found an awl to punch some holes along the edges of the makeshift body bag. He used some rawhide strips from an old bull whip that was hanging on a hook inside the stable to sew the canvas up as tight as he could. Buffole's bad leg and sore arm were not yet strong enough for him to hoist the body onto his shoulder and take it over to the grave Shag had dug. I ran up to the door of the house to make sure the women were not in eye sight of what was about to happen. Buffole tugged, pushed and finally got the body into a rough old wooden wheel barrow and rolled it over to the grave. The body was dumped from the wheelbarrow into the grave and Buffole hurriedly returned the wheel barrow to its place next to the corral. It didn't help that the last thing in the wheel barrow was horse dung. With shovel in hand and Shag using his hoofs and me using my paws we covered up the body as quick as we could. When we were done

Ole took a flat board he found near the old wagon and carved in the date as a start of a grave marker. We didn't get the man's name so we figured when the women were ready we could finish up the grave marker. Shag wandered off to some fine meadow grass for a little feed time and Buffole and I sat down by the creek in the shade of a tree to wait for the women.

I heard the women come out of the cabin and told Buffole they were looking around and must have seen the grave for they were making their way over to take a look. Buffole turned and watched them approach the grave site. Jo dropped to her knees and we could hear her sobs as the reality of the situation took hold. It was hard to tell from the distance how Krystal was handling things. Krystal knelt by her daughter and put her arms around her to comfort her. For the time being we once again figured it was best to leave them be until they were ready to have our company.

The ladies spent some time at the grave as well they should have. They saw Shag off in the distance and they looked rather surprised to see a lone buffalo so close to their ranch. Lena had been near the grave site with them and she took over the lead as they made their way over to Buffole and I. Sometimes it takes a canine to show a human what they should do. Lena's people followed her and they all walked over to us. Jo asked us if it would be all right if they sat down. I gave a soft bark and Lena pulled at Krystal's skirt which seemed to be enough of an answer that they joined us on the bank of the stream.

Buffole was never real good with words when it came to women. In fact he and Kate had not talked much for some time and I often wondered if their marriage was all right. Here we all sat and I could tell Buffole was tongue tied. Sort of like one of those dime novel cowboys too shy to talk to women but great at talking to his dog or a horse or in our case a buffalo. Finally I urged him to say something with the universal language of both dogs and humans. "Buffole speak boy speak."

"Krystal. Are you and Jo all right? I hope we didn't offend you by taking the liberty of burying your husband. I was hoping it might be less painful if someone else did the job so you and Jo did not have to suffer any more than necessary. Well, ma'am I don't know what to say, I know your suffering and I'm just trying to help out if you will let me."

Krystal looked at the ground as she spoke, she seemed either sad or ashamed by what she was about to say. "Mister you have no need to be sorry. You did a mighty nice thing for Jo and me. Times have been tough since we came out west. We came from a small logging town in Minnesota. A place you probably never heard of. My husband had grand plans to raise race horses and he hoped to take them to the big race tracks and make a fortune. Seems he could spend our money a lot faster then we could make it. I wanted a normal life for Jo. Not a life of going from race track to race track. I thought he was in agreement with me to settle down out here away from the temptation of gambling and racing. I was wrong. He was about to leave Jo and I and head off on another farfetched scheme of his when that man came here and shot him dead."

To my surprise Buffole stepped right up and answered her. "I'm right sorry to hear you were having man troubles. Your man must have been plump crazy to want to leave a pretty lady like you and a right fine looking daughter like Jo. I had me a wife and son till that rattlesnake Popeye and his friends killed them. I didn't appreciate her like I should have and now it's too late to change my ways. A man and a woman ought to talk more and share their feelings. I think that's what they ought to do to make their lives together meaningful for both of them. My loss is too fresh to think about a future right now but just talking to you gives me hope that there is at least one mighty fine female out here in the west. You will do all right for yourself. You're strong and brave and you got a good mind set and a child to help you out. Yes ma'am I think you will make out all right. By the way we might have been neighbors at one time I'm from Minnesota myself, little place called Sauk Rapids, dead center in the middle of the state. You ever heard of it?"

"I grew up in Brainerd and moved to Fort Ripley during the war. We came out west about a year ago. The ranch was just starting to become home. Vegetables are growing and we have a milk cow, some beef cattle out on the range and of course some mighty fine horses. For the time being Jo and I will stay here and work the place. It has potential. I just learned I better keep a gun handy and not trust anyone. Accepting maybe you."

"Ma'am I got a question for you, you don't have to tell me if you have a mind not to. I saw that pistol of yours and your rifle was in the far corner of the room. Just how did you drive ol' Popeye out of your cabin? He came running out the door with his hands over his face and screamin' like a banshee."

"He got the drop on me when he threatened to shoot Jo. He hustled us into the cabin and was holding us at gun point and then he started giving orders. Said he had come a long ways and two pretty women were just what he was looking for. But first he said his throat was mighty dry and that he was powerful hungry. He told me to get him some of the hot coffee I had on the stove and then I was to rustle him up some vittles. I could see him leering at Jo. I told him I would do what he wanted if he let Jo go. He sneered at me and said he was holding all the cards in this game and he would do whatever pleased him. Maybe I'll take you first woman. He said. You are a mighty pretty thing. When I get done with you I'll let you watch as I teach your daughter how to be a woman. By this time I was close enough to him and I had a hot pot of coffee in my hands. I threw the coffee in his face and I screamed at Jo to grab the pistol on the mantel of the fire place. He must have known we would shoot him and his face had to have been scalded by the hot coffee. He ran for the door and somehow he holstered his pistol on the way. Then we heard the shots and you came through the door."

Buffole looked right at Krystal as he spoke. "It was mighty brave of you ma'am you did the right thing. Popeye would have had his way with you and Jo and then he would have done one of two things. If he thought he could control you he would have tied you up and taken you to the nearest Indian camp or found him some Mexican banditos to sell or trade you. Not saying you was lucky I came along when I did but I'm glad I was here to make sure Popeye kept on running. By the way ma'am was you gonna shoot him with the same pistol you were holding on me?"

"Yes I was. Well maybe I wasn't but it's a good thing he didn't stay around to find out or I might have been in a heap of trouble if he knew as much about that old gun as you did. It's getting late so how about you and your dog come up to the house and I'll fix us all some vittles. You can put your horse up in the stable before we eat. By the way I never did see the horse you rode in. You weren't on foot were you?"

I could see Buffole hesitate on giving the answer. "Well Ma'am I didn't come in on foot. Yet I ain't rightly riding no horse either. See that buffalo over there?" Buffole pointed over in Shag's direction. "That's my ride ma'am. It's sort of a sad story 'bout how it happened but my dog Sven and that buffalo Shag, well were sort of like our own little family."

"I think maybe you should come on to the house and you can tell us all about it. Jo and I are mighty good listeners and we ain't had much company in a long time." Buffole walked over to the hand water pump that had been installed in the kitchen and pumped up some fresh water to wash up. He reached down and cleaned up my muzzle for me as he whispered. "Sven we best look respectable for the ladies here. I'm sure that little dog Lena likes a good looking male." If I was a human I would have blushed at what Ole just said.

Krystal and Jo served up a fine dinner and we all sat and talked and ate and ate and talked. Buffole helped to clear the table and even went to the sink to give Krystal a hand with washing and drying the dishes. Some folks think it's unbecoming for a man to help a lady but Buffole makes no never mind to what other folks think. To him helping each other be it a man or woman is how things should be. Jo, Lena and I went out to feed and check on the livestock. Shag was over by the edge of the forest sound asleep. It was quiet and peaceful with the stars twinkling in the sky. Lena kept close to me and the moon light glimmering on her white coat was mighty pretty and I told her so. Being with Lena kind of made me think about settling down and having me a wife. Except Buffole, Shag and I had work to do. There would be no settling down for any of us until we caught that lowdown side winding snake Popeye.

Krystal and Buffole finished cleaning up after supper and made their way out to a willow bench on the cabins porch. Of course they each sort of hugged opposite ends of the seat to be proper.

Krystal started the conversation. "Is it all right if I call you Buffole?"

"I would prefer if you did ma'am."

"All right I'll call you Buffole if you will quit calling me ma'am and start calling me Krystal. I don't have an adult to talk to and I do not even know if we have any neighbors. A lot lays heavy on my mind and I hope you do not mind if I unload my burdens on you. After all you are a complete stranger. It would help me a lot to have someone to confide in. I know you will be leaving soon so I guess that's why I was hoping you might be willing to listen to me. I cannot say anything to Jo because she loved her daddy and I do not want to ruin her image of him."

"Well ma'am, I mean Miss Krystal."

"Please just call me Krystal. No miss, no ma'am, just Krystal."

"Krystal I am a good listener and I can keep a confidence till my dying day. I only got two friends left in this world that I totally trust and one is Sven and the other is Shag the buffalo. Both of them have saved my life. Just so you know I might share some secrets with them during some lonely night by the campfire."

"I think I can trust a dog and a buffalo, in fact I've shared a lot of my hurts and feelings with Lena. But talking to a dog is just not the same as talking to a human. You may have noticed that I was not very upset when my husband was killed. Well I was upset but it was more for Jo then it was for me. I loved him once but he killed my love just as if you tore the heart from my breast. Back in my own home town I found out he was having a love affair with my best friend. I tried to forgive him for Jo's sake. We came out west for a fresh start. A few days ago he told me he only brought Jo and me here until he felt we could handle things on our own. He was going to saddle up a horse and go back to the other woman tomorrow morning. He told Jo he was going away on horse business and he would send for her later. Maybe

I'm glad he's dead. I would fight him tooth and nail before I would let him take my daughter away to live with that cheating floozy that I thought was my friend. Now you know my story. Do you think I'm a bad person for feeling the way I do?"

"Krystal you have no idea how close you are to my home with what you just said. If you're a bad person I think you are in good company with me. If you would like me to stay around for a few days and help you get things sorted out I can do that. Popeye can wait but to be honest his trail will get colder day by day. Right now I think both of us need to take a little revenge on him and I consider myself the avenging angel for the job."

Jo, Lena and I showed up on the porch and there was a brief lull in the conversation. Jo seemed to see that the two adults seemed uncomfortable and so she decided to get everyone talking. "Sven is quite a dog Mr. Buffole. He's alert and seems like he would be a good watch dog. I also think he and Lena really like each other." Lena looked at me and once again. If we were humans we would have blushed.

"Mister Buffole are you and Sven thinking of staying here for awhile? We sure could use some help around the place?"

Krystal broke in. "Jo we have no right to ask Buffole to stay and help us. We just met the man today and he was just telling me he has important business to tend to. He's the man who is going to track down your daddy's killer and bring him to justice."

"I'm sorry momma I didn't think. Of course Mr. Buffole needs to find him. Just when do you plan on leaving sir?"

"Jo it's got to be mighty tough for you losing your pa and helping out your mother around here. I wish I could stay and help but if I'm to catch Popeye the sooner I leave the better. Sven, Shag and I would be best hitting the road bright and early in the morning."

When morning arrived Buffole had had second thoughts. "Sven these two ladies have had a mighty rough time of it in the last twenty four hours. If it's all right with you I think we should hang around for a day or two and help them out."

I had no misgivings at all about hanging around. It would give me time to get to know Lena better. Any way Buffole was right it would be wrong of us not to make sure this family was taken care of before we left.

Buffole and I approached the house and knocked at the door. Krystal was already cooking breakfast and Jo was bringing in wood for the stove. Once we were seated Krystal suggested that her, Jo and Buffole hold hands during the saying of grace. It was rather heartwarming if I say so myself.

Buffole asked if it would be all right if he stayed and helped for a few days. He made it look like a favor if the ladies would allow it. "Krystal, Jo I would be very grateful if you would let Sven, Shag and I hang around here for a few days. My leg is mighty sore and it will give me some time to mend. I can still work some, maybe chop some wood, help you plow up a little more land for crops and do a few odd jobs. That is if you don't mind?"

Krystal smiled at Jo as she spoke. "Buffole we would welcome your company. We can most certainly use some help. I don't want you working too hard though, like you said you need to tend to that injured leg."

I could see Jo liked the idea. "Mr. Buffole I think it would be fine for you to stay a few days. I'll help all I can."

We helped out for the next two days. Jo occasionally was there to lend us a hand. Yet at times she was rather stand offish. She seemed to like Buffole but she had a sense of loyalty to her father which was only right for her to have. I think she knew that maybe her mother and Buffole had already developed a bond between them. Was it because they both shared a similar loss or was it one of those natural attractions that two humans can have for each other?

Each night after super all of us sat out in front of the house and marveled at the night sky. We visited and learned a few things about each other. Krystal sent Jo to bed about an hour before her and Buffole retired for the night. In that hour the two of them had some nice talks. Lena and I stayed up and listened so I knew there were feelings of the heart growing between those two.

Buffole respected Krystal and he seemed to see that she was loyal and trustworthy as a companion. He also mentioned to me that she was probably the most beautiful woman he had ever seen. It was not meant as a slur to his now deceased wife but I had to admit to myself that Krystal was one nice looking female for a human. I felt the same way about Lena.

Lena told me in confidence and I had to swear not to tell Buffole that Krystal pretty much felt the same way about him. I started to hope that maybe when this man hunt of ours was over that this might just be a nice place for us to return to. It might hold bad memories for Krystal and Jo. If so we could always move on and start our own home somewhere else. That night I had pleasant dreams about a future with all those here on this little ranch.

Each night Ole, Shag and I slept in the stable. Shag mentioned that he could understand now why horses liked stables. A soft bed of hay and a roof over his head to keep him dry and cozy were unknown comforts to our buffalo friend. Ole and I piled up some hay for ourselves and with Ole's blanket as a cushion we curled up together for a good night's sleep. I wanted to ask Ole if he was tempted to stay here longer. After all Krystal seemed nice and Jo was as good of a kid as anyone could ask for. Yet I knew we had a job to do and I best keep my thoughts to myself.

I was the first to awake in the morning to the smell of fresh frying bacon. I gave Ole a doggie nose kiss on his cheek and told him to get up and ready for breakfast. Shag also smelled breakfast but it was not a menu item for a buffalo. He stood up and shook his mighty body. Dust and derbies from his coat filled the air and Ole and I both sneezed. Shag looked at us with a buffalo smile and said. "Sorry guy's just straightening myself up with a little morning shake down. Think I'll head over to the stream for a bath and then have me some of that fine green grass along the creek for breakfast. Let me know when it's time to hit the trail."

Buffole spoke to Shag. "Actually Shag come back here in about half an hour. The ladies have some cattle out there that needs rounding up. Sven and I have rounded up a lot of dairy cows in our day but they are pretty domesticated. We aren't cowboys so we will have to depend on you to help us find and round up beef cattle and longhorns.

Shag passed his answer on to me. "Longhorns, beef cattle makes no difference to me. I can track 'em and control 'em. They are just a bunch of pansy ass cows compared to riding roughshod over a herd of buffalo"

Buffole talked to Krystal and learned that they had maybe two dozen head of cattle scattered around. They had bought them from a rancher on their way west. They only had to be driven about two days from their home range. The rancher that sold them the cattle had his men deliver them. All she knew was that the cowboys called them shorthorns and they had a 'MC' brand that the seller had special made for them. He told them the 'MC' was for Minnesotan cattle.

We rode out early in the morning and Shag held his nose high in the air. "The cows are not far. There is a lot of lush grass and water in the area so no need for the cattle to roam very far from home. By mid day we had spotted fourteen cows. We checked their brands and they were all 'MC". We left the cows bunched up as they were and Shag led us to a meadow that was located between some rock outcroppings. Without Shag we would have never found this place. Eight more cows were now located. Ole was about as good with a rope as he was at understanding women. So Shag took over. "A bovine is a bovine" he said. "I'll just tell them they gotta come back to the main herd. After all I am the alpha bull so they know they best follow my orders.

Now we had twenty-two cows in one bunch. Shag walked amongst them talking to them about the two missing cows. He learned one had fallen and broke its leg. The wolves put the poor beast out of its misery. The other missing one was a young bull who liked to wander off and act tough. He was seen a few miles away in a shaded area by the mountains base. Seems the young bull had found two longhorns and was busy courting them.

Shag found the bulls tracks and we followed them. The bull was standing in the shade munching on some prairie flowers. The two longhorns were a couple yards away and neither of them had a brand. The bull ignored our approach until we were right on him. Then he lifted his head and snorted. He turned and looked at us as he lowered his head and pawed the ground. Shag held his own and let the young bull blow off some steam and show off for his longhorn sweethearts. Then Shag spoke quietly to the young bull so the lady longhorns would not hear him. "Listen here youngster. You may think your tuff stuff but you don't have my experience, my size or my instincts. I hope you are smart enough to come along peaceful like because if we tangle you'll end up as wolf bait. You can bring your lady friends along and you can be boss bull when we rejoin your herd."

The young bull was smart enough to know a good deal when he heard it. He didn't have any witnesses to say he backed down and he could be boss of his herd. So we all meandered back to the main herd. It was late in the day so we made camp for the night. If we hit the trail before daybreak we could be back at the ranch for breakfast.

It was two hours before the sun came up when we started driving the cattle to the ranch. As the sun came over the horizon we could see smoke from the cabins chimney. We pulled in about nine in the morning and settled the herd on a pasture within eyesight of the ranch house. Shag had a talk with the bull and the youngster promised to stay in the area to help the human women out for awhile by not letting any of the cows stray.

Buffole unsaddled Shag and brushed him down. Shag made his way to the stream and after a good long drink he laid down for a well deserved rest in the soft grass.

Ole refreshed himself in the water trough with a few splashes of cool water to his face. He pulled an old razor from his saddlebag and scrapped the stubble off his chin as best he could. His wet hand ran through his hair to keep it somewhat in place. A quick swipe round his mouth with a well worn toothbrush and he was as presentable as he would ever be.

We made our way to the cabin and the door was open. The smell of fresh baked bread, bacon and pancakes filling the air. The window in the kitchen was propped open and a breeze helped to carry those delicious scents right to us. If I didn't know better I would think that Krystal had set up the window and door on purpose to get our attention. If she did it on purpose she's as sneaky as any Indian.

Krystal looked at Buffole and gave him a big smile. Lena looked at me and ran over to give me a nose kiss. Jo quickly ushered us to the table and started serving us breakfast. Ole, always the gentleman told Jo we would not start eating until everyone was seated. He stood up and pulled out a chair for Krystal as she approached the table. She was busy wiping her hands on her apron and was straightening herself up to look like a proper lady should. I could see in Ole's eyes that he thought Krystal was every bit as much of a lady as any woman he had ever seen.

"Mom, maybe Mr. Buffole will say grace for us?" Jo's comment sure did put Buffole on the spot. "Come on you can do it" is what I said to him. I knew Buffole had sort of forsaken the Lord some time ago when his own marriage was going sour. With the death of his wife and child it would be hard for Buffole to have much to be thankful for. Yet he had Shag and me and now three new friends with Krystal, Jo and Lena. I prodded him once more as he sat in dumb founded silence. "Buffole you can do this, thank the lord for letting you save three lives by coming here. Then you can add in your new friend Shag."

Buffole cleared his throat and Lena and I could hear him all right because we have canine hearing but I know that Krystal and Jo had to strain their ears to pick up the words. "Lord, thank you for letting Sven, Shag and I find a place to stay amongst good friends. Also thank you for letting me stay alive so that I can avenge the deaths and hurt for this family here and my own. God Bless this household that took us in. Lord please watch over Krystal, Jo and Lena. Please keep them safe and healthy. Amen." Well, it wasn't the best blessing I ever heard but it would do.

After breakfast Buffole tried to help clean up around the kitchen but Krystal insisted that Jo and she would take care of that. She knew that Buffole needed to get back to the hunt for Popeye. Buffole went outside and called for Shag. He grabbed his gear and saddled up our big shaggy friend. Jo, Lena and I sat on the porch saying our goodbyes as we watched Buffole getting things ready for us to leave. Shag and

Buffole were at the front of the cabin when Krystal came outside to say her farewells.

She walked over to Buffole and I could hear her softly say. "I've only just met you but I can tell you're a good man. You should take time to let yourself heal up. I want you to know your welcome to stay here and I would be more than happy to take care of you for a few days. Yet I know you must do what you have to do. You take care of yourself and watch after Sven and your buffalo. Thank you for all your help with that scoundrel and with burying my husband. You're welcome back here anytime you want. I would be much obliged if you decide to come back here when your job is finished" She took Buffole's hands in hers and then she leaned over and kissed his cheek. I know he wanted to do the same but he was just too shy. I ran over and gave Lena a doggie kiss goodbye and then Buffole scooped me up and put me in the saddlebag on the back of Shag. "Buffole softly said. "Krystal you're a good woman I wish I could stay and get to know you better. Right now I've got work to do, so if hell doesn't take me maybe heaven will be waiting here for me when my work is finished. I think you might just be the angel at the end of my journey." We rode off and I looked back wagging my tail at Lena, Krystal and Jo, of course my tail was hidden in that darn saddlebag and no one could see it but I think they knew I was going to miss them.

CHAPTER 7

It was mid morning by the time we were on the trail. Shag agreed with Ole and I that the rest we had at Krystal's was good for all of us. It gave us time to get our heads straight. Now it was back to business. We were refreshed and on the hunt. Popeye's horse was well worn and it showed in his early tracks. One of the horse shoe nails had fallen out and Shag said this made it much easier to trail Popeye in case he might cross tracks with other horses. We didn't know if Popeye knew it was us that shot at him at the ranch house. He may have thought it was another member of the family or a neighbor who had heard the gunshot. If we were lucky Popeye would think that he had left Buffole and all the other humans at the wagon train dead or dying.

Popeye had a good lead on us but we were determined to make up for lost time. Buffole and I shared some jerky and remained in the saddle for the whole day. Shag refused to eat anything until we camped for the night. A few water stops was all the rest that we took. The trail was heading for a town up ahead of us. Shag had roamed these hills and valleys for a long time and he knew where every town and cabin was located. To him each settler meant less land for the grazing buffalo herds. Yet he seemed to understand that he and his kind would have to share their land with others to survive.

We came into a sleepy little town which had been vacated by most of its residents when the local gold rush had proved to be nothing more than a few scattered veins of poor grade ore. A rundown hotel was a few doors down from a saloon that still seemed to be doing a good business. Buffole paid the local stable keeper an extra dollar for a stall to keep Shag in. The owner of the stable gave us a strange look but the money kept him from saying anything about our rather unique form of transportation. We had spotted Popeye's horse at the railing of the saloon and that was where Buffole and I were now headed.

Buffole made sure his holster was tied down. A loose holster would of course be a disaster if it came to a quick draw of the gun. We stopped in the shadow of a building and Ole pulled out the LeMat and checked the cylinder of the gun to make sure it was loaded and ready. The usual empty chamber he kept for safety reasons now had a bullet slipped into it. We crossed the street towards the saloon. Small puffs of dust from the street rose with each step of Buffole's boots. Even my four paws caused their own little dust storms. We now stood in front of the saloons batwing doors. Beads of sweat trickled down Buffole's face. This would be the first time he would face a man down. It would not be a cold blooded killing. It was justified revenge and in the west that was as good a reason as any for killing a man.

Buffole swung open the batwing doors and we both stepped inside. Some sun was filtering in the windows and dust particles mixed with smoke from hand rolled cigarettes hung in the air like an early morning fog. A few men were at the table playing cards. Two more cowboys were at the bar. There was no sign of Popeye.

The bartender and a few of the men glanced at us but nobody said a word. I guess it was permissible in a town like this for a dog to be in a saloon. Buffole ordered a SvenBrew beer for the both of us, mine in a bowl. The strange order did not even faze the bartender.

"Where's the owner of the horse at the far end of the rail outside" asked Buffole. One of the cowboy's at the card table looked our way and spoke. I could see his hand resting on the butt of his gun. "That's a mighty inquiring question for a stranger to ask. What business is it of yours?"

"The skunk that was riding that horse killed some folks that I knew. I mean to make him pay up." Buffole's hand was poised and ready to draw if need be. I tensed myself up to take action and leap at the cowboy to give Buffole an advantage. After all Buffole had never faced down a man under circumstances like this. Sure he had been challenged by death many times in the Civil War but this was different. This was a face to face challenge and not the heat of battle.

The cowboy then asked. "Was those folks killed in a fair fight?"

Buffole held back his feelings as best he could. "Nope, the hombre shot 'em in cold blood, never gave any of them a chance. Killed a woman, a young boy and their trail guide."

The cowboy relaxed and reached for his drink. "Seeing you put it that way I feel obliged to help you out. Barkeep give the man a drink on me. The fella you are looking for came in here and bought drinks for the house. Said he was in a hurry to catch a train heading down Texas way. Told us his ma was there and she was mighty ill. Her dying wish was to see her son as he had been gone a good many years. He needed a fresh mount and offered to trade me his horse for mine plus he tossed in five gold dollars. Hell my horse wasn't worth half that much plus I got me his horse to boot. What's the fella's name you're chasin?"

Buffole accepted the drink and gulped it down. "His name is Popeye. How long since he left here?"

"He didn't stay long. I'd say he's got a two and a half day start on you."

"Thanks for the drink. You've been real helpful. I got to get moving I've got me a man to catch,

"By the way stranger what's your name?"

"They call me Buffole and this here dog is my partner, they call him Sven. Is there anything you can tell me about the horse Popeye took? His markings or anything unusual about the hoof prints?"

"The horse is a plain old roan. Come to think of it there is a chip out of his left front horseshoe. I was meaning to replace it but that fella seemed to be in a hurry to buy so I didn't mention it. Good luck to you two, hope you get your man."

We went back to the stable and Buffole apologized to Shag for only letting him get such a short rest. "Sorry Shag but we got a lead on Popeye and we need you to check out some hoof prints near the saloon. The scoundrel switched horses on us. He's got a fresh mount and we best keep moving or we might lose him. Sven and I were told the horse he's riding has a chip out of his left front horse shoe, figured that will help you indentify the tracks."

We mounted Shag and rode over to the saloon. Shag soon located the tracks of Popeye's new mount and we made our way out of town. The three of us had a good laugh as we were leaving. From the cowboys in the saloon to what looked to be half the town's population had stopped whatever they were doing to watch a stranger and a dog riding on a buffalo.

It was a good thing the weather had stayed dry and still. Shag picked up Popeye's tracks and we followed them out of town. It was dry and dusty and Ole shared the water from his canteen with me. Shag told us he could go for a long time without water and it would be best for us two to drink often and keep ourselves hydrated.

The railroad was a good two day ride from where we were and Popeye's tracks seemed to veer off in the wrong direction. He was heading towards Texas but it sure did not seem that he was planning on taking a train. His story back at town was most likely fabricated to throw anyone who might be hunting him off track.

We made camp for the night and if anyone would have come upon us we would have made quite a sight. We really felt we had nothing to fear so Ole had our campfire burning bright. Shag and I were lying down facing the fire and Ole was sitting on a piece of log cooking up beans for him and me. We discussed what moves Popeye might be taking. Even if there was a posse after a few days he might just figure that a posse would give up. In Popeye's mind he might have even thought of going back and killing whoever shot at him and then he could finish what he started with the women. Then again Popeye was more the running scared type of guy. He proved that when he lit out from camp after killing Ole's and my family.

We traversed everything you could imagine. Beautiful grass filled valleys. Hills, streams, rivers, prairies and desert like areas of nothing but heat and sand. Whatever was on the mind of Popeye must have told him to keep on moving and that he did. We travelled later in the day and stopped only for water and to let Shag get a rest. Shag said the tracks were getting fresher and we should find our prey very soon.

As the sun set we made camp near the base of a mountain. A depression in the face of the rock made for a nice shelter and kept the slight evening breeze at bay. I gathered wood for the fire and Ole brushed down Shag's coat for him. Shag mentioned once again that maybe being a horse was not such a bad thing. After all horse's get stables and their humans brush them down and supply them with feed. It seemed like a pretty even exchange for having someone riding on your back.

Ole was cooking up what seemed to be a regular fare for us. Beans and hard tack bread. The smell of hot coffee filled the air and even I had come to be a coffee drinking dog for it was warm and soothing on a cool evening. I heard a noise and warned Ole and Shag that someone or something was approaching our camp. Shag took a deep breath and snorted. "It's a human on a horse I can smell him." Ole had learned to keep his gun belt on at all times unless he was sleeping and tonight was no exception. He thumbed off the leather thong he kept over his guns hammer to keep it from falling out in case of trouble. Ole reached over and cocked his rifle as quietly as he could and laid it at an angle to give it a quick grab and fire position.

The stranger rode up on his horse with one hand holding the reins and the other hand in the air. He looked at our motley crew in a rather surprised way before he spoke. "Howdy mister. I heard you cock that rifle. I don't want any trouble just looking for a place to bed down for the night and I smelled your coffee. I'm a lawman and my names Pat Garrett. Would you mind some company?" We could see the badge he wore glitter in the moonlight confirming his status as the law so we offered our hospitality.

As Pat was taking care of his horse Shag made a comment. "I smell buffalo death on that human. He was an old buffalo hunter I have no doubt. Ole you should kill him."

I relayed Shag's comment over to Ole. "Tell Shag I can't just kill a man for being a buffalo hunter. Hell they would string me from the closest tree for that. It's just not the way of humans. Tell him if we see him shoot a buffalo or if he is still hunting them I'll see what I can do about it."

Shag got up and shook himself off. The dust he made filled the camp as he made one last comment. "Humans are hard to understand.

They are a lot like wolves. They hunt in packs and sometimes kill more then they need to survive. You can let this one live but if I see him even hurt another buffalo I will kill him myself."

"Fair enough" I answered for both Ole and me. Pat came over and sat down by Ole and me. Ole handed him a cup of hot coffee and a plate of beans and hard bread. Pat held the hot cup in his gloved hands to help warm them up. "It's very hospitable for you to invite me into your camp. It seems sort of odd seeing a man sitting at a campfire with a buffalo. A dog I can understand that, hell any dog makes for a mighty fine companion. Even a horse can be a good friend out on the trail when you're by yourself. A buffalo, I ain't ever heard of a man hanging out with a buffalo. Used to hunt them big shaggy's a few years back. Sort of regret killing them now. I hear they have been almost wiped out. It was a bad thing for men to kill such a majestic creature. I hear some of the old time buffalo hunters like Buffalo Bill have started protected reserves for the buffalo. I sure wish them old critters the best. The west is dying and we all got to do what we got a do to save it. By the way stranger what's your name and what you doing out here all alone?"

"They call me Buffole and my dog partner's name is Sven. The buffalo standing over there is called Shag. We are hunting for a man called Popeye. He killed my family and one other man that we know of. I'm no lawman but this being the west there comes a time when a man has to take the law in to his own hands. You being the law I can only hope you agree."

"The law can only do so much. If a man does what is right the law of the west will usually look the other way. I wish I could help you out but I never heard of Popeye. As for me I have my own man to hunt. Couple of rustlers are my main objective. I am also keeping an eye out for a young man named William Bonney. Some call him Billy the Kid. There's a warrant out for his arrest but for the moment he is not on the top of my list. By the way where's your horse?"

"I don't have a horse I'm riding Shag the buffalo."

I can't describe the expression that was on Pat's face but to say the least it was somewhere between surprised and amused.

Pat was up early and had coffee on the fire. His horse was already saddled and ready to go. Buffole saddled up Shag and then he and Pat sat and had coffee as they said their goodbyes. Buffole was heading for Shag when he stepped around a small boulder with some rocks piled up against it. Like a lightning strike it happened. A Gila monster had been dozing in the pile of rocks and Ole not seeing it had stepped on its tail. The lizard sank his teeth into Buffole's leg and he went down in agony. Pat rushed over and grabbed the lizard by the tail. He held the Gila monster up and away from Buffole's leg as he pulled out this knife and pried the lizard's jaws open to get it to release its deadly grip from Buffole's leg. Once the Gila monster let go of Buffole's leg Pat sliced its head off and tossed it aside. He tore open Buffole's pants leg and made two slits with his knife along the line of the lizard's teeth marks. He squeezed out as much of the poison as he could as Buffole lay withering in agony. I looked at Shag with worry on my face. "Shag is Buffole going to die?" was all I could say.

Shag looked seriously at me and answered. "The Gila monster is poisonous but I have heard of many an Indian being bitten and they do get very sick but seldom do they die"

Shag was saddled and ready and he walked over by Pat and Buffole. Pat looked at Shag and said. "Listen buffalo I don't know if you can understand but Buffole is hurt bad. I'm going to hoist him up onto your saddle and I hope you will let me take your reins and lead you to the nearest town. It might be the only hope there is to save Buffole." Of course Shag and I both understood but we could not tell Pat that. Shag did as he was told. He stood still and let Pat help Buffole into the saddle. Buffole was still conscious but he was already turning pale. Pat took a leather thong from his saddle bag and tied Buffole's hands to the saddle horn. "Buffole listen hard, I tied your hands so you don't let go of the saddle horn. You just hold on as best you can. There's a town about a half days ride from here. There's a doctor there and I'll get you there as fast as I can."

Pat didn't know that I usually rode in Shags saddlebag but that was all right. I ran alongside Shag as we made our way on the road into town. I was saying every doggie and human prayer I knew to help

Buffole. It crossed my mind more than once that maybe we should have stayed with Krystal, Jo and Lena and none of this would have happened. Sure Popeye deserved to pay for his crimes but my Buffole deserved a chance to be happy with a good woman.

Buffole was slumped over in his saddle with his body resting on Shag's neck as we entered a dusty little town called Lutherhell. A few of the townspeople were loitering along the wooden sidewalks and we had soon gathered a crowd. Pat hollered out. "Somebody get a doctor this man's been bit by a Gila monster."

A round little lady came out from the saloon and started giving orders. "You men get this man down off that buffalo and take him to one of the rooms above the saloon." The local wagon salesman was standing nearby and the lady ordered him "Scotty quit gawking and go get the Doc like the man told you."

Scotty ran for the Doctor while some of the townsmen carried Buffole up the stairs to the rooms above the saloon. Pat flashed his badge and told one of the men in the crowd to take his horse and Shag to the stables.

We followed the men upstairs and once Buffole was in bed Pat drove away all the bystanders. The saloon lady started taking off Buffole's pants so the doc would have a clear view of the injured leg. Pat gave her kind of a strange look like maybe she was just a little bit to knowledgeable at removing a man's britches. "Ma'am you look like you've done this before. You sure don't look like no nurse."

The lady gave Pat an evil eye and said. "Listen mister it ain't none of your business what I done before. My names Trixie and I own this here establishment. I ain't no bar maid floozy if that's what you're thinking. Being in the saloon business I get to deal with lots of gunshot, stabbings and banged up bodies from just plain fighting. I guess I know what the doc expects and I'm getting your friend ready for his examination. If you don't approve of what I'm doing then you can do it yourself."

Pat got sort of red faced and answered. "No Ma'am I approve whole heartily of the way you is handling things."

The door of the room opened and the Doctor came in. "My name's Doc Payne. Tell me what happened to this man?" He set his bag on the nightstand and washed his hands in the water pitcher while he looked over Buffole's leg. Trish had removed the blood stained bandage and the leg was black and swollen around the bite marks.

Pat answered the Doc's question. "He was bit by a Gila monster. I got him here as soon as I could. It happened about five or six hours ago."

The Doctor examined the wound and told Trixie to get some laudanum from his bag. "Get some of the laudanum down this man's throat it will help ease the pain. What's your name cowboy?"

"Name's Pat Garrett. The man you're doctoring is called Buffole."

"Well Pat Garret you come over here and hold this man's leg still so he doesn't jerk around on me. Trixie you take hold of his wrists and don't let him squirm around. There's poison swelled up around this bite and I have to drain it." Doc Payne went to his bag and pulled out a scalpel. He lit a candle under the blade and got it red hot to sanitize it. I sat there watching and my eyes were as big as milk saucers. I could hardly believe he was going to cut my Buffole. Cut him he did. He slit the puffed up bulges around that wound wide open. What ran out I can't describe because about that time I threw up on the floor. I saw Buffole squirm a little and then he went limp. My God they killed my Buffole. I was about to take a flying leap and tear out the Doctors juggler vein when a dog's voice stopped me.

I glanced at the doorway. A Shih Tzu with a whitish brown coat who was built a lot like Trixie was standing just inside the room. She was looking at me when she spoke. "Your human just passed out from the laudanum. It's better that way he won't hurt so bad. I've seen lots of injuries around here and the Doc is taking good care of him. Just settle down and listen to what the Doc has to say." She came and sat by me and having here near gave me a calming feeling inside.

The Doctor pushed and prodded until he was satisfied that the wound was cleaned out of as much poison as possible. A man from the saloon had brought up hot water and the Doc used it to bath and clean up Buffole's leg. Trixie supplied fresh bandages and they soon had Buffole resting comfortably in the bed.

The Doctor started packing up his medical bag as he spoke. "Pat you got your friend here in time. Lizard bites like that are serious but not usually deadly. Buffole's got a fair amount of poison in his system and it's going to take a few days for it to work its way out. I suggest you make arrangements with Trixie to leave him stay here until he's strong enough to get up and around. Trixie make sure he gets lots of fluids and keep him in bed for at least three or four days. Find out if he's got any money. If he does I'll collect on my bill before he leaves.

Pat picked up Buffole's pants and rummaged through his pockets. He found some money and paid off the doctor. Doc Payne told Pat the bill was two dollars including the laudanum he would leave for pain. If Pat wanted the Doc to do a follow up call in a few days it would be another dollar which Pat paid advance.

Doc Payne left and it was Trixie, Pat and the little round dog and me. Pat looked over at Trixie. "So how much does Buffole owe you for the room and messing up your bed?"

She looked at Pat and said. "I'll worry about that when your friend gets better. You need a place to stay?"

"No ma'am I'm a lawman and I got some scoundrels to catch. I was on their trail when I met up with Buffalo last night. He got bit just as we were splitting up. I sure couldn't just leave him lying out there to die so I brought him in to town. I best get back to work. You wish him the best of luck for me when he wakes up. Thank you for your hospitality."

Pat walked over to me and patted me on the head. "Sven you take care of Buffole ya hear. By the way Trixie I'll pay the stable to look after his buffalo for him. Tell him it's my way of saying thinks for the coffee and beans he gave me for supper."

CHAPTER 8

The little Shih Tzu that had joined me was called Tesse. Her human Trixie came over and scratched me behind my ears and welcomed me to her saloon. She told me I could hang out with Tesse and we had free run of the entire place. Ole needed to rest and he was out like a light so Tesse gave me the grand tour of the establishment.

We visited the kitchen and got treats from a bald guy called Bessie. Next we hung out in the main saloon. A long ornately carved oak bar with some well placed spittoons was along one wall. Lots of tables and a grand looking stairway that led to the rooms upstairs were along another wall. It was getting late and the regulars were filling up the empty spots. A well dressed black man was playing the piano. Behind the bar was a life size painting of a scantily clad lady lying on a bed, her bare top was discreetly hidden by a small dog in the painting. I did not notice who it was until Tesse pointed it out to me. ""Sven did you see the picture of my human hanging behind the bar, that's me making sure she did not show enough to get arrested for indecent exposure." All I could say was "woof" that was a close call.

Tesse and I hung around the saloon for awhile watching the saloon girls hustle drinks for money. The locals, cowboys and drifters tried their luck at poker and faro. Trixie was ever present and made sure the peace was kept. I think it helped that she had supplied the bartender with a sawed off shotgun and according to Tesse there was a well concealed derringer somewhere on Trixie's person.

It was getting late and after a few drinks offered us by the saloon patrons Tesse was getting a little to frisky for my taste. I excused myself and went to Buffole's room. He was still sleeping soundly as I jumped on the bed and curled up by his side. He must have sensed my presence as he wrapped his hand around me and I quickly fell asleep.

I must have slept well as I should have. The previous day had been long and stressful. From the time Buffole had been bitten, the trip to town, Buffole's life hanging somewhere between life and death and a night of drinking with Tesse had worn me out. Trixie woke me with a little scratching behind my ear. I rolled on my tummy for a belly rub which she obliged me with. Then she whispered. Sven you best go outside and do your duties. I'll change Buffole's bandages and clean him up some."

When I came back into the room Buffole had his eyes open and smiled when he saw me. "Sven old partner come up here on the bed and give me a hug." I didn't need no invite as soon as I saw Buffole recognize me I was on my way to greet to him. I gave him a doggie kiss on the nose and he hugged me with his arm and cuddled his nose into the fur of my neck. I knew right then and there that everything was going to be all right.

Trixie walked into the room and gave us an order. "Sven out with you it's time for Buffole to have some breakfast. If he doesn't eat he won't get well.' She had made up some chicken broth and coffee and she sat on the edge of the bed to feed him. Tesse had appeared in the doorway and invited me downstairs to share her breakfast which consisted of leftover scraps from the night before plus a bowl of fresh milk. I had to admit saloon life was not so bad.

Over the next few days Buffole's leg was healing nicely. His fever finally disappeared and other then a slight limp which he had never really gotten over from the gunshot wound he was moving around pretty well.

We had been lucky when we had our run in with the buffalo hunters that they never had time to rob us so we were living off the money we had brought with us to start our new lives. I went to the livery stable every day to hang out with Shag. It was a nice break from Tesse who seemed to be trying to get her paws into me. You never know what a woman really thinks. I was always on my best behavior around Tesse but I think she figured I was the settling down kind. Maybe I will some day, but right now ain't the time. I bided my time for now between being with Buffole or Shag. You always feel safer when you're with your best pards.

Buffole offered to pay for his room and board but Trixie would have none of that. She refused to accept a cash payment. Her excuse was that she had to neglect a few of her own duties to care for Buffole so it would only be right and proper that he should work off his debt around the saloon. Next thing you knew Buffole was sweeping floors, chopping wood, bartending and a few nights he even ran the faro table.

It was late one evening and Buffole had finished his shift at the faro table. Trixie was busy fraternizing with the customers. She played the perfect hostess and usually kept everyone in line. Drinking, gambling and a room full of men could be an explosive combination. Buffalo sat down to a game of poker with three men he did not know. I lay down by Buffole's feet to keep an eye on things. Tesse was making the rounds with Trixie although she often looked my way to see if I was watching her. I had to admit that little Shih Tzu had a way of swinging her hips that was hard to ignore for any warm blooded dog.

I was listening to Buffole and the three other players. Two of the men were cowboys from the River Bar ranch and seemed like genial enough fellows. Both had gun belts that were loose and high up at their sides certainly they wore their guns for protection and not for making a living. The other man was called the Scotsmen and he wore his gun low and tied down. He had an air about him I did not like and I told Buffole to watch him. He seemed cocky and over confident in his card playing. Worse still he was drinking heavily and losing a lot of money, most of it to Buffole.

As a dog I can sense when an animal is about to attack and the Scotsman had that air about him. I told Buffole to slowly ease his gun from his holster and keep it under the table with the barrel slightly tilted upward towards the Scotsmen. It's always better to be safe than sorry. My eyes and ears picked up the motion of Trixie off to the side of us. She was making her way to the bar and I could see her mouthing the words 'shotgun' to the bartender. She must have had her own type of 'human' sense that said there was danger in the air.

Buffole was playing well and lady luck was smiling on him. The two cowboys had dropped out of the current hand and it was Buffole and the Scotsmen. The Scotsmen was down to his final few dollars when it was time for Buffole to call or raise. In a sense of fair play Buffole decided to give the Scotsmen a break. A raise would have busted the Scotsmen and he would be out of the game. A call gave him a chance to show a winning hand and if the Scotsmen was smart and had that winning hand he would take his money and call it quits.

The Scotsmen was not as smart as I had hoped he would be. Buffole called his hand and the Scotsman lay down a mighty weak pair of jacks on the table. Buffole didn't smile or even flinch as he laid out three deuces to win the pot. The Scotsmen's face turned red as he spoke. "Buffole you're a cheatin' no account sidewinder and I'm taking my money back. If you got the guts try and stop me." As the last words came from his mouth the Scotsmen stood up and drew his gun.

I caught the Scotsmen's movement a little quicker then Buffole and I shouted "Shoot Buffole, shoot!" Buffole stayed seated his gun drawn under the table and pointing upward. A pull of the trigger was all it took. The shot from Buffole's gun roared as the bullet tore through the top of the table and into the Scotsmen's chest. The Scotsmen flew backwards from the concussion of the bullet and he knocked over his chair as he fell to the floor.

Trixie had by now retrieved the shotgun from the bar but it was too late to stop the gunplay that had already occurred. Trixie and one of the cowboys from the table knelt next to the fallen Scotsmen and checked to see if he was still breathing. It only took a few seconds for Trixie to make an announcement. "The Scotsmen is dead. Everyone who saw what happened I'm sure will agree it was self defense on Buffole's part. Boys take this hunk of trash out of here and deliver him to the mortician. Buffole you shot him so you can pay to bury him. Everybody back to what you were doing. Drinks are on the house, complaints of Buffole."

We had won quite a bit of money but by the time we paid the undertaker and bought drinks for the saloon we used up a good half of our winnings. As for Buffole some of those present counted this as the first notch on his gun. They knew we were hunting Popeye and they figured Buffole might just add a few more notches before he was through. Of course no one was aware that Buffole had killed Bully the buffalo hunter and under the circumstances the fewer notches on Buffole's gun the better. The last thing we needed was for Buffole to become a known gunslinger.

When things had settled down for the evening we went off to bed. Buffole was still shaking a little from the gunfight when he started talking to me. "Sven it's mighty nerve wracking to kill a man. Even though it was self defense. One good thing came of this. Now I know I can stand up against Popeye and put him in his grave."

"Buffole you're not alone you got me as your partner. We'll both do the hunting and the killing together." Buffole hung his gun belt on the post at the head of the bed. From this day forward we both knew that a gun had better be close at hand at all times.

We went down to the Saloon for a little breakfast as the sun was just peeking over the horizon. Trixie was already up and making ham and eggs for a few early risers that were in the saloon. She gave us a few words to start our day out. "You best be ready to answer some questions about last night. The sheriff was out of town but he's expected back today. He's a different sort. Likes to talk a lot and don't listen much. Those of us that saw what happened will vouch for you that it was self defense but the Sheriff has a mind set of his own and it usually ain't got nothing to do with right or wrong. Whatever he thinks is right is what he's gonna do. You and Sven got two choices. Sit down and have some breakfast and hang around till the Sheriff shows. Or high tail it out of town and hope the Sheriff lets it slide on what the townsfolk tell him."

"Thanks for the advice Miss Trixie but I think Sven and I will do what's right and stay here to explain the shooting on our own. Like you said it was self defense. This is the west and no man should be found guilty for defending himself."

Miss Trixie was setting out our food and added in a new bit of information. "You and Sven don't know the whole story. The Scotsmen works for a man named Carlos Gracious who runs the stables and a wagon and buggy shop at the edge of town. Some say he was driven out of the Dakota territories for shady dealing, horse stealing and lying and cheatin' anyone he could. He's been doing the same here but nobody can do anything about it. He's a mighty dangerous man to rile up and your killing one of his men ain't gonna set to well with him."

"Well, ma'am maybe I'll just let the law deal with him if and when the time comes."

"Buffole what I'm trying to tell you is this. Carlos Gracious is not only a scoundrel and a lying cheat. He killed our town sheriff in a gunfight when he tried to arrest him for bilking a local widow woman out of her land. After he shot the sheriff he walked over to his body and ripped the tin star from his chest. Then in front of a town full of witnesses he declared himself the new sheriff and renamed our town Lutherhell. Not a man in town was brave enough to stand up to him or his band of horse stealing, wagon selling desperados. Now did that little bit of information sink into that thick Norwegian skull of yours? You're dealing with a Sheriff that would as soon shoot you as look at you. I suggest you and Sven get out of town while you're still walking upright."

"Well the way I see it Miss Trixie is if I back down from this Sheriff Gracious than I might not have the nerve to face the man I'm hunting. This might just be a good test for me. If I lose maybe I am guilty for killing the Scotsmen. If I face Gracious down and he figures I'm innocent well then I can go my way with no problems. Leaving now would be the same as me admitting to being guilty of killing a man. Nope, I ain't leaving."

I had to admit Buffole was doing what he figured was right. As for me I never learned to back down myself. I fought a lot of dogs who figured they were bigger and better than me and I always managed to come out on top. Sometimes I was pretty bruised and beat up but I was the winner. Buffole knew that about me and he knew I would be watching his back come hell or high water.

We had just finished our breakfast when this weasel of a fella named Travis poked his head in the door of the saloon. "Sheriff's heading this way Miss Trixie. I'll be back after the shooting to collect my free drink for warning you."

Miss Trixie was behind the bar and just shook her head. "Thought you boys might want a little warning. If you offer that snivlin' little polecat Travis a drink he'll snoop around and gather up everything going on in town from truth to gossip."

We could hear footsteps on the wooden boardwalk of the saloon. The steps were very deliberate and a jingle of spurs gave the steps an almost musical quality. The batwing doors of the saloon swung open and in stepped the Sheriff. It was hard to make out his features as the sun was at his back and the dim lighting in the saloon shadowed his face.

The Sheriff slowly looked around the room. He knew everyone there except for one man and his dog. Trixie stood behind the bar pretending to be cleaning some glasses. In reality she had her shotgun within easy reach. Why she should think about protecting Buffole seemed almost incomprehensible? She owed him nothing. If she had any feeling for him they were dispelled when she heard him cry out during his delirium while the poison worked its way from his system. He screamed a name she didn't know, Krystal, Krystal. Sometimes he mumbled for Sven and even a few mentions of someone named Shag, but Krystal came most often from his lips. Still she liked this fella and maybe it would be a good thing if he shot and killed the Sheriff and rid the town of this blight.

The Sheriff's eyes settled on the one man he did not know. That man was Buffole. I could sense the Sheriff had a power complex about him. He was not very tall and nothing about him would bring out fear from a man. Yet he seemed like the kind who wanted men to fear him. He was defiantly of Mexican descent with medium dark skin and black hair. He dressed all in black with lots of sliver ornaments on his outfit. From his shiny silver sheriff's badge to the conchos on his belt and holsters right on down to his silver spurs. Even his bolo tie was held by a small silver wagon, which I guess was the symbol of his wagon selling business. Two pearl handled revolvers completed his ensemble.

The sheriff made his way to our table. He swung a chair so the back was towards us and he straddled it. We could both see that this move kept his guns out in the open and ready for quick use against us. He stared hard at Buffole and I stared hard at the Sheriff. Buffole knew the rule about he who talks first loses so he kept quiet. Finally the Sheriff broke the silence.

"You must be the man they call Buffole. I saw the shaggy beast you ride in the stables. My name is Carlos Gracious, Sheriff Gracious to you. I hear you killed one of my men. In fact the man you murdered was one of my best wagon salesmen. It will be of a great monetary loss to me not to have this man selling for me anymore."

Buffole broke in. "Sheriff, you may not have all the facts." With the word's barley out of Buffole's mouth the Sheriff started talking again.

"Listen gringo you hear me out. I don't care what you have to say, the facts are what I say they are and that is the way it will be. You shot a citizen of this town. I as Sheriff have two choices. I can arrest you and conduct a trail which will cost the towns people money for me to put you up in jail and feed you until the hanging. I have already decided you are guilty of murder so why waste time. So I give you a break."

Carlos gave a big smile like he was Buffole's best friend before he continued speaking. "I'll tell you what amigo you and me will be friends until four o'clock this afternoon. We'll have some drinks and play some cards. Then we'll go out in the street where the whole town can see us. I'll hold your trial right there. Forty paces apart we will have a good old Mexican showdown. If you win you are innocent and you can go your way. If you lose you are guilty. Of course being guilty also means you are dead. When you are dead then maybe I shoot that little dog of yours too. I think that dog he looks guilty to me. Accessory to murder I will put on his little doggie tombstone."

I told Buffole not to worry as a team I was sure we could take this sweet talking Mexican. "Well Sheriff I guess I have no choice let's have a drink and play us some cards. I don't suppose you're ready to listen to my side of the story?"

"Gringo you have no side of the story. If you try to tell me your lies I will shoot you now and get it over with. I think even though we are now friends you should put your gun on the table and I will keep it safe for you until it is time for us to go out into the street." Buffole figured he could probably not out draw the Sheriff and did as he was told.

Trixie brought us drinks and gave Carlos a disgusted look as she spoke. "Carlos, Buffole is no gunfighter and you may have threatened him into not telling his side of the story but you don't scare me. You don't dare shoot a woman or this town would lynch you in a heartbeat. Buffole didn't make the first move. The Scotsmen was a sore loser at cards and he drew his gun on Buffole. The shooting was self defense and everyone in the saloon witnessed it. Someday you'll go too far and this town will rebel and put an end to you and your hired gunman."

"Go away woman, there's worse things I can do to you than kill you. You keep your mouth shut and keep the drinks coming. Now go and lock up the front doors. Me and my new friend are going to have a nice quiet game of cards. My boys over at the bar and the tables will keep an eye on things until the trial. You make sure you keep them refreshed and happy. Maybe you roust a few of your bar wench's out of bed to keep my boys company."

Trixie got two of her girls to come downstairs to mingle with Carlos's boys. I lay down by Buffole and told him my plan of action. When he got to the street he should be ready to draw and shoot. At the last moment I would be standing on the boardwalk across from the Sheriff. I would bark as the Sheriff went for his gun to distract him. If it works you can take your time for a clean draw and a straight shot.

Tesse came and sat down by me and told me that Trixie had sent one of her bartenders to the stables to saddle up Shag and have him ready to ride. I let Buffole know about Shag and it was a relief to both of us. No matter what Carlos said his smiling Mexican face and pretense of being a friend only meant that he could lie to a man's face and shoot him while he smiled at him. Although Trixie had no way of knowing that Buffole and I could communicate so that we both knew Shag was ready I was pretty sure she would somehow let

Buffole know what was going on through some type of normal human communication.

Buffole sat back and relaxed as he shuffled the cards. He knew I was keeping an eye on things from my position on the floor next to his chair. As he dealt the cards he started in on some small talk. "Sheriff seeing we're such good friends can I call you Carlos? Just how is it that this town came to be called Lutherhell? Seems to be a mighty strange name for a town."

"Friends, which we are gringo, at least until I kill you. When I first come here the town was very small, tiny you might say. I work for a man who collects towns for a hobby. He own many towns I think as of last count maybe twenty six towns he owns. This town it give us lots of trouble at first. The people fought us and did not like to see us take over. It was founded years ago by a German man named Besser. This man he wanted the American version of his name used for the town so he called it Bettertown. My boss well he had so much trouble here with the old timers in town he sort of punished them with a joke about the town. He named the town after himself. His name is Luther. He added the hell part to remind the people what would happen to them if they did not follow his laws. Good joke is it not?"

"Good joke I'm not so sure of that Carlos. Appropriate name for a town with you as Sheriff that I would say rings true."

"Good thing I like you gringo or I would have to kill you now for a comment like that. By the way I saw your buffalo at the stables. Why would a sane man ride a buffalo? When you are dead I think maybe we butcher and roast your buffalo and have a big celebration in town for killing you. Many men in town they liked the Scotsmen they would love to have a party to celebrate the death of his killer."

"Carlos I wouldn't be roasting my buffalo just yet. What if you lose and I win? Would you give me your word right here in front of Trixie and your men that I can ride out of this town with no interference?"

"Gringo, Carlos never lies. Men you heard the gringo if he beats me out in the street you let him ride out on his shaggy beast. Steve and Chad did you hear me?"

Chad answered for the two of them. "Yeah boss we heard you. If the gringo wins we leave him go all peaceful like. We know he won't win so no need for us to worry about it."

A quiet mummer of acceptance went through the room. I whispered to Buffole. "Don't you trust that smiling Mexican any farther than you can throw Shag." Buffole looked down at me and mouthed the words. "I don't. If we kill him we best be ready to make a dash for the livery stable and make our stand until we can get on Shag and high tail it out of here."

The card game was about over. The bets had been small and Carlos and Buffole were about even in their stack of chips. Carlo's stood up and announced. "Buffole it's time we settle this matter man to man. Are you ready?"

Buffole took his gun from the table slow and easy so as not to cause Carlos a reason to start the gun fight early. "Carlos, I hope you don't mind but I want to make sure my first chamber has a bullet. I usually carry an empty first chamber just for safety." Buffole clicked the cylinder over a notch and the gun was ready. He stood up and slipped the LeMat into his holster

"No problem gringo, you'll need any advantage you can get. I have many notches on my gun already and you will just add one more." Carlos held his hand out for Buffole to shake it. I was surprised that Buffole accepted this token gesture of false friendship from the Mexican. Then Buffole surprised Carlos when he said. "God bless you Carlos and if not may the Devil have his way with you."

Carlos said nothing he just led the way out of the saloon and out into the street. Nobody actually counted how many paces they were apart. That was just for fancy dudes over in Europe or maybe on the east coast of colonial America. This was the west where formalities were not required. The fastest gun, the surest shot or in some cases just plain luck is what counted.

The two men faced each other as a crowd of on lookers gathered on the boardwalk. I took my place directly across from Carlos on the boardwalk of the saloon. Trixie stood just outside the saloons batwing doors with a shotgun cradled in her arms. One of her bartenders was on the balcony above us along with two of her saloon girls. Each of them had rifles in their hands. Across the street I noticed a few other townsfolk had armed themselves. Tesse was next to Trixie and she told me that Trixie had sent out word to the other town's people that this may be the chance they had all waited for. If Carlos lost, his men would have no leader and it would be the perfect opportunity for the town to rid themselves of the evil that had befallen it. I was too far from Buffole to let him know that not only did his life depend on what was about to happen but he also held the fate of a whole town in his hands.

The sun was just setting in the west but there was still enough light cascading over the tops of the false front buildings for the showdown to take place. Carlos had his guns at the ready and it was a rare sight to see a man poised to draw two guns at once. Buffole had released the leather thong from his guns hammer and stood waiting. I doubt he had any fear of death for himself. His motivation was to stay alive until we hunted down Popeye and killed him.

My hunting eye sight saw the slight muscle twinge in the Sheriff's hands as he was about to make his draw and he was not going to wait for Buffole to make the first move. I barked and the Sheriff jerked his head my way as he was drawing his guns. Our plan worked to perfection. Buffole had time to draw his gun and straighten his arm for a well aimed shot. Carlo's stumbled backward as his guns cleared their holsters. He was still conscious enough to pull the triggers on both guns. One gun was pointing downward and its bullet bit the dust. Trying to regain his balance he took aim at Buffole but his backward momentum over rode his effort to gain his footing and his other gun hand went into the air firing a bullet harmlessly into the sky. Falling on to his back his body slammed onto the road and the dust settled on his clean black outfit. I could see a few beats of his heart were still pumping as small spurts of blood rose from the bullet hole just below his Sheriff's badge and stained his black shirt a crimson red.

Carlo's two main henchmen were right behind me. They were as good at their word as was Carlos. Steve pulled his gun and took aim at Buffole. My instincts took hold and I lunged for his gun hand knocking his pistol from his grip.

Chad then pulled his gun and Trixie stepped in front of him with her shotgun lowered. She pulled the trigger and the blast of her well aimed shot blow a hole in Chad's chest the size of a man's fist. Buffole holstered his gun and looked around him. The townspeople had their assorted weapons leveled at what remained of Carlos's men. Trixie shouted out orders. "Carlos Gracious is dead and so is his stranglehold on this town. All of you men who worked for him had best clear out now while you're still walking upright." Steve looked at his bloodied hand complements of my fangs and then he looked at his gun lying on the boardwalk.

"Don't even think about picking up that gun Steve. I suggest you load Chad's and the Sheriff's bodies into one of Carlos's precious wagons and leave this town and never return." Said Trixie.

Steve stood there rather dumbfounded. What was left of the Carlos crew were looking at him as the next man in charge now that the Sheriff was dead. "Men you heard the lady. Go get a wagon and pick up those bodies. We best be moving on." Steve walked into the streets and looked at the body of his dead boss and glanced back at his blasted away partner Chad. I ran out to Buffole with my tail in full wag screaming. "We did it partner, what should we do now?"

Buffole picked me up and hugged my hard as he gave me a kiss on the forehead and I gave him a doggie kiss on the cheek. "Sven you're the best partner any man could ever have." We walked over to Trixie as she stood looking at us. The wagon was already roaring up the street driven by one of the Carlos's men to collect the bodies.

Buffole cleared his throat to start talking but Trixie interrupted him. "Buffole I know what you're going to say. You've got to find that man Popeye. So I understand that you need to take you're leave. I've sent one of my bartenders to get that thing you call a ride from the stables. Tesse and I would like to see you stop back and say hello if you're ever passing this way. I have a feeling that it isn't just Popeye you're hunting for. I think you may be searching for a woman named Krystal too."

Buffole was a little red in the face when he answered. "You might just be right on all accounts Trixie. Thanks for saving my life. That Chad fella would have shot me dead to rights if you hadn't stepped in. If this town has any sense at all they should elect a woman as their next Sheriff. I think you would be a perfect choice for the job." Trixie came forward and gave Buffole a kiss on the cheek as she said. "You're buffalos here, best you saddle up and skedaddle out of here. I've been asking around and word is that Popeye is two towns south of here in a town called Caraline Valley. I hear he's getting a reputation for a few killings and is claiming to be the fastest gun around. Maybe you and Sven can take him down a notch." Then she turned and went back into the saloon.

Tesse sat looking at me and I think I detected a tear in her eye. I went over and told her she was a great friend to me while we were in town and thanked her for making me feel at home. I think she was hoping for more but I had Lena on my mind. Guess maybe Buffole and me were thinking that our trail might end up back at a little ranch someday.

As we rode out of town the streets had cleared and Carlos's men were nowhere to be seen. A man was scratching out the name on the towns sign as we rode by him. I looked back from my perch in Shag's saddlebag and watched as the man wrote New Bettertown under the crossed out town name of Lutherhell.

CHAPTER 9

We wandered along down the road and Shag finally started talking. "Sounds like you two had one heck of an adventure according to talk around the stables. Makes me kind of glad I was warm and snug in my own stall. Now that you two had all your fun I hope we can get back to the matters at hand."

Buffole just smiled and then asked me a question. "Sven how do you suppose Trixie knew about Krystal and what made her think I had any interest in going back to her?"

"Buffole when you were under the influence of the Gila monsters poison and the Doctor's prescribed laudanum you did some mighty strange talking. From cussing out your family for driving you out of Minnesota to casting hell and brim fire at those buffalo hunters that killed Kate and Zeb. Mostly though you thinking Trixie was Krystal and talking like you should have never left her. Your darn lucky Trixie was the understanding kind or she might of just let you up and die. If you got Krystal on your mind it's no never mind to Shag and me. I'll tell you one thing though I wouldn't mind seeing Lena again and Shag sort of liked that little valley full of sweet grass and clear water."

After that we rode on in silence. Buffole was keeping his thoughts to himself. I updated Shag on Sheriff Carlos and his men. We even talked about Trixie and Tesse. It was a pretty interesting time in Lutherhell.

Our first night back on the trail Buffole built us a nice fire and we gathered around for a quiet evening. The night was clear and the stars shone brightly. A coyote howled off in the distance which sort of spooked Buffole. He still had some country boy in him and not the experience of the west that he would continue to gain as time went on. He had a thought that maybe it wasn't a coyote, maybe it was an

Indian. Being a part of the canine family myself I quickly assured Buffole that it was not an Indian it really was a coyote. He was not just howling at the moon he was looking for a mate. Buffalo just gave me a rather strange stare as if I was hinting at something. Me. I just wagged my tail and suggested we get some shuteye.

When daybreak came we hit the trail again. We came upon a road that had been recently traveled and it made for easy riding. We had to figure there was civilization nearby as both the hoof prints from horses and the wagon wheel tracks looked fairly fresh. Some cattle grazing off in the distance suggested a ranch was nearby.

The sun was in our eyes yet we could discern a lone rider on horseback approaching. With the sun to their back we couldn't make out the riders features. The way the person rode looked causal and relaxed so we figured it was a friendly encounter, but Buffole still slipped the leather thong from his LeMat's trigger just in case.

As the rider got closer we could tell, and boy I mean we could tell it was a beautiful lady. Slim, dark long hair tied in a pony tail under her hat and wearing a man's shirt and man's britches. Men's clothes or not there was no mistaking this was a lady. Alongside her trotted a black mongrel dog who weighed about forty pounds. Dogs have a sense about each other and I took a liking to this canine even before we were introduced.

She pulled her horse right up to us. This was a gal who was bold and straight forward. Not afraid of anything from what I could tell. "Howdy mister, my names Ilsa and this is my dog Tanner. I saw you from a distance and I just could not believe my eyes. I could have sworn you were riding a Buffole and doggone it if you aren't. I was out east going to school and I visited one of the circus' out there and saw an elephant. I figured in all my born days that had to be the most unusual thing I ever would see. But you mister, you take the cake. A man riding a buffalo and a little dog hitching along in the saddle bag. I swear I think you are even a stranger sight then an elephant. By the way what's your name?

"Name's Buffole ma'am. My dog's name is Sven and this here buffalo's name is Shag. Sven and Shag don't belong to anyone we three are sort of partners."

She smiled and her pearly white's just sort of sparkled in the sunshine. "Mister Buffole I would be mighty pleased if you would ride back to the ranch with me and have some supper with my family. If you have a mind to you could stay overnight. I could even arrange for a soft bed for you and a nice stall for Shag and Sven to bed down in."

I told Buffole to accept under one condition. I was not sleeping in a stall. "Sounds to inviting to say no to Miss Ilsa. I have just one small request. Would it be all right if Sven stayed with me during the night? Shag he snore's something fierce and poor Sven would not get any rest staying with him."

"I think that can be arranged." Said Ilsa.

We rode side by side down the road leading to the ranch. Ilsa was very friendly and talkative. "I hope you don't mind if I show you three off to my family. My parents like to keep us all together so we all share work on the ranch. It's actually more than a ranch now days. In fact we have our own little town. I have eleven brothers and sisters and some of them are married with spouses and kids of their own. To keep some privacy for everyone we built homes for all of the families to live in. It works out very well and now we have our own little main street about a half mile from my folk's large ranch house. Daddy and the boys raise beef and grow crops. The rest of us do the chores as needed. As for me I like to ride the range and locate stray cattle. I am also in charge of the vegetable and flower gardens. Well here we are."

We rode up the main street of the ranch and it was filled with neat homes, white picket fences and flower gardens. It was like one of those picture perfect towns you see on a fancy hand tinted postcard from out east. Some of Ilsa's sisters and sister-in-laws plus a bushel of kids all watched us ride by. The woman folk had strange and sort of unbelievable looks on their faces. The kids all ran out to run alongside Shag and touch him. Shag sort of snorted but allowed the little human critters their curiosity. "Sven you tell Buffole I'll put up with these tiny humans this time but don't make a habit of doing things like this." I of course relayed the information to Buffole and he just smiled.

Ilsa led the way to the stables and I must say they were nicer then a lot of house's we had stayed in. The stalls were white washed and the floors were made of wood and scrubbed clean. The older boys offered to unsaddle Shag and brush him down. Buffole helped Ilsa take off the saddle from her horse and he placed it on a saddle stand along the wall. Bridles, saddles, ropes and anything a good stable should have were placed or hung neatly along the walls. Buffole walked over and patted Shag on his big wooly head. "It will be all right partner. These kids will take good care of you." Shag snorted and he told me "Buffole's right, I could get used to being treated like this." A young girl offered Shag a handful of oats and that was the last we heard from him as we left the stables and headed to the house.

The house was a huge two story affair with a balcony on the second floor and a railed porch all the way around the main level. The place was spotless outside and a massive set of double oak doors were opened by one of Ilsa's sisters who had seen us from the kitchen window as we rode up.

We were soon up to our ears in sister's and kids. We learned their last name was Pest and it seemed amusingly appropriate to Buffole and I because there were already enough of them that they were becoming pest's with all their questions about why we rode in on a buffalo. Mrs. Pest told the ladies of the house to get busy and finish setting the table. They made sure that an extra place was set for their guest and also to make sure that a place next to Tanner in the corner of the room was set up for me. I guess they were not the let the dogs eat at the table type of folk. Although I heard Ilsa whisper to Buffole that when guests were not present Tanner would sit next to her on the floor by the table but her father felt it was inappropriate behavior around strangers.

Mrs. Pest made her way to the porch and rang a huge brass bell that was mounted to one of the pillars at the entryway to the porch. I was standing in the doorway with Tanner when we saw a swarm of men folk come streaming out of every building, nook and crevice with-in sight. Eventually they converged with each other and became a dust raising mob of men with hunger in their eyes. "Wash up before you come in for supper! We have a guest so clean yourselves up well and be on your best behavior!" Shouted Mrs. Pest. She certainly had authority because those men hit the water pump and washed and spiffed themselves like it was a Sunday go to meeting day.

Once everyone was inside the seating ritual began. The women all approached their chairs as the husbands, finance's, and even brothers pulled out the chairs for the ladies and let them be the first ones seated. Mr. Pest came over by me and held out his hand. "Hello their young man. My names Jack Pest, you can call me Jack. I heard from some of the kids that my Ilsa brought you home. Just like her rounding up strays and bringing them to the house. Just joshing with you sir, have a seat next to my Ilsa I'm sure her fiancé won't mind." Buffole shook hands with Jack and sat in the chair next to Ilsa. Her fiancé was on her other side and he did not look to happy about the arrangement.

Jack said a blessing and it was the first time there was silence as he told everyone to bow their heads and think about the gifts God had given them. I thanked God for Buffole and Shag, oh yes also for a great meal and a place to stay for the night that wasn't outside.

The food was passed and plates were filled. It seems it was tradition that everyone in or connected to the family ate supper together. It was like eating with a small army. Lots of small talk and conversation filled the room until Ilsa clinked her glass with her spoon. "Can I have everyone's attention? "I would like to introduce our guest Buffole and over by Tanner is Sven. I found them riding along the road through our ranch. For those of you who may not have heard Buffole rides a buffalo."

Jack took up the conversation at this point. "Yes I heard about our buffalo riding guest. Tell us Buffole just how does it happen that a man picks a buffalo to ride over a horse?"

I could tell by the look on Buffole's face that he was not comfortable with being the center of attention but he had no choice as all eyes and ears were now on him. "I don't think a man picks a buffalo to ride. It just so happens that the buffalo picked me. To make a long story short the buffalo came into my camp and just sort of hung around. The horses had run off and it was a long walk to civilization. After a few days the buffalo which is called Shag and I befriended each other with some help from my dog Sven. Sven just seemed to have a way with Shag and it did not take long before I tried to put a saddle on Shag and he let me. We rode on out of there and here we are." Buffole tended to leave out some parts and embellished some others but the story was sort of truthful and seemed to satisfy our audience."

Buffole's hand was on the table and Ilsa reached over and put her hand on his as she spoke. "I think that is a wonderful story. A man and a buffalo becoming friends. Back east people would pay to see a man riding a buffalo. I myself am quite impressed with you Buffole." A number of the people at the table gave a resounding "Here Here!" to Ilsa's statement. I noticed her fiancé seemed to have fire in his eyes as he looked at Buffole.

Tanner had not said much to me up until now. "Sven, if you can figure out some way to let your human know you better do it. Ilsa's fiancé is studying law and he is very jealous. He's not much with a gun but he could come up with some reason to get your human in trouble with the law. It would be best for him to stay clear of Ilsa. I know her well as she is my human and I think she has some feelings towards Buffole. Her Fiancé is a widower with a daughter and Ilsa feels obligated to give the child a mother but if too much temptation comes her way it could mean trouble for all concerned. She likes your human Buffole a lot but it may just be fascination because he is sort of rough and rugged. Ilsa's used to being around a more refined type of man and her curiosity might just get the best of her."

Ilsa's fiancé figured he better get his two-cents worth in. "Buffole just what brings you to this neck of the woods? Are you running or hiding from something." That comment hushed the whole room except for Jack. "Listen, you may be my daughter's fiancé but I don't feel that's an appropriate question to ask a guest."

It almost looked like hatred in Ilsa's eyes as she stared at her fiancé. All eyes were on the three of them and it looked as if a showdown was about to take place. Buffole figured he better say something to try and calm down the situation that was developing. "Jack don't you worry none about that question. Out here in the west it's not uncommon to run into men trying to start new lives. As for me I'm not running from anything except maybe the memory of a family I left buried back on the prairie. I'm just a drifter looking for a new start."

"Why that is so sad," said Ilsa.

"Just plain old heart breaking I'm sure" said her fiancé.

Jack figured it was time to take control. "I think that is about enough about our guest and his past. Let us leave him alone to enjoy this fantastic meal the ladies have provided for us." The table was soon a buzz with ranch talk between the men and lady talk between the women. I looked at Buffole and could see he was relieved that he was no longer the center of attention.

Supper was over and the ladies started to clear the table. The men retired to the front porch and spread out into little groups. Jack broke out some fine bottled wine and cigars for after dinner relaxation. Tanner and I curled up by the back door of the kitchen. It looked like it might just be a quiet relaxing evening.

I saw Buffole heading towards the stable and Tanner and I trotted over to see him. By this time I had mentioned to Tanner that Buffole and I could communicate which he of course thought was a very unusual thing to happen. Yet being a canine he took it in stride.

"Buffole what are you doing? I asked.

"Too many people in one place make me nervous as a prairie dog with a hawk overhead. Figured I would get some quiet time and check on Shag. Tanner nice to have you along for a visit maybe we can get to know each other better. Your Miss Ilsa is quite a lady. A little headstrong but I like that in a woman." We entered the stable and Buffole went to Shags stall. "Shag old boy how you doing? How about I brush you down for the night?" Shag looked at Buffole and snorted. Then he shook his mighty head up and down as a yes to Buffole's question.

Tanner and I sat watching Buffole brush Shag. Tanner did not seem to say too much but he finally started talking. "Sven I like you and your friends. You three really seem to have a bond with each other.

Remember what I told you inside. You best warn Buffole to watch his step around here. Anyone who pays to much attention to Ilsa gets her fiancé gets mighty riled. He and some of the guys will be heading off to town to do some drinking after they finish visiting up on the porch. Once he gets liquored up no telling what he might do. He's already jealous over the attention Ilsa paid to Buffole during supper. I like your company but it might be best you three pull out in the morning."

I was too late to relay my information to Buffole. Ilsa came walking into the stable and went right up to Buffole. She grabbed a brush and started to work on Shag's opposite side. "Buffole I was looking for you and here you are keeping company with a buffalo instead of me. The least you could do is go for a walk in the moonlight with the lady that brought you to her home and fed you." Said Ilsa.

Ilsa took Buffole's arm in hers and led him from the stable. Tanner and I went along to keep an eye on things. We heard the men at the house mounting their horses and riding off towards town.

Ilsa led us along a path towards a wooded area that led us to a lake. A wooden bench swing hung from a huge oak tree branch that overlooked the moonlit lake. She and Buffole sat next to each other and she took Buffole's hand in her's. Buffole was being his normal shy self but he did hold hands with her. I knew him well enough to know that he would have probably pulled his hand away from hers except he did not want to offend her. My best hope was that he still had thoughts of Krystal on his mind and was not going to fall for the charms of the beautiful Ilsa.

Ilsa had a way of speaking that seemed to mesmerize Buffole. "I like you Buffole. You seem like a man a woman can talk to who will understand. Around here everyone is family or about to be family. My father has arranged for me to marry a widower with a little ten year old girl. For my father it is a matter of practicality. The man I am supposed to marry is studying to be a lawyer. With the size of our ranch and our family it would be an advantage to have a man in the family that practices law. I like his little girl and she likes me. The child needs a mother and I am well past marrying age with no children of my own. I just do not know if I should marry someone I don't love.

I will probably learn to love him but is it the right thing to do? You are an outsider, someone I can confide in. You don't know any of us or what is expected of us. What do you think I should do?"

I could tell Buffole was skitterish as a lamb being stalked by a mountain lion. "Ilsa you seem like a nice lady. I just don't feel I'm qualified to give advice on matters of the heart. Sounds to me like your fiancé's daughter really loves you and she needs a mother. He seems a little too high strung and jealous to me but I'm sure he loves you or he wouldn't care. Only you know what is best for you to do. I ain't no praying man but if you are maybe you can find an answer there. Just don't marry him because your father or family tell you to. Marry him because you want to. You got a mighty nice spread here and a huge family to support you in whatever you feel is best. One thing I'm sure of is that your family will always make sure that any man that marries you will take care of you and treat you right."

Ilsa's next statement was a shocker. "Buffole what if I wanted you to take me away from all this? We could saddle up and ride out tonight."

Buffole must have been ready for he gave his answer without hesitation. "Ilsa it's a mighty tempting invitation. I think you are a fine looking woman and you tempt me to say yes. My old man taught me that if you tell the truth you never have to remember what you said. I told part of the truth at the supper table. I need to start a new life. I just ain't ready to start it right now. I'm hunting the man that killed my family and I won't rest until I find him. I killed that man's partner right after they killed my wife and boy. Then I got in a gunfight up in Lutherhell and two men are dead because of me. It was self defense so there ain't no wanted posters out for me. You can see I ain't no godly man, if anything the devil seems to be riding with me. Just to be totally honest I met a gal after my family was killed and I sort of hope to make my way back to see her when I get through doing what I got to do. I think you best stay with the people that care for you and love you."

All of us sat in silence for awhile. After about half an hour Ilsa stood up and took Ole by the hand. They walked back to the ranch arm in arm. No one said anything until Ilsa showed Buffole his room in the house. She kissed Buffole on the cheek and said. "Thank you I think staying here and giving that little girl a mother and marrying her father are the right thing for me to do. Anyway it will make my father happy to get a son-in-law who is hoping to become a lawyer."

Buffole washed up in the water bowl on the nightstand and left his gun belt hanging on the front poster of the bed within easy reach. "Never hurts to be cautious." Is what he said to me. I had to agree I didn't trust Ilsa's fiancé and if he came home drunk no telling what he might do. Even worse if he found out we had been down by the lake with Ilsa it might just set him off to do something really stupid.

It was after midnight when my canine hearing heard horses and the boisterous voices of drunken men enter the ranch yard. It took some time but after unsaddling and putting away their horses the men finally dispersed and things quieted down. Buffole tossed and turned some but sleeping in a soft bed was almost a novelty for him and a little noise was not about to disturb his sleep.

Once things finally settled down outside I relaxed and stretched out at the bottom of the bed. Buffole was softly snoring and I was used to his sounds so it helped to lull me to sleep. Suddenly my ears perked up and I heard the door of the house creaking open. Clumsy heavy footsteps were coming down the hall towards our room. Whoever was in the hallway was unsteady on their feet and I heard them bump against the wall as they approached the door to our room. By now I was sitting up and fully alert. I saw the door handle to our room start to turn. I growled loud enough to alert Buffole. He knew my growl and knew it meant danger. Quick as stink from a skunk he pulled his pistol from its holster and slid it under his blanket. He lay back down and pretended to be asleep. He knew I was on the lookout and would alert him if needed.

The door to our room opened and I could see a glint of moon light from our window glimmer on the barrel of a rifle. A man stood in our door way and lit a match. He reached over and touched the match to the kerosene lamp hanging on our wall. The silver coated dish behind the lamp lit up the room like daylight. I told Buffole the fiancé was in the room and loaded for bear. Buffole slowly opened his eyes as he feigned just waking up. I knew his pistol under the bed covers was aimed at the fiancé where it would do maximum harm if needed.

The man leveled his rifle at Buffole and shaky as he was I was a little worried he might just pull the trigger of that rifle by mistake instead of on purpose. I sensed he wasn't really a killer he just wanted to put a scare into my partner. I told Buffole to talk to this guy and calm him down. Whatever it took to get him to lower that rifle had to be done.

Buffole did not let the man know he had a gun under his blanket. He just started to talk soft and easy like. "I know you. You are Ilsa's fiancé. Beautiful woman you got there your mighty lucky to have her. She told me you have a little girl that needs a mother. I think the three of you will make a great family. You know if you kill me you will ruin everything for your little girl, for Ilsa and yourself. Killing a man in cold blood would either get you hanged or at the very least a long stretch in prison. Why don't you lower your rifle and tell me what you want?"

Ilsa's fiancé lowered the rifle barrel enough so that it was pointing at the floor. Buffole and I both breathed a sigh of relief. "Buffole I have been checking up on you. There were some men at the saloon that came in from Lutherhell. They told me and the boys that they had been working up there until you came along and spoiled everything. Seems you killed two men in that town and one of them was the Sheriff. You claimed self defense and the town backed you up so there are no wanted posters out on you. Yet those Lutherhell boys would probably give me a reward for killing you. What you said about my little girl was right. Killing you would only ruin my life. I'm studying to be a lawyer and I guess killing you is not worth ruining my life. Ilsa is my women and you best remember it. I want you off this ranch first thing in the morning or I might just change my mind and come gunning for you. You understand me?"

Two good things were coming out of this conversation. Buffole, Shag and me had work to do and we had to pull out in the morning anyway. Buffole was almost tempted by Ilsa's offer to take her away from this yahoo she was engaged to but it was none of our affair. Anyway Krystal and her daughter were well placed in the back of Buffole's mind and Krystal was a women that might just need a man like Buffole. I knew that no matter what Buffole was thinking he could really use a woman like Krystal. As for me, Lena was also a strong reason to think about settling down when the time was right.

Buffole relaxed his own gun hand from under the blanket. "Listen fella I meant no harm stopping in here. I just accepted a friendly invite from Ilsa and a nice place to get some grub and sleep. Your bride to be seems like a nice lady and she loves your daughter very much from what she told me. I planned on taking off first thing in the morning anyhow. I'll be on the trail by sun up no need for you to worry none."

The fiancé turned and walked towards the door. "You be sure to be gone before breakfast cowboy."

CHAPTER 10

Buffole shook me awake and told me it was time to hit the trail and make dust. It was still pitch black outside like printers ink. The moon and stars had moved beyond the horizon and the sun had yet to peek its rays in from the east. We gathered up what few things we had in the bedroom. Buffole carried his boots and proceeded out the door in just his stocking feet. Once on the porch he slipped his boots on and we went out to the stable and rousted Shag from a sound sleep. Buffole whispered to Shag. "Be quiet you big hunk of fur. No snorting and shaking like a dust storm we got to get saddled and out of here before anyone hears us. As we rode away I looked back and I could see Ilsa and Tanner in her upstairs bedroom window watching us leave. I could have sworn even in the dark that my canine eyes detected tears running down Ilsa's cheeks. Maybe being a canine and having good night vision is not always the best sense to have.

I cuddled up in my saddle bag as the sun began to rise. It always gets colder when the early morning heat from the sun pushes the cold night air towards the ground and this morning was no exception. Buffole pulled his leather sheepskin lined coat tighter to his body as Shag plodded us towards Caraline Valley.

By noon the sun was beating down and starting to cook us. I decided to trot along on the ground by Shag. As we passed a prairie dog town Shag started up a conversation. "See that prairie dog town that's one of the worst enemies a buffalo can have."

That statement sort of bewildered both Buffole and me so of course we had to ask why.

"Well" said Shag. "A herd of buffalo might have stampeded for any number of reasons or even if you come across one of those towns after dusk them darn little holes those critters dig for their homes can be right deadly for a buffalo. You step in one of those holes with your hoof and you are most likely to break a leg. A buffalo with a broken leg is a sure goner. If the wolves don't get you then you most likely will starve to death or die from lack of water. Whichever one it is your buzzard bait in the end. If them little doggies and I use the term loosely because they are really rodents weren't so darn cute I might just wish them harm. Maybe if humans started eating them and making clothing and blankets out of their hides instead of buffalo they might just wipe out every prairie dog in the country."

I was glad to know that prairie dogs aren't really dogs otherwise I might have felt bad about the whole situation. Plodding along as we were was mighty dry and dusty for our throats. Shag held his head high in the air and snorted. "There's water about a half mile over in those rocks. Smells like a small pool let's go check it out."

We meandered over to the rocks and sure as Shag said there was a trickle of water coming from a cleft in the rocks. It was running slow but a small basin in the rocks had gathered up enough for Buffole to fill his canteen. The shade of the rock surrounding the small pool kept it from evaporating. Shag insisted Buffole and I drink our fill before he partook of the life sustaining liquid. When Shag had finished drinking the rock basin was only a moist memory. In a few days it would refill for the next thirsty traveler.

We were resting in the shade of the rocks when I saw a curios little critter sunning himself on a small rocky ledge near me. I figured to check this little bugger out and slowly started to sneak up on it. I guess I was not as stealthy as I thought. The little critter looked at me and its eyes blinked. I was about four feet away when a stream of blood shot right out from this little devils eyes and splashed onto my lips. A quick lick of my lips with my tongue told me this foul tasting beast was not worth pursuing. I ran over to the basin of water which by this time had barley filled to a tongue full of water which I quickly lapped up. Next I bee lined to Buffole and asked for a cup of water from the canteen. Anything to wash down the foul taste of devils blood that thing had shot me with.

Shag had been watching the whole episode and his body shook with laughter at my plight. "Sven you just had your first taste of horny toad blood. He's not really a toad he's a lizard. They are known as a horned toad or more appropriately a horned lizard. Those little horns on his head are real bone underneath. As you just found out he can squirt a stream of foul tasting blood from his eyes up to five feet to dissuade predators from wanting to eat him. It works very well on canines and felines. If a bird attacks him he flattens himself out and raises his horned head so that it is almost impossible for a bird to get its beak under him to pick him up to eat him."

The horny little fella looked at me and said. "Listen to your big shaggy friend dog he knows what he's talking about. You must be new to the west or you would have known better than to try to sneak up on me. Go away now and let me try to catch a bug for my dinner."

Buffole did not understand the horny toad but I interpreted the whole discussion between the lizard, Shag and I. Buffole of course thought it as funny as Shag did and they had a good laugh at my expense. The horned lizard disappeared from sight figuring all the noise and too much activity was ruining his chances at snagging a nice plump ant or bug for his meal.

We hit the trail again and made our way towards Caraline Valley. We figured it best to move off the main trail and cut our own path to our destination. If Carlos Gracious' men had made it to the last town we were in they might just beat us to the town ahead of us. We figured it best that no one knew our whereabouts or it might spook Popeye if he managed to put two and two together and figure out that we were hunting him.

We followed the route that Shag had taken as a calf with his family. It moved us into lush grasslands and picture perfect valleys. I doubt if ever a human or a dog, well excluding coyotes and wolves had ever seen some of the country we were now travelling. Towering trees and shimmering lakes were in my eyes only something that god could have created.

For a little while we all thought that this was god's country. Until we came upon the remains of a cabin. The corral was still standing although no livestock was in sight. What had once been someone's log cabin now lay in burned out charred ruins. Buffole and I got off Shag and went to the blackened rubble of the cabin to investigate. The smell of burned wood was still in the air so the fire could not have been more than a few days old.

I was the first to discover what looked like a large piece of charred wood was actually a man's body. I called Buffole over to investigate. It is no pleasant task to find someone dead and charred. Buffole went over to the small stable by the corral and found a shovel. He started digging a grave not far from the remains of the cabin. As for me I was not so sure this man died because of the fire.

As Buffole continued digging the grave Shag walked over near me and started talking. 'Sven this was no accidental death. Look around, anything of value is gone. There are no guns in sight. A man living alone out here was sure to have a rifle if not also a handgun. While you and Buffole were examining this place I took a quick look around the stable. There was a horse corralled there but not anymore."

I glanced in the direction of the corral before I said anything. "Shag the corral gate is open the horse probably wandered off. Maybe someone came along after the fire and took what valuables might have been here including the man's guns.

Shag shook his mighty head back and forth. "No Sven I think this man was murdered. There is no saddle in the barn and one set of tracks rode in from the direction we came. Two sets of tracks left here. Looking at those tracks I'm sure one set belongs to Popeye's horse. You best tell Buffole to check that body over for bullet holes before he buries it."

I did as Shag said and unpleasant as it was Buffole located a hole in the man's chest. He flinched as he dug his fingers into the hole and located a bullet. There was no doubt that the man had been murdered. From the position of the body near the charred ruins of a table it looked as if the man most likely had a guest and was being hospitable when he was shot. The three of us could well imagine Popeye being friendly right up to the time he murdered this man. We had one more reason for finding the murdering skunk.

Buffole finished burying the man and he placed some stones at the head of the grave to mark it. The best he could do was to scratch some letters into a large flat stone with a piece of metal he found in the ruins of the house. The only epitaph we could come up with was 'Unknown Man lays here, Rest in Peace.'

Shag located the trail and we followed it. Coming over a rise we finally spotted our destination. Caraline Valley lay below us. A nice little town laid out well. A few buggies and street traffic were visible. The main street looked well kept and respectable. One of the side streets seemed a little shabby with some rundown buildings and what appeared to be a livery stable at the edge of the town. We took our time riding into town and made a point to acquaint ourselves with the layout just in case trouble brewed up and we needed to make a quick exit.

Shag lost Popeye's trail in the jumble of hoof and wagon prints from this busy little town. Knowing the kind of man Popeye was we figured we best head to the seedy part of town and check out the local saloons. The sun was setting and the saloons were slowly filling up with cowhands and what looked to be some of the towns less desirable citizens. Buffole directed us to a particular busy looking establishment called Buffalo Dicks. Shag gave a loud snort as we dismounted by the horse rail. He shook his mighty head and said. "I smell death in that building. The souls of buffalo, deer, elk and big horn sheep reek from the crevices of that building. Maybe I should go in with you and find the murderers of animals." I told Shag it was best he wait outside. A buffalo in a saloon would draw undo attention to us. Buffole looked at Shag and I as he said. "As if a man riding a buffalo had not already attracted undo attention."

Buffole and I entered the saloon through the batwing doors. The air hung thick with cigar and cigarette smoke. The floors were stained with years of accumulated whisky and beer spills. Tables were filled with men drinking and playing cards. A female card dealer was running a faro game in one of the back corners. She looked as old as the building if not older but she still had the men's attention as she was the only thing that vaguely resembled a female in the place.

Shag was right about the dead animals. Trophy heads lined the walls with a full mounted bobcat taking honors on top of the back bar. The trophies were old and some were moth eaten. I doubted that whoever killed these animals was still around but I nudged Buffole in the leg and told him to make sure he checked on who supplied the trophies for the saloon. "Buffole whispered under his breath. "Sven I think we might have enough trouble around here without taking on a bunch of hunters, but I'll ask just to satisfy Shags curiosity. I only hope we don't find the animal hunter or we might not be able to control Shags vengeance."

I was doing my best to pick up Popeye's scent but no luck. Buffole bellied up to the bar and ordered two SvenBrew beers, one in a glass and the other in a bowl for me. No one seemed to take notice of a beer drinking dog in the place.

Then we heard a familiar voice. "Why if it ain't my Gila monster buddies Buffole and Sven. I heard you two were out and about. Let's find us a table and talk about what you been up to." Sure enough Pat Garret was in town.

Pat motioned for me to hop up on a chair next to him and poured Buffole and me a shot glass full of whisky. Buffole grabbed an extra beer as he came to the table so the three of us had chasers for our shots. Once we were all seated Pat started talking.

"I've been hearing some stories about you two and that buffalo of yours. The word round the campfires and the saloons is that you killed a card shark and a sheriff up in Lutherhell. Most of the folks say it was self defense although a few of the sheriff's boys are claiming you shot both men down under unfair circumstances. The new sheriff in Lutherhell which I heard was renamed Bettertown claims you boys are innocent of any wrong doing and has refused to press charges against you. By the way this new town sheriff just so happens to be a woman. First time I ever heard of a town having a lady sheriff. I think her name was Trixie and if I remember right that's the name of the saloon owner who took you in after you were bit by the Gila monster. Just what are boys doing down this way."

Buffole took his shot of whisky and downed it with a beer chaser before he answered. "First let me say thank you Pat for saving me out there in the wilderness. I most likely would have died if you had not brought me to Lutherhell for medical care. Sven, Shag and I are still on the trail of Popeye the man who killed my family. The last we heard was that he might be here. Have you heard anything of him? He's easy to recognize with his eyes bulging from their sockets and his dirty appearance."

"I just came to town about two days ago. Had me a prisoner that I turned over to the town marshal. I wasn't looking for information on your man but I heard talk of someone who meets his description. In fact he supposedly hung out in this very bar. That hag over there dealing faro I believe had a rather close relationship with him from what the men I been playing cards with said." The bartender brought us more beer and Pat asked him to relay a message to the lady faro dealer that we would buy her drinks if she wished to join us. We watched as the bartender approached her and she gave us a toothless smile and called over one of the male employees to take her place at the faro table.

She came to our table and I'll do my best to describe her. She was skinny as a rail and her knee high saloon dress was well worn and dirty. Her black stockings were filled with holes that had tufts of hair sticking out of them. The black shoes on her feet looked to have been worn by a mule they were so dirty and dusty. Her once blonde hair was filtered with gray. The long boney fingers were capped by smoke stained yellow finger nails. What teeth she had left which amounted to maybe four in the rear and one top front tooth were stained and blackened with decay. Her voice would have made the squeal of chalk on a chalkboard seem almost pleasant. To put it simply a beauty she was not.

"Buy me a drink boys, whisky and SvenBrew beer will do." She said. "My name is Olwish. Once you've been with me y'all wish you could be with me again. What you fella's want?"

"We're looking for man and heard you might know of him. He's a skinny guy, sort of dark complexion and bulging eyes" answered Buffole as he did his best to look at his beer glass and not at Olwish.

Olwish took a swig of beer that would have made many a man proud before she answered. "Sure I know him. I heard from Jeb at the livery stable that he bought two horses from Popeye so I knew he had some cash burning a hole in his pocket so I got friendly with him. He's not only skinny and ugly he smells like a rotting dead buffalo. At first I thought it was his buffalo vest that stunk but after we bedded down together I found out the smell had permeated that man. Took him to my room four times I did. Paid me well in gold coin and anyway he not only smelled like a buffalo well he was also, well you know the man was hung like a bison. Sorry I should probably watch my language in front of the dog he might not be of age yet."

Pat and Buffole both got red in the face but I could tell they were trying not to laugh and as for me I had to sit tight on my tail to keep it from wagging in laughter myself.

Pat finally gained his composure enough to keep talking. "Olwish can you tell us where Popeye is right now?"

"He left here a few days ago. Some cowboys from Lutherhell had heard talk that a man was looking for him. Popeye swore he did not have a price on his head but the man that was hunting for him was plump crazy and he blamed him for the death of his family. Popeye told me he had two partners that might have killed the man's family but he had nothing to do with it. I told Popeye to go to the law but he figured it was his word against this other fellow and that would get nobody anyplace. One of you the men that are hunting Popeye?"

"Did he say where he was going" asked Pat.

Olwish was staring at Pat's vest and she got a glimpse of the shining star he wore. "You the law? Are you the one after Popeye?"

"He ain't wanted by the law, at least not yet, unless Buffole here wants to file charges against him. Like you said ma'am it's his word against Buffole's. As for me this ain't my fight just trying to help my friend here."

"Well he might have been my last chance at having a man and the sidewinder left me so I don't owe him nothin'. He talked about heading down to Mexico. I think he figured once he crossed the border he was safe. If either of you two want to come on up to my room I could show you a good time. No charge this one's on the house."

Buffole and Pat looked at each other. I just wagged my tail and waited to see how they planned on getting out of this predicament. Buffole quickly said. "Ma'am mighty fine offer you made there but I got a man to find and I need to get some rest. Come on Sven we best take care of Shag and get us a room at the hotel."

Pat sputtered out the words real quick like. "Yes ma'am mighty fine offer you made but being a lawman if I accepted it might be considered that I owed you a favor in the future and I just can't compromise my position like that. I best tag along with Buffole and Sven and get me a little shut eye. I've gotta be leaving early in the morning to get back to my wife."

Pat left the saloon with us and we agreed to meet him for supper at the hotel which was located in a nicer part of town. We walked Shag down the street to the livery stable and a young man came out to greet us. "Howdy my names Jeb I own this here stable what can I help you with?"

"Nice to meet you Jeb. I'd like to put my buffalo in your stables think you can handle that?"

"This here critter friendly to man? If so I can handle him just fine. Four-bits for the night and for an extra four-bits I'll brush him down, clean your saddle and tack and feed this here shaggy fella a meal fit for a king's horse."

"You got yourself a deal Jeb. I'll pay in advance because I don't know how early we'll be taking out of here and I might not see you in the morning." Buffole handed Jeb the money and as we walked away we heard Jeb holler after us.

"I sleep in the lean to attached to the stables mister. Nothing happens night or day in my stable that I don't know about. You all have a good evening now ya hear?"

The hotel was on the main street with a fancy false front and was two stories high. It was called the Caraline House. The entrance had two fancy doors with oval stained glass windows and lots of brass trim. Inside the place was done with red carpets and we were greeted by the man behind the desk who was dressed in a suit and tie and slicked up like a dude ready to get married. We checked in for the night and asked if Pat Garret had checked in yet. The man told us Mr. Garret was in the dining room waiting for us. "You may wish to go to your room and clean up a bit before entering the dining room" said the clerk. It seemed like a rather bold hint that we were not quite up to snuff in our present condition. Yet what could Buffole say? We did look sort of scruffy and the clerk was right.

We made our way to the second floor and found our room. I jumped up on the nice soft bed to check it out. Buffole washed up in the basin on the night stand. Just as we were ready to leave Buffole grabbed me and ruffled up my fur real nice to shake the dust out of my coat. He ran his fingers under my eyes to remove the dust crusted sleep that had hardened there from our many days on the trail. Now we were both presentable enough to go downstairs and join Pat for supper.

Pat was having a glass of wine as we made our way to his table. I leapt up on one of the chairs and nobody seemed to notice that a dog was dining with his human. Or if they did notice they didn't care. The waitress came to take our order. She gave us a menu and for Buffole and me this was the first time we ever ate in a place fancy enough to have a menu with choices of meals. Our usual dining spots had one or two items to pick from and the person in charge told you what they were. We did our best to look like we knew what we were doing and the waitress excused herself to give us time to make a decision. The wine bottle was on the table and Pat reached over and poured a glass for Buffole and for me he dumped out the sugar bowl that was on the table and poured my wine in that. This really was a high class place.

When the waitress returned Pat ordered a steak rare and I had the same. Buffole had steak also but wanted his medium rare. He said he didn't like his meat to bellow at him when he ate it.

Pat relaxed in his chair and asked. "What are you going to do when you catch up with Popeye? He's not wanted for anything and you never swore out a complaint. You should really bring him in for a trial. If you kill him it could be you that's a wanted man. Unless of course you shoot him in self defense but then you better have some witnesses. I'm just telling you this because I sure would hate to have to hunt you down and bring you in for murder."

Buffole looked at me and then took a sip of his wine before he said anything. "You know Pat I hadn't really thought about ever bringing Popeye in for a trial. It would just be my word against his. Guess I'll just have to kill him. I won't shoot him down in cold blood I'll give him an even break which is a lot more then he gave my wife and son. Maybe if I kill him south of the border you won't have to concern yourself with it."

"One thing that may just be Popeye's undoing although I doubt if there's any proof there for you to find. I came across a burned out cabin about a half mile north east of here. There was a dead man in the ruins. He was charred and not recognizable, except the fire didn't kill him. He had a bullet in his chest. I buried him and left a marker. The only tracks coming to his place were from Popeye's horse. The tracks leaving showed three horses' two did not have riders"

Pat smiled "Well if I had time to check it out and the tracks were still there that would make both our lives easier. I would have liked to ride with you for awhile but under the circumstances I think we best part company by morning. Me being a lawman I just can't condone what you a planning to do. I also don't blame you for wanting revenge. If I was in your boots I'd probably do the same thing. Just a little friendly warning if you do go down Mexico way. There's a bandit down there calls himself Poncho Villa. Stay clear of him he's a mean hombre from what I hear tell and he's got a small army of followers that do whatever he tells them."

"Thanks for the warning Pat. Sven and I will both do our best not to cross the line. Last thing I want to do is to have you hunting me. By the way I still owe you for paying the livery stable to keep Shag and helping me out after that gila monster bit me. What do I owe you?"

"You don't owe me nothing and don't ever offer again. We're partners on the trail and partner's just plain old help each other with no thanks necessary."

"Pat that's mighty nice of you. I'm paying for this here spread were eating and that's all there is to it. That be all right with you."

"Sounds like a plan partner" and Pat took another sip of that ten dollar a bottle wine. I think the livery stable fees for Shag might have been a whole lot cheaper.

CHAPTER 11

It was nice to share a soft bed with Buffole. I slept at the bottom of the bed so I could keep an eye on the door. With me as watch dog it was much easier for Buffole to get a good night's sleep. We awoke early before sun break and I thought it was fine that Buffole still shook out his boots to make sure there were no strange critters inside of them. The two of us were really becoming westerners.

We crept into the stable as quietly as possible. Shag was still sleeping when I nudged him with my nose and told him it was time to rise and shine. He shook his mighty body and we could feel the earth shake beneath our feet. From out of the lean to attached to the stables we heard. "What the hell is going on out there? Whoever you are freeze I got me a rifle and I know how to use it!" Next thing we saw was Jeb standing in the doorway his gun leveled at us. Buffalo raised his hands in the air and spoke. "Jeb, it's just Buffole and Sven here to pick up Shag. Remember we told you we would be leaving early in the morning."

Jeb lowered the rifle. "Yeah I remember. You need any help?"

"No we're doing just fine you can go back to bed."

"Think I'll do just that. You boys have a safe journey now ya hear."

Buffole continued to pack up our gear and tie things down on Shag's back. Shag was finally getting his senses about him after a night's sleep. "Sven did you find out who shot those animals mounted in Buffalo Dicks saloon?"

Shag we plump forgot in all the excitement going on. It's too late to find out now we got a lead on Popeye and we have to get on his trail. Buffalo Dicks won't be open till we are long gone from here." Shag shook his might head 'no'. "We are not going anywhere until I have a chance to revenge those animals."

I told Buffole what Shag said and he said the last thing we needed was to go after or kill some hunter. Shag insisted we find out who the animal killer was. He said it was no different killing his kind then a human killing a human or an animal killing a human just for pleasure. For food or protection killing was all right but not for sport like getting a trophy head to mount on the wall.

Buffalo ran his fingers through his hair and thought for a minute. "I've got an idea. You boys come along with me." Buffole went to the door of the lean to and knocked loudly. "Jeb it's Buffole I need to ask you something."

The door of the lean to opened. Jeb stood before us barefoot and wearing just a night shirt. "You told me to go back to bed. What the hell do you want waking me up again?"

Buffole pulled a dollar from his pocket and handed it to Jeb. "Just wanted to give you a little extra for taking such good care of Shag. By the way I had a bet with someone about those trophy mounted heads over at Buffalo Dicks. They looked sort of old and moth eaten to me and I bet the hunter that bagged them was probably old and dead by now. You know anything about him?"

"Yeah he was old and he is dead. Last hunt he made killed him. They say he went after a big old bear up in the woods north of town. Biggest bear anyone around here had ever seen. Paws were as big as a large skillet. On this hunt the bear won. They found that old hunter clawed up and his head was tore off and sitting on a rock just as pretty as them there trophy heads over at the saloon. Unless you want to do any more talking I think I'm going back to bed."

"Thank you Jeb, you've been a big help" said Buffole.

Shag was in a good mood now and we headed out of town at a lively step. There were too many hoof prints and wagon tracks for Shag to discern Popeye's tracks so we just headed south to the border.

We made camp that night and enjoyed the evening stars and the cool night air. Shag told us stories of when he was a young bull and travelled with vast herds across the prairies. Sometimes there would be buffalo as far as the eye could see. Eventually the young bulls like Shag would challenge their older brethren for the right to have their own harem of cows. Shag was strong and powerful and when we found him he was in command of the herd of buffalo we had encountered. Sadly Shag told us that fresh young bulls were challenging his leadership. When Shag could not protect his herd from the human hunters he figured it was best to move on and let the younger bulls take command. Now we were Shag's herd and his friends. Just the three of us. To me I thought of us more as a family.

We had been riding for a few days and nothing unusual had come our way. It was mid afternoon when we saw a herd of horses roaming free. We were not even sure if we were in a territory or a state. We figured we had at least reached Texas by now. The horses seemed tame enough and as we neared them we could see they had a 'BS' brand. Shag told me that humans should not really own animals and as far as he was concerned the 'BS' stood for buffalo shit. His thoughts on the matter were that animals and humans worked and stayed together because they wanted to. It was no more right in his mind to brand an animal than for a husband to brand his wife. Maybe he had a valid point but I don't see humans changing their ways any to soon in the future.

Riding towards the afternoon sun we could make out four riders. With that big bright ball of fire in the sky at their backs we could not make out their faces. Three of them were broad shouldered and looked to be men. The other was small in stature and even smaller in body, it was most likely a woman but she rode like a man.

Buffole lifted me from my saddlebag and lowered me so I could jump safely to the ground. If needed I could spook some horses or attack a man that was down. Then he pulled his rifle from its gun scabbard and laid it across his saddle horn with his finger on the trigger in one hand and the barrel in the other. If need be he could make a slight move and fire a shot where it would do the most good. Any rider coming up would know that we were ready for business if need be.

The more burly of the three riders shouted out to us. "Sven and Ole, well I'll be damned what the hell you doing way down here in Texas all by your lonesome." We were surprised to see Tearhart from our wagon train days talking to us. With him was Korn's wife Sindee, his son Lake and the other wrangler Bubba.

Sindee spoke right up. "Tearhart you watch your language when your around a lady ya here. Ole where's your family?"

Ole sort of choked up a little before he answered. "There all dead ma'am. Just me and Sven and my new mount Shag here is all I got for family now."

"We are all mighty sorry to hear that. Well you best come back to the ranch with me. Korn will be glad to see you. You boys must be thirsty and famished. Lake, Tearhart and Bubba you boys gather up the horses and bring them in we'll have us a real shindig tonight to welcome our friends."

I glanced up in the hills and saw a figure on a horse watching us. Quickly I warned Buffole that it might be Popeye or a renegade or an Indian watching us. He in turn mentioned to Sindee that we were being observed by a lone rider in the distance.

She nonchalantly looked towards the hills and caught sight of the rider. "No need to worry boys he's one of us. We've been having a fair share of Indian trouble and that man up there is one of the best scouts in this or any other territory. If Indians are about he'll find them. Lake you ride up and make sure our scout comes to the Shindig tonight. Tell him it's an order from me or he will have all kinds of excuses not to show up."

Sindee and we rode on together towards their ranch. She seemed deep in thought and no one said a word until she started the conversation. "Ole I'm so sad to hear about Kate and Zeb would you mind telling me what happened. If it pains you too much to talk about it I understand and not another word will be spoken about it."

"It's all right Sindee. It seems like a lifetime ago even though it's only been a few months. We met up with some buffalo hunters after your group left the wagon train. They seemed a little shady right from the start but me being a tenderfoot I try to find the best in people and to trust them. It was the biggest mistake of my life. Dancer was still with us and I figured if any trouble brewed up he would step in and handle it."

"Well trouble brewed up all right, boiled itself right up and over the top. The buffalo hunters shot and killed Dancer. I didn't know they had shot him until I went out looking for him. He was gut shot but still alive when I got to him. I made him as comfortable as I could and then he insisted I take his belongings to use for myself and to leave him with his gun and go back to my family. It was darn hard to just leave him there to die all alone like that. Yet I figured he knew best him being a man of the frontier. I bid him farewell and did as he told me to do."

"When I got back to the wagon the buffalo hunters were in the process of raping my wife and holding my son captive. On pure instinct I fought them. I killed one of them and then Shag, by the way that's who I am riding right now, well he came charging into camp and smashed one of those hunter's to death with his mighty head. I shot and killed one of the others and took a bullet in the process. The third one escaped. That third hunters name is Popeye and he's the reason I'm here. I've tracked him this far and I won't stop hunting him until I bring him to justice for killing my family."

After what Buffole had said we rode on in silence. It seemed almost strange to hear someone call Buffole by his real name again. I couldn't tell for sure if he liked being called Ole again or if it just brought up bad memories of the past.

Some time passed and I knew Buffole was still contemplating our past so I suggested that it would be polite to ask about Korn and the horses. "Sindee how's Korn? Did you arrive safe with your horses and everything intact?"

I think she was still unsure of how Buffole felt after he spilled his guts to her. With Buffole breaking the awkward silence she smiled and looked over at him. "We are all just fine. All our horses survived the trip and Korn and the boy's have been busy working on our new spread. We've hired some local men to build the house and the stables are already finished. Korn always teases me that my horses are more important than a house for us. I think he might just be right."

As we rode to the ranch we could see the house was still a work in progress. It was a large two story affair with a porch that wrapped around three quarters of the house. Some workmen were shingling the roof and some others were putting up trim. The place had not yet been painted and was maybe three fourths of the way finished.

Korn was pitching hay as we rode up. Sindee called over to him. "Korn look what I found roaming around out on the prairie."

Korn turned and almost dropped his pitchfork in surprise. "Ole and Sven! It's great to see you two alive and kicking. Where's the rest of the family? My god man is that a buffalo you're riding?"

Sindee came to our rescue. "Korn not so many questions. Take Ole's horse, I mean his buffalo and put him in the stables, unless you have some good excuse not to and don't tell me your allergic to buffalos. Ole and Sven you two come with me and I'll show you around the place. Korn when you get done stabling Ole's buffalo tell the cook and the boys to get ready for a party tonight to welcome our guests."

Sindee showed us around the stables as Korn unsaddled Shag and brushed him down. The horses here had better living conditions then a lot of the shacks, houses and even some of the hotels that Buffole and I had stayed in. This place was even nicer than the Pest stables that we had used a few days earlier. The stalls had fresh water pumped into them and fresh feed was at the ready for the horses to enjoy. Saddles, tack and blankets were hung neatly on the walls. Each horse had its name on a plaque in its own nice cozy living quarters. Outside there were Corrals sectioned off for the ranches work horses and also for Sindee's three prize race horses.

She took us over to introduce us to the horses that were to make the BS ranch famous. There was Romeo who had yet to be beaten by any other horse and was already holding track records at race courses throughout Texas. Jess and Not a Cheap Date were the other two horses and had made good showings on the race track although they were not near the caliber of Romeo.

Korn came over to join us. "Ole I can't believe you're riding a buffalo it must take you forever to get any place. How the heck did you ever saddle break that beast?"

Buffole smiled and said. "Korn I don't know if you can train a buffalo. This one picked me as his friend when his herd was in danger and my family was in danger. I guess the two of us just sort of bonded. Next thing you know I made a saddle for him and he let me ride him. We been on the trail ever since my wife and boy were killed. By the way my buffalo is called Shag."

"Sorry to hear about your family, how did?" Sindee touched Korn's arm and shook her head no. "Korn I think Ole could use a rest I'm sure he has had a long hard day. Ole we have a guest room it is not painted or finished yet but it has a comfortable bed and a place to clean up if you would like to relax before the party tonight."

We took up the offer for a little rest before the night's shindig. Once in our room Buffole brushed out my coat with his fingers as best he could. He washed up and put his clothes outside the door as Sindee suggested. She told him they had a lady hired to do the laundry and maintain the house. Buffole did have a spare set of go to Sunday meeting clothes which he figured on wearing for the evening festivities so there was no rush to get back his everyday duds. We both decided to get a little shuteye and Buffole hung his gun belt and gun on the bedpost at close reach more out of habit than necessity. For once in a blue moon we felt safe in the Besser house.

A feeling of security must have overcome Buffole and I for the next thing we heard was a knock on our door. The shadows of the setting sun were filling our room. A dark skinned lady with a rather plump figure popped into our room with Buffole's fresh clothes folded neatly in her arms. "Massa Ole my names Jasmine and I've got your clothes here all fresh and clean." She looked over in the corner and saw Buffole's dress outfit hanging on the chair in the corner of the room. "Why Massa Ole you should have told me you had another outfit and I would have cleaned that one for you to. It's too late now the festivities is about to start. You get yourself spruced up now 'cause the party ain't gonna start until you get there. By the way Miss Sindee says no guns are allowed at the party." I did a tail laugh as I was watching Buffole do his best to cover up his long john covered body with the bedding when Jasmine burst in on us.

Buffole got dressed in his finest and slicked back his hair. A shave finished him up and he looked down right presentable. We made our way downstairs and out to the backyard. While we had been sleeping a wooden dance floor was set up and the word of a party must have spread like wildfire. Neighbors from miles around had somehow managed to pack up their families and made their way to the shindig. There was even some locals making up a make shift band with guitars, banjos, fiddles, a washtub contraption, and a washboard that some fellow seemed to really enjoy strumming up and down with a stiff bristled brush.

As soon as Korn saw Buffole he grabbed him by the arm and hauled him up on the makeshift dance floor. I of course was right on Buffole's heels all the way. "Friends this here is an old buddy of mine. He came west from Minnesota on a wagon train with me and my family. Why don't you all give a warm welcome to Ole and his dog Sven." There was a round of applause, some whistles, and a few yahoo's from the crowd. It looked like we were in for a humdinger of a night.

Korn took us over to a hog that they had started roasting almost as soon as we had gone to our room. The beast was ready to eat on the outside but his insides were awful rare for most humans tastes. As for me I don't mind my pork being on the raw side.

A long table was set up for the guests to eat and use for visiting and we made our way over and sat down. A man approached us with his hat pulled low down on his forehead and it was hard to make out his face. He had a plate heaping full of meat and potatoes. A cigar was clinched in his teeth. I thought right of way of our wagon master Dancer as he used to clinch his cigar in his teeth the same way. The man had a jug of what one would assume was home brew liquor in his other hand. He threw his leg over the wooden bench and made himself right at home across from us.

Buffole and I looked at the man. Something seemed familiar about him. Finally our mystery man looked up and titled his cowboy hat away from his face. It was Dancer and yup he was alive and kicking.

Dancer smiled wide as the Rio Grande as he spoke. "Ole and Sven you old rattlesnakes bet you thought you would never see me again.

I suppose you want to know what happened? After I ordered you two back to your family I sort of blacked out. I must have been unconscious for three maybe four days or more. I woke up occasionally and had a drink of water but everything was a blur. Then I heard a horse pawing the ground next to me. I opened my eyes and my very own horse had his head down by mine and nudged my face with his nose. Hell I figured if I had survived this long maybe I wasn't meant to die. A horse sometimes has more sense than a man and if my horse was still waiting for me he must have knew I was going to live. Weak as a newborn babe I crawled onto the rocks where I laid and managed to get onto the back of my horse. We wandered over to your camp and found it abandoned except for two buzzard eaten buffalo hunters' bodies and a big mound of dirt with a grave marker. I don't remember that marker real well but I knew you wife and boy were in that grave. I must have been delirious because I thought I read something on the grave marker about a bunch of dead buffalo buried in a grave there too. I found enough food to last for a few days and managed to get some of my strength back. A few of the horses from your wagon and the buffalo hunters meandered back into my little camp. I guess they figured they were better off being around a human than out on the prairie by themselves."

The Indians must of have had business elsewhere for I never did see hide nor hair of them the whole time I was at your wagon. Once I got strong enough I gathered up the saddles around the camp and enough supplies and food to head for the nearest town. I took the horses with me and sold everything I didn't need once I reached civilization. Now I had me a grubstake to start over with. I wasn't sure exactly what had happened to you and Sven. I saw the buffalo tracks around the campsite but figured some stray bison had made his way into camp and was scavenging around. It never dawned on me that you would ride a buffalo out of that camp."

"Dancer it's darn good to see you. I'm really sorry I left you out there to die. Can you forgive me?" I could tell what had happened had upset Buffole, heck it upset me.

"Ole there's nothing to forgive. I told you to leave me. I figured I was a goner and just wanted to die alone and in peace my own way. After I got back on my feet I heard some rather disturbing news. Seems I made two mistakes while I was guiding your wagon train. One of course was thinking I was going to be die. The other one was something I neglected to tell you folks. When the Anderson's were attacked by Indians I know I saw their boy Trapis with two arrows in him. When Casey and I went to bury the Anderson family the boy Trapis was gone. I figured the boy might have still had some life in him and the Indians took him to torture him for fun. I swore Casey to silence on the matter so as not to upset the rest of you folks."

"I was wrong about that boy just like I was wrong about me when I told you I was going to die. The boy didn't die. The Indians actually nursed him back to health and filled him with hate for the folks that left him there to die. They taught that boy how to be an Indian and hunt and kill like a wild animal. I heard from some friendly Indians that I ran across that the boy kept his hatred bottled up in him like some demon. He turned on the Indians that had nursed him back to health and took him in as part of their tribe. One night he snuck through the Indian camp and killed every one of the Indians that had raided his mother and fathers wagon. The last I heard of him was from a trapper who came across the boy in the mountains."

"Seems this tapper and his partner found the boy half starved on a rundown Indian pony. They took him in and nursed him back to health. He told them how the Indians killed his family and how he pretended to fit in with the tribe to gain their confidence. Finally he told them how he killed those savages with a knife and escaped."

"While the trappers were helping Trapis to regain his strength they would hear him talking in his sleep about killing the whites that had abandoned him and his family. My name of course came up and so did yours and even the Besser's. The trappers tried to reason with the boy. Told him they heard his dreams and that sometimes things can go wrong when you're travelling in the west. They tried to convince the boy that hatred and revenge were not the answer. Killing everyone from the wagon train that he traveled with was just plain foolishness.

Trapis lashed out at the two men and grabbed one of their rifles. He shot one of the trappers and killed him. The other trapper managed to grab a horse and escape when the boy's rifle jammed."

"As best as I've been able to figure it Trapis is heading this way to kill the Besser's, Bubba and Tearhart. I've tracked him this far and I know he's in the area. It's my fault the Anderson's got bushwhacked. If I had been doing a better job as scout it should have never happened. Then I left them there while the Indians finished attacking them. I made mistakes and it's my job to fix them. So for the time being I ride for the BS brand until I catch the boy and either reform him or kill him."

"Now for something that's really bewildering me. I asked everywhere I went about the surviving members of the wagon train. The Eichman's had settled in that little town where I took them when Nicole was having trouble with her baby. Sounds like they settled in and Henry, Nicole and the little one are doing fine. I figured Trapis had no concern for them as they were gone before his parents were killed. Casey and Kilroy are still somewhere in the Black Hills looking for gold. The Besser's of course are right here. Yet no one seemed to have heard the whereabouts of you and Sven. Ole you seemed like you just plain old fell off the edge of the world. Where you been hiding all this time?"

Buffole pondered the question as Dancer and Korn sat in rapt anticipation. "There's a good reason you couldn't find me. After I left you I had a show down with the buffalo hunters and as you know two of them are dead. Popeye escaped and I'm on his trail as we speak. Those men killed my family and I mean to have justice. As for not finding me by asking around there is a rather simple explanation."

"I sort of took your advice and re-outfitted myself to better survive in the west. My buffalo Shag, Sven and I decided I needed a new identity. A new name and a new look would be sure to throw Popeye off and he would not expect anyone other than Ole to be hunting him. So I changed my name to go along with my new mount. Folks now know me as Buffole."

Dancer smiled and said, "Well if that don't beat all. You went and changed your name and identity." He rubbed his stubbled chin with his hand for moment as if deep in thought. "Buffole, you know now that you mention it I have heard of the new you. You're getting quite a reputation. I heard a man named Buffole shot and killed two men in the town of Lutherhell and one of those men was the sheriff. Add that to the two buffalo hunters you left dead at your wagon means you've got four notches on your gun. You best be careful or some young gun wanting to make a reputation might just come after your ass."

"Buffole was quick to make a correction to Dancers assumption. "I only killed one of the buffalo hunters. Shag my buffalo killed the other one. As for the other two men they were both killed in a fair fight, it was them or me. There's no price on my head and I plan to keep it that way. When I finally find Popeye I'll give him more of a chance than he gave my wife and boy. Then I will kill him."

Buffole figured it was best to change the subject. "Korn I saw the brand on your horses. Just what does 'BS' stand for? I assume Besser is the 'B'. Do I dare to venture what the 'S' stands for."

Korn smiled and answered. "Well Bubba is a hard working guy but he occasionally has a knack of getting things a little confused. The ranch and the horses are really Sindee's passion more than mine so we decided to call the ranch the 'Sindee Besser." I told Bubba to make up a few branding irons with the letter 'SB'. Somewhere in his mind he mixed up the letters and made the branding irons with the letter's 'BS'. By the time I caught his mistake he and Tearhart had already branded so much of our livestock I figure it was easier to change the name of the ranch to Besser Sindee."

The party was now well under way. The musicians were playing and couples had made their way to the dance floor. It was getting to noisy to have a nice visit so Korn suggested we make our way behind the stable to his target practice range. Some torches had been set up all over the immediate ranch grounds so even the target range was well light with its bales of hay lined with bull's eyes and there were even a number of stuffed scarecrow figures dressed like Indians. Some of the scare crows were facing us, some were turned to their side and a few were in a kneeling position. It made a rather eerie sight under the flicker of the torch lights. You almost felt as if you were under attack.

Lake had seen us heading towards the practice range and he soon made whatever excuse's to the young lady he was with and joined us. Buffole told the group he would have to go back to the house to get his guns but Korn stopped him short. "On this range we use bow and arrows. If you remember from the wagon train days Lake is extremely proficient and I'm not too bad myself. The advantage out here on the prairie with the bow and arrow is that they make no sound. If you are shooting game no one will hear you. If the Indians don't hear you they won't know where to find us. The advantage of a quiet kill for food is that it does not scare any other animals in the area away. I know Dancer won't use a bow but he has another skill which may not be quite as good but it sure is effective. Show Buffole and Sven what I mean Dancer."

Dancer unsheathed his hunting knife and with a mighty swing of his arm the blade hit its mark in the chest of one of the Indian scare crows. Buffalo and I remembered hearing of Dancer's expertise with his knife once before at the saloon where we first met.

Korn had strung his bow and took two shots. His arrows both made hits just off center of the bulls eye on the hay bales. He handed the bow and one arrow to Buffole. "Here you give it a try. Hold the bow tight but keep your arm away from the bow string. Pull the string back about three quarters of the way to give it enough power to make it to the target."

Buffole pulled back on the bow string and let it fly. I saw him rub his forearm and I'm sure there was a nice red welt under his shirt sleeve from the sting of the bow string. To top matters off the arrow fell about four feet short of the target. "Not bad for a first try, here's another arrow try again." Said Korn. "That's all right" said Buffole "I think I'll stay with my guns. "Lake why don't you show us how a real bow expert does it"

Lake took his stance and readied his bow. Almost as fast as a man with a six shooter he let fly one arrow after another. Six arrows quivered in a tight formation dead center in a bull's eye. Lake took the next arrow and shot it into the heart of one of the Indian dressed scare crows. "That's the fate that awaits Trapis if he dares to come after any of us" said Lake.

In the dark edges of the targets one of the scare crows looked to have fallen down. Suddenly it rose from the ground and a tomahawk flew towards us. The blade of the tomahawk embedded itself in Lake's leg. He went down withering in pain.

Dancer hollered "it's the young buck Trapis, I'll get him."

Korn shouted at Dancer and Buffole before they had made a move. "Both of you look after Lake. Trapis is mine."

The figure of Trapis was running towards a horse which we could barely make out in the moonlight past the light of the torches. Korn aimed his bow and let an arrow fly. We saw the figure of Trapis stumble and then regain his footing as he leapt on to his horse. "You will never catch him in the dark Korn" said Dancer. I may not catch him tonight but I'll damn well track him." Korn ran to the stables and threw a saddle on Romeo the fastest horse on the ranch. By now a crowd had gathered around us from the party. Tearhart had gathered some food and water for Korn and helped him mount up and get on the trail of Trapis. Dancer, Buffole, Bubba and Tearhart carried Lake to his bedroom in the house. Buffole told Korn he would never track Trapis in the dark and he added in. "If you would allow it, Sven, Shag and I can track at night. Korn was already mounted and ready to ride." "If you three can track at night then you will find me out on the trail." That was the last words from Korn's mouth as he put the spurs to Romeo and rode off into the night.

We helped get Lake to his room and Sindee made him as comfortable as possible. Dancer told us to leave the tomahawk in his leg until the doctor arrived. For the time being the tomahawk seemed to be sealing Lake's wound and keeping down the flow of blood. Sindee did her best to stuff bandages around the blade of the tomahawk and then she tried to comfort her son as best she could.

Bubba had saddled up Not-a-cheap-date which was one of the other race horses and rode as fast as he could to nearest town to bring back the doctor. If all went well Bubba would be back with the doctor in about two hours. For now all we could do was hope for the best as far as Lake was concerned.

Dancer made an announcement to the guests that as far as anyone could tell this was just an attack by a rouge individual that had been taught to fight like an Indian. The danger of a real Indian attack was very slim. He suggested the guests wait until daylight to return to their homes. Some of the men wanted to help hunt down Trapis when morning came but Dancer assured them the matter was well under control. Korn had a hunter's instinct and if anyone could hunt down Trapis he would be the one to do it. The ranch help found blankets for everyone and the men bunked in the stable while the women and children were placed in any available room inside the house.

Buffole, Shag and I saddled up and requisitioned some provisions from the kitchen. We headed off in the direction that Korn had taken. Shag shook his mighty head and breathed in the scents of Korn's horse Romeo and of the blood trail from the wounded Trapis. "Which one do you want me to follow" asked Shag?

"Best we follow Korn's trail for now. He may not want any help but tracking a man in the dark is not easy for a human." We were less than two hours out when Shag told us that Korn was near. We were almost upon him when we were hailed from a rocky out cropping. 'Stop right there and toss down your weapons or you're a dead man." It sure enough was Korn's voice that we heard.

"Korn it's me Buffole. Sven, Shag and I came to help you track Trapis."

"All right dismount and come over by the fire after you settle that buffalo down. You can tether him over by Romeo if you want." Once Shag was unsaddled and given a quick rub down by Buffole we joined Korn by the campfire. We shared his coffee and some beef jerky. "You know I don't need any help tacking that little renegade." If nothing else Korn was a stubborn and proud man when it came to his hunting and tracking skills.

Buffole felt it best to tread lightly in this conversation. Korn I ain't saying you need help I'm just offering my assistance. I know you're good at tracking anything that moves yet I got a mighty fine set of animals here that can track by smell and don't always need their eyes to find what their looking for. Sometimes out here in the wilderness just tracking your prey is one thing, tracking water to drink can be almost as important. If a man dies of thirst his prey is going to escape. If you don't mind Sven, Shag and I would like to help you out. I promise that Trapis is all yours we're just here to help locate him."

Begrudgingly Korn accepted our offer. We all bedded down for the night. That renegade Trapis had been trained by the Indians and he would know a lot of their tricks. Yet the boy was wounded and it would slow him down. The smell of his blood would be easy for Shag and Sven to track. For our own safety we decided to set up a watch on our camp. I would take first watch followed by Korn and then Buffole. Buffole made sure to give Korn the middle watch so he would be less tempted to sneak off without us.

The night went without a hitch. We made some coffee and Buffole had some eggs and bacon from the ranch kitchen that made for a good breakfast. Korn was on foot scouting around for Trapis' horse prints and any sign of blood from the boy's wound. Shag told me to relay to Buffole that we were at least a half mile off the trail. One thing Shag could scent easily was a blood trial. When Korn returned from his scouting mission Buffole told him that I was the one who was giving indications that we should head west to pick up the trail. We figured that Korn might be a bit skeptical if he knew a buffalo was leading our group. He would be even more skeptical to think we could communicate with a buffalo.

It took us about an hour to cross Trapis' trial. A piece of cloth that the boy must have used for a bandage had caught on some brush and Korn was quick to see it. Examining the make shift bandage there was a small stain of blood on it. From the looks of the boy's horse tracks he was a good half day ride ahead of us. Most likely Trapis only briefly rested during the night. He must of figured that his enemies were hot on his trail and he knew he had to get us up into the far country filled with rocks and ledges to either lose us or ambush us.

We travelled all day with a hot sun cooking us. I found riding in the saddlebag was better than trotting alongside as Korn and Buffole rode.

The saddlebag was hot but it used a lot less energy and thus less loss of moisture from my body. Trapis' trail finally led us to a small basin of water that should have been enough to get us by. Unfortunately Trapis had figured we would be thirsty and he had filled the basin with sand that he found about a hundred feet away that had washed out from the rocks above us. The Indians had trained him well.

As we rode along Korn's horse Romeo seemed a little agitated. I could hear the discussion between Shag and Romeo and Romeo felt it was degrading for a horse of his caliber to have to travel with a buffalo. Shag had finally had enough and challenged Romeo to a race. Two miles start to finish and may the best animal win. It was now my job to convince Buffole to set up the race with Korn to keep the peace between our mounts.

Buffole was actually excited by the prospect of a race. "Korn you say Romeo is the fastest horse your own?"

"Fast is an understatement. Romeo holds the fastest track record in all of Minnesota. I have no doubt he'll be on the top of his game here in Texas. I doubt if there is a horse in this whole state, maybe even in the whole darn country that can beat my Romeo."

Buffole throw out the challenge. "How about we put down a little wager that my Shag here can beat Romeo in a two mile race?"

"Korn had a rather surprised look on his face as he answered. "Two miles. Nobody races for two miles. Romeo is a quarter horse and a quarter mile is what he is bred to race. I'll make it a half-mile to make it fair to you. By the way what is the wager?"

"No, no a half-mile won't do at all. Shag here weighs a lot more than Romeo and I might be able to cut the race down to a mile and half. I figure we'll wager that you don't sneak off and go hunting Trapis on your own against you staying with us and letting us help you find him."

Korn sat silently in his saddle as we rode on and it took a full five minutes before he gave his answer. "All right I'll tell you what I'll do. We'll race for one mile. If Shag wins I'll abide by your conditions. If I win then anything goes. I might let you stay with me to the end of the hunt or I might not. It will be my choice."

I listened as Shag and Romeo talked over their rider's decision and neither animal was very happy with the one mile term of the race. Romeo definitely had the advantage for a short race. Shag was a long distance type of runner. In one mile Romeo would be wearing down while Shag would just be hitting his stride. It looked like this would be a very interesting contest to say the least.

Buffole looked over at Korn and said. "I agree to the terms when do we start."

"Now!" Hollered Korn as he gave the spurs to Romeo.

Buffole did not have to say anything for Shag took the intuitive on his own to take off after Romeo. We were way behind right from the start and Korn's rather sly way of taking the edge at the start lost us some extra ground. At the half mile mark Shag was still dropping behind. By three quarters of a mile Shag was about two lengths behind Romeo. At the end of the mile which both Korn and Buffole had designated by a large boulder being the finish line both Romeo and Shag were nose to nose.

Once we had stopped Romeo was lathering like a man ready for a barbershop shave. Shag was breathing a little hard but no worse for the wear of the race. Korn and Buffole argued for awhile but finally decided to call the race a draw. For the time being nothing was settled about the hunt for Trapis.

One thing the race did was to increase our thirst for water. Romeo was hit especially hard for a drink. Korn shared some water from his canteen with Romeo. Shag told us he was fine as buffalo were used to going long periods without water. Buffole and I shared a small sip of water each as we did not know how far the next source of water might be.

Trapis was using every trick in the book. He back tracked a few times and he often moved his horse over to hard rock surfaces. The horse he was riding must have been stolen from some white man as it had horse shoes and those shoes left small scuff marks that Korn was easily following. We stopped when we noticed that Trapis had dismounted his horse and the grass in that area was well packed as if something was being done to his mount. The tracks almost seemed to disappear and lost the sharpness of the hoof print. Korn told us that Trapis had wrapped his horse's hoofs in leather to keep them from scuffing the rocks. For Korn the trail was growing cold.

I left my perch in the saddlebag and got down on the ground to help with the tracking. I was doing all right and with Shag's sense of smell I was soon looking to Korn like I was the best tracking dog in the whole darn country.

It was nearing nightfall and we decided to make camp. Shag had led us to a water hole at the foot of a small mountain range. We were close to Trapis and I think all of us could sense his presence. Buffole got a campfire going and I gathered up some dry wood for us. Korn went on a scouting mission on foot. You could tell he had done some serious tracking before. He slipped off his boots and pulled a pair of moccasins from his saddle bag. This allowed him to move silently and more quickly than a pair of cowboy boots. Shag and Romeo made themselves at home in the grass along the edge of the pond. Buffole and I started cooking supper.

Korn returned and said he had not found a trace of Trapis. We had our meal and settled in for the night. Korn seemed rather distracted and aloof from Buffole and me. We bedded down near the campfire to keep off some of the nights chill. Korn took his bedroll over by Romeo. He said he did not want to risk the chance of Trapis sneaking into camp and stealing his horse. We had no need to worry about Shag, nobody would try to steal a buffalo.

The sound of crickets lulled us off to sleep. I woke first and made my way over to some bushes to do my morning duty. I glanced over to see how Korn and Romeo were doing and noticed they were both gone. I ran over and alerted Buffole to their absence. The two of us hurriedly got ready to go after them. Shag came meandering over slow and easy as if nothing was wrong. "I saw those two leave here as soon as you two were asleep. Korn can be mighty quiet and sneaky when he wants to. Can't blame him for wanting to get Trapis himself. After all that little wanna be Indian darn near killed Korn's son. For all any of us know Lake could be crippled up for life after taking that tomahawk in his leg. I think we should just let Korn take his revenge and leave well enough alone. After all Buffole and you to Sven would want to be left alone to take care of business with Popeye when you find him."

Shag had a point and I told Buffole what he had said. Buffole shook his head no but it was more out of uncertainty then refusal. "Shag has a point. Who am I to be judge and jury for any man? Still I think it best we track down Korn just in case he might need our help."

Buffole hurriedly loaded up Shag and I ran alongside as Shag picked up Romeo's trail. Korn must have been in a hurry for he had not bothered to try and hide his tracks.

We rode for half a day before I noticed a sign that we might be nearing our quarry. I told Buffole and Shag to look up in the sky. Buzzards were lazily circling overhead about a mile in the distance. Something or someone was most likely dying and the buzzards were gathering for a meal.

Following the circling buzzards we wound a path through huge boulders with a few occasional areas of open sand. We were now near to the area the buzzards were watching. A large buzzard sat on a high rock outcropping and he seemed to be getting antsy for a meal that would soon be ready to eat.

We came around a big boulder and there sat Korn in the shade of a rocky over hang. A trickle of water ran from between the stones next to him and emptied into a small pool at the base of the rocks. In the hot desert sand lay Trapis. His arms and legs were staked out in a spread eagle fashion. One leg was wrapped with a blood stained bandage. We knew that was the wound from the day he attacked us at the ranch. His other leg had two arrows from Korn's quiver sticking from the flesh into the air. Those wounds were still seeping blood but it had started to congeal from the heat of the sun. Trapis' shirt was torn open and his chest had been cut with a knife just deep enough to cause pain without death. The bottoms of his now bare feet were also slashed along with his tendons. If he did leave here alive he would most likely never walk again. Yet those wounds were not the worst of Trapis' troubles.

His face seemed to be covered in grease and red ants were feasting on his lips and eyes. We soon realized that what looked like grease was actually honey that Korn must have had in his saddlebag. The boy was more dead than alive. Buffole, Shag and I turned our heads at the hideous sight that was before us. Korn just sat on his rocky ledge and stared at Trapis. Finally Buffole said something. "Korn I know I am in no position to judge how you feel but it looks to me as if this boy has suffered enough. He's going to die there's no doubt about that. Don't you think it's about time you put him out of his misery?"

Korn had a blank look on his face as he gave his answer. "Suffered enough? My boy could be crippled for life or maybe even dead for all I know. My boy did nothing to deserve being attacked by that little savage. The kid's mind is warped from seeing his parents killed and than being taken in by the Indians. He wanted revenge on those who did not deserve it. Now he can die the way Indians kill those who have no honor in how they fight."

Buffole was becoming hardened to the way of the west but he still held a sense of decency. "Korn I consider you a good friend and if there was trouble I would want you by my side but I can't let you go on torturing the boy like this. If you don't put him out of my misery I will." I saw Buffole slowly pull his gun from its holster as he stared down Korn. "Korn I don't mean to use this gun on you, but I do mean to use it on this boy unless you finish what you have started and kill him now. You do that and I'll never breathe a word of what happened here. As far as I'm concerned you caught up with the boy and it was either you or him that had to die."

Korn's expression did not change when he spoke. "I caught up with this savage about two hours after you and Sven fell asleep. That darn buffalo of yours was watching me and I was afraid he was going to make some type of buffalo noise to alert you but he just watched me lead Romeo quietly away so as not to wake you. Trapis was asleep and his Indian senses are not so good because I snuck up on him and had my knife at his throat before his eyes were even open. I've been torturing him ever since. I guess maybe your right he's probably had enough. Anyway he'll be dead soon enough." As stealthy as a bobcat on the prowl Korn had his bow loaded and aimed. The arrow shot out with a slight twang of the bow string and went through Trapis' temple and out the other side of his skull. "We'll leave him for buzzard bait. They deserve a good meal for being so patient." Said Korn as he came down off the rocks and saddled up Romeo.

We rode in silence as we headed back to the ranch. Buffole and even I were contemplating what we had just witnessed. Were we revenge minded enough to do something similar to Popeye? Only time would tell.

There was dust in the air off in the distance which could mean a number of things and some of them were not good. Indians would normally do their best to keep any dust clouds down so as not to be noticed so we dismissed that threat. Buffalo could raise some dust but Shag was quick to point out in less it was a stampede it was doubtful the dust cloud was from buffalo, wild horses or cattle. Men, now that was a logical conclusion. We stopped and Korn took a spyglass from his saddle bag to check out the situation. When he was done he handed the spyglass to Buffole to take a look. "Looks like men riding hard to me. Five of 'em by my count," said Buffole.

Korn put the cover over the lens on the spyglass as he slid it back into his saddlebag. He took a swig of water from his canteen and said. "Yup five of 'em. My guess is it's my men from the ranch. Most likely Bubba must be in the lead or they wouldn't be so damn obvious as to their movement. That boy never did have a lick of sense but he's faithful as an old dog. We best hurry along to meet them before they run my horse's that their ridin' to death."

We soon met up with Bubba, Tearhart, Dancer and two Mexican ranch hands named Joe and Willie. Bubba did the talking for the group. "Korn where the hell have you been? Sindee sent us out to find you. Lake is going to be all right the tomahawk did not cut any major arteries or muscles and the doc says he may limp for a few weeks but he should heal up just fine."

Dancer then entered the conversation. "What about Trapis did you find him?"

Buffole and I looked at Korn to give the answer. "Yes we found him. He'll not be giving us trouble any more. I'd like to say he has joined his parents but more likely he might just be in a place a little lower down living with the devil."

Once we were back at the ranch Sindee insisted we stay for a few days. Buffole tried to worm his way out of the invitation by explaining that we had already lost time that should have been used for tracking Popeye but she would have none of his excuses. "Ole or Buffole? Whatever your name is now, I don't want no guff from you. Your party was ruined by that little savage and sleeping out on the prairie with Korn as company sure was no picnic. You and Sven go get washed up and relax. We'll have a good meal tonight and you boys can get a few nights of well deserved sleep in a real home with a real bed. When I see you and Sven well fed and rested than you can leave. Now you do what I say ya here? Bubba you take care of Shag and brush him down good so Buffole don't have to worry about him."

Buffalo looked at me and then at Korn. Korn added in his two cents worth. "You best do as she says boys ain't no arguing with that woman once she sets her mind to the way things should be."

For the next two days Sindee and everyone else at the ranch made us feel like family. Lake was finally out of bed and hobbling around with a cane. His leg was sore and stiff but he was on the mend.

Sindee would have liked us to stay longer but Korn intervened on our behalf. He understood that revenge is a powerful force for a man to deal with. Bubba saddled up Shag for us and the cook from the kitchen supplied us with enough food for at least a week, including honey from the ranches very own bee hives.

We said our goodbyes and Dancer had also saddled up and was leaving with us. He offered to ride with us and help track down Popeye. We were not the only ones with a vendetta against the buffalo hunter. We accepted his offer and rode off towards the Rio Grande for the last we heard Popeye was over the border in Mexico.

CHAPTER 12

We traveled for number of days before we came upon the town of Santa Angela. It was a good sized town and it was a welcome sight after eating trial dust for so long. We tied up our mounts on the railing outside Miss Hattie's Cafe and Saloon.

Entering Miss Hattie's we were surprised to see a number of women about the place. It was late afternoon and the place was almost as busy as a hive of bees making honey. The women looked well used and were scantily dressed. A number of men were being led up or down the stairs to and from various rooms which were most likely being used for things and secrets best kept behind locked doors.

Dancer and Buffole stepped up to bar and ordered drinks. As for me I stayed close by Buffole figuring I was less likely to be tripped over or stepped on by the crowd. A rather comely wench was soon at Buffole's side and started talking. "Hey cowboy you going to buy a lady a drink." Buffole being rather shy just said 'Sure' and let the lady 'if you would call her that' order whatever she wanted. Dancer just stood off to the side with an amused look on his face as the lady progressed the conversation. "You're new in town I ain't never seen you around here before. I see you got a cute little dog with you what's his name?"

"My canine partners name is Sven and my name is Buffole. We're just passing through ma'am." She smiled and took Buffole's arm in hers. "Why don't you come upstairs with me and I will show you a real good time Mr. Buffole. You can bring your dog along if he likes to watch. My name's Carrie and I can make your dreams come true." Buffole sort of pulled away and unlocked his arm from hers. "Ma'am not meaning no disrespect for your profession but I think I best pass on your offer. Sven don't like me consorting with strange women.

Dancer I think we best move on and find us a place to stay for the night." Carrie muttered some nasty words just loud enough for us to hear and then she moved on to the next most likely candidate for her sales pitch.

Dancer smiled and downed his drink. "Yes sir Buffole I think your right let's find us a hotel to stay in."

We found a livery stable and put our mounts up for the night. Buffole and Dancer both took time to groom and feed their rides. Shag I could tell really enjoyed having Buffole brush him even if he was too proud to say anything about it.

A few blocks from the Livery stable was the Longhorn Hotel, it was a fancy two story building with a second floor balcony. Its white painted front with blue trim looked pretty inviting. The double oak doors had oval stained glass windows and brass door handles. Once inside a red carpet on the floor was a nice change from the wooden floors we usually traversed. The clerk put down the book he was reading to greet us as we neared the check in desk.

"Good day gentleman you look a little tired? Have you been on the trail long?"

"Long enough that we would like a bath and a good shave" said Buffole. "Yeah what he said." Added in Dancer.

The clerk told us we could get cleaned up across the street at Long's Barber and Bath. He also mentioned that if we were looking for any female companionship we might try Hattie's Bordello. So it was not just a saloon and café as the sign said. Guess we knew it was a house of ill repute all along and the hotel clerk certainly confirmed our suspicions.

At Long's Barber Shop and Bath we were greeted by a well dressed gentleman in a crisp white shirt, narrow black tie, pressed pants and highly polished black shoes. "Hello gentleman my name is Aaron Long and I'm the proprietor of this establishment. What can I do for you gents?"

Dancer removed his hat and stood in the doorway almost afraid to move. The place was so neat and tidy none of us wanted to mess it up with our dusty bodies. "Mister Long me and my partners here need haircuts, a shave and most of all a good bath." Buffole added in to the requests. "A bath and trim for Sven my dog would be much appreciated too if it's all right with you. If you have anyone that could wash our duds that would be also much appreciated."

An oriental boy was sitting in the corner of the barbershop and Aaron politely asked the boy to take us into the back room for our baths. A steam boiler was stoked up and buckets of hot water were steaming on metal grates ready for use. The boy started pouring the water into two of the waiting bath tubs and he said to us. "You fella's take off clothes and put on pile on floor. Then get in tubs as I fill them. You bathe, I take clothes to my mama's laundry be back quick as soon. Dog he come with me and mamma wash him to." Well what could I do but go with. Anyway it was probably better to go with the Chinese boy then to see Buffole and Dancer naked.

The Chinese boy led me and his bundle of clothes down the street to his mother's laundry. It was actually just a tent set up at the end of the block where the town ended. A wood sign on one of the poles holding up the tent had a crudely lettered sign in English that read Washy-Washy Laundry.

The boy's mother was an attractive lady with dark hair pulled into a bun behind her head. She was maybe four and half feet tall. Her hands were red and raw from scrubbing laundry but she carried herself with dignity. The boy spoke to her in Chinese and the next thing you know I was picked up by the lady and deposited in a tub of soapy water. She scrubbed and rubbed me till my fur was almost raw. Then out I came for a rub down with a coarse towel. She brushed me and pulled out knots of matted hair that had built up over our travels. Once she had me scrubbed, brushed and all fancy looking she had the boy take me out in the sun to dry while she did Dancer and Buffole's laundry. It was good hour before we returned to the barber shop. The men's clothes were clean pressed and folded.

We walked into the barber shop and Buffole and Dancer were dressed or should I say covered up in some old wool house coats. The house coats looked like they were made from colorful old horse blankets but at least they were clean. Buffole was in the barber chair with lather over his face and his hair had already been cut short. Dancer was eager to grab his clothes and get dressed. Sometime while we were gone a local boy had come in and polished the guy's boots. Dancer already had his boots on along with his housecoat and it made for a rather interesting sight. Buffole was still barefoot and with his missing big toe looked rather strange sitting in the barber chair. The boy was just finishing buffing out Buffole's boots as the barber started shaving him.

As Dancer took his clothes from the Chinese boy the lad told him. "You owe three dollar. Two dollar for the clothes and one dollar for washy dog." Dancer gave the boy his money and the lad went scurrying out the door for home. The boots cost the guys another dollar and add that to the bath, haircut and shave and it looked to be a total of ten dollars well spent.

When everyone was dressed and ready we strutted our stuff in front of each other and the barber. Everyone agreed we all looked like the gentleman we were pretending to be. Buffole asked the barber where we could get a good meal and maybe a drink. "Most of the drinking is done at Miss Hattie's and she's got lots of shall we say soiled doves to keep you company."

Dancer was quick to answer. "We been there and didn't much care for the place or the company. Do you have any other places that might be more befittin' for a couple of fancy dudes like me and my friends here?"

"You might try Guido Ottinio's dinner theater on the far side of town. They have great food and each night a play is put on by traveling actors. This week a traveling troupe is putting the musical burlesque play called 'Robert and the Devil' or 'The Nun, the Dun and the Son of a Gun." It was written by the playwright W.S. Gilbert. You best hurry over there because with Guido's superb meals and real live entertainment the place sells out very quickly. I've seen the show and in this god forsaken land a little cultural entertainment is very welcomed. It reminds me of my days growing up in England. America is a great place but it was far behind Europe in culture. Best you gentleman hurry over to Guido's. I hope you have a nice evening." With those words Aaron hustled us out the door of his shop.

We walked to the far side of town and it was a lot different from the other side of town where the Washy-Washy Laundry was located. A large two story building with a false front was painted in gaudy green, red and white. A lot of fancy gold letters proclaimed the name of Guido Ottinio's Dinner Theater, fine dining and Exceptional theatrical Shows and Revue's. Billboards of the current show and future entertainment were pasted on the walls. Two large arched doors made of mahogany with large ornately colored glass windows done with scenes of Italy greeted us. A man with an Italian accent was dressed in an outfit that looked like an officer's uniform but I think it was just a doorman's costume. He opened the door for us and welcomed us to Guido's the finest dining and entertainment establishment west of the Mississippi.

Guido himself led us to a table near the stage. He accepted me just as he would any other guest and he even pulled out a chair for me to sit at the table with Dancer and Buffole. "Welcome gentleman and furry guest." He said that as he tied a napkin around my neck for me. Now this is what I would call a first class establishment. "I will be taking your dinner order tonight. May I bring you some of the house wine? It comes from my father's very own vineyards in Italy. He ships it to me on a regular basis. Nowhere in the America's will you find a finer wine to satisfy your palates." Buffole cleared his throat as he played the part of a worldly gentleman. "Yes Guido I think we will accept your gracious suggestion on the wine. Please bring us two glasses." Guido smiled and winked at me. "For your four legged friend I will bring him a bowl of wine. If you would be so kind as to permit me to do so. Seldom do I have such a handsome canine grace my humble theater." Buffole swallowed hard as he tried to come up with the right words for an answer. "I think my friend Sven would greatly appreciate your offer Mister Ottino. By the way my name is Buffole and the gentleman accompanying me is Mister Dancer." Signore's please call me Guido. There is no Mister in front of my name for my friends."

When Guido returned Dancer and Ole had our orders ready. Dancer wanted the biggest steak in the place done on the rare side. I think he slipped out of the gentleman character when he ordered it in these words. "Guido I'm might hungry. Give me the biggest thickest steak you got and make it rare, just cooked enough so it ain't bellowing when I cut into it. Toss a few potatoes and gravy next to my meat. A whisky and a beer chaser to drink if you please."

Buffole was a bit more discreet with his order. "Guido I would also like a steak. Medium rare with a baked potato on the side and a roll with butter and jam. Sven will have the same as me. If it is not a bother Sven and I would also enjoy some fresh milk if you have it. We have not had milk since we left our farm in Minnesota and it would be a treat much appreciated." At Guido's suggestion we also ended up with a side dish of pasta with a mushroom and wine sauce glaze. Of course this made sense since Guido's was considered an Italian restaurant.

We watched as Guido handled his guests much like a professional juggler would handle his juggling items. That man was quicker than stink from a skunk at taking orders and making small talk to keep his patrons happy.

Like a flash the house lights were dimmed as waiters appeared and turned the wicks of the side lights down, even the chandeliers were lowered and dimmed so that the theater was lit like the soft glow of an evening sun fall. Lights on the front of the stage were turned up with silvered chrome disks behind them to illuminate the show. Guido was suddenly on stage in his black waistcoat and black pants with a grey stripe running down the length of the leg. His white shirt with its pearled buttons glimmered like stars in the midnight sky. He held up his hand to quiet the over filled room of dinners and guests. "Ladies and Gentleman Guido's Theater is proud to present for your enjoyment the renowned troupe of Pierce's Players in a play written by the world famous playwright W.S Gilbert. 'Robert and the Devil' or as we like to call it 'The Nun, the Dun and the Son of a Gun.'"

The audience all clapped and as Guido left the stage the curtain with its painted backdrop was lowered to coincide with the first scene of the play. As we sat watching the actors the waiters busily hurried around the room filling the tables with meals. Buffole had seen some plays back in Minnesota and even a few while he travelled with his regiment during the Civil war. I don't know if Dancer had ever seen a play before but he seemed to be enjoying it. Some of the ladies played the parts of men, and full grown adults sometimes played the parts of children. It was all rather amusing to say the least.

A young lady on stage started to sing and Buffole suddenly stopped eating with his food half to his mouth. He sat spell bound just staring at the woman on the stage. He swallowed hard and said. "I know that girl. Sven you know her too." Dancer gave us a quizzical look as he had heard Buffole talk to me. Dancer went back to butchering his steak and acted as if he was mistaken about Buffole talking to a dog as if I understood and was supposed to answer. I looked more closely at the girl on stage and doggone if Buffole wasn't right.

Buffole went back to eating his meal and kept an eye on the girl on stage. She was blonde and rather young compared to the rest of the actresses and actors in the troupe. I could see Buffole was agitated about seeing the girl so I asked him. "It might just be someday that looks like her." Buffole looked at me so I could see his face and read his lips. "It's her I'm sure of it."

Guido stopped at our table to check on us. "Gentleman and furry one are you enjoying the show? Is your meal satisfactory? May I send over additional beverages for your enjoyment?" Dancer looked at Buffole and my empty glasses and answered. "Everything is great. You can bring us more drinks though. Guido you really know how to treat a customer."

Buffole reached up and touched Guido's arm than motioned for him to come closer. Guido lowered his head down by Buffole. For a brief moment the actors were speaking with no background noise so Buffole was able to whisper to Guido. "Guido I think I know the young blonde girl on the stage would it be possible for me to meet her after the show?"

"Sir if I believed every man that told me he knew one of the actresses really did know them the unfortunate ladies would have to visit with every gentleman in this room every night. It was a good try but it is against house rules for the actresses to associate with the customers."

"Guido it's very important that I talk to her. Her name is Jo and I knew her and her mother from my travels. I just want to know that her mother is safe and all right. If you would just tell her that Buffole the man who rides a buffalo wants to see her I'm sure she would be willing to talk to me. Maybe you can arrange a meeting away from the public so none of your other customers would know." Buffole then slipped five gold dollars into Guido's hand.

Guido looked in the palm of his hand before he said anything. "I'll give her your message but it is up to her and not to me. I'll let you know what her answer is."

Guido disappeared from sight and soon after we had fresh drinks as the play continued. The best I could make of the whole thing was that humans are tempted by the Devil. Sometimes the humans are strong enough to resist the temptations of sins but lots of times they fall prey to the ways of evil. Here in the west, Buffole, Shag and I have witnessed lots of evil, in fact maybe hunting Popeye makes us no better than anyone else in this wicked world. In fact we may be even worse then some.

I could tell Buffole was getting nervous about Jo. Guido had not returned and our new round of drinks was about empty. According to the play bill that Buffole had the play was about three fourths of the way over. If Guido did not come through we would need to find another way to see Jo. I knew Buffole had been thinking a lot about Jo's mom Krystal and he had a worried look on his face. If Krystal was not in the play was she at least here with the troupe of actors or had something happened to her? If Jo was alone we could only expect the worse.

Guido finally appeared at our table with another tray of drinks too wet our whistles. He served Dancer and me first than he leaned in by Buffole to fill his glass. "Sir the young lady would like to meet alone after the play has ended. You can send your friend on his way and stay here until we close. She did say your furry friend could stay."

Buffole and I impatiently waited for the play to end. Every time Joe was on the stage we both had our own thoughts to deal with. Buffole was of course worried about Krystal. As for me, I was worried about Lena.

It seemed to take forever for the crowd to leave. Buffole tried to be polite as he asked Dancer to go back to the hotel. "Dancer why don't you go back to the hotel and get a good night's sleep? I saw an old friend of mine in the play and I am hoping to meet them and talk about the old days."

Dancer definitely had a few too many drinks and slurred his words. "So you want to get rid of me do you? I ain't good enough to meet your friends. Why just look at me dressed up as well as any dandy ever was. Well I know when I'm not wanted. Goodbye!"

"Dancer I didn't mean any offense, I just wanted a little time alone with an old friend." It was too late Dancer was already huffing out the door. In the morning when he sobered up he would most likely forgot about the whole thing anyway.

Eventually the place cleared out except for the cleanup crew who were busy clearing tables and mopping up the floor. Guido was there directing the clean-up operations and he insisted that our table be cleared and washed immediately. Once that was done a fresh bottle of champagne with two crystal glasses and a cut glass bowl were set up for us. "Drinks are on the house, my compliments" said Guido. I whispered to Buffole. "I think Guido might have the wrong idea, he seems to be under the impression that this might be a romantic interlude or maybe that you are trying to impress the lady."

We left Guido to think what he may. Jo finally came from the side stage door and approached our table. Buffole stood and clasped her hand in his. "Jo it is great to see you, thank you so much for meeting with me. He pulled out a chair for her and then helped to push it in just as a gentleman should. I was rather proud of him. Jo reached over and scratched my ear. "Sven it's good to see you. Lena is with mama but I know she will feel really sad that she missed seeing you. What brings you two to the theater? How are you both doing and where have you been? I have so many questions. I'm sorry. I must let you talk I am just happy to see someone I know. Momma and I have been apart for weeks now and I miss her so much."

Buffole was moving in the same direction as Jo when he spoke. "Jo what about your mother. Is she all right. What are you doing here on the stage? I had no idea you were an actress. By the way I thought you did a marvelous job with your part in the play."

"Momma and I had some trouble with Indians after you left. First we saw them off in the distance watching us. After a while they become more bold and rode right up to the house. One of them asked if they could use our water. Momma was standing in the doorway of the cabin with a rifle in her hand and figured it best to be hospitable. Every few days they would come by again asking for water. Finally the one who spoke English asked where the man of the ranch was. Momma told him he was away on business. After two weeks the buck who spoke English told Momma her man was not going to return. No man would leave his woman and child for so long alone. He said if her man did not return in a week he would take Momma and me to his village. Momma would be his woman and they would find a young brave for me to wed. We had no choice but to get away. That very night we packed up our wagon and by daybreak we were on the trail to the nearest army outpost. It was a two day trip but we made it without incident. Momma drove the wagon and I drove what livestock we could round up along with us."

"At the fort the soldier's welcomed us and set us up with an empty room in one of the barracks. Some of the soldiers had their wives and children with them. A few of the soldiers had even married local Indian girls and they too were staying at the fort so it was nice not being the only women there. Momma has never been one to accept charity from anyone so she made it known that our extra livestock was for sale. She also took up doing laundry and cleaning for the unmarried soldiers. Within a few days we were settled in and making money to live on. Within a few weeks enough settlers had passed through the fort that we had managed to sell off our excess live stock."

"We now had enough money to go somewhere and start over. We were about to hook up with the next wagon train that passed through when Momma had a change of heart. The troupe of actors that I am with stopped at the fort to put on a show. It just so happened the manager is related to us. One of the actresses from the show had run off with a young gentleman at the last town they were in and they needed a replacement. Momma convinced her cousin to let me try out for the part and he liked my acting enough to offer me this job, so here I am. I did not want to leave my Momma but she insisted that I go with the stage troupe for she had things that she had to do."

"She sat me down and explained her reasoning to me. Although she loved my father he was dead and gone. We were in a strange new world out here in the west and things moved faster than they had back in Minnesota. It was time for me to be an adult and make my own way. Many girls out west were already married and having children when they were my age. Well I was not ready to get married and I certainly was not ready to start a family of my own. Having a job with a relative Momma could trust seemed like a logical thing to do."

"Momma told me something that at first shocked me but then as I thought about it I did my best to understand how she felt. My daddy hurt her a lot when he announced he was leaving us. I think Momma knew deep down in her heart that it was going to happen sooner or later. Then she told me her plans. First she said she felt much like you must feel about taking revenge on Popeye. She bought herself a gun and a holster from a trader at the fort. She has been practicing drawing and shooting but her hands are sort of small for the size of the gun. I guess handguns were designed more for men than women. As a back-up weapon she bought a rifle and had the barrel cut down and a larger loop put on for cocking it faster. The gunsmith that sold it to her said they call it a mare's leg. She designed a shoulder holster for it so it could hang on her back. It was now easy for her to grab and pull it out with one hand. I've watched her practice with the mare's leg and she is pretty proficient with that compared to the handgun. She is my mother and she's strong minded she'll do what she feels has to be done."

"There is one thing you should know. I am not sure if I agree with her on this matter but it is important to her and I want her to be happy.

My daddy has not been dead very long but I am trying to accept that things were over between him and Momma a long time before he was killed."

"So here it is straight and to the point. Momma told me that there was a spark between you and her and you've kindled feelings in her that she thought were just dead ashes that would never come to flame again. The only problem for her was she does not know how you really feel. She told me what you said to her when you left. You said. She was possibly the angel at the end of your journey. Buffole I think she wants to be that angel. I also believe that her excuse to go hunting for Popeye has more to do with finding you than of killing him. She figures wherever Popeye is you are probably not far behind. I am no artist but I drew her a picture of how Popeye looks so she can show it around, it should help her to trace him down."

"Momma and I have both heard some stories about you at the fort. In fact I have heard even more about you since I have been on the road with the acting troupe. They say there were three buffalo hunters that attacked your family and you have already killed one of them, no one seems to know how the other one died and Popeye is the only other survivor of the three. Then we heard that you killed a gambler and a sheriff in the town of Lutherhell. So far all the killings have been in self defense from what they say and there are no warrants out for your arrest. Is all of what we hear really true?"

Buffalo took a sip of his drink before he answered. "Yes what you heard is true. Those stories make me sound like some sort of gunslinger and I assure you that is not a reputation I want to have. Seems I just sort have fallen into the wrong places at the wrong times."

"You know it is a dangerous undertaking for your mother to travel alone looking for me. Most men in the west respect a woman and would never think of harming one. Yet there are a lot of bad men who would not think twice of taking advantage of her or maybe even killing her. Remember what Popeye wanted to do. Men like him are the scourge of society and someone needs to stop them."

"Is there any way you can contact your mother and have her wait wherever she is. I would give her my word that as soon as I am finished with Popeye I would come and join her. Jo if you could would you draw me a likeness of Popeye it sure would be useful in my hunt."

Jo had some paper in her hand bag and started drawing the likeness of Popeye even as she kept talking. "Momma has a schedule that my cousin gave her as to where our troupe will be playing. I always go to the post office in each town as soon as we arrive to see if she has sent mail. If there is not a letter from her I check the mail again before we leave town. So far I have received only two letters. The last one had her in the town of Lutherhell where she wrote of meeting a lady who she said is not only a local saloon keeper but also the town Sheriff. I think the Sheriff's name was Trixie. She told Momma that you had come to town half dead from the bite of a Gila monster. After you healed up you had a run in with the towns corrupt Sheriff and some of his men. She said you killed the Sheriff in a showdown right on main street. Trixie told Momma if it were not for you she would not have been appointed Sheriff. I guess the townsfolk changed the name of the town to Bettertown to give it a new image. Momma is on the move a lot but said when she finds Popeye and you she will write and let me know. I do not have a way of knowing where she is from day to day. If you were to stay put here I bet she would show up soon. You're getting to be a well known figure in the west and there's nothing people like to talk about more than a hero or a bandit."

Buffole sort of fumbled for words. "Jo I would love to stay here and wait for Krystal but if the trail gets to cold Popeye might escape. Like the west itself things like this are tough choices. I have enough money that I could give you to stay here and wait for your mother to return and then keep her here until I finish my job. Knowing you were both here safe and sound would take a mighty heavy load off my mind. What do you say? Will you stay and wait for your mother?"

"Buffole I can't desert the troupe. After all my Momma's cousin gave me a job to help her. He's paying me a good salary and they would be short one actress if I left them. No I cannot stay here I have an obligation to keep. Maybe you and I are not so different. We are both bound by our word to do what we have to do. I must go and get some rest for we leave early tomorrow."

As Jo stood up to leave Buffole rose and took her hands in his. "You be careful now ya hear? If you see your Momma you tell her that I will come for her as soon as this is finished. Try to keep her safe if you can. Both of you will be in my thoughts."

I broke into the conversation. "Buffole tell her to make sure to keep Lena safe too."

"Jo one more thing, I know Sven wants you to know that he's thinking about Lena and make sure your mother keeps her safe."

Jo leaned over and gave Buffole a kiss on the cheek and she looked a little sad as she gave me a goodbye pat on the head and left for her room.

CHAPTER 13

We met Dancer at breakfast the next morning. He seemed to have forgot all about the previous evenings little tirade. "Buffole I have to change my plans. I stopped at the Sheriff's office before I came here to see if there were any wanted posters for Popeye. The man is not wanted for anything that we know of. The Sheriff has heard of him and seems he is riding with a group of renegade Mexicans led by an hombre by the name of Doroteo Avango, but he likes to call himself Poncho Villa. You could swear out a complaint for Popeye and that would help a lot in getting him brought to justice. After all you saw him kill your wife and boy. You were also a witness when he killed that rancher and attacked his woman and his daughter."

"Anyway what I'm trying to say is that I've been offered a job as a tracker by a local Pinkerton agent I met in the hotel lobby after I left you to meet your friend. Some hombre they call Pauly nine-toe and his gang just robbed a train not too far from here and I sure could use the reward money they have offered for his capture. Maybe you should go talk with the local Sheriff and swear out a warrant for Popeye at least then if you kill him everything would be above board and legal."

"Dancer I don't want a bunch of wanted posters spread out all over the countryside for Popeye. If that happened the law would offer a reward and every bounty hunter and peace officer would be hunting him. Popeye's hide belongs to me and I aim to get it. If you're so darn fired anxious to have a reward posted on Popeye why don't you file a complaint. After all he and his friends shot you and left you for dead."

"I can't swear that Popeye even shot me. It could have been any one of those three and the other two are dead. Hell maybe you, Sven and that buffalo of yours already avenged the man that shot me. I'm not positive which of the buffalo hunters shot me. I can't just go rushing in and kill a man without positive proof. You and Popeye that will be justified revenge in any court in the west if you kill him. If he kills you all I can say is I hope heaven takes you before the devil grabs you."

"Thanks Dancer and I hope you catch Pauly nine-toes and his gang. I'm off to Mexico, adios Amigo."

Dancer had his horse saddled up and out front ready to ride. We went back to our room and packed up our own gear. Shag was happy to see us even if he pretended not to care. Buffole stroked his big old shaggy head and said hello as Shag snorted in acknowledgement. I stood on my hind legs in front of Shag and he lowered his head down to mine for a good old animal nose touch greeting.

Buffole settled up with the livery stable's owner and then he saddled up Shag. I decided to ride in the saddlebag for at least a while. We were making our way past the train station when we noticed Jo and the acting troupe boarding the train. Buffole pulled Shag's reins for him to stop. "Shag do you see Jo boarding the train. You remember her, she and her mother were the ones we rescued when Popeye killed their man."

Shag turned his mighty head towards the train. "Yes I remember her, where's her mother?"

"Her mother is hunting for Popeye and for us from what Jo told me last night. Jo belongs to a theater troupe and is heading off to their next engagement. As for us we best be on the trail to find Popeye. Krystal is far enough behind us that we should have no problem locating him before she does. Well boys it's off to Mexico for us.

Our travel was hot and we all grew weary with the sun beating down on us. We met a family with a burro heading in the opposite direction. The man and a young boy were walking while a woman sat astride the burro. They had bundles of clothing, food and water enough to show they expected to be travelling for many days. They all had on white clothes that were dusty and well worn. The boy was fascinated by Shag as he had never seen a buffalo before. The man and the woman gave Shag a wide berth as if they were afraid of him. Most likely they also had never before laid eyes on such a beast.

Buffole spoke first. "Howdy folks I wonder if you might be able to help me?"

The man took charge as if he meant to protect his family in case of harm. His hand rested on the handle of a machete that was tucked into the red sash round his waist. "See senor. We have never seen such a beast as you are riding. I have heard of the shaggy bison from the plains but never have I seen one before. Even more unusual is I have never heard of a man riding such an animal." The boy had ventured close enough to run his hand up and down Shag's neck. Shag of course enjoyed the attention. The man had a look of horror on his face as his boy touched Shag. "Manual you get away from that animal there is no telling what it might do to you."

Buffole smiled to get the man to relax. "Senor no need to worry. This is my buffalo Shag he will not harm your boy or anyone else unless I ask him to. I've travelled far and am looking for a very bad man." Buffole pulled the drawing Jo had made for him from inside the crown of his hat. He dismounted from Shag and walked over to the man and held the drawing so the man could see it. "This is the man I am looking for have you seen him?"

"No senor I have not seen him but from the picture you show me I believe I have heard of him. There cannot be many men so ugly with bulging eyes. I have heard of such a man, a gringo mercenary they say. He has hired his gun to ride with Poncho Villa in Mexico. They like to raid villages south of Columbus, New Mexico. Poncho Villa calls himself a champion of the people but the Federale's call him a renegade and murderer. He and his men are wanted for many crimes by the Mexican government. He helps many of the peasants and the poor so they protect him and hide him from the government troops. I would suggest you not go after the man with bulging eyes as long as he is with Poncho."

Buffole slipped a dollar coin from his pocket and pressed it into the man's hand. "Take this my friend and be safe. Thank you for the information." We mounted up and the boy backed away from petting Shag. "Senor I like your buffalo" he said.

As we rode away the family waved goodbye and we heard the man say "Adios amigo may god be with you."

The trail we followed into New Mexico territory was dry and dusty. A few tumbleweeds caught up by an occasional cactus were the only sights that broke up the monotony of the desert we were crossing. Buffole had packed some extra canteens so water was not a problem as long as we rationed it appropriately amongst ourselves.

When riding the trail on a buffalo's back it took us seven days from our start point to the town of Columbus in New Mexico territory. Most of the trip is miserable with just the lizards, snakes, buzzards and a few road runners to keep us company.

When we finally arrived in Columbus we found a nice clean livery stable run by a colored man with a rough growth of curly black whiskers and dressed in the remnants of a soldier's uniform. Buffole dismounted Shag and the stable owner took his reins. Buffole asked. "I see your uniform were you with the 10th Calvary. The man smiled and answered. "Yes sir I was. Mustered out a couple years back. Fighting Indians was looking to be a darn right dangerous job. When my hitch was up I came here and started myself this livery stable. Ain't so glamorous as being a soldier in some folk's eyes but it sure as hell is a lot safer. You know my regiment was known as the Buffalo Soldiers, so it seems mighty fitting that you give me a buffalo to take care of here in my stables. I almost feel akin to this big shaggy beast. I'll take real fine care of him for you. How long you staying?"

"We should be leaving in a day or two if I can get the information I need. By the way have you seen or heard anything about a man named Popeye. Here's a drawing of him if that might help you remember."

The colored man looked over the picture that Buffole handed him. "Yes I've seen this man. He boarded his horse here a few weeks back. Darn right rude and nasty he was. Smelled like a dead and rotting buffalo. By the way no offense to your ride here. He hung around for a few days called himself Popeye. He claimed to be a mercenary looking for work. Wanted to find Poncho Villa and join up with him. Eventually a few Mexicans came to town and recruited him to work for Poncho and his army as he calls it. They are really just a bunch of bandits disguising themselves as champions of the peasant's from what I hear. You don't look like the law are you a bounty hunter?"

"No I'm not a bounty hunter but I have a score to settle with Popeye. Would you know how I can find this Poncho Villa fella?"

"He moves around a lot, the Mexican Federale's are always looking for him. The peasants hide him out because he helps them with food and money. Sometimes he ransacks a town and burns and pillages it. If you find one of those towns they may lead you to him for revenge. Except in those towns the peasants are often afraid of reprisals if they tell anyone where Villa is. If you offer money to the right peasants they may help you out. If not they may go to Poncho and tell him about you. If they do that you are going to die. If I were you I would leave here and go back to where you came from."

"I'm here for one reason and one reason only and that is to find Popeye. Is there any place in town that I might be able to get more information on Poncho Villa's whereabouts? I could also use a place to stay until I get the information I need. Do you have any suggestions?"

"Well sir if I was you I would try the saloon. It's down about a dozen buildings from here. You can't miss it they just got themselves something called gas lights and the place looks like day time all night long. The name is lit up on front bold as sunshine. It's called Pezta's Palace and it has rooms for rent upstairs. Sort of a noisy place to stay until the saloon closes for the night which is usually about one in the morning. Liza the owner likes to make sure the saloon closes up by then so her boarders upstairs can get some sleep. They don't open until noon during the day so you can sleep in if you want. If anyone might know the rumors about where Poncho might be hiding out it will be Liza."

"By the way my name is Buffole, this is my dog Sven and my ride here is called Shag. I didn't catch your name sir."

"Name's Ivan and yup I know that's a strange name for a colored man. My family was slaves for a Russian Czar back before the war and the Master there he named all the babies born on the plantation. So here I be at your service Ivan Czarnoff."

Buffole shook Ivan's hand as he pressed a dollar coin into his palm. "Nice meeting you Ivan. Here's a little extra for the information. You take extra good care of Shag for me. He likes to be brushed down and scratch his ears some. Come on over for a drink when you have some spare time, I'm buying."

"I'll take care of ol' Shag real well. The drink sounds mighty inviting. If you're still in town tomorrow I'll take you up on that offer. Tonight the misses and the kids are expecting me home for supper."

We walked over to the Pezta Palace and it was busy as a bee hive. Buffole had to step over a drunk who had been tossed out the batwing doors and was now lying on the board walk. Once inside Buffole fanned his hand in front of his face to try and clear the smoke from the air enough so he could see the bar. Being a dog I was low to the ground and the floor smelled of spilt beer and liquor but it was better than breathing in stale smoke.

Faro games were being played at a few tables. A roulette wheel whirled with the soft clink of the steel ball and a wheel of fortune spun with clinking sounds as the canvas strip worked its way over the pins on the board. Cigars, cigarettes and stale liquor filled our nostrils not to mention the steady hum of the voices that made it hard to distinguish what anyone was saying.

Once at the bar I had to suggest that Buffole move over a bit so I did not have to stand next to one of the many brass spittoons. Being on the floor and next to a spittoon which is being used by a bunch of drunks is not a good idea. Buffole looked down and saw the predicament I was in so he reached down picked me off the floor and set me on the bar.

"Bartender a tequila with a SvenBrew chaser for me and a bowl of SvenBrew for my friend Sven." There was another dog in the room sitting next to an attractive slim lady with long dark hair who was dealing faro at one of the tables. The dog was about forty pounds and looked to be of mixed descent. I could sense some Schnauzer and Border collie in him and maybe a hint of a few other breeds. The lady, well she looked to be very well bred by the thoughts I was picking up from Buffole as he looked her way.

The saloon gals were in full swing and flirting with customers like there was no tomorrow. A few of them approached Buffole and a few even approached me and I must say having a pretty lady scratch your ears and tell you how good looking you are is pretty darn flattering even for a dog.

I noticed a dandy at the opposite end of the bar and he had not taken his eyes off Buffole since we had come in. The guy was young and cocky looking. He was dressed all in black with Mexican silver spurs and two pearl handled guns in a tooled leather holster. Each gun had a dollar sign engraved in the handle in what appeared to be solid gold.

Buffole downed his first tequila and it surprised me when he ordered a second. He was not really much of a drinking man and hearing him order a second was definitely a shock me. He glanced at me and said. "Don't worry little buddy I'm not getting drunk just building up some courage to talk to this Liza lady. You know me I'm not very good with talking to women." The bartender poured Buffole's tequila into a shot glass and Buffole downed it quickly and took a bite of lime to calm his taste buds. A quick swig of SvenBrew beer as his chaser and he asked the bartender. "I'm new here in town and I'm told I might find a woman named Liza here. I was wondering if you could maybe help me out as bartenders' usually know everyone in town."

"I know who you're looking for mister but she don't talk to just any yahoo who comes into town. You tell me your business with her and I might see what I can do. Of course information will cost you."

"How much?" asked Buffole.

The bartender rubbed his chin with his hand and thought for a moment. "I think an introduction should be worth at least five dollars. I also need to know your business if I'm to take the trouble to introduce you."

"I'm looking for the man that killed my family and I heard Liza may be able to help me find him." Buffole reached in his pocket and put five dollars on the bar. The bartender picked up the money and walked away.

Buffole and I continued nursing our SvenBrews and I kept an eye on the young fella in black. Two other men joined him and they started talking. Now all three of those hombres kept looking over at Buffole and me. I'll admit I didn't like the look of those three.

Buffole and I watched the bartender as he made his way to the slim lady at the faro table. He talked to her for a minute or so and then he came back to the bar. The faro dealer called one of the other saloon girls over to take her place as dealer and then she went to a table in the corner of the room. I'm not sure what she said but the two men and their lady friend vacated the table awful fast after that lady approached them. She sat down and looked our way. By this time the bartender was across the bar from us and told us that Liza was waiting for us at the table we had been watching.

We made our way through the crowded saloon to Liza's table. Buffole removed his hat and introduced us. "Hello ma'am my name is Buffole and this here is my best friend Sven. Thank you for taking the time to see us."

She smiled and I could see it was one of those lady smiles that can melt a grown man's heart and it was working its charm on Buffole. "Please sit down Buffole and you to Sven. My name is Liza and the dog sitting by my chair is Einer. Just what can I help you two with?" Before we answered the bartender supplied us with drinks.

Buffole took the drawing from his hat and handed it to Liza. "We are looking for this man, his name is Popeye. He killed some people I cared deeply about. I have heard that he was in town and he might have gone to join Poncho Villa and his men. Ivan at the livery stable suggested that I contact you. Can you help us?"

Liza looked the drawing of Popeye over and handed it back. "It would be hard to miss a man like that. Yes he has been here. I've seen a lot of ugly men in my time and a lady can put up with a fella that don't look so good. This Popeye had to be right up in the top ten for ugly which ain't so bad but he smelled of death. Reeked like a rotting corpse he did. Wasn't one of my gals would have anything to do with him. He was mean and ornery and it was probably because he couldn't stand the smell of himself either. He liked to brag about being fast with his gun. Claims he killed a dozen or more men in fair fights. Some of Poncho's men were here about a week ago and Popeye left with them."

Buffole quickly asked. "Liza do you know where Poncho Villa's hideout is?"

"The last I heard they were camped near Poncho's home town of San Juan Del Rio in Mexico. If you go after Poncho Villa you might as well leave Sven with me because it is doubtful you will be coming back."

"I've heard of you Buffole. You have a reputation as a shootist and I could use a good man around the saloon. Someone like you to keep law and order when things get a little rowdy around here. You could deal some cards and keep the drunks in line. With your reputation folks that frequent places like mine will either listen to you or stay clear of you. I'll pay you well. What do you say?"

Buffole looked at me and we both knew the answer. "Ma'am that's a mighty tempting offer but we got us a man to hunt down and that's what we mean to do."

Liza reached over and put her hand on top of Buffole's. I knew that was a woman's trick to soften a man's heart. "Buffole I could really use your help for at least a few days. There are a bunch of men in town that came from North of here. They had taken over a town called Lutherhell and I think they have plans to do the same thing here. I overheard some of them talking and your name came up as the one who killed their boss. I was hoping you could drive them out of here like you did at Lutherhell. We don't have any law in this town. I'll take up a collection of the town folks to pay you however much it takes. You just name your price. Please Buffole we need your help."

Damn doggies. I knew we had no choice. We would be staying long enough to help. I looked at the three men at the bar and they were staring at us again. Now I knew that I had seen them before. They were from Lutherhell.

Liza put us up in one of her upstairs rooms free of charge. We were in our room getting ready to bed down for the night when there was a knock on our door. Buffole was down to his pants and nothing else as he grabbed his gun from the holster hanging on the bed post. He stood off to the side of the door and called out. "Who is it?"

"It's me Liza can I talk to you?"

"Yes. Just a minute." Buffole grabbed his shirt and was still buttoning it as he opened the door. "Come on in."

"I'm sorry were you already in bed?"

"No, no Sven and I were just relaxing a bit." Liza had entered our room dressed in a flowing white night gown. She looked almost angel like with all the white and her beautiful shining black hair. It was a sight that Buffole was more than aware of. She sat on a chair by the bed and crossed her legs. A small amount of bare ankle above her slipper peeked out. Buffole sort of blushed at the sight. My human he is a shy one for sure.

Einer had also entered our room but he was quiet as a mouse, much like he was when we first met in the saloon. He sat just behind and off to the side of Liza's chair. Liza straightened the folds of her housecoat as Buffole watched her slender fingers. "Buffole you look nervous. Certainly you have had a woman in your room before? Or are you married and afraid your wife would disapprove?"

Buffole swallowed hard and sort of mumbled his words. "No, no. I mean no to both questions. We'll wait, no to the second question. Sort of. Well actually I was married but my wife is dead. Yes to the part of having a woman in my room, but to tell the truth having someone as beautiful as you in my room and, well you know, dressed like you are. This situation is new for me."

Liza gave one of those watch out for me type of coy smiles to Buffole. "I thought maybe we could discuss your temporary job here. I don't think there is a man I know that I would feel comfortable in front of dressed as I am. Yet there is something safe and comforting about you. I feel you are trustworthy and would do nothing that would in any way show disrespect for me. Am I right?"

"Liza you're right I respect women and besides that I'm too shy to make a move that I may feel sorry about later. I'm sort of old fashioned when it comes to the ladies. I still think anything serious should wait until after we have declared our love for each other and are married.

Just to set the facts up front I met a woman up north. Popeye killed her husband and left her a widow with a teenage daughter. I like this woman a lot but I'm not sure the feeling is mutual. Yet in my heart I would like to find out if she has any real feelings for me."

"Buffole your feelings are on thin ice. I will tell you that from experience. I was married once to a widower with a teenage daughter. I found out trying to be a step parent is sort of like the old fairy tales you heard when you were a child. No matter how hard you try to be a good parent you will end up being the evil step mother or in your case the evil step father. When it comes to a parent and its child the parent will always side with the child. It will be a no win situation for you just as it was for me. Here I am alone again and wondering if there is anyone out there for me. You and I are a lot alike maybe we should give each other a chance. I am not asking for any commitment. Let's just get to know each other and be friends. We can see if anything grows from that. Is that agreeable to you?"

I looked at Einer and asked. "Einer is she sincere. You're a dog just like me and dogs don't ever tell lies. I can communicate with my human and his decision might just be based on what you tell me. Tell me what you think about this because in the future we could end up being step brothers."

Einer looked me right in the eye as he answered. "Liza felt a spark right away with Buffole. It was no lightning bolt or fireworks but it was a good healthy spark. She is pretty gun shy about men after having a bad marriage. Buffole is the first one since that time that she has felt anything for. If it is all right with you and your human I say let them try being friends and we can see where it leads."

I gave Buffole a quick rundown of my conversation with Einer and I told him to leave his options open. Sure Krystal seemed like a great woman and he had a spark in his heart for her. She may even have a spark in her heart for him. Yet what Liza said about a parent and a child has weight in what the future might bring.

Buffole walked over and sat on the bed close to Liza. "Liza I think the two of us might just be on the same track. If we can take it slow as a train on a steep grade I might just be your man."

She smiled and stood up. She leaned over and gave Buffole a slight kiss on the cheek. I could see his eyes bulge as he got a glance down her slightly opened night gown. He may be shy but he's still a man. As she and Einer left for their room she said. "Sven, Buffole you two sleep well. Breakfast around here serve's late. I'll let you know when it's time to eat."

CHAPTER 14

It was nice having a warm soft bed to sleep in. As usual Buffole kept his gun close at hand hanging from the bed post by his head. I slept at the bottom of the bed facing the door. Like any dog my hearing is excellent and it was my job at night to be ever alert for intruders.

Buffole had a rather restless night. I asked him when morning came what was wrong. "You know how it is just my bad leg and old wounds acting up. My leg seems to get cramped up whenever I get to sleep in a soft bed. I guess I'm better off roughing it."

Like I was going to believe that was the only thing wrong. "I know you better than that. You were tossing and turning half the night. I heard you mumble something about Krystal and then Liza. You've got woman problems on your mind my friend. Come on you can tell ol' Sven the truth."

"All right you nosey dog I was dreaming or maybe it was nightmares. Those two women just totally confuse my mind and my heart. Liza is almost offering me a chance to let love into my life and even more important to have somebody of my own to love. Krystal is someone I think I could really fall for and yet I really have no idea what is in her heart and she's not here for me to find out. You think you're so smart about what I think and feel what would you do?"

"Well you've been waiting this long to find out about Krystal. I think you should talk with her before you make any decisions. Although Liza is one mighty fine looking woman and she has a thriving business established here. With Krystal you would have to start over from scratch and build a new life and find a job. Might even be that Liza is right. Jo might get in trouble and need help and if it came down to being with you or being with her daughter you might end up on the short end of the stick. Hell I guess I don't know what to tell you."

A knock on the door and a voice from the hall announced that it was breakfast time. It was a man's voice so it must have been one of the bartenders or the cooks. Buffole was washed up and dressed and just needed to buckle on his gun as we headed to the door. He looked at me and sarcastically said. "Thanks old buddy you been a big help."

Ilsa was dressed in a black leather riding skirt and had on a orange silk blouse with a black leather vest. Her black boots were polished to a shine so bright you could see yourself in them. She was seated at a large table along with a few of the cooks, bartenders and saloon girls who all lived full time in the rooms above the saloon. Breakfast was on the table and everyone acted just like an extended family. They all ate together and shared stories and events in their lives. It was a very comfortable place to be and we were made to feel at home.

After we finished our meal Liza stood up and walked behind Buffole. She put her hands on his shoulders and gently rubbed his neck. "Buffole I hope you don't mind but I took the liberty of having Shag saddled up and brought to the Saloon. My horse is also outside. I thought maybe we could take a ride out in the country and talk. Einer and Sven are both welcome to come along."

Wasn't much Buffole could say. He got up from his chair and thanked everyone for making us feel at home. Outside Buffole held Liza's horse while she mounted up. Einer and I decided to run alongside for awhile. As we left town I noticed the black clad cowboy from the saloon standing in the shadows of a doorway watching us leave. I told Buffole to beware and he whispered he too had seen the cowboy watching us.

We left town and about two miles down the road Liza led us towards a large grove of trees. A small lake was situated there and it was an idyllic spot for a picnic which it just so happened Liza had brought along with her. Buffole helped her with the picnic basket and they laid out a large blanket to sit on. Einer and I made for the water and went swimming and chased a few frogs. I was shocked when I looked back and our two humans were both out of sight. Then I figured that nature must have called them away and went back to having a good time with Einer.

To the surprise of Einer and me our two humans came out from the bushes which were on opposite sides of the picnic blanket. Buffole was in just the bottoms of his long johns and was covering his bare chest with his arms in embarrassment. I looked at Einer and said. "I told you he was shy, wait till he tries to hide his foot that's missing the big toe, which really makes him self-conscious. Liza came out in a one piece swimsuit which covered her from shoulder to ankles. Not knowing much about ladies clothing it looked to me like a loose fitting version of a man's full length long underwear. Bear arms and bare feet on a woman are still quite a novelty out here in the west. The two of them met by the picnic blanket and smiled at each other. Then hand in hand they headed towards the lake. Buffole played the part of the no nonsense man and took a running leap in the air as he pulled in his knees to his chest cannonball fashion. He hit the water with a huge splash and when his head appeared above the water we heard the deafening scream of a man who just discovered how cold this lake water really was. Liza was more lady like and slowly waded in to join Buffole for a swim. Einer and I were soon in the water and enjoying a relaxed afternoon with our humans.

Liza and Buffole were like two children playing in the water. They splashed each other, had races across the lake and diving contests to see who could find the most interesting thing on the bottom of the lake. Buffole came up with a rock which he thought was gold but it ended up being just pyrite or in layman's terms fool's gold which Liza was quick to point out. Liza's little treasure from the bottom was a clam and it was alive but having no legs it was not kicking. She held it in front of Buffole's face as she squeezed the shell together with her hand. Buffole of course was squirted in the face with water as it shot out of the clam shell. Einer and I barked and wagged our tails in joy to see the look on Buffole's face. Liza also started laughing and as the look of surprise left Buffole's face he joined in with the rest of us. We were all having a grand time.

When everyone was wore out and exhausted from playing and swimming we all retired to the picnic blanket. Einer and I were ordered to stay far away until we shook off our coats and were at least somewhat dry and no longer dripping water on everything around us. Liza had brought towels for her and Buffole and they took turns drying each other off. When they had finished it was our turn. What moisture was left on our coats Liza and Buffole with lots of wrestling and tug of war matches with the towels finally got us dried off enough that we were allowed to share the picnic blanket with them.

Liza opened the picnic basket and we enjoyed fried chicken, corn muffins and SvenBrew beers. She told Buffole what she knew about the men who had come to town to take over. There were three of them and they worked for a man named Luther. Luther was located in another state and from what she had heard none of his employees ever saw him. He sent telegrams or letters with instructions as to what he wanted done. Occasionally one of his agents might appear to check on how things were going. Luther supplied the money and the know how to set things up and to take over the towns he wanted. Once the operational phase was in place and his men were running things he would receive his weekly cut of the money they took in.

As of this time three men are here doing their best to buy up property at rock bottom prices. They make an offer and if the owner does not wish to sell it seems that some catastrophe will befall him. Barns on ranches mysteriously catch fire. Store windows are broken and merchandise is stolen in the dark of night. Livestock is run off or an owner may find himself bushwhacked and dead. One of the homesteaders that left here told how he was dragged from his house and taken to the river where his masked attackers filled his trouser legs with stones. Then they then tied ropes around his ankles and waist so the stones would not fall out. When that was done they then tied a rope around his waist and tossed him off a bridge into the river. After a few minutes they would pull him to the surface and he was told if he wished to live he would have to sign over the deed to his property. The first two times he refused. Each time they tossed him into the river they kept him there longer. By the third time he signed away the deed to his property. The next morning he packed up his wagon full of belongings and left town. We have no law here and no one wants to risk their lives to stop these men. Buffole I have heard of your reputation in dealing with the Luther gang. This is the same gang that took over the town of Lutherhell which you cleaned up and gave back to its citizens. I and this town need you to do the same thing for us.

The tall hefty built one is named Steve and he seems to be in charge. Of the three he seems to be nice enough but I have heard from those that have seen him get angry that he has a quick and nasty temper. Bill the heavy set one has a sharp tongue and uses it to degrade people like some men use a knife to cut up their enemies. All in all I think he is pretty harmless compared to the other two. The young cock of the walk that dresses in black is the one who seems to be the most dangerous. They call him Kid Finance. He brags that he got his name from robbing banks and putting whole towns in to financial ruin. At his last bank robbery a customer who had his hands in the air during the robbery made the mistake of telling the Kid he would never get away with it. The kid shot the man right between the eyes. The victim's friend was standing nearby and the kid said are you friends with that bastard that I just shot? The man answered in the affirmative and the Kid shot him dead. When the bank teller asked the kid why he shot the man's friend the Kid answered. "I figured if the first guy was no good his friend was no good to. They both deserved to die." The teller did not argue he just gave the Kid the banks money and left him go. The Kid is definitely the hired gun of the three. He's the one you have to watch out for.

I had a terrible thought yet I knew I had to share it with Buffole. "Buffole has it crossed your mind that Liza's being nice to you and acting like she might be falling in love with you might just be a trick to get you to do what she wants you to do. Taking on those three Luther employees' could get you killed. What if she's in cahoots with them in taking over the town?" Einer looked at me with surprise in his eyes. "Liza is my human and I know her well enough to know that she would never do such a thing. She just wants Buffole's help and her feelings for him are real. She would probably give her own life if she felt Buffole was in danger. She wants someone to be on her side to fight this battle with her. She does not expect Buffole to do this alone. Buffole's presence may be just enough to scare those hombres out of town."

Buffole had a gift with dogs and he understood Einer as well as I did. He looked at me and whispered. "Yes I've thought that maybe I'm being used. But a guy my age and not being too good looking, well maybe being used ain't so bad. I would like to think Liza likes me. Either way I figure if we had not forced this bunch out of Lutherhell they would not be here bothering this town. I feel obligated to drive them out of here."

I had to admit that I had not thought about Buffole and I being sort of responsible for those no good Luther boys being here. I also figured as long as Buffole had considered that Liza might or might not be using him we should be all right staying here and helping out. After all if Popeye was riding with Poncho Villa he should still be there by the time we finished our work here.

Buffole and Liza lay on the blanket and talked for a long time. Einer and I took a nap in the shade of some trees. When I awoke it was getting late so I went over to see how my partner Buffole was doing. He was on his back sound asleep. Curled up next to him with her head on his shoulder was Liza. I watched them both for a minute or so. They seemed so peaceful sleeping like a couple who had the comfort of each other for years. I slowly walked over by Buffole and nuzzled my nose to his ear. "Get up sleepy head it's time to go." He opened his eyes and turned his head to look at me. "All right partner," was all he said as he gently roused Liza. We packed up our picnic items and headed back to town. The sun was slowly dipping into the western horizon and a beautiful orange hue lit up a few clouds in the distance. I'm sure for Liza and Buffole it looked like a very romantic sunset.

The town seemed peaceful enough as we rode in. A few people were milling about but not much was happening. As we rode by the general store I noticed that Bill one of the Luther group was standing in the shadows watching us. He hurried away as fast as a big man can hurry as soon as he saw us. I did not want to alarm Liza or Einer so

I did not say anything. I was sure that Buffole had noticed him from the look in his eye.

We rode our mounts to the stable and Ivan met us at the entrance. He offered to take Liza's horse and Shag inside and stable them for the night. Buffole helped Liza down and said. "Liza why don't you and Einer head to the saloon, Sven and I would like to take care of Shag ourselves if you don't mind." Liza smiled and gave Buffole a quick kiss on the cheek. "Don't you boy's take too long I know how it is when you leave men alone to talk about their buffalo." She laughed and went along her way with Einer at her side. I was glad to see Einer keeping a close eye on her. He was big enough and strong enough to be a respectable guard dog and protector for Liza.

Ivan led Liza's horse to a stall as Buffole did the same for Shag. As the guy's unsaddled our mounts and started brushing them Buffole started a conversation with Ivan. "Ivan you know Liza seems kind of worried about the Luther boys in town. She thinks they want to take the town over. I have a mind to think she might be right. I had a run in with some of that bunch back in Lutherhell. Three of them died when I was there and two of them were laid out for the undertaker by me. It was self defense mind you, but still they are dead by my hand. I'm sure the three of them in town right now don't take to kindly to my being here."

Ivan kept grooming Liza's horse as he answered. "Those three Luther boys seem to keep pretty much to themselves. Steve he's the leader from what I can tell. If anyone does the talking it's him. When they do talk it usually has to do with trying to buy someone's property or business. They ain't approached me yet and best be they don't. I keep a loaded shotgun over by the door and if them boys try to buck me I'll fill 'em full of lead if I have to. I think they got some big money behind them to buy this town and control it. There's been some good mineral strikes around here, mostly silver but some gold to. There's money to be made here and I think they want it all to themselves. What's your stake in all this mister Buffole? You gone sweet on Miss Liza? She ain't ever hankered no other man that's gone after her since I knowed her. She sure seems to have takin' a likin' to you though."

Before Buffole could give Ivan an answer Bill came into the livery stable. He was a big heavyset man. He wore his gun belt loose so he was no gunslinger. He put one foot on the bottom board of the stall we were in than he leaned his arms onto the top rail and sort of peered at Buffole and Shag. I'm not so sure he noticed me sitting on the floor in the front corner of the stall.

"You're the fella they call Buffole ain't you? I saw you when you gunned down Sheriff Gracious up in Lutherhell. You had to be good with a gun to kill ol' Carlos in a fair fight like that. I saw Carlos kill many men in showdowns before. Guess he met his match with you."

Buffole kept brushing Shag as he spoke. "Just who are you and what do you want?"

"They call me Big Bill. Carlos used to be my boss. He was a son of a bitch and to be perfectly honest I didn't mind seeing you kill him. I got me a new boss now. He sort of stepped in to replace Carlos. Of course we had to leave Lutherhell seeing the whole darn town turned against us. Now we are here and damn if you don't come riding into town trying to spoil all our fun. Anyhow the new boss wants to talk to you. His name's Steve he's waiting over at the Pezta Palace for you. Best not keep him waiting he gets sort of impatient and he's got a quick temper with his words when he ain't happy. Well I gave you the message and I best be getting back to the Palace."

Everything remained sort of quiet after Big Bill left. Buffole just took his old sweet time bedding down Shag. When he finished he started to walk out of the livery building when Ivan walked up beside him. "Buffole I believe you promised me a drink. I think I would like to take you up on the offer. Never hurts to have a friend at your back when you're drinking."

"Ivan I appreciate the offer but you got a family waiting for you. I would hate to come between you and your wife. Women ain't always so understanding when their men go drinking instead of going home."

"Don't you worry none Mister Buffole she'll understand just fine. Anything getting done to get those low life bushwhackers out of our town will more than please her."

Buffole had buckled on his gun when we left the meadow after our picnic. Ivan picked up his shot gun by the livery stable door and made sure it was loaded. When we arrived at the Palace it was busy as ever. Walking through the batwing doors the only ones to take notice of us were Big Bill and Kid Finance who were having a drink at the end of the bar. Steve was at a table busily fondling two of the local saloon gals. Liza was nowhere to be seen but Einer was at the opposite end of the bar keeping an eye on things. We settled at the end of the bar by Einer and Buffole ordered drinks for Ivan, me and with a quick pat on top of the bar he had Einer jump up to join us.

Einer and I were lapping up our SvenBrew beer from our bowls as Ivan and Buffole were talking to each other. I asked Einer where Liza was. He told me she was still upstairs changing clothes. A glance at Steve told me he was getting impatient for his meeting with Buffole. He shooed the two girls away from his table and motioned for Big Bill to bring Buffole over to his table. Kid Finance was stroking the handle of one of his guns like he had a love affair with it. In his other hand he held a drink and from the looks of him he had had too many drinks already.

Big Bill set his drink down and walked slowly over to Buffole. He seemed to be searching for what to say and finally blurted out the words. "Buffole Mr. Steve is waiting to talk to you. I mean if you have the time."

Buffole looked Big Bill right in the eye. Big Bill was shaking and looking mighty scared. Finally Buffole smiled. "Ivan would you and Einer mind staying here for a minute while I attend to business with Steve?" Ivan rolled the glass of SvenBrew in his hand and said. "You go right ahead I think Einer and I have things covered well enough. Let me just lay my shotgun up here on the bar so I don't accidently knock it over." I noticed that the barrel of the shotgun just so happened to be pointed right at Kid Finance.

Big Bill wiped the sweat from his brow and led Buffole over to Steve's table for an introduction.

"Steve this is Buffole he's here to talk" said Big Bill and then he hurried back to the bar and stood a respectable distance away from

Kid Finance. I think he saw the shotgun on the bar next to Ivan and figured he was safer if he kept some distance between himself and the Kid.

Steve motioned to one of the saloon girls by holding up three fingers for the number of dinks he wanted. "Buffole you and your furry friend sit down and let's have a little talk." I jumped up on the chair next to Buffole. The saloon girl quickly appeared with three SvenBrews. Two in glasses for Steve and Buffole and one in a bowl for me.

Steve took a sip of his beer and said. "Buffole I remember you. It was back in Lutherhell you shot and killed the Scotsman and Carlos. That Trixie friend of yours shot my buddy Chad. Now here you are like a festering cactus needle under my skin. I don't want any trouble with you. I'll tell you what I'll do. I've got five hundred dollars in my pocket and its all yours. It's not a gift just an offer for you to come to work for the Luther group. I heard you came from Minnesota. My boss has his headquarters in Minneapolis sort of makes you and him neighbors. So as a neighborly gesture we are offering you a job to come work for us. We'll pay you five hundred a month just to be around and show your face when we need you. Now I might not be as pretty as that hussy Liza that runs this place but sure as hell I will pay you more then she will for working here. What do you say cowboy? We got a deal?"

Buffole was holding his temper well until the 'hussy' remark about Liza. I noticed someone who had just come through the saloon doors and was standing there looking around the room. It was a woman her dark hair in a pony tail hanging form under her cowboy hat. She had on a man's plaid wool shirt with the butt of a short rifle sticking out the back just above her shoulder. Her pants were something fairly new in the west they called them Levi's and she wore a holster with a colt sidearm that was tied down like she knew how to use it. Her brown boots were dusty from travel. I glanced at her face and I knew this woman. Before I could tell Buffole what was happening he had made a move that was not characteristic of him. I had always known Buffole to hold his temper and try to work things out without violence. But not this time.

Buffole rose from his chair and with a hard right he nailed Steve's jaw. Steve went to the floor like a rock. As Steve regained his sense's his hand went for his gun. Buffole's gun was already drawn and aimed at Steve's head.

A blast of gunfire erupted form the bar and I turned in time to see that Ivan's shotgun had blasted Big Bill's gun hand to a bloody pulp as his gun dropped to the floor.

The Kid had his gun out and I barked to Buffole to look out. A bullet form the Kid's gun grazed Buffole's left arm as he turned and fired. The first shot caught the Kid in the stomach. The Kid staggered backwards a few steps and took aim once again at Buffole. Buffole took his time to aim and his second shot went into the Kids heart. The Kid fell to the floor knocking over a brass spittoon which splashed across his face. It was plain to see the Kids future finances were denied.

Steve had regained his senses and had his gun out and was ready to put a bullet into Buffole. Suddenly a loud gun blast rang out form the doorway of the saloon. We turned to look at Steve and half of his forehead was gone.

Standing in the doorway with her sawed off mare's leg shotgun barrel still smoking was none other than Krystal. She looked at Buffole and smiled. "Sorry to intrude on your fun but it looked like you might have needed some help." Then she twirled the rifle and like a pro she slid it into the holster on her back.

Suddenly I felt a wet nose nuzzle my cheek. It was Lena and she had come running from behind Krystal as the gun smoke in the room still hung in the air. Liza came rushing down the stairs in one of her fancy saloon dresses to see what all the commotion was about. Most of the customers had hit the floor or were taking cover behind anything they could find and were now coming out to see just what had transpired. Ivan had walked over to Big Bill and apologized for shooting him in the hand. Ivan asked the bartender for a bar towel and helped Big Bill wrap up his bloody hand. "Sorry there Bill but I couldn't stand by and let you shoot my friend. Once I get your hand wrapped up you might just want to consider leaving town real quick like."

Liza rushed to Buffole and threw her arms around him. "Buffole are you all right? Your arm is bleeding." She stood back and looked him over. Your knuckles are scraped too, what happened here?" The bartender was already next to us with some hot water and a bandage for Buffole's arm. Liza cleaned his wound and started to wrap it.

Buffole explained what had happened. He told her it all started when he hit Steve. Liza looked down at Steve's body on the floor. "You must have hit him awfully hard half his skull is gone" Buffole said. "He's dead all right but that was not from me hitting him." He looked up and Krystal was looking at him with fire in her eyes. I couldn't tell if that fire was directed at Liza or Buffalo or maybe at both of them. Buffole did his best to look calm. "Liza I'd like you to meet a friend of mine. This is Krystal. She just saved my life. It was her mare's leg shotgun that killed Steve when he was trying to put a bullet into me."

Krystal sat down at the table and watched as Liza attended to Buffole's wound. Liza was too busy taking care of Buffole to note the jealous tension that was emitting from Krystal. Einer and I could sense a problem brewing. Two women and one man. Ivan came over to check on Buffole and said. "I'll handle the mess we just made here. Big Bill has already decided to leave town. Looks to me like you got two mighty fine looking women to care for you. One that shoots your enemies and one to doctor you up. Maybe tomorrow night we can have another drink together under less stressful conditions."

CHAPTER 15

Poor Buffole was in between a rock and a hard place. Liza was fondling over him like a horse with a new born colt. Krystal was looking as possessive as a canine bitch whose puppy was being taken away from her. My suggestion to Buffole was to let Liza finish bandaging him up and then we should get the hell out of Dodge. He took my suggestion and as soon as Liza finished Buffole excused himself and said. "Liza thanks so much for doctoring me up. Krystal you don't know how glad I am to see you here but my arm is aching something fierce and I best go to my room and lie down for awhile." With those comments over and done Buffole high tailed it out of there and headed to his upstairs room. I gave Lena a quick doggie nose kiss goodbye and ran off to join Buffole.

Once in our room Buffole took off his gun belt and hung it on the bed post by his pillow. He had some trouble pulling off his boots now that his arm was starting to hurt. Both of us finally settled down on the bed to rest. Buffole closed his eyes but I knew he had a lot on his mind and it was not from just having to shoot a man for that was done in self defense.

I figured I best get him to talk so I started the conversation. "Buffole I know you got a problem downstairs. Liza and Krystal in the same room at the same time. Partner you know those two are going to talk. There's no doubt Liza cares about you. I also know you have feelings for Krystal even though you don't know her very well. As far as I can see you got two choices and I don't just mean Krystal or Liza. You have to decide if you want to hook up with one of them women or skedaddle out of here and finish what we started with Popeye."

"What the hell Sven. I had to face everything from Indians, buffalo hunters, gunfights and gila monsters and none of them scared me as much as facing these two women. I'd rather catch a rattlesnake with my bare hands then have to deal with this. I don't suppose you have a preference as to which one would be the best choice?"

I rolled from my side to my stomach and looked at Buffole. "I like them both. Liza has Einer and he is sort of hard to get to know but I like him and he would probably make a good big brother. Then there's Krystal and she has Lena with her. Lena is one cute little doggie. I don't know what to tell you. It might be nice for me to have my own gal and then again I'm sort of getting to like being a bachelor."

"Yeah Sven I know just how you feel. You and I have had some adventures together and we've made us a few enemies. We still need to track and find Popeye and one or both of us could get killed in the process. It might be best if we don't have any women in our lives at this time. Liza's more my age if it came right down to it she might be a good choice. Krystal stole my heart right from the first time I saw her but she's mighty young for me. I think it might be best we make a trail for Mexico and see if we can find Popeye. When we finish with him we can always come back and see if Liza and Einer or Krystal and Lena still have any interest in us. If not it might just be that we are destined to be alone and partners till the day we die.

The day's events must have tired us out for after our talk we both slept soundly. The fact that the Luther gang in this town had been wiped out I'm sure allowed us to finally relax for a change. That and the knowledge that we had friends in this town to watch our backs. Liza, Krystal, Ivan, Einer and Lena. Since we had come west we had never developed such bonds as we had here. Sure we had Trish, Dancer, the Besser's, Krystal's daughter Jo and even Pat Garret but this group of people had an element mixed in that we had not had before and that was feelings. I had some for Lena but nothing that had been strong enough for me to get excited about. Buffole on the other hand was torn between two women. Humans have two ways to fall in love. One is that love at first sight as he had with Krystal. The second type of love starts as a friendship and grows with time to become love. Buffole had both gnawing at him at the same time. I only hoped that he realized that love at first sight had to work both ways and yet I did not envy his position one bit.

A ray of sunshine hit my eyelids and woke me up. I could hear some activity outside our open window. I jumped out of the bed and went to the window to see what was taking place on the street. Standing on my hind legs with my front paws on the window sill gave me a good view. It must be early morning as the shop keepers were just unlocking their doors. A few were sweeping the board walks or cleaning windows. Buffole was dead to the world so I curled up on the floor by the door to do my job as watchdog. My partner had had a rough night and I felt it best to let him sleep for as long as he wanted to.

It was almost an hour later when a knock was heard on our door. I was on my feet and growling faster than warts grow on a toad. "Buffole, Sven it's me Krystal can I come in?"

Buffole opened his eyes and even though his throat was dry and raspy due to some of the dehydration he had from blood loss he forced out the words. "Krystal, just a minute I'm coming." He sat up and took stock of his condition. He had clothes on so that was a good thing for answering the door. He stood up and found he was a little dizzy from his wound. He steadied himself on the bed post at the foot of the bed. A few slow steps and he regained his balance. He ran his fingers through his hair in a vain hope to look presentable.

He opened the door and Krystal took one look at him and said. "Buffole you look like something the cat drug in. Lie back down on that bed and let me take a look at you." Lena was with her and she ran over to greet me with a doggie nose kiss. Buffole was still a little wobbly and Krystal grabbed his arm with her free hand and helped him back to the bed. In her other hand was a bowl of clean hot water, a towel and fresh bandages were draped over her arm. She put the palm of her hand on Buffole's forehead. "You've got a fever, it's not bad but you need to rest for a day or two. Let me see that arm of yours."

She removed the bandages which were sticking to his skin and the hair on his arms from the blood that oozed out of his wound during the night. He mumbled "ouch that hurts woman."

She smiled as she bathed his arm with warm water. "Listen you big baby this needs to be cleaned and dressed with fresh bandages or it will become infected. You already have a slight fever so shut up and do what you are told. To think a big strong man like you gets shot and does not even whimper and I pull a few hairs out of your arm and you squeal like a pig."

Buffole relaxed as she changed the bandage on his arm. Krystal it's mighty good to see you again. By the way thanks for saving my life. You've been on my mind a lot since I left you back at your ranch. I saw Jo not too long ago and she told me what you were up to. I was worried about you but I can see now that you can take care of yourself."

Krystal got a little rough with the cleaning job on Buffole's arm and he winced with pain. "Thinking about me were you. Was that when you were wooing that hussy Liza. You're like every other man a pretty gal pays you some attention and you melt like butter in a hot frying pan. The only reason I'm here bandaging you up is to make sure it gets done right. If I let that hussy take care of this wound you might get infected and die. Than my killing that man downstairs would have been done for nothing." She finished her work on Buffole's arm and grabbed the dirty bandages and water bowl off the nightstand and huffed out of the room. I was sitting with Lena watching what was happening and quick as a racehorse Lena got up and followed Krystal from the room. The last thing we heard was the slamming of the door.

I jumped up on the bed next to Buffole. "That went well didn't it? Not only have you alienated Krystal but you messed up my time with Lena. Thanks a lot Partner." Buffole just sort of mumbled something about 'women' and then he picked up a dime novel that was on the nightstand about Kit Carson and read it out loud so I could listen. After a while we both drifted off to sleep.

We slept for about hour and then made our way downstairs. The place was empty so we decided to take a walk outside. Buffole was feeling a little better and once up and around he seemed to regain his balance. We made our way to a small restaurant called Larry's Place and had flapjacks, bacon and eggs for breakfast. The owner let me sit at the table with Buffole and served me just like any other customer. Seems he had heard about yesterday's showdown and the whole town was grateful to be shed of the Luther gang.

Our meal was on the house so we were all in a good mood as we made our way to Ivan's Livery Stables. Shag was happy to see us and we told him all about the gunfight at Liza's place. He told us he had heard some of the story from customers and he mentioned that Big Bill had looked sort of funny as he tried to saddle himself on his horse with only one good hand. Seems Big Bill was in quite a hurry to leave town.

Buffole spent some time using his good arm brushing down Shag and making sure he had fresh water and feed before we left. The three of us talked over our plans and figured to be shed of this town within the next two days. I was curious as to just how Buffole was going to present that fact to Krystal and Liza. As for me I figured on spending as much time as possible with Lena and maybe even get to know Einer better.

We took our own sweet time exploring the town. They had a nice dry goods store where Buffole picked up some new long johns, under shirts and socks. I picked up a new red kerchief for myself. At Lorin's gunsmith shop we loaded up on spare ammunition, some spare springs and gun oil to keep our weapons in tip top shape. Being out on the trail is no place to have a gun that misfires or won't work from neglect. Buffole even purchased a new Colt .22 caliber single action revolver for what reason I could not comprehend, but then again he was becoming a westerner and westerners can never have too many guns. He claimed it was a good hideaway gun because it was smaller and lighter than the heavy caliber weapons.

The barber shop was our next stop and Buffole got his hair cut and a shave. He left a long handlebar mustache and I thought it looked good on him. As for me I got a good face trim and had the hair plucked from my ears. Being the watch dog it is very important to keep your hearing as acute as possible.

Back at Pezta's Palace we were surprised to see Liza and Krystal sitting at the same table as we walked through the batwing doors.

They invited us to join them. Lena was on a chair by Krystal and I jumped up next to her. We did the doggie nose kiss thing and it felt quite enjoyable to me. Einer was lying on the floor by Liza and seemed to just ignore Lena and me. I figured he was either too proud or too jealous to show any emotion. Buffole sat down and the ladies took him into their conversation as if all three of them were the best of friends. Heck who am I to say? Maybe Krystal and Liza had become friends. If so it ought to be mighty interesting as to how things were to develop as far as Buffole was concerned.

It seems the ladies had planned to have a fandango in the evening. The celebration was to be on Main Street and Buffole and I were the guests of honor. A number of the town's people felt they owed us a little party for helping to rid the town of the Luther gang. Buffole was quick to point out that there were others more worthy than us. Ivan the blacksmith for one and what about Krystal. If not for those two the chances are that Buffole would not even be alive right now.

Liza was quick to point out some facts to Buffole. "The town will certainly honor Krystal as well as Ivan as being instrumental in ending the Luther gang's strangle hold in this territory. Yet if you had not come here and taken the bull by the horns in confronting those villains they might still have been in control of our town. Your past action in Lutherhell had them running scared. You led the charge against them so you might as well accept the fact that this town needed a hero and you are elected whether you like it or not." As for me I had to wonder why she didn't mention me, I was right there at Buffole's side through the whole ordeal. I guess being a dog just makes me sort of a silent partner.

Buffole gave one of those forced smiles to the two ladies. "It sure is nice to see you two getting along so well. I take it introductions from me are no longer necessary?"

Krystal answered. "Introductions? You were too busy shooting people and getting shot to give any introductions. Liza was telling me about how you and her have been busy cleaning up the town. I'm sure it was a lot of work going on picnics and eating suppers together or having little private discussions in your room. Lena come along I think we need some fresh air." With that said Krystal and Lena headed outside.

Buffole looked at Liza with a puzzled look on his face. She smiled and said. "Being a man you have no idea what's wrong here do you?"

"None what so ever" said Buffole.

Liza put her hand on top of Buffole's. "Krystal likes you a lot. Given a chance she could probably fall in love with you. She's a bit concerned about the age difference you being a good twelve to fifteen years her senior but I told her age makes no difference if you really love someone. There is one other problem that bothers her. She thinks you and I are in love. Now you know why she stormed out of here. If you ask me good riddance to bad rubbish. She's dressed like a man and she handled that mare's leg gun like a professional gun slinger. Surely you could not see anything feminine about her to interest you?"

I urged Buffole to think before he answered. After all I had Lena on my mind and his decision would affect my life as much as his. "Well Liza I never thought that she might be jealous of you. I like you a lot but we're just good friends aren't we? As for Krystal I like her a lot but I hardly got know her in the short time we spent together but that don't mean I wouldn't like to get to know her better."

Liza gave Buffole an icy stare. "Why, why you're just a typical man. You have absolutely no idea what a woman thinks or what is in her heart. I'll see you later tonight at the fandango." She and Einer stormed up the stairs to her room in much the same manor that Krystal and Lena had stormed out of the saloons front door.

Buffole looked at me. "Sven, what the hell just happened here?"

I shook my head as I answered him. "Buffole you know I think you're broken when it comes to love and I don't mean broke like a wild horse gets broke. I mean you're broken like a smashed saloon window. I just don't know if there is any fixin for you anymore. Between your mind and your heart you can't see when a woman's telling you she's interested in being more than just friends. You got two women giving you every sign possible and you're as a blind as a bat in the sunshine as to what's going on. Until you figure out your heart and clear your mind I think it best we be moving on real soon.

Maybe we need to spend some more time alone for you to appreciate what it is to have a human love you and care about you. At least out on the prairie you know you have Shag and me to confide in and look after you with no strings attached."

Buffole still looked a little perplexed about the whole lady type of thinking. "Sven you might just be right. Somewhere deep down I would like to be able to love a woman. Liza sure seems to care a lot about me and she would be a fine wife. Yet somewhere in my mind something about her worries me. Maybe she's just too good for me."

I cut in on Buffole's thinking. "Maybe she's just not enough of a challenge for you partner. You ever think of that?"

"Might just be so Sven. Liza's a lovely lady and she has money and her own thriving business a man would be a fool not to pick her for a wife. Yet from the first time I saw Krystal she stole what little heart I've got right away from me. She was as beautiful as a single star shining on a cloudless desert night. I'm just smart enough to know I'm too old for her. She's young and full of life. Me I'm still moving around all right and I got some good years still left in my life but there ain't any good reason for her to want someone like me in her life. I'm just an old fool wanting something I can't have and not taking what's offered to me. Will be pulling out in the morning. You may want to go and let Shag know. I'm going to our room and get myself spruced up for tonight's shindig. Figure I might as well go out looking like a gentleman instead of the old fart that I am."

Buffole and I met back at our room at the Palace. I could see my partner's arm was bothering him and suggested we get some shuteye before the nights festivities. With his gun on the bed head within easy reach we both dozed off. A few hours later we heard movement outside our window. Buffole sat up and looked outside. The street was lit up with torches and local vendors had tables set up selling everything from liquor, food, flowers for the ladies and assorted sundries. A wooden platform had been set up as a dance floor. A group of Mexican musicians were warming up and the fandango would be starting very soon.

Buffole put on his Sunday go to meeting clothes and then he brushed my fur and straightened out the red kerchief I wore around my neck. He put his boots on the chair and gave them a quick spit shine polish although it did not do a lot of good. Buckling on his gun belt we made our way downstairs and out on to the street. Looking around we spotted Ivan and his family at a taco stand. The lady running the stand was breast feeding a baby in one arm and making tacos with her free hand. When we approached Ivan whispered to Buffole. "Not the most appetizing sight in the world but the kids wanted tacos and the lady's husband was killed by the Luther gang so the least I could do was to give her some business and help her out some. She's independent and won't accept any charity from anyone."

Mighty nice of you Ivan," Buffole whispered back. Then he dropped a couple dollars on the lady's table and said. "Nothing for right now ma'am you just remember I prepaid in case I might get hungry later."

"Ivan have you seen Liza or Krystal around anywhere?" asked Buffole.

"Yes I have they are over by the dance floor. There are tables and chairs set up over there and I think they are talking with the town's hardware owner. I heard something about him being an important town personality and he should give a speech before the music and dancing begins."

Buffole and I made our way to the table area and Buffole politely asked if he could have a seat next to Krystal. Lena was on Krystal's lap and Einer was on a chair next to Liza so I made myself at home and jumped up on the chair next to Buffole. The ladies of course welcomed us to sit next to them. The store owner introduced himself as a Mister Zarnoff and he thanked Buffole for all he had done to help the town. The crowd was getting restless and it was now time for the speech to be given and then the fandango could begin in earnest.

Mister Zarnoff stood in the center of the dance floor that had been erected for the night's festivities. He raised his arms in the air to quiet the crowd of people that were now gathered to hear him speak. Just raising his arms in the air did not seem to do the trick so Krystal took matters into her own hands. She was now dressed in a flowing skirt with a rather tight bodice at the waist. She lifted one side of her skirt and produced a derringer which was strapped to her upper thigh. Holding the tiny firearm above her head she pulled the trigger. Silence now prevailed as the crowd looked our way. Krystal had already hid the gun from view by sliding it quickly into her hand bag. Buffole stood up and addressed the crowd. "Folks' sorry for the gunshot but Mister Zarnof has some words for all to hear and he needs a little quiet to give his speech." Buffole sat back down and all eyes were now riveted on Mister Zarnoff. Krystal put her hand on top of Buffole's and said. "Thank you for taking the attention away from me. I don't know what got into me. Poor Mister Zarnoff just seemed to need a little help in quieting the crowd." Buffole smiled at her as we sat back to listen to the speech.

Mister Zarnoff cleared his throat and looked at the hastily scribbled notes that he held in his hand. "Citizens of Coldero del Diablo I have a very brief speech and then we can commence with the nights festivities. As all of you know the Luther Group came to our town and by means of deception, threats and even murder did their best to take control. Thanks to the bravery of a few exceptional souls these evil men are now dead or driven from our midst. Order is now restored so that we may live in peace and watch our town prosper."

"When I read your name please stand and be accounted for your acts of bravery and unselfishness that you have performed for our town and its citizens. Ivan the blacksmith. Liza owner of the Pezta Palace." The crowd clapped and whistled with approval. "Folks we have more heroes in our midst. Just new in town is Krystal without whose quick thinking and brave actions might have meant disaster for us all." Another round of applause was heard. "Last and certainly not least was a man and his canine partner who have been here only a short while. Let's give a big round of applause for Buffole and Sven. Let the festivities begin."

To say the least we were embarrassed but once Mister Zarnoff started walking off the stage everyone started to celebrate. Drinks were flowing, food was being consumed, the Mexican band started playing music and the dance floor was filled with activities. We sat and took in the sights around us. A beautiful senorita moved gracefully onto the dance floor and everyone made room for her. The band stopped for a moment as the Senorita readied herself. With castanets in her hands she slowly began to move. The band began to play and kept rhythm to her movements which became faster and faster. She was a beauty to behold and her dance captivated everyone within sight. Soon she started to focus her attention on Buffole. She danced across the stage and made her way directly to our table. Her lithe body slid across the table top and she lay on her back and lifted her head right up to Buffole's face. She removed a red rose from her hair and put it into her mouth. Her lips touched Buffole's as he took the rose stem from her mouth to his. Like the flash of a gun she was up from the table and back on the stage. It was her dramatic way of honoring the hero of Coldero del Diablo.

Liza stood up and grabbed Buffole by the arm. "Come along let's dance," Buffole hates to dance but he had no choice in the matter. A farmer had stepped up on the stage to give the Mexican band a breather. His son pulled out a fiddle and the famer started calling a square dance. At least Buffole would have some directions being called to help him make it through the dance. With a bum leg and a still healing wounded arm I had to give Buffole credit. He was doing all right with the square dance. When the dance ended Liza threw her arms around Buffole and gave him a kiss. The two of them went over to one of the booths and shared some punch that the farmer's wife had prepared. Krystal seemed to be seething at the sight of the whole ordeal. I invited Lena onto my chair and the two of us did our best to ignore the human activity that was taking place.

Finally Krystal rose from her chair knocking it over as she did so. She didn't even bother to pick it back up. She went over to Liza and Buffole like a desert dust devil. She grabbed Buffole by the arm and came close to dragging him onto the dance floor.

Krystal looked at the musicians with a look only a woman can give to a man. It is a look that means "do what I tell you to do and do it now. You boys play something slow that we can dance to. While you're at it make it romantic."

A lone guitar player stepped forward. Soft chords of love emitted from the strings of his guitar, His voice was sweet and low as words of love blew like a warm summer breeze from his lips. Krystal and Buffole moved as if one across the dance floor. Other couples surrounded them as the music continued but they seemed oblivious to all except for each other. I was feeling proud that my partner was doing so well at dancing with Krystal but I became distracted as Lena cuddled up close to me.

When the music stopped I looked up and Krystal and Buffole were kissing. I heard Einer who was three chairs down from me say. "That's one way to make Liza mad as a hornet. Sven I suggest you and your partner leave town before Liza stings you both."

I glanced at Liza who was watching Krystal and Buffole. She had fire in her eyes and cuss words on her lips. I think Einer was right we should plan on leaving town and the sooner the better. Battling gunslingers may not be the safest of professions but getting between two women could prove to be downright deadly.

Lena, Einer and I decided to roam around the area of the fandango. You would be surprised how much good food gets dropped by people when they are having a good time. Kids are especially good targets for dogs. The majority of children seem to love sharing their food with any canine who gives them the slightest amount of attention.

I kept an occasional eye on Buffole to make sure he was not getting into trouble. Krystal seemed to be monopolizing him much to the chagrin of Liza and Einer. I was glad Lena was with us as it kept Einer from saying anything about what Liza might be thinking or feeling. As for me Krystal and Lena were a matched set and I was leaning in that direction if Buffole had to make a choice.

I'm not sure what was going on between Krystal and Buffole although I did see them at times walking arm in arm. In fact one time I glimpsed them looking in a dress makers shop and Buffole had his arm around Krystal's waist. Lena noticed it to and said "Sven, look at our humans isn't that just the sweetest thing you ever did see?" Unfortunately Einer also witnessed the scene and he left us in a huff.

He said something about finding Liza and making sure she was all right.

It was near midnight and I started noticing a few strange Mexicans around town. I figured they were here for the fandango. Yet they all seemed awful well armed for being at a fandango. It was getting late and the party was winding down. A number of the torches that had been lighting the street were flickering out. I heard Buffole call for both Lena and me. We started at a good trot to join our humans which were calling us from the boardwalk in front of Pezta Palace. We were crossing the street from the Palace to join or humans when the shadow of a man caught my eye. From what I could see he was dressed in animal skins and he had on a large sombrero that was pulled down on his forehead to hide his face. I smelled a distinct and familiar odor from the man as a slight breeze wafted across my nostrils. I could not place it right away but it made the fur on my back prickle in the air. Lena and I joined Liza and Buffole and we went inside the Palace for a good night drink. Ivan was playing cards with some fellows we didn't know. But he took time to greet us. "I saw you two a few times this evening and you looked to be having a mighty good time. I saw Liza and Einer too she seemed to be mighty moody. In fact she came in here a while ago and huffed right on up to her room. I said hello but she ignored my like a plague."

Buffole felt it best to change the subject. "Ivan what you doing here playing cards shouldn't you be with your family?"

"I got a lot of stock at the livery right now with all the goings on in town. A bunch of Mexican's left their horses' in my care a few hours ago. I sent the family home so the kids could get to bed. They got school to attend in the morning you know. Once the town shuts down for the night I have to check on the stock and make sure they are all bedded in nice and proper."

As we sat down for a drink two Mexican's approached our table. Both were dressed mighty fine and they wore their guns low slung and tied down. It was a sure sign that they were professional pistolero's. One of them put his hands on our table and leaned over to get a good looked Krystal. He smiled with a big grin and it was hard not to notice one of his front teeth was made of silver and reflected the light like a mirror. "Mighty pretty senorita you have with you gringo. Maybe me and my friend dance with her." The Mexican slid his hand back and wrapped it around his the butt of his gun as he waited for Buffole's answer. Lena let me know that she could see under the table that Krystal had lifted her dress and slipped out the derringer that was strapped to her upper leg. I glanced over at Ivan as I gave off a low growl. Ivan caught my meaning and pulled the gun he had hidden under his coat in the waistband of his pants. I let Buffole know he was covered by both Krystal and Ivan.

Buffole returned the Mexican's smile as he answered. "Sir I don't believe the lady cares to dance or even converse with you or your friend. Might just be best you two mosey along and just enjoy yourselves with some less dangerous activities."

"Gringo you wish maybe to die? Your woman will not have much of a choice with you lying on the floor in a puddle of blood."

The Mexican heard a gun cock and looked over at Ivan. Krystal had a big smile on her face as she said to the Mexican. "Senor you just saw the man with the gun over at that card table, well he is the least of your worries. I am holding a gun under this table and if you don't want to look like a neutered steer I suggest you and your friend take my man Buffole's advice and find some other pursuits to keep you occupied."

The Mexican had a look of surprise on his face. "You are the one they call Buffole? I've heard of you. I'm the least of your problems. My friend and I we are sorry we bothered you. Adios amigos."

Krystal looked at Buffole. "What do you suppose he meant about the least of your problems?"

Buffole just shrugged it off. "I've no idea. Most likely he just thought to put a scare into us."

We were about to call it a night and Buffole was escorting Krystal up the steps to her room when my sensitive canine ears heard a low bellow. It was Shag and that bellow meant something was wrong. Ivan must have heard it too for the folded his poker hand and excused himself from the card game. I told Buffole what was going on.

"Buffole I just heard Shag call to me. I see Ivan is heading for the livery and I think Lena and I will tag along with him to see what Shag wants. You just see to Krystal and we'll be back soon.

Lena and I ran up alongside Ivan as he made his way to the livery. Ivan looked down and saw us. "Well howdy Sven you comin' along to check on that big furry beast you call your partner. I see you got your little lady friend with you. You and Buffole seem to be mighty popular with the ladies tonight. You know I thought I heard that old buffalo let out a bellow and figured I best hurry down and see if he's all right. I'm a feared if he gets ornery he could cause an awful lot of damage in a pretty short time."

When we arrived at the livery stable I could see that Shag was agitated. I ran over to Shag with Lena close at my heels. "Shag what's the matter?" "A Mexican came in a short while ago with three horses. It can be sort of difficult to distinguish a specific scent when you have three sweaty horses in such close proximity to each other. Yet I knew there was something familiar about the scent of one of those horses. It was the scent of a human mixed with the smell of death from my own kind. After the Mexican left the stable I asked that particular horse what its riders name was. The name of that human hit me like a bolt of lightning. I should have recognized that scent immediately but the smell of the livery and other animals had mixed up my senses. Sven you have to hurry back to Buffole and warn him that Popeye is in town."

I turned and told Lena to follow me. I told her about Popeye being in town and she knew as well as I did that Krystal and Buffole were in danger. The torches from the fandango were now extinguished and the town had no street lights. As we raced to the Palace a few lamps and candles were giving an eerie glow from the windows of those folks who had not yet retired for the night. Those flickers of light were helping Lena and I to try and make out any figure that might be lurking in the shadows.

I glanced up at the second floor window of Buffole's and my room and I saw the silhouette of Krystal. The shade of our window had been drawn but there was light enough from a lamp in the room to make out what was happening. My attention was riveted to the window as I saw Krystal's dress fall from her shoulders. The shadowy outline of her bare back was what humans would call downright shapely. A cry of warning from Lena brought me back to reality.

I glanced in the direction that Lena had warned about. Across the street from the Palace and our second story room was the dark shadow of man next to some wooden barrels on the boardwalk. The awning of the building he was located at and the barrels almost blended him into the darkness in invisibility. My canine eyes adjusted quickly to the darkness and I could see his rifle barrel pointing in the direction of our room's window.

Lena and I made a wild rush towards the shadow of our supposed assailant when I heard the shatter of glass breaking from the bedroom window. I made a leap into the air at the shooter's trigger arm and as I did so I glanced at our hotel room just long enough to see Krystal's body fall from sight. The report of the gun blast did not reach my ears until my teeth had latched on to the assailants arm. Lena hit his ankle with just enough force to knock him off balance. I could smell the scent of dead buffalo from the man's clothing and I knew it was Popeye. He grabbed me by the scruff of my neck and tore me from his arm. I was happy to know that I tore a good chunk of flesh from him as he threw me through the air and out into the street. Popeye was on the ground now and Lena was nipping at his ankles and hands in quick succession to keep him down. He kicked and swatted at her until one of his hands made contact and sent her sprawling against the wall of the building. Both Lena and I were dazed and it gave Popeye enough time to get to his feet grab his rifle from the ground and make a run for it.

Most of the town was dark but it was surprising how many people came rushing out of the buildings after they heard the gunshot. A few patrons' from the Palace came out and some of them had pistols in their hands ready to do what was ever necessary under the circumstances. One of the Palace's bartenders had a shot gun and he looked like he meant business. Popeye was already gone and out of sight so there were no human's that had seen him or would be able to suspect him of the shooting. Even if they did see him no one had actually seen him take his shot at the window except for Lena and me.

The two Mexican's we had met up with before came out of the saloon last and they hurried off towards the livery stable as if they knew it was time to get out of town. I groggily made my way to Lena and nuzzled her with my nose. She was dazed and the breath had been knocked out of her. I could feel a soft spot on her ribs and I knew she was badly bruised. The bartender saw us and came over to check on us. He could see Lena had been injured and he handed his shotgun to another man. He gently picked up Lena and carried her back to the Palace. I put on a good front and acted like I was not in pain as I followed him and my poor injured Lena to the saloon.

As we entered the saloon one of the bar girls came running down the stairs. "Quick! Someone go get Doc Johnson. I need some boiling water and lots of clean towels. Krystal's been shot." Lena struggled to free herself from the hands of the bartender so he set her down as gently as he could. Hurt or not she was going to check on her mistress and I was right there with her as we made our way up the stairs to Buffole's room.

We entered the room and I could see a puddle of blood by the window. Krystal was lying on her stomach on the bed. The bed had been pushed away from the wall and Liza was sitting on a chair by Krystal. She had a bloody stained towel in her hand and was holding it pressed to Krystal's back to slow the bleeding from the bullet hole. Lena immediately jumped on the bed and licked Krystal's face. Krystal gave a weak smile and said. "Lena my baby I'm so glad you're here. Krystal squeezed Buffole's hand as he knelt on the other side of the bed with tears running down his cheeks. He was dressed in just his pants and a blood stained undershirt which I knew must have come from carrying Krystal from the floor to the bed. I went to Buffole's side and laid my head on his leg. I told Buffole what I knew. "Buffole it was Popeye that shot her. Lena and I attacked him but it was too late he had already fired his rifle. He fought back and I did my best to stop him but he escaped. " With his free hand Buffole stroked my head.

Krystal's breathing was becoming shallow and Buffole moved his head next to her ear and whispered. "Krystal I love you, don't you dare die on me." I saw the tears fall from Buffole's cheek and land by Krystal's ear as he kissed her cheek. I could feel his pain and it hurt like hell.

Doc Johnson finally arrived and he hurriedly opened his black bag and took out his stethoscope. He brushed Liza away and took the chair next to Krystal. He held the stethoscope to her back as he pulled the bloody towel from her wound. I saw the look of shock on his face as he asked. "What the hell was she shot with a damn cannon?"

Buffole found enough voice to give an answer. "Doc I know who did this and I know his rifle. It was a Sharps buffalo gun. I can only figure the wood frame work holding the glass of the window panes deflected the bullet enough that it didn't instantly kill her. You have to save her Doc. I love her and all I got to say is you save her you hear me?"

Doc Johnson shook his head as he looked over the wound. "I'll do what I can but it's serious. Help me turn her over." Buffole and Doc lifted her gently and laid her on her back. Doc ran his fingers along the skin just above her left breast. "As you can see the bullet didn't pass through. I can feel a lump where it's lodged under the skin. If she's to have any chance I have to remove that bullet. Liza you get that bottle of chloroform out of my bag and some wads of cotton. This poor lady is still conscious and the only thing that keeps her from screaming out in pain is that she's in shock. Pour a little of the chloroform into the cotton and hold it over Krystal's nose. Make sure she keeps her mouth closed and let her breath in the chloroform. Liza keep your head back and away from the cotton I don't need you passed out on the floor. Buffole you go to the bottom of the bed and hold her legs down. She should be passed out but I don't want any involuntary movement or jerking around. Make sure she stays still. Lena had to leave the bed while they worked on her mistress and she came and curled up next to me. The two of us moved up on a chair away from the bed to give all the humans room to work on saving Krystal's life.

Lena closed her eyes and buried her head against my side as Doc Johnson used his scalpel to cut open the bulged flesh on Krystal's chest. The chloroform must have been doing its job as she made no movement as the Doc used a small forceps to find and remove the bullet. Looking at Buffole's face I think he was hurting as much inside as poor Lena. Doc held the bullet up for all to see and remarked. "That bullet can kill a buffalo and yet this woman is still alive. It's a damn miracle if you ask me. I'll stitch up both of the holes and then all we can do is pray for the best. If she is still alive in twenty-four hours she has a chance. Don't get your hopes up though she's lost a lot of blood and that bullet came awful darn close to her heart. I don't think any major arteries or veins were broken so she might have a chance." The Doc looked pretty proficient as he sewed up the bullet hole and the new hole he had to make when removing the bullet from her chest. He cleaned up the wounds and bandaged Krystal up nice and neat like.

Doc Johnson washed up in the basin on the wash stand and cleaned up his tools as best he could under the circumstances. "Liza don't just let the poor gal lay there half naked find her some loose fitting night clothes and cover her up. Buffole your job is to keep her covered and warm. When she regains consciousness keep her still. Try to get her to drink some water. She lost a lot of blood and she is going to need as much fluid in her body as she can stand to help her start healing. I'll stop back early in the morning to check on her."

Liza and Buffole did as Doc Johnson instructed. Once Krystal looked comfortable Buffole thanked Liza for all her help. "Liza I don't know how to thank you for what you've done. You go get some rest I'll stay here with Krystal."

Liza had sort of a sad look on her face. No doubt she figured that she had no chance of winning over Buffole's heart. "Buffole I'm really sorry about Krystal. You know I was a little jealous but I still liked her. She will be all right just you wait and see." Liza walked over and kissed Buffole on the cheek. She was about to leave when she looked at Lena and me. She came over picked up Lena and put her on the bed next to Krystal. Lena was sore and hurting but she made no sound as she was picked up. She curled up by Krystal's neck and exhausted she fell fast to sleep. Liza than told me as she left. "Sven you take care of Buffole ya here?"

Buffole put a few blankets and a pillow on the floor. He and I lay down next to each other before he said anything. "Sven we gotta kill that Popeye and we gotta do it soon before he hurts anyone else. As soon as we know Krystal is going to be all right we're gonna find that low down rattlesnake." We both had a fitful night as Buffole would often check on Krystal and every time he did he kissed her cheek. I checked on Lena at the same time and always gave her a nuzzle with my nose to let her know how much I cared about her, hell maybe I even loved that little gal.

CHAPTER 16

When morning came I was sprawled out on the floor enjoying the warm rays of sunshine that streamed into our room. After the shooting a blanket had been hastily tacked over the broken window but now that it was a warm sunny day Buffole had taken the blanket down to let in the fresh air. Krystal was still unconscious. Lena was lying at the bottom of the bed and enjoying the warmth of the sun on her fur. I had asked her to join me on the floor but she wanted to stay close to Krystal in case she woke up.

The door to our room slowly creaked open and Liza stuck her head in. "Everyone decent in here? I've brought you, Lena and Sven some breakfast. How's Krystal doing?" Liza set the tray of food on the wash stand and then went to have a look at Krystal. She put her hand on Krystal's forehead. "She has a high fever. Doc Johnson should be here soon." She tried to pick up Lena to comfort her but Lena let out a week cry of pain so Liza just petted her for a bit. "You poor little girl I'm sorry I hurt you. You just stay with Krystal and comfort her."

Buffole was sitting in the chair by Krystal. "Lena was injured last night by the man that shot Krystal. Sven's mighty sore too. The two of them did their best to stop the assailant. Thanks for the breakfast and all your help Liza. It's much appreciated."

Liza had a quizzical look on her face as she asked. "How do you know Lena and Sven attacked the man who shot Krystal?"

Serious as could be Buffole answered. "Just a cowboy's intuition I guess."

Liza just shook her head and started to leave. "Einer will be right outside the door to keep away any intruders. If you need anything you just tell Einer to find me."

None of us felt like eating but Buffole figured we best have something off the tray or Liza would feel bad. I took a piece of bacon to Lena and forced her to eat it. Buffole brought her a small bowl of milk which she readily drank. I could tell she was in a lot of pain and after her little breakfast she went back to sleep. I went over to Buffole but my ribs hurt too much for me to jump on his lap. I did not have to say anything he just sensed my predicament so he gently picked me up and I gave him a few doggie kisses to help ease the pain he was feeling for Krystal. Then I curled up in his lap and fell asleep myself.

My ears picked up footsteps on the stairs and then coming down the hallway. With canine hearing you have to be alert at all times to protect your loved ones and yourself and my job was to pick up any strange or unusual noises that might affect our well being. The next thing I heard was Einer's tail thumping against the door to our room. If Einer was wagging his tail that meant the visitor was friendly.

There was a soft knock on our door. The door opened without an invite from Buffole. It was Doc Johnson. Good morning Buffole, Lena and Sven. "How's are patient today?" He walked over to Krystal and rested his hand on her forehead. "Fever is still high. That's not good but it's only been about twelve hours so we'll hope it starts to drop. He removed the bandage from Krystal's chest and cleaned the wound. Once he had fresh bandages applied he asked Buffole to help roll Krystal onto her stomach so he could take care of the bullet wound on her back. When he had finished he and Buffole rolled Krystal onto her back and made her as comfortable as possible. Doc took a bottle from his bag and left it on the nightstand. "Buffole if she wakes up she will be in a lot of pain give her a teaspoon of this every couple of hours as needed. It is laudanum and it can be addicting so don't give her any more than necessary. I'll stop back this evening to see how she's doing."

I could see the look of concern in my Lena's and my partners eyes when Buffole asked the big question. "She will be all right, won't she doc?"

The expression on Doc Johnson's face remained sober as he answered while leaving the room. "From my experience with a hole that big in her she shouldn't even be alive. If I was you I would spend as much time with her now as you can. Hold her hand and tell her you love her. Just hope to God that she can hear you. It might be of comfort to both of you just in case. I'll stop back tonight to check on her and change her bandages."

I'm not sure if what the Doc said upset Lena or Buffole more. In some respects I think Lena took it the hardest. Right after Doc left she went up to Krystal's pillow and curled up next to her head. Gently Lena rested her head on Krystal's cheek. Buffole held Krystal's hand and whispered to Lena. "I promise you Lena if anything happens to Krystal I'll find Jo for you if you want to go and live with her. Or if you want you have a home with Sven and me for as long as you want. One more thing, Sven, Shag and me will find Popeye and kill him. It won't be a quick death either that low down buffalo killing, woman shooting varmint is going to suffer right up to his dying breath."

I could see that Lena and Buffole were tired from last night's terrible ordeal coupled with a lack of sleep so I made a suggestion. "Why don't you two take a nap while I go and check on Shag?"

Lena let out a deep sigh and looked at me with what I took as love in her eyes before she closed them and relaxed to sleep next to Krystal. Buffole stayed in his chair and laid his head on the bed while he held Krystal's hand in his. "That's a good idea Sven. Say hello to Shag for me." He was sleeping before I left the room.

I slipped out the door and Einer greeted me. "How's Krystal doing?" he asked.

"The Doc isn't giving much of an opinion but it doesn't look to good."Einer cocked his head as he spoke. "That's too bad. I know that you know Liza was falling in love with Buffole. Still I know she feels pretty bad about Krystal. The two of them had become sort of friendly rivals. As for me I sure do feel bad for both Krystal and Lena. It must be hard for Lena to see her mistress in such a bad way. I gotta admit I was little mad about Buffole hurting Liza the way he did when he choose Krystal over her but I would never have wished such a hurt on him. I just hope Krystal makes a turn for the better. In the end I think it would be best for everyone. My Liza is pretty understanding and she told me no matter what she wants Krystal and Buffole to be her friends for a long time. Hell if they decided to get married I bet she would throw them a beautiful wedding right here in the Palace."

Einer was all right in my book and I asked him if he would like to accompany me as I went to see Shag. He explained that Liza had left him strict instructions to stay and guard our room and that is just what he was going to do. I had to give him credit for being true to his word.

Ivan had put Shag in the corral outside the livery stable so he could get some fresh air and sunshine. When my big furry friend saw me he pawed the ground with his front hoof and made a soft bellowing sound hello. He lowered his big head and a nuzzled his beard to my nose in greeting.

Shag was too excited to tell me what had happened for me to get in the first words. "Sven it's about time you show up. I wanted to come and get you but I knew the Palace was not going to let a buffalo come into their establishment. I heard a gunshot last night and right after that two Mexicans showed up and saddled the three horses that they had left here earlier. They were talking about Popeye shooting Buffole but they had heard from some towns folks that it didn't look like a man in the window that Popeye was aiming at. They figured it was a woman and if that was the case and Popeye shot her there would be a lynch mob for sure. Popeye came running into the livery just as his friends had the horses ready to ride. I kicked open the door of my stall and I managed to back into him and his horse. He had blood on his arm and leg and seemed to be rather unsteady in the saddle. He came close to falling off but one of his friends grabbed the reins of Popeye's horse and helped him get out of the livery stable before I could do them any more damage. I wanted to go after them but I knew I had best wait and make sure you and Buffole were all right."

I was shaking with anticipation to tell Shag what had happened on our side of the story. "Shag if only you had been with Lena and I last night. After we left here we saw the shadow of a man aiming a rifle at our room in the Palace. By the time we heard the gun shot it was too late. Popeye had fired and Lena and I attacked him. He was too big for us to take him down and hold him. Lena received a serious rib injury from Popeye and I had the breath knocked out of me. He ran off towards the stable and well you did what you could to stop him. If you had known what had transpired before he got to the livery I'm sure you would have done your best to kill him on the spot. In fact you probably did your best to do so." I was just glad to know that Lena and I had inflicted some damage on Popeye.

"Buffole knew of course that Popeye wanted him dead but what Popeye did was more typical of that rattlesnake's character. It was Krystal whose back was towards the window when Popeye fired. I glanced up at the window just before Popeye shot his rifle and I can tell you there was no doubt that it was a woman's silhouette in the window and not a mans. Popeye was using a 50 caliber Spencer buffalo rifle just like the one he used to kill your family and friends from the herd you were in charge of. By all right's Krystal should be dead and she could still die unless God sees fit to save her. Buffole figured the only thing that saved her life was that the bullet came from a steep angle shooting upwards from the street to the second floor window. The bullet hit the wood cross trim on the window as it shattered the glass and the deflection slowed the bullet down enough that it didn't shatter Krystal's chest. It came to rest about a quarter inch from exiting out of her chest. If that bullet would have gone all the way through she would have bled to death in no time at all. She's still alive right now but she's in a coma. The Doc ain't to sure if she's gonna pull through or not."

Shag looked distressed when he asked. "What about Buffole and the sweet little dog Lena are they both all right?

"Well like I said before Lena got hit hard by Popeye and her ribs are mighty sore but physically I think she will be all right. Krystal is her human and the way poor Lena is mopping around its easy to see her heart is breaking. As for Buffole he's about the same as Lena in the hurting heart department. He finally opened up to let a human into his life and then Popeye comes along and shoots her. The only thing that I figure will keep Buffole going if Krystal dies is his desire for revenge to kill Popeye. If Krystal does die you and I better do everything we can to make Buffole figure he has a reason to stay living even after we find and kill Popeye."

"Oh yeah I almost forgot to tell you. Buffole offered Lena two options just in case Krystal does not make it. The first option is that he would find Krystal's daughter Jo and Lena could go to live with her. The other option is that Lena would stay with the three of us and be part of our family. I figure that was a great idea. Would that be all right with you partner?"

"Of course it's all right with me Sven. The little I've seen of you and Lena makes me believe you like that little lady quite a bit."

"You're right Shag. I guess there ain't no hiding my feelings when I'm around you." I hung out with Shag for a few hours and we enjoyed the warmth of the sunshine on our fur coats. As the sun started to set Ivan came to the corral and led Shag back to his stable.

Ivan gave me a pat on the head and said. "Sven I see you've been visiting with Shag today. It does that big old furry beast some good to have his friends around. Why do you know he broke out of his stall last night? He made quite a commotion just as those Mexicans' were leaving here. You tell Buffole I'll stop over later to see how he's doing. It's a mighty sad thing about Krystal being shot. I sure hope they catch whoever did it."

When I got back to our room things were about the same as when I had left. Einer was guarding the door and I noticed he had a fresh bowl of food and water that Liza had brought to him. In our room there was a plate of steak and potatoes also compliments of Liza for Lena, Buffole and me. Lena refused to eat but she did drink a little water that I offered her. Buffole took about two bites and said he wasn't hungry. I ate about half the food. I figured one of us had to try and be the strong one in the group. I was feeling pretty bad myself but it was up to me to take care of Lena and Buffole.

It was almost nine at night when I heard footsteps coming down the hallway towards our room. The thumping of Einer's tail on our door told me the visitor was friendly. Doc Johnson did not bother to knock he just came in. He looked at Krystal lying on the bed and then looked at the rest of us. "Buffole you look like hell. Lena you don't look much better. Sven you are not looking just too bad so you best take charge and get Lena and Buffole out of this room for awhile. By the way that's a doctor's orders and I expect them to be carried out. Now let's take a look at the patient I'm really here to see."

Doc Johnson checked Krystal's temperature and it was lower than from his last visit which he said was a good sign. He changed the bandages and noted that the bleeding had stopped so for the next few days the bandages would need to be changed only once a day. Fresh bandages would help keep down the chances of infection. Her breathing was more regular now and that was also a positive sign. When he had finished he said. "She's doing better than I had expected. I am not saying she's out of the woods yet but she's got a chance. If she would wake up and be cognizant as to her surroundings and what's going on around her I would say she has a better than fifty-fifty chance of recovery. If she wakes up confused and irrational she might have damage to her brain. Remember she's lost a lot of blood and if the oxygen to her brain was cut off because of her injures it could cause irreparable damage. I don't mean to alarm any of you but its best you know the worst case scenario. Right now in my professional opinion I think she's got a good chance of surviving. Sven you do what I told you when I came in. Get Lena and Buffole out of this room and get them some fresh air and food and maybe even a few drinks at the bar. I'll stop and ask Liza to spell you for awhile. For the next few days don't ever leave Krystal alone. If and when she wakes up someone needs to be here to make sure she stays still and she gets whatever attention she needs. I gave her a little sip of water and she swallowed it. That means the involuntary muscles are working in her throat. That's a good sign so every two hours give her a small drink to help get her fluid content back up. I'll be back tomorrow night to check on her."

After Doc Johnson left the room I did my best to convince Lena and Buffole that we should go downstairs and get some food and have a few drinks. It would be good for them to mingle with people and relax. I stressed that everyone knew that they cared for Krystal with all their hearts but their friends would also know that they had to go on with their own lives. I was not doing too well on convincing them until a quiet knock came on our door. Liza and Ivan came in to the room to see how things were going. Liza was the first to say something. "Buffole I just talked to Doc Johnson and he told me that I was to order you out of this room for awhile. I brought Ivan along to make sure you do as the doctor ordered. Take Lena with you she needs to get out in public and you make sure she eats a good meal. Sven I know you've been out already today but you go with them and take Einer along he needs a break. I'll sit with Krystal so don't none of you worry. Go on get out of here and enjoy yourselves. I own this place and the bartender and my girls have been told that whatever you want is on the house. Now skedaddle on out of here."

Lena was the most reluctant to leave. In fact she flat out refused. Buffole finally went over to the bed and picked or should I say pried her away from Krystal. Lucky for Buffole Lena was too tired to put up much of a fight. I could also see the pain in her eyes and knew her ribs still hurt her. I whispered to Buffole to be gentle with her even though I knew he would be.

Once we reached the saloon we were surprised to see how crowded it was. Ivan told us that a lot of people were here to check on Krystal and Buffole. It seems we had made a lot more friends then we could have imaged. As soon as the crowd of people saw us they all gave us words of encouragement and a lot of folks said they were saying prayers for Krystal's recovery. A table suddenly opened up for us to use and the folks at the table told us that we deserved the best seat in the house.

A redheaded bouncy little lady came and took our order for food and drinks. She was sweet as apple pie and for a human I thought she was rather cute. Ivan started telling us stories of the strange things he had seen in his life on the trail and at the livery stable. He figured this was as good as any way to take our minds off our troubles for at least a little while. Doc Johnson came in to the saloon and joined us for supper. He was a welcome addition and the first thing he said was. "Mind if I join you for supper. No shop talk just a friendly visit is all I want to hear."

Some of Ivan's stories were rather graphic for a little lady like Lena but she was not paying real close attention so I let Ivan ramble on. "I'm going to tell you all about the time I was on the trail of the famous Indian Chief Sitting Duck. I was riding with the army's Buffalo Soldiers. Just in case you don't know we were an all black regiment except for our commanding officer who was a young wet behind the ears white boy.

We had been sent to the New Mexico territory to hunt down Chief Sitting Duck and his Comanche warriors. One thing with Comanche's that we soon learned was that they were masters at hit and run warfare. Why them boys could be sitting on a rock in plain sight picking us off one by one with their rifles and by the time we had regrouped to attack them they would disappear like a whiff of smoke. There was no pretending amongst any of us. We would all have preferred to be somewhere else but we had a job to do and being Buffalo soldiers we had a pride in our outfit that wouldn't let us quit. A lot of the white folks and army brass was just looking for a reason to discredit us and we weren't about to let that happen.

We were on patrol when we saw black smoke in the distance. As we got closer we could see a cabin and barn still smoldering from a recent fire. The owner and his wife were tied to a pole in the corral. They were scared stiff but still alive. They told us Sitting Duck and about six warriors rode up and asked for food and water. The farmer did not offer resistance and told them they could have all the water they wanted but they had no food to spare. Sitting Duck had been taught by missionaries how to speak English and he told the farmer that seeing he offered water and did not put up a fight they would spare the lives of him and his wife. The warriors tied them to the post and then they plundered the house and drove off the few horses and cows that they had. As they were leaving two of the warriors torched the house and barn. Sitting Duck told them to leave this land and never return. He said this was Comanche land and the whites were not welcome. This time he spared their lives next time they would not be so lucky. Let the Buffalo soldiers know that this is a war they will not win were his last words as he and his warriors rode away.

With horses and cows being rustled by the Indians it was easy to follow their trail. Half a day's ride and we came upon another burned out family of settlers. This time they were not so lucky. The man of the house had grabbed a rifle and was ready to defend his family and his home. Two arrows in the back caught him by surprise as he was talking to Sitting Duck. Yet Sitting Duck showed some compassion. He left the man's wife and two small children live. He told them that Sitting Duck and his warriors were men of honor and only killed combatants in their war against the white man.

We tracked that rascal through territory that would make hell look like a picnic ground. I never saw so much desert and rocks in my life. Water was almost non-existent. When we did find a small pool of water in the rocky outcroppings it was hot and brackish but we drank it anyway. We soon came to respect are adversaries as being better warriors than we were. Sitting Duck and his men knew how to live in this hell on earth. Us buffalo soldiers were totally out of our element. Our Captain was going mad with thirst and hunger. I can tell you now that I'm no longer a soldier that that white boy leading us had no business being in charge of anything other than a spring social back in his hometown back east. That boy was useless. He led us in circles and set up our nightly camps in positions that we could not defend if the Indians decided to attack. Which they did.

Our enemies were Indians not white men. The rules our Captain was hoping to follow said that we would be attacked like an army attacks. The enemy would mass his men into formation and rush us. That is not the Indian way. Sitting Duck knew he had to conserve his limited manpower so he used stealth as a weapon. Each night we set up camp and every night a few Indians would sneak up on our sentry's and kill them. They were like ghosts. We never saw them and we never heard them. Every night we lost men and the Indians took our slain soldiers weapons and ammunition with them. We started with thirty six soldiers plus our Captain. Now there were only twelve of us left.

After two weeks of tracking Sitting Duck we finally met up with him face to face. We followed his trail towards a large river. That flowing water was the sweetest tasting drink I ever had. The Captain posted three men as sentries as the rest of us watered the horses and washed them down. Then it was our turn for a nice cool dip and a good scrubbing to get the dust and grime off our bodies. There were no Indians in sight but we knew they were watching us. We caught some fish and finally ate and started to feel like we were humans again. That night we were feeling better but we knew that Sitting Duck was planning something. We felt sort of like a fatted cow being led to the slaughter.

During the night and completely unseen by our sentries Sitting Duck had positioned himself on an island that was in the middle of the river. It was about three hundred yards away and he sat on a large rock with his rifle cradled in his lap. Some of us were still pulling on our pants and boots and our Captain just stood there in his long underwear staring in disbelief. He could hardly comprehend the audacity of the Chief. The Captain shouted out orders his voice pitched like a scared little boy. 'Men, grab your rifles and shoot that man!'

Sitting Duck held up one hand to hail us and I shouted at the Captain and the men. Hold your fire boys the Chief wants to parlay. The Captain shouted back at me with fire in his eyes and I could see pee wetting down his underwear legs. "Don't listen to that man I'm in charge here and I say shoot the Indian." The men were smarter than the Captain and they held their fire to let the Chief speak.

Sitting Duck motioned his arm towards the trees, brush and rocks on the Island and then towards the area surrounding our camp. Indian warriors appeared from their hiding places. They were all well armed with repeating rifles and if they had a mind to they could kill us all where we stood. Our Captain was now in hysterics and shouted. "What are you men waiting for, kill them, and kill them all. The filthy red savages." Sitting Duck raised his hand in the air and then quickly brought it down as if he were chopping wood. Two gunshots rang out. One from behind us and the other from the Island. They hit the Captain at about the same time so that he stayed upright for a few seconds. We could see blood spurting from the back of his head and more blood turning the front of his undershirt a crimson red from the hole in his chest. There was no doubt he was dead before he hit the ground.

I held the rank of Sergeant and I was next in command of our rather decimated troop. I held my hand in the air and ordered the men to hold their fire. I had my pants and gun belt on with just my undershirt on top. I holstered my side arm and spoke to the Chief. Sitting Duck you are a great and noble warrior and the troops and I would like to hear the words you have to speak.

The Chief stared at us for a few moments before he spoke. Buffalo soldiers you have tracked us and you have shown bravery. My warriors and I respect that. Your leader he was no good. It is good now that he is dead for he would have taken you with him in death if he had been allowed to live. I offer you a chance to leave in peace. Our people are starving on the reservation. The promise of the white father from your Washington is no good. The Indian agents steal our food and clothing and sell it to others. We left the reservation to find food for our people. We now have cattle and horses like we had been promised. We also have guns to hunt for game. We killed no one unless they tried to stop us or kill us. For us this is a war of survival. Now you need to make a choice to fight us here and die or to understand our motives and leave us in peace and live. What is your answer Buffalo soldier?

I'll tell you right now my mama didn't raise no idiot for a son and I figured Sitting Duck had a good point about just caring for his people. A lot of my men had been brought up on plantations and some of them and their families had been slaves. Not always being able to depend on white folk and their promises was something we all understood. I looked at my men and I knew we were all in agreement as to what to do. "Chief" I said. We appreciate your offer to leave in peace and we accept it. Me and my men wish you and your people a good life. In a blink of an eye them Indians disappeared from sight including Sitting Duck. I don't know how they could just vanish so fast but they did. My men and I buried the Captain and put up a marker on his grave. The marker just gave his name, rank and the date he died. We figured as little said about him the better. Then we packed up our campsite and went back to the fort.

Being the highest ranking officer left in our patrol I had to make a report to the commanding officer of the fort. I told him that we had valiantly tracked and had engagements with Sitting Duck and his warriors. Our Captain was killed in the line of duty while trying to lead an attack on the renegades and we buried him near where he had died. In the end my report said that Sitting Duck and his warriors were crossing into Mexico and we had no authority to follow them across the border so we returned to the fort. Overall the report was pretty much the truth. We were near the border and if Sitting Duck and his braves had killed us they may well have continued on to the Mexican border.

The fort's commander accepted my report at face value. He even told me if I were not a colored man he would put in for a promotion to make me a Captain. Both he and I knew that the United States Army was not yet ready for a man of color to attain a Captains rank so a Sergeant I stayed. I was given the responsibilities of a Captain but not the rank or the pay. It didn't really matter much for in another week my hitch with the army was over and I was not about to re-enlist.

I drifted for awhile after leaving the army. I did on occasion hire on as a civilian scout for the army once and a while. I learned the country pretty well. Lived with some friendly Cheyenne Indians and even had me a squaw for a short time. She was killed by soldiers who figured the only good Indians were dead Indians. They attacked our village early in the morning while most of us were still sleeping. I never had much opinion of the army after that. I realize every race has a few bad ones but an awful lot of them seemed to be in charge on the western army bases.

After my wife was killed I was tempted to hunt down and kill the soldiers that were involved but how I could justify killing a whole regiment of men. Anyway I'm sure they would have caught me sooner or later and either shot me or hung me.

I roamed for a while doing some cow punching and ranch work. One of the ranches had an old blacksmith that was getting on in years and figured me for a good replacement. I worked with the old man for two winters and learned me a mighty good trade. When the old man died it sort of broke my heart. So I left the ranch and headed back east where I found me a wife. She was working as a domestic for some rich folks and I offered her a chance for the freedom that a person can only find in the west. Now I got me a good wife and family and I own the livery stable free and clear.

Buffole I suppose you're wondering why I told you all this about myself. Sometimes a man just has to rid himself of his past demons and move on to better things. A pretty woman like Krystal or even Liza would be a mighty fine choice for a man to settle down and raise a family with. Maybe Popeye is a demon you should let someone else take care of.

Doc Johnson looked hard at Buffole as he spoke. "You know Ivan might have a point there. If Krystal survives which I'm feeling more confident that she will then she could use a man around to help her get back on her feet."

I was all for this little parable to work. Well at least for Lena and me. Buffole I could see had doubts in his mind. His feeling for Krystal was very strong. I could sense that his feelings for revenge against Popeye might just be stronger.

Buffole excused himself from the table saying he had to go for a walk outside and clear his head. Of course I went with him. We walked in silence for awhile but I could see where we were headed. Buffole had not seen or talked to Shag for some time and I think he was feeling a little guilty about not visiting his big furry partner.

We made our way to the livery stable and Shag was standing outside in the corral soaking up the sunshine. I ran up to him and he lowered his shaggy old head down to give me a nudge on my nose to say hello. Buffole stood by and started scratching Shags ears for him. "Shag I sure have missed you. I'm sorry I've left you here alone for so long but we humans can tend to be a little selfish once and awhile. I'm sure Sven told you about Krystal. She seems to be on the mend but the doc says she could still go either way so I been watching after her. It was my fault she got shot. She was in my room and I figure Popeye either thought she was me or he shot her to get back at me for hunting him all this time. As soon as I know she's out of the woods and on the mend the three of us will get back to work hunting Popeye."

Shag closed his eyes and kept enjoying the ear scratching he was getting from Buffole. "No need to worry partner I understand when someone cares about a woman. I had a lot of cows in my life because I had to propagate the herd. Yet every once and a while one of them cows would be special. Almost made me want to be loyal to just her and no one else. I have heard humans usually prefer a monogamous relationship and for you I think that would be a right choice. You're a loyal friend and I'm sure you would be a loyal husband to any woman that would have you."

Buffole gave Shag a nasty look. "Have me? Just what do you mean by have me?"

Shag lifted his head and gave us one of those strange buffalo smiles of his. "I've heard about Krystal. She's pretty, she's three quarters of your age, and I hear she's smart. You're half way over the hill, nothing special to look at and your getting a little soft around the middle. Hell if she wakes form her coma her eyesight and mind might be clear enough to stay clear of your rangly old ass. If so you know Sven and I would never desert you."

Buffole tried to look serious but he knew what Shag said was mostly true. "Your one hell of a friend Shag. Next time you want to be truthful try to add a little sugar to your words it might help ease the sting. Sven come on we best get back to Krystal and Lena."

As we were returning to the Palace something caught Buffole's attention as it hung on the front of the Palace's wall. Tacked up as obvious as could be was a broadside advertising a theater troupe that was coming to town. Buffole stopped dead in his tracks and read the advertisement. He looked down at me as he spoke. "Sven I can't believe I never even thought about her."

"Thought about who?" Was of course my answer.

"Jo. I should have thought about Jo. You know Krystal's daughter. I should have went through Krystal's things and found out where Jo was. Remember Jo told us her mother had a list of towns that Jo would be playing in with her acting troupe. This broadside says that Jo and the troupe will be coming here to give a show at the Palace in two days. How am I going to tell her about her mother? At least Jo will be here. Maybe hearing Jo's voice will be enough to shake Krystal out of her coma."

Ivan and Doc Johnson were gone when we got back. I figured Lena was already back upstairs with Krystal. We stopped at the bar and had a few drinks as Buffole contemplated how he was going to handle Jo when she arrived.

Liza came down the steps and of course that jolted both Buffole and me into action. We figured if Krystal had been left alone we better get our butts upstairs to her bedside and pronto but Liza stopped us.

"Settle down you two Doc Johnson is upstairs with Krystal. He's going to watch over her until you two get back up there. Lena is by her side and you know that no one will keep a closer eye on Krystal then Lena."

Liza stood next to Buffole and put one foot on the brass rail like any other relaxed customer would do. Then she shocked us when she spit into the brass spittoon on the floor. She smiled at the surprised look on our faces and said. "Just so you two know I might be a lady but I can be one of the guys when I need to be. Running a place like this means you have to learn how to handle all kinds. I spent years reading people and the looks on their faces are like windows to their minds. Buffole I see a lot of worry on your face but it's not the same worry I've been seeing since Krystal was shot. Something else is bothering you. Why don't you pretend I'm one of the guys and tell me what's ailing you."

Buffole took a shot of whisky and followed it with a SvenBrew chaser. He slowly looked at Liza from head to toe. "Well you sure as hell don't look like one of the guys. Yet I think I'll take you up on your offer to talk. I seen a broadside posted outside by the door about an acting troupe coming to the Palace. One of the actress's in the troupe just happens to be Krystal's daughter. I should have tried to contact her when her mother was shot but it completely slipped my mind. Now I don't know how I'm going to tell her about her mother when she gets here. I'm supposed to be her friend and now I feel like a darn fool having forgot all about her and her feelings. I know Krystal has an itinerary of where Jo is supposed to be and I should have looked for it but I never even thought about it. I was selfish thinking about myself and how much I hurt for Krystal. Hell my feelings ain't nothing compared to what a daughter is going to feel for her mother."

Liza followed Buffole's example by taking a shot of whisky and a chaser of SvenBrew before she answered. "Listen good you big galoot. You got feelings too and you just forgot about something that wasn't on your mind. When Krystal's daughter gets here you just meet her on the stage and take her to a quiet table in the far corner of the saloon. Tell her just what happened right from the beginning when her mother came in the saloon doors and saved your life. Her mom's a hero in this town and she should know it. It's only been a few days since she was shot and even if you had sent a letter to Jo she would not have received it yet. Just leave the contacting her part out of your story. You been doing the best you could and this Jo girl better appreciate it. That's my advice and you best heed to it. Do you understand? I can tell you are antsy as a dunk begging for a drink to get back upstairs to Krystal so go on now and get your butt upstairs."

"Thanks for the advice Liza you're a good friend." Einer was back on guard duty when we arrived and his tail thumped our arrival on the door. As Buffole opened the door Doc Johnson was just reaching for the door handle from his side of the door and it startled all of us. In fact I had to whisper to Buffole to take his hand away from his gun. It was only the Doc and we sure as hell didn't want to shoot him.

Buffole apologized to Doc Johnson for being so skitterish. Doc Johnson said he understood. After all Krystal was shot and the bullet could just as well been meant for Buffole.

Buffole looked at Krystal and could see no change from when we left. "Doc how is she doing?"

Doc Johnson's expression stayed the same. "No change yet. She's holding her own and the fever seems to be steady which is all right for now. If her fever goes up then we might have to worry. You just keep holding her hand and talking to her now and then. With any luck maybe your voice will get through to her and help her come out of her coma." Then Doc Johnson looked right at me and whispered. "Sven you hop on the bed and give Lena some comfort. That poor little things heart is breaking for her mistress. I'll stop back in the morning to see how things are going."

We spent our night and most of the next day just as the doctor ordered. Lena seemed to take comfort in curling up next to me. In fact I enjoyed the feeling of having her close by and it made me think that someday Buffole and I should have wives and settle down. Buffole held Krystal's hand and occasionally whispered things about missing her and once in a while I think I even heard words that mentioned love. Tomorrow Jo would be here and maybe her presence would jar something inside her mother to bring her out of her coma.

CHAPTER 17

When morning came we waited for news of the stage's arrival. Doc Johnson stopped in as he was now in the habit of doing and still there was no change in Krystal's condition. At two in the afternoon Liza showed up and told Buffole the stage was due in any minute. Some cowboys at the bar had seen it off in the distance as they rode into town.

Liza offered to stay with Krystal and we all figured it was best Lena stay with her otherwise Jo would know something was wrong if she saw Lena without Krystal.

Buffole and I went to the street to meet the stage. We were surprised to see two stage coaches arrive. There were four people in the first stage and five in the next. This was the main group of players in the acting troupe. They came in early to set things up and mingle amongst the town folks to let it be known they were in town and of course drum up as much business as possible for their stay.

In any western town it was big news to have any type of out of town entertainment and this would be no exception. The citizen's of Coldero del Diablo were more than eager to ante up their money to see a real live theater performance.

A big man exited the first stage followed by what could only be termed a 'dandy' by the way he was dressed with his ruffled silk shirt, long backed waist coat and a shining silk top hat. Then we saw Jo as the 'dandy' took her hand and helped her from the stage. We didn't pay much attention to the others. A crowd had gathered to see this unusual spectacle in a town of this size so we had to bide our time in getting to talk to Jo.

The actors and actresses shook hands and did their best to endear the crowd of townsfolk with their cultured charms. We stayed in the shadow of the Palace doorway until the crowd slowly dispersed. A number of the local men were taking our distinguished guests luggage upstairs to their rooms in the Palace. As they passed by us Buffole reached out and softly touched Jo's arm.

"Jo it's me Buffole." at first Jo seemed a little surprised that someone would dare to touch her for most men just stood in awe of her beauty and position of prominence on the stage. Her escort the 'dandy' turned abruptly and grabbed Buffole's wrist. "Sir I beg you to keep your hands to yourself. If I ever see you touch this lady again I will give you a sound thrashing." He held his silver headed cane tightly in his hand as he backed away pointing it at Buffole.

Jo quickly saw who we were and stepped between her escort and Buffole. "Rupert this man is an old friend of mine. There is no need for us to be rude to him." She clasped Buffole's hand in hers and said. "Buffole it is so nice to see you again. Please excuse my fiancé he was just trying to protect me. We meet so many ruffians in these small towns that we visit." She stepped back next to her fiancé and introduced him. "Buffole this is my fiancé Rupert. He joined our troupe a short time ago and we have fallen in love. I have told him I would not marry him until we find my mother and then he has to officially ask her for my hand. From the last letter I received I thought she might be heading this way and if so maybe we can finally see each other again."

Buffole looked Rupert up and down and he must have felt the same as I did. This guy sure didn't look like husband material. In fact he looked down right shady in my opinion. Now we weren't there to judge Jo's choice of a husband. We had a much more important task at hand and Buffole wanted to get it over with as quickly as possible.

Buffole talked softly trying to exclude Rupert from the conversation. "Jo I really need to talk to you about something in private if you don't mind."

Rupert was looking at Buffole like a cat looks at a mouse. Jo seemed to ignore Rupert's rudeness as she answered. "Why of course we should have a nice visit. It's been some time since we last spoke. In fact it was a number of towns back when you caught me in my last stage play. Since then I have become the star of the theater. Buffole, just between you and me I'm making a bundle of cash and in another year or two I should have enough saved up for mother and I to travel the world and do whatever we want." She saw that Rupert was staring at her. "Of course I almost forgot that Rupert is not only my fiancé' but also my manager. I'm sure mother will love to have him as a son-in-law. As soon as I rest up a bit and get refreshed we shall dine together at this town's fanciest eating establishment. I'll meet you here in the lobby about seven this evening. Will that fit in to your schedule?"

Buffole really wanted to talk now. What if Krystal should die before then and he hadn't got Jo in to see her while she was still alive. Jo's voice might be the one thing that would give Krystal the will to live and might just wake her from her coma. "Jo we really need to talk now."

Jo smiled. "Buffalo you are just like so many men of the west. You just want to say your say and be done with it. I'll have none of that. We need to have a nice meal together and a relaxing conversation. With my father gone and mother taking a liking to you I feel as if you are sort of a substitute father. You just let me have my way and we'll meet at seven. Come along Rupert let's find our rooms."

I looked at Buffole and said. "Well partner you handled that well."

We went to the bar and there was Ivan having a drink. "Ivan what are you doing here in the middle of the day."

"I came to see the theater troupe and to buy tickets for my family before they were sold out. We don't see much culture come to this town and my kids need to know that there's a whole other world waiting outside the boundaries of Coldero del Diablo. One thing is sort of bothering me though. I saw a man I should remember. He was going up the stairs with a pretty young lady. He had on a ruffled shirt and waist coat. I've seen him somewhere before I just can't seem to place where it was. I'm sure he wasn't dressed like that and he wasn't no actor the last time I saw him. I'm sure it will come back to me sooner or later. You know how it is, it just sort of weigh's on a man's mind when you see someone from the past you should remember. My gut feeling is that the last time I saw him it was not a good thing. I gotta get back to the livery. The show starts at eight-thirty tonight will I see you and Sven there?"

"Yup we'll be there." Ole gave his answer rather absent mindedly. He was still wondering about what to do about the Jo situation. A few whisky and beer chasers for each of us was sure to help us make a decision. Whether it was a right or wrong decision only time would tell.

We finally got up our nerve and Buffole went to the check-in area for the guests which was located in a room off from the saloon area. No one was at the desk so a quick check of the guest register told us what room Jo was in. We made our way upstairs and Buffole stood still as a statue with his hand poised to knock on Jo's door.

I finally got tired of him just standing there. "Knock already she ain't going to answer the door if she don't hear anyone knocking on it."

I guess what I said finally jolted Buffole into action. "Yeah, yeah I was just rehearsing in my mind what I was going to say."

Buffole finally knocked so softly even with my dog sense of hearing I could just barely tell he had knocked at all. I finally rose to my hind legs and using my paws I scratched on the door loud enough to be heard by half the people in the rooms along the hallway. It took only a few seconds before we heard Jo. 'What's going on out there? Just a minute I'll be right there no need to scratch my door down."

The door opened just enough for Jo to peek out and see who we were. Once she saw it was us she threw the door open and welcomed us in. She was in a fancy robe with a fur collar and cuffs. I had to think that Shag would not approve of the trim on her outfit.

Jo took a seat at a fancy little dressing table and started combing her hair in the mirror. "Ole and Sven what brings you here? I was getting ready for our dinner date."

Ole took a seat on the chair by the wash basin stand. I sat next to him on the floor. He cleared his throat looked at me and I nodded to him to spit out the words he had to say. "Jo I. I mean Sven and me. Well I have something very important to tell you. When we were downstairs you just didn't give me a chance to say what I had to say.

This place here, I mean here alone with you is better for what I need to tell you. You should sit down. I'm sorry you are sitting down. Now don't get all worried just listen to me. Do you understand what I'm trying to tell you?"

Jo just sat there with a confused and bewildered look on her face. I couldn't blame her because so far Ole had said a whole lot of nothing. If Jo could have understood me I'd take over and tell her about her mother. Jo finally said something to get Ole to finish what he wanted to say. "Ole just what do you want to tell me. I'm a big girl just spit it out."

Buffole swallowed hard and forced the words from his mouth. "Jo it's about your mother. She's right here in this very hotel."

Jo almost screamed with delight. "My mother is here! Why in the world didn't you tell me this right away?"

"Listen close Jo your mothers been injured and she's in a comma. I've been sitting with her ever since she was shot by that scoundrel Popeye. She was in my room and I'm sure he meant the bullet for me so I feel like I'm to blame. The Doctor has been doing all he could for her. We are hoping maybe if she hears your voice it might bring her around."

It was hard to tell if Jo was scared or angry. "Take me to her now!"

We went straight to the room and I asked Einer to step aside and make room for Krystal's daughter. Liza was at her bedside and she quickly made room to let Jo take her place. Lena's tail was wagging at full speed when she saw Jo and she literally leaped from the bed into Jo's arms. "Lena I'm so glad to see you are here with mom." She held her mother's hand and spoke to her. "Mom it's me Jo I'm here to take care of you. Please wake up." Jo buried her head in the pillow next to her mother and wept. Liza had moved to the door and stood by me. Ole approached the bed and said. "Jo you can't imagine how bad I feel. I love your mother and I wish it would have been me instead of her."

Jo looked up at Ole as the tears streamed down her cheeks. "Buffole this is all your fault. If you would not have come into our lives we would have handled Popeye ourselves. My mother would have killed him back at the cabin and you let him escape. Now my mother is lying here near death because of you. Get out of this room and leave us alone. Better yet get out of my sight forever. We don't need you or Sven. If you still have that big smelly buffalo you two should mount up and leave this town before I say or do something I might regret." With that said she pulled a derringer from her handbag and pointed it at Buffole. "Leave now and never try to see my mother or me again!"

Buffole turned and walked out the door as I sheepishly followed. Liza was right behind us and she reached out and grasped Buffole's arm. "Buffole, Jo's just upset this was a total surprise for her. She's in shock and she doesn't know what she's saying. Just give her some time to calm down and I'm sure she'll regret what she said to you."

Buffole just kept walking as Liza loosened her grip on his arm. The three of us went downstairs to the bar and had a few drinks in silence. Liza waited for a while until she spoke up. "Buffole you know Jo's just upset. She's young and she's worried about her mother. I'm sure she didn't mean any of what she said. She's just angry with the world right now. I bet if you wait around for awhile she'll come to her senses. You know when Krystal wakes up she's going to want you to be here."

Buffole just shook his head and answered. "No Liza, Jo's probably right. I'm just plain old bad luck when it comes to woman. I couldn't save my wife and I couldn't save Krystal from a bullet in her back and look at what I did to you. You treated me like a king and I ignored your advances. Nope I think you gotta admit I'm just not good material for any woman to work with. I'd like to ask you to do something for me. Once Jo settles down up there I need you to get my things out of the room so I can get back on the trail. Sven and I have some unfinished business and we need to take care of."

"I've no problem getting your things for you but I think your wrong about you and women. You're just too ignorant to know when to open up your heart to someone of the opposite sex is all. I'm going upstairs to try and comfort Jo." Liza left us alone to drown our sorrows in more whisky and SvenBrews. Ivan was just coming into the saloon and I saw Liza stop and talk to him before she went upstairs.

We must have been at the bar for a long time because the next thing you know the sun had gone down and the saloon was filling up for the night's big show. Ivan stopped to say hello and mentioned that the dandy Rupert had a serious poker game going on in one of the private gambling rooms. He told us that hearing about Rupert and the poker game had jarred his memory.

"Liza mentioned to me as she was going up the stairs that you're thinking of leaving here by morning. You do what you gotta do but I want to tell you something before you go. Buffole you know I said I knew that Rupert fellow from somewhere well now I remember where I seen him before. He used to hang around the army posts. He wasn't so fancy then just dressed like a down and out drifter. He'd make a few friends amongst some of the soldier boys and even the miners, hunters and Indians that hung around the fort. Everyone passed a lot of our free time playing cards and gambling and he just sort of stayed off to the side and watched us. His name wasn't Rupert then it was Adam. Had him a fancy little gal with him that he had picked up at one of the ranches. Promised to take her away from her hard scrabble life and give her all the luxuries the world could offer once he hit it big. She was a sweet trusting little thing. Definitely too good for the likes of him."

"One night someone drops out of a high stakes poker game and they invite Adam to sit in. He accepts and looks like a new born colt trying to stand up. The boys have to tell him how to shuffle the cards and give him instructions on how the game is played. Adam or I guess Rupert is clumsy as a new born babe dropping cards and acting all innocent like. Yet the boy is winning like there's no tomorrow. This kids got a streak of dumb luck like none of us had ever seen. After an all night game Adam walks away with about a thousand dollars. Now the other players want a chance to get their money back so they set up another game for the next night."

Now I was just sitting off to the side watching them play and I noticed the kid had this big shiny ring on his finger. I was thinking to myself that the ring was awful unusual for a drifter like him to be wearing. Another strange thing was that little gal that was with him.

She sort of coyly got the others players attention by saying or moving around just enough to get everyone to look at her. Now I ain't no professional gambler but after awhile I figured out what them two was up to and it weren't no good."

"I observed the same behavior from the two of them the next night as the evenings poker game progressed. A few high roller card players had come into the game after hearing about Adam's lucky streak. They figured the kid had lots of cash and they meant to win it. These new players were seasoned enough to look for the signs of a dishonest player and they let the game go on until early morning. By now Adam had amassed a small fortune. When I had left the game to get some air I noticed that Adam's horse was saddled and ready to ride just outside the building. It seemed sort of strange though that only his horse was ready. I had to wonder if he was going to make a run for it after the game. If so what was he planning on doing with the girl. Most likely he figured if he got caught he could get away and no one would bother accusing the girl of any wrong doing after all she was just watching the game and not playing. Or maybe he figured to get shed of her and keep all that money to himself."

"It was near midnight and Adam was raking in a lot of cash. Finally one of the other players mentioned Adam's ring. He says that big old ring sure looks like a shiner to him. In case you ain't familiar with the term professional card cheats use a shiner ring to read the cards their dealing to get an advantage. That shiner is just big enough to reflect what a card is to an experienced eye. The other five players tended to agree with the first man that noticed the shiner. Then they started talking about how the girl was being used to distract them. I backed away from the area as I could see all hell was about to break loose any second."

The accusations of cheating were heating up. One of the players rose from his seat and went for his gun. Adam no longer playing the innocent slipped a 4 barreled derringer from the sleeve of his shirt and let the gun drawing player have the first bullet. Adam jumped from his chair and grabbed the girl to use as a shield as he backed towards the door. One of the other players had already fired before he saw Adam grab the girl and the bullet entered her body instead of Adam's. Adam let the girl fall and bolted for his horse. Everyone in the room ran to the aid of the girl and thus allowed Adam to escape. That girl died before morning and none of us ever saw Adam again. That is until today. He didn't actually shoot her so I guess he's not guilty in the eyes of the law. In my eye's he's the one who killed her not that man that fired the shot. The town held an inquest the next day and the girl's death was ruled an accident."

"Buffole if you do anything at all for Krystal before you leave here make sure that you get Jo away from Rupert. I ain't saying you should kill him but there has to be some way to get rid of him."

Buffole took another swig of whisky and skipped the SvenBrew chaser. "Ivan where'd you say this poker room was?"

"Right over there partner. I'll tag along and keep an eye on things. Barkeep hand me that shotgun from under the bar I might want to use it if the occasion arises." I think we already knew we could trust Ivan and this just made it more so.

Buffole knocked on the door and we heard an invite to come in. There were four men plus Rupert sitting at the table. The room was smoky from the fancy cigars all the men were puffing on. Glasses of whisky and bottles of beer dotted the table by each player. The four players that had joined Rupert were some of the wealthiest men living in Coldero del Diablo. They included the town Banker, two of the area's largest and most profitable ranchers and the owner of a silver mine located a few miles out of town.

A quick glance showed at least five thousand dollars in the current pot in the middle of the table. I knew Buffole still had about four thousand dollars on him that he had squirreled away to buy land and build us a new home. He didn't touch the money up until now. It was our nest egg and I could see in his eyes he was going to risk it all to take down Rupert.

Buffole made one of those clearing his throat noises to get the attention of the poker players. "Would you gentleman have room for another player?"

The owner of the silver mine folded his hand and answered. "Sir you can gladly take my place at this table. I'm down over twenty thousand dollars and I can't afford any more for tonight." The man got up from the table and took his coat from the back of the chair. As he was leaving he said to Buffole as he walked by. "Watch that Rupert fellow he's either got the darndest luck or he's one hell of a good cheater."

Buffole took the seat at the now empty chair and placed three thousand in cash on the table. I saw a smile come over Rupert's face as he looked at the money. Ivan took a chair along the wall and I jumped up on a small table next to Ivan to help keep watch on things. The men at the table all introduced themselves to Buffole and he did likewise. There was a one hundred dollar buy in per hand. That left no doubt that these men were playing for high stakes and by the size of the money pile next to Rupert he was doing very well.

Rupert offered Buffole a cigar which was accepted with grace. The bartender showed up with a tray filled with whiskeys and SvenBrew beer. Buffole passed on the whiskey but took a SvenBrew to help him wet his whistle as he started matching the large bets that were accumulating on the table. Buffole was playing well and he started to amass a fair amount of cash. Ivan and I kept our eyes on Rupert. It was questionable if Buffole was really playing well or if Rupert was suckering him in by dealing him good hands.

The other players slowly started dropping out of the game after heavy losses. By my estimate there was at least forty thousand dollars on the table and Buffole had gathered up nearly half of that amount. I tried to communicate to him that maybe we should quit and be satisfied with a hefty profit. I guess I got caught up in the value of the money and not the reason we were here.

Rupert and Buffole were sitting across from each other. Ivan and I had both noticed that Rupert not only used his ring as a shiner to detect the cards he dealt he was also using a slider up his sleeve to keep an extra card or two in reserve. He was figuring on using Buffole as a sucker until the time was right.

The pot in the middle of the table was growing and both players must have had good hands. Buffole had been fairly silent up until now. It was time to drop the hammer and Buffole did it. "Rupert just what are your plans with Jo. I know her and her mom and I feel sort of a bond with them both. Her dad is dead and I guess maybe as a friend I should know your intentions."

Rupert tossed a few hundred more dollars into the pot to raise Buffole's last bid. "Well sir I love her and I plan to marry her. I also plan to be her manager in the theater. You know she has turned herself into quite a little gold mine on the stage. She needs someone like me to manage her money."

Buffole looked at his cards and raised the stakes again. "Rupert I've heard some things about your past that concern me. I believe you might just have a little of the con artist up your sleeve. Could it be you're marrying Jo for her money?"

Rupert raised another five thousand dollars. "Sir if you were not looking out for the interests of Jo as her friend I might just have to take offense at your last insinuation."

There was now over fifty thousand dollars up for grabs. Both men held their hands. "Rupert I hear you were a card shark out west. Seems that you were involved in a game that caused the death of a young woman. The woman I hear was your partner until you used her as a shield from a well deserved bullet meant for you."

Sweat appeared on Rupert's brow as he fought to hold his temper. "Sir I don't know what you've heard or who you think I might be but any more talk like that and I may have to kill you."

Buffole glanced sideways towards Ivan. "Rupert or Adam as the case may be. Do you see that man standing there with the shotgun? He's my witness. He was there when you got that girl killed."

By this time the sweat was rolling down Rupert's face. Suddenly a derringer slipped out of Rupert's sleeve and he wrapped his hand around it to get a shot at Buffole. Before I could jump in to help Ivan slammed the barrel of the shotgun down on Rupert's hand. Rupert screamed in agony as the derringer fell from his grip. Buffole reached across the table and pulled up Rupert's other sleeve to reveal a card slider attached to his arm. The slider held two aces.

Buffole scooped up the derringer and told Rupert to finish the game. The two aces lay face up off to the side where they had fallen. "Come on Rupert show the hand your holding. The aces ain't yours to use this time." Rupert laid his cards on the table. Two aces, a king, a jack and an eight. If he would have got to use the two aces in his slider Buffole would have been up against four aces and a king. A tough hand to beat.

Buffole laid his cards on the table. Three kings and two jacks. "Rupert looks like you lose. In fact you not only lost all your money but you're going to lose Jo to. I suggest you let Ivan escort you to your room so you can gather up what things you need and get out of town now. If I ever hear of you coming near Jo again things won't be as pleasant as they were tonight."

Rupert was shaking more now in fear than in anger. "I don't have a horse and the next stage won't be here for three days. How do you expect me to leave town? Plus your friend there most likely broke my wrist how do you expect me to make a living?"

Buffole looked over at Ivan. "Ivan you got any suggestions?"

"As for his wrist it will eventually heal and I figure he brought his problems on himself it's not really our worry."

Ivan smiled and continued. "I think I might just be able to help this young man get along his way. That fancy gold watch and chain he's wearing would be just about the right payment for that old mule I got at the stable. The critters sort of wore out and sway backed but he's got a few good miles left in him."

Buffole smiled and added in a suggestion. "Ivan you don't expect a high class gentleman like Rupert to ride out of town bareback do you? I bet that shinny ring of his must be worth the price of a saddle."

Ivan asked to see the ring which Rupert reluctantly took off. "Why you know I have a saddle back of the livery that's stored outside in the weather. It's pretty rough but if I tossed in a blanket the old mule won't notice. I think this here ring might just cover the cost of that saddle and blanket. Yes sir mister Rupert I think we got a deal. Not let's you and me and this here shotgun go up to your room and gather your stuff. Then we can make our way over to the livery and I'll help you get along your way."

Rupert got up to leave and asked for a favor. "Buffole you can't just make me leave without at least leaving Jo a note. She'll think I abandoned her and it will break her heart."

Buffole always kept some paper and a pencil in his pocket just in case he might want to send a letter. He never sent any but he thought he should be prepared in case the thought ever crossed his mind or if he had someone to write to. He put a piece of paper on the table and handed the pencil to Rupert.

Rupert was shaking as he was about to start writing. Buffole then reached out and held Rupert's wrist as he spoke. "Rupert I think maybe I'll tell you what to write. You write this down just as I say. If you don't it might be hard for you to take up your profession with two broken wrists."

Now write this down. "Jo. I've been misleading you. I am a gambler and a cheat and I was only using you to profit from your success. I have seen the errors of my ways and have decided it best for me to leave now and seek out the graces of god so that he might forgive me of my sins. Rupert."

Buffole picked up the paper and read it aloud so that Ivan and I could hear it once more. "What do you think Ivan?"

"I think that's a mighty fine letter Buffole. Why don't you let me have it and I'll make sure Rupert slides it under the door of Jo's room so she can find it."

Ivan and Rupert left and I jumped up on the poker table to help Buffole count our winnings. Fifty-one thousand dollars less our stake of three thousand gave us a profit of forty-eight thousand dollars.

I looked at Buffole and said. "Partner that's a lot of money we could settle down here and have a darn good life."

Buffole smiled and reached over to scratch my ear. "Sven I think if we keep some and give some away we would both feel better. We still have to track down Popeye but maybe we can do some good with some of this money before we leave."

It was seven in the morning and we left the poker room to see Liza still in her robe having breakfast. "Boys I didn't think you would ever come out of that room. Come join me for some breakfast. I just saw Ivan leave with that Rupert fellow. Rupert told me he was leaving and short on cash. I was about to confront him for payment but Ivan said you would take care of Rupert's bill. Ivan then proceeded to prod Rupert out the door with the barrel of a shotgun."

Buffole smiled as we sat down to have some breakfast. "Liza I'll pay his bill. I have a favor to ask. Sven and I would like to get a few hours shuteye before we hit the road. You got a room we could use for a few hours."

"No problem. You can use Rupert's room as it seems he won't be needing it. You know I still wish you would change your mind and stay. Krystal will be disappointed if you're not here when she wakes up."

Buffole took a sip of cold milk before he answered. "How about you Liza. Will you be disappointed if I leave?"

"Yes I can honestly say that I will."

"I'm flattered to hear you say that. You're a mighty fine woman and maybe someday I'll come through this way again. Krystal's a fine woman too but you know she's really too young for me and sooner or later she'll wish she had a younger man. Now that Jo's here with her I think she'll recover just fine without me around. I'd like to apologize for being a man and thinking about things with something other than my mind. You're a lady through and through and I'm going to miss you. Excuse me but Sven and I best hit the sack for a rest."

As Buffole stood up Liza did the same. She wrapped her arms around Buffole and kissed him. I started towards the stairs and walked slowly until Buffole caught up with me. We were both dog tired when we hit the mattress of the bed we slept well until mid-afternoon.

CHAPTER 18

When we awoke it was after three in the afternoon. Liza had moved our things from our bedroom where Jo and Krystal were now residing to the foot of our bed. Buffole washed up and changed into his traveling clothes. I got a fresh red bandana around my neck to use on those dusty rides ahead of us. Buffole picked up his saddlebags and we made our way down the stairs to the bar. Liza was dealing a game of faro when she noticed us. She called one of her girls to take over so she could see us off.

Liza and Buffole sat at a table for a last drink goodbye. I excused myself to Buffole and told him I would back in a few minutes. I ran upstairs to where Krystal was and Einer greeted me with a tail thumping welcome against the door.

Jo said "come in" so I did. I looked at Lena who was looking better now that Jo was here. "Lena would you like to come downstairs and have a drink with me? Buffole and I need to be leaving in a little while." Lena looked surprised but she jumped off the bed and the two of us walked side by side downstairs. Lena and I shared a chair at the table with Liza and Buffole and Buffole ordered two bowls of SvenBrew for us. I quickly told him, to make it just one bowl as we would share.

As Lena and I talked the soft strumming of a guitar could be heard. Liza had hired a Mexican guitar player to play music for the guests. I told Lena that I cared about her a lot but like my partner I had a job to do and that was to find Popeye. I explained to her that we really cared about her and Krystal but sometimes a man has to do what a man has to do. I could see the sadness in her eyes but she said she understood. At least Jo was here and Lena had her family back together. I told her I was sure Krystal would get better.

As for Liza and Buffole I was too busy with Lena to catch much of their conversation. I did hear Liza ask Buffole to write her a letter now and then. She told him she would gladly write back and let him know how things were going with Krystal and also with herself. It was about time to go and I walked Lena back to her room. A doggie kiss goodbye sealed my departure.

Back at the table Liza held Buffole's hands in hers. She had tears in her eyes. Krystal or no Krystal if was evident that Liza still had deep feelings for Buffole. She made him promise that he would write to her and if he was staying in any one spot for long he was to expect a letter back. Buffole stood to leave and Liza did the same. As he said a final goodbye she wrapped her arms around his neck and kissed him like I've never seen two humans kiss before. I believe it would be termed extremely passionate.

Buffole picked up his saddlebags and headed towards the door. Liza grabbed me from the floor and gave me a hug and kiss on the forehead goodbye. "Sven, you take care of Buffole you hear. Make sure he drops me a line from time to time." I don't know if she knew Buffole and I could communicate but she seemed to expect us to do so.

As we left the guitar player started to sing. "I'm just a poor wayfaring stranger. I'm traveling through this world or woe. Yet there's no sickness, toil nor danger. In that bright land to which I go. I'm going there to see my mother and father. I'm going there no more to roam." Well at least the wayfaring stranger part seemed appropriate as we left the Palace and headed towards the livery stable.

Ivan was busy standing in the bed of a wagon pitching hay up into the livery stable's loft. "Buffole, Sven looks like you two are ready to travel. I brushed Shag down for you and I think he's been penned up here long enough. He's been developing an attitude lately that he's the king of my stables and all the other critters just let him have his way. He's first to the food and first to the water trough. I like the big brute but I think he would prefer the open range to this dark dusty place."

Shag lowered his head and we touched noses in greeting. Buffole scratched Shag behind the ear and whispered to him. "I missed you big buddy. Remind me in the future not to neglect you. Sometimes a man's heart over rules his common sense." We saddled up and rode out of the stable to see Ivan still hard at work pitching hay.

We stopped long enough to say goodbye. Buffole removed his hat and set it on the pommel of the saddle. He looked into Ivan's eyes as he spoke. "Ivan you've been a good friend to me while I was here and I'll never forget it. I want you to have a little something in the name of friendship. I also want to ask one more favor of you. I have two envelopes here I would like you to give to Liza and Krystal for me. The third envelope is for you. I ain't much at accepting thanks from folks so maybe you could wait and open your envelope at the supper table with your wife and kids. By the way thanks for taking care of Shag for me." With that last comment he tossed a twenty dollar gold piece to Ivan.

Ivan caught the gold piece in his hand and without looking to see how much it was he slipped it into his pants pocket. Jumping down from the wagon he walked over to us and took the three envelopes from Buffole. He shook Buffole's hand and said. "You're a good man Buffole and I'm proud to call you my friend. May the angels of heaven ride with you."

We slowly rode down the street and Buffole and I took one long last look at the Pezta Palace as we rode by. We might miss that place but not near as much as we would miss those inside.

We rode in silence for some time before I finally asked. "Well partner just how much money did you put in those three envelopes?"

"I gave them each five thousand dollars. I figured that should help Krystal get back on her feet. Liza probably doesn't need it but I know she'll invest it well for her future. As for Ivan I figure he and his family deserve the better things in life. This should give them something to build a future on. Sven I hope you don't mind that I gave away fifteen thousand dollars?"

I wagged my tail and answered. "Partner if we can't make it on the thirty some thousand dollars we have left we best pack it in right now. Maybe down the road we can get us a nice place and settle down with women of our own and raise a family. Who knows after we finish with Popeye we may have a new outlook on life."

Shag just sort of snorted at our talk and then he said. "You know boys I'm part of this here family myself how come no one told me about all this money?"

I gave Shag his answer. "We're telling you now Shag. You know you're one of our family and you were included when I said we might someday all find women of our own and have a family. I can see it now a bunch of little Shag's running across a prairie that we own with no one to threaten them."

We rode for the rest of the day and then made camp along the Rio Grande. It was a moon lit night with the stars twinkling messages of beauty across the ink black sky. We all settled in around the campfire. An occasional howl from a coyote or the hoot of an owl broke the silence. Oh yes a few croaking frogs and crickets singing their songs soon filled our ears with sounds that we had been missing from our nights on the prairie. We slept better out here with nature then with the music of pianos and the songs of drunks in the street. A soft bed is nice but it's hard to beat a nice bedroll with a campfire and nature's creatures to sing us a lullaby goodnight.

We crossed the Rio Grande river and we were now in Mexico. Popeye's trail had been long lost to us by this time so our only hope to find him was to find Poncho Villa's camp and hope he was there. Once in Villa's camp we would have to hope we could be accepted as visitors and not the enemy. Finding Popeye and then killing him would most likely not go over to well when he was surrounded by his amigos.

The next day we rode into a sleepy little Mexican town called Los Cactus. It was just a few adobe buildings with a dirt street. There was a Cantina with no windows and one of the batwing doors was hanging open by one hinge. There was a dog outside the place scratching away at his fleas. I gave him a wide berth as fleas were the last thing I needed to deal with on our journey.

We left Shag outside to act as a lookout in case of trouble. Inside the Cantina it took a few moments for us to get used to how dark it was inside compared to the bright sunlight we had left behind us.

The bartender had a few days of dark growth on his face and his hair was jet black and stringy as it hung down loosely around his face. I jumped up on the bar and no one seemed to take notice. The bartender approached us and said. "What will you and your dog have amigo?"

Buffole slid the leather thong down that was over his guns hammer that kept it from falling out of the holster when we traveled. He leaned on the bar and kept an eye on the three men who were playing cards at one of the tables. "My dog and I will each have a shot a whisky and a SvenBrew beer."

The men at the table looked up at us and the bartender laughed as he answered. "Whiskey I have but you are south of the border now my friend no SvenBrew here. I have some home brewed beer that will have to do."

The poker players smiled at our ignorance of beer choices. They all had large sombreros with them. Two were hanging loosely from the men's necks over the back of their chairs. The other man who seemed to be the most important of the group still had his sombrero on his head and it tended to hide his face. Buffole downed his whisky and I lapped mine up from its glass. It was strong and made my tail stand straight up. I was glad my beer was in a bowl so I could quickly lick up a chaser for myself.

Buffole took the drawing of Popeye from inside his hat and put it on the bar with a twenty dollar gold piece. The bartender looked at the drawing and then at the gold piece and finally he looked at Buffole. My partner softly said. "That's for the drinks and any information you can give me about that man. If you've seen him or can tell me where he might be you can keep the gold piece. If not I expect my change."

The bartender hesitated as he reached for the money. He leaned over and wiped up a wet spot on the well worn bar top right next to our drinks. He discreetly pointed at the men sitting at the table and whispered. "They know this man you look for. Be careful they don't like strangers." The bartender quickly scooped up the gold piece and exited from behind the bar to the back room of the cantina.

Buffole slipped a derringer from its hiding place in the watch pocket of his pants. It was small enough for him to conceal it in the palm of his hand. He turned and spoke to the group of card players at the table. His elbow on the bar would make the men at the table figure he had no chance of using his gun if that happened to cross their minds.

"Gentleman I would like to ask you a question." Buffole held up the drawing of Popeye so the men could see it. "Have any of you men seen this man."

The man with the sombrero shading his eyes answered. "Why are you looking for this man my friend? If you are the law this is Mexico and your gringo laws are no good here."

"I'm not the law. This man killed my family and shot someone who meant a lot to me. I mean to find him and take out my revenge. If you men have ever had anyone do you wrong you know it is a code some men live be to exact an eye for an eye. Have any of you seen this man or not?"

I could see the bottom halves of the two Mexicans nearest to us and they both had their hands on the butts of their side arms. The third man with the sombrero who was doing the talking seemed to be the leader. His one hand held the cards he was playing. His other hand had its fingers wrapped around a glass of beer. I communicated to Buffole that at present the odds if a gunfight should erupt were two to one in their favor.

"Amigo it is a very interesting story you tell. I am a man of justice myself. Your story it touches my heart. I know of this man you seek and I will take you to him. First though you must give me your word that he will be allowed to tell his side of the story. Then I will be the judge of how this problem shall be handled. If you do not agree or try to pull any tricks on me I will of course have to kill you." The man tilted his sombrero back on his head and gave us a big smile as he waited for our answer."

Buffole glanced at me for my approval and then he gave his answer. "Just who are you that I should trust you?"

"My name is Poncho Villa. If you cannot trust the man who is the savior of Mexico amigo, then who can you trust?"

Buffole smiled for we knew now that Popeye was riding for Villa. "You are well known to me and I know that you are a man I can trust. Let me buy you and your men a drink."

My canine instinct told me that trusting this man was like trusting a coyote. Don't get me wrong coyotes are part of the dog family but they tend to be sneaky and not the most trust worthy of canines.

Poncho asked Buffole to join him and his men at the card table. I stayed on top of the bar and nursed my drink. From my vantage point I could keep an eye on our new friends just in case they were not as friendly as they seemed.

My partner has always had an easy way with talking to people and gaining their trust and tonight would prove to be no exception. "Mr. Villa how goes your battle with the Mexican Federale's troops?"

"Buffole you are my friend we call each other by our first names. You will call me Poncho, see? The Federale's they are ill trained to deal with me and my men. The villagers they protect us. Your government they wish to stay clear of any political stance so that way whoever wins will still like the United States. I fight for my people. You wait and see in the end we will be victorious. Then Mexico will belong to the people."

Buffole did his best to not say anything that would stir up Poncho. "So Poncho I have heard that the man I am looking for might be riding with you as a mercenary. His name is Popeye. I realize you have a lot of men but maybe you know personally of this one."

"Poncho gave a belly laugh and his two friends did the same. "Popeye he is a nasty one. I know him well. Often times I have to tell him do not be so mean and cruel to the enemy. He kills for sport and the women. The poor women they are not safe around him. Sometimes I think I should kill him but he is a good soldier and he gets the job done. Maybe you kill him for me then my problems with him are over. Then again maybe he kill you then things will just stay the same."

By this time my partner was in the poker game. As the game progressed into the night the bartender brought out tacos and beans for the poker players. He set a plate of chicken and beans by me which I quickly devoured. As the night wore on I decided Buffole was safe for the time being and I decided to take a nap.

I awoke when a ray of sunshine hit my eyes. I was still sleeping on the top of the bar and the saloons owner must have felt sorry for me because I was covered with a bar towel to keep me warm from the chill of the night. I noticed a small room to the side of the bar with a blanket acting as a door. I rushed over and peeked inside the room. Four cots contained the four men sleeping off a night of too much whiskey and beer. My partner was passed out with one boot on and one boot off. His arm dangled over the edge of the cot. He was curled up with his gun and gun belt like a babe holding onto a teddy bear. It would have been cute if it wasn't so disgusting. The place and my partner reeked of cigar smoke and liquor. I nudged his hand to wake him and told him to get outside and wash up.

It was early morning and already the sun was baking the earth to the point that the hot ground hurt my paws. Buffole pumped some fresh water into the combination horse trough and fountain in the town square. Soon the three Mexicans came out and joined us. They all washed up and went to saddle their horses. Shag was standing in the shade of the saloon his saddle on a broken fence post nearby. He was giving Buffole a nasty look as we approached. He looked at me and said. "Lucky for you two that a young boy came along and took an interest in me. The lad looked in the saloon and figured everyone inside was too drunk to worry about me being left outside with a saddle on. He came over took off my saddle and even brought me some hay. If you look over yonder you will see him at the end of the street in the doorway of his house. I would suggest Buffole give him some money for taking care of me."

Buffole saddled up Shag and I made sure he apologized to our big furry friend. We rode out to the street and our three Mexican friends were mounted on their horses and ready to ride. As we rode out of town the boy who took care of Shag was standing by his home watching us. Buffole flipped the lad a dollar coin as we passed him.

The Mexicans had a good laugh at our form of transportation. Buffole, Shag and I just took their snide remarks in stride.

Poncho rode next to Buffole and me regaling us with tales of his exploits. He was quite a talker and was very proud of his service to the Mexican people. He told of the villagers he had helped and of the many women that he let love him. We got the impression that he might be more of a braggart then the hero he wanted the world to think he was. He was known to us from stories that we had read or heard back in the states. Although he seemed to be congenial enough right now we knew he had a dark side that included brutality, murder and the taking of women against their will. Yet we rode with him now to fulfill our own lustful desires. I had to wonder if maybe we were no better than he was. We were doing what we felt was right and needed to be done. I believe Poncho felt the same way about his cause.

We crossed the heart of a small desert and then made our way up a mountain path before we reached Poncho's encampment. The closer we came to the camp the more sentries we saw. Poncho had men placed in strategic locations so that no unwanted guests could enter the area unseen. Riding into camp was like attending a gala fiesta. The women and children all rushed up to greet Poncho and his men as if they were returning war heroes. The children seemed to be drawn to Shag. Some of them ran up to touch him others stayed a safe distance away. We must have been a strange sight for the youngsters most of who had never seen a buffalo before.

The encampment was more of a traveling village then an army camp. Many of the soldiers had their wives and families with them to help do the laundry and the cooking. Poncho introduced us to his followers and told them that we were to be treated as guests. From that point on we had the run of the camp. We even had a tent for our own private use and it was suggested we get some rest for tonight there would be a party in our honor.

Buffole tried his best to be subtle when he asked. "Poncho, if you remember I am here to see a man and take care of business. You gave your word to help me. Is that man here?"

Poncho smiled and answered. "Amigo do not be so impatient. Tonight we celebrate my return to the camp and to honor you as our new friend from the United States. There will be plenty of time later for you to see Popeye. He is not in this camp right now for I sent him and some of my men to do a job for me. I will send for him now. It may take a day or two for him to arrive."

Poncho looked about until his eyes fell on a man who was sitting in the shade of a tree. The man had a bottle of tequila in one hand and there was a rather hefty woman at his side. The two of them were obviously drunk. Poncho barked out an order. "Pedro you drunken slob get up and go and find Popeye. You tell him I want to see him immediately."

Pedro took his arm from around the woman and she fell in a drunken heap on the ground. He stood up and staggered a bit as he gave a salute to Poncho and mumbled the words. "Yes Poncho I will go and get Popeye immediately like you say."

Poncho shook his head in disgust as he answered the man. "Pedro you call me General in front of guests. Remember we are an army. No more calling your leader Poncho, it is General Villa. Now you remember that all right Pedro."

"Yes General. I mean yes General Villa. I go now and find Popeye for you." Pedro stumbled off towards the horses and Buffole thanked Poncho for his help. Poncho told us as his guests we could call him Poncho, but his men were soldiers and they must learn to respect him and call him General.

We retired to the tent that Poncho had provided for us. It had a cot and blanket plus a small stand with a fresh pitcher of water. Buffole unbuckled his gun belt and hung it on the edge of the water stand. He lay down on the cot and covered himself up. His handgun was kept by his side with one hand ready for its use. I positioned myself on the ground under the cot facing towards the tents doorway. Buffole could sleep well as long as he knew I was alert to anything that might happen.

An hour passed and Buffole could not sleep any longer. He got up and used the water basin to wash up a bit. We left the tent just as the sun was lowering itself below the horizon. The area was filled with torches and tables that had been set up for the fiesta. The women of the camp were preparing food and setting up the tables with plates and beverages. We wandered about and took note that there were wagons filled with rifles, pistols and even a Gatling gun. If nothing else Poncho's army seemed to be well equipped for a small scale war.

It did not take long before Poncho found us. "Buffole my friend you are awake and ready to have a good time. Come we will start the festivities now." With that said Poncho pulled a pistol from his shoulder holster and fired three shots into the air. Of course that got everyone's attention. Once all eyes were on him he made an announcement. "Amigo's it is time to celebrate. We have two new friends in camp tonight. All of you welcome Buffole and his little four legged partner Sven. Come let's all feast and have a good time."

I sat next to my partner as everyone took their places at the table. Poncho was seated at the head of the table and we were on one side of him. His second in command was opposite from us. It was a boisterous crowd and it took a gunshot from Poncho's gun to quiet the gathering. Once it became quiet Poncho stood up and held his drink in the air. It was time for a speech from General Villa.

"Soldier's and friends of the revolution let us all toast to the freedom of Mexico. Viva Mexico!" Buffalo joined in as the whole group shouted in unison "Viva Mexico." As for me I barked the words but no one understood except for Buffole.

As the night progressed and the food had been consumed everyone drifted off for other activities. An impromptu race track was set up for horse racing. Poncho looked at Buffole after a few of the men had raced their horses and said. "Too bad you have no horse amigo or you could have entered him in the races. That buffalo you ride he is much too big to be any challenge to a horse. Me I have a fine horse and I will race him last to show these men what real horse flesh can do."

I knew just what my partner was going to say and I also knew it could cause us nothing but trouble. "Poncho would you like to make a little wager. I'll bet you one hundred dollars my buffalo Shag can beat your horse in a one mile race."

Everyone within hearing distance became quiet as they waited for Poncho to answer. "Buffole my friend I hate to take money from a fool but I accept your bet." Two men rode out to figure our starting point. The finish line would be in the camp with all of Poncho's people to witness what they figured would be our defeat.

Poncho and Buffole saddled up their mounts and got ready to ride out to the starting line. Poncho decided to make a new offer before the race began. "Buffole what you say we forget the money and bet for something more interesting."

My partner leaned on the pommel of his saddle and looked at Poncho. "What do you have in mind Poncho?"

Poncho gave a big grin and answered. "Let's say if I win you ride with me as one of my men for six months. If you should win I give you the man Popeye. You can then do what you want with him with no questions asked.

I heard Buffole whisper to Shag. "Are you sure you can beat him Shag?" Shag snorted a yes as he pawed the ground with one of his front hoofs. That was all my partner needed to know as he said. "Poncho you have a deal." The two men shook hands and slowly rode to the starting line.

It was dark by now and we could barely see the flicker of the two torches that marked the starting line. As they rode toward the starting line the last quarter of a mile was lined with the people of Poncho's traveling army and they were holding torches and cheering for their leader.

As the two contestants came into sight Poncho was leading by a full length. Shag was coming up fast and Poncho's horse was doing its best as it tried to hold its lead. The closer they came to the finish line the stamina of Shag was just coming into his stride. Poncho's horse gave it all he could but the distance favored my two partners.

Shag crossed the finish line a full two lengths ahead of Poncho and his horse.

I had a bad feeling about Shag winning this race. Poncho did not seem like the sort of man that would take losing in stride. The men dismounted and Poncho's horse was lathered in sweat. Shag was breathing a little faster than normal but he was still in darn good shape for just having finished a one mile race.

Poncho was walking towards Buffole and I was glad that he had shed all his weapons before the race to save weight. My partner had done the same so my best hope was for a battle of fists instead of a shoot out.

Poncho came up close to Buffole and threw his arms around him giving him a great big bear hug. A big Smile crossed Poncho's face as he said loud enough for all to hear. "Buffole it was a good race. I thought I had you beaten until that last moment. Maybe I should buy that buffalo from you he is much better than a horse."

My partner accepted the hug and stepped back sliding his hand into a hand shake with Poncho. Then almost in a whisper that my canine ears picked up I heard my partner say. "Poncho a buffalo is best for the long run. Most horses tire out after about a half of a mile. That horse of yours is a good one he almost beat my Shag. You keep that horse and I'll keep my buffalo. It was a good race amigo."

Two nice looking senorita's greeted the two men and handed them jugs of mescal. Poncho slapped one of the ladies on the rear and said. "Inez you keep my friend Buffole company tonight. Treat him well and see he get's anything he wants. Buffole in the morning I will have your prize for you. Tonight you drink with us and enjoy the festivities."

We decided to do as Poncho suggested. There was a foot race between two of Poncho's men and the betting was heavy. We placed a bet on the lanky skinny fella to win. His opponent was hefty and it looked like a buffalo against a horse. The race was one hundred yards. When it was over we had lost ten dollars. Much like Shag against the horse the bigger of the two racers came on strong at the finish line and won the race.

Inez was the young lady that was now to accompany us. She took us under her wing and kept us feeling safe amongst all the wild activity going on around us. Neither Buffole nor I spoke Spanish so it would not be too difficult for us to find ourselves in a bad situation with no way to talk our way out of it. Luckily for us Inez spoke English and Spanish equally well.

We soon found ourselves as spectators to a knife throwing contest. One of the men asked Buffole to give it a try. With Inez as our translator and with the man gesturing and pushing us to the throwing line we got the point. Buffole was no knife thrower so I knew this would prove to be interesting. With everyone gesturing and giving him pointers Buffole finally took the knife and threw it at the target. The knife hit just off center of the bulls eye. Unfortunately the knife hit butt first which got a lot of laughs, hoots and hollers from the spectators. As if my partner wasn't embarrassed enough I followed him to the next contest with my tail between my legs. When your partners if one of you does something to embarrass' himself we both take the blame. Any way the contestants were moving from knives to machetes and a machete throwing Buffole would not be safe to be around.

At the edge of the camp some of the men had set up empty bottles for a target shooting contest. Handguns were being used and each man took his turn with the gun he carried. Once again the Mexicans took Poncho's advice to make their guest feel welcome and they asked Inez to let Buffole know that they expected him to join in on the contest. Five dollars was put in the pot as an entry fee. Winner take all. Buffole is a fair shot but good enough to win a shooting contest I had my doubts. But we were game and it would give my partner a little more practice before we faced our sworn enemy Popeye.

There were six bottles set up at varying heights and distances. One bottle for each bullet of a six gun. Buffole was the fifth shooter out of twelve. The first shooter hit three bottles, the second and third shooters hit five bottles, shooter four took out all six bottles and the poor young boy whose job was to run over and set up new bottles after each round was looking exhausted. Buffole got five hits and we were now officially out of the running for first place. We stayed and watched until the end and the number four shooter took first place.

A glance at the moons position in the sky told us it was nearing morning. We mingled amongst the different groups of people. By this time many had already retired for the night. A fairly large number of the men and even some of the women were passed out from too much liquor. A few were doing things that my partner and I felt should not be done out in the open. At least all the children had been hustled off to bed by this time.

Buffole told Inez he would like to call it a night. We had a job to do in the morning and it would be best if my partner was not to hung over and had a descent night's sleep. Inez smiled and wrapped her arm around Buffole's arm as she led us back to our tent. Buffole collapsed on the cot. I could tell he was light headed from the mescal and as for me I was dog tired.

Inez had a questioning look on her face. She looked at Buffole lying on the cot and finally asked. "Buffole I'm here to make you happy. Poncho told me to give you anything you want. Do you not want me?"

I could tell that this caught my partner completely by surprise. I must say I was curious to hear his answer. Inez was young, very pretty and she expected Buffole to have his way with her.

Buffole sat up like a bolt of lightning had hit him. Suddenly he seemed to be completely sober and fully aware of what was happening. It was rather surprising to see a man half passed out and drunk regain his senses so fast.

His hand rubbed the stubble on his chin as he searched for just the right words. "Inez you're a beautiful young lady. Now I ain't meaning no disrespect and your offer is awful tempting but I got me my own set of morals. Sort of like a code of the west. I don't lie, I don't kill unless it is self defense, I respect women and I don't make love to a woman unless I figure I'm going to marry her and settle down."

It was hard to say if Inez looked surprised or hurt as she spoke. "I thought all American cowboys just took woman when they wanted one. I hear them talk of the whore's in the saloons and brothels in your western towns. Are you not a cowboy?"

I looked at Buffole as I had to wonder how he was going to answer. "Most folks consider a cowboy to be someone who rides the range, fixes fence, rounds up cows and brands them. They also tend to have a lonely life and I suppose any kind of love they can get from anywhere is the best they can hope for. I'm not that kind of cowboy. But ma'am if milking dairy cows in Minnesota is considered being a cowboy then yup I'm a cowboy. I also like to think I'm a gentleman and how about you I have a little arrangement. You sleep here on this cot and Sven and I will curl up on a blanket on the ground. Poncho will think you made me happy and by doing this for me I will be happy and no one has to be any the wiser as to what went on in here."

Inez smiled and gave my partner a kiss on the cheek. She even reached down and gave me a pat on the head. She curled up on the cot and we made our bed on the ground. She looked over at us and said. "Buffole I think you are a real cowboy and a gentleman to."

CHAPTER 19

We awoke to the aroma of something that smelled awful good. Inez had been up since who knows when and had fixed us breakfast. She even thought of me and had scrounged up a bowl of goat's milk to add to my already scrumptious serving of fried eggs and tortillas filled with meat and peppers. Buffole and I are not too fond of peppers but as luck would have it these were rather mild and we ate them to be polite.

Inez insisted that we have our breakfast outside while she tidied up our little living quarters. We went outside and found a couple of beat up chairs to sit on. My partner put my plate on the chair seat for me and we ate while enjoying the morning sunshine. The camp was just beginning to stir and a number of tired and inebriated people both men and women were zigzagging paths to their respective living areas.

A bugle call sounded revelry and a mad dash of men rushed past us. It was almost comical if not a little sad that many of the men were still half dressed and doing their best to clothe themselves as they sped by us. The most fun was watching those men who were busy trying to put on their pants while running. A few actually got dressed on the run. Most of them fell flat on their faces or did a few small barrel rolls with their arms and legs flailing in the air.

Buffole and I waited until the soldiers had passed and then we got up and followed to see what all the commotion was about. Poncho and his officers were standing on a wooden table that had been set up for a review of the troops. At least Poncho and his officers were dressed up and looked very presentable compared to the troops that did their slovenly best to stand at attention.

Poncho walked the line like a good General should and inspected his troops. We heard him order some of the men to tuck in their shirts, clean that rifle, stand up straight and don't drink so much before inspection. He also added in a few personnel notes such as Jose has your wife had her baby yet? Poco how's the wound on your arm is it healing well? Raul have you made an honest woman out of your mistress yet? It was obvious this was not the best disciplined army in the world but everyone seemed to be loyal to Poncho and to the ideal of a free Mexico.

Poncho saw us standing off to the side and came over to greet us. "Good morning amigo and my little furry one. Inez did she take good care of you? Have you had breakfast? Come with me I have something for you. Never let it be said that Poncho Villa does not keep his word."

Buffole gave quick answers yes to Poncho's questions. I thought it was nice that the General took time to include me in his good morning greeting. We walked for a distance away from the main camp to a sandy section of land behind a small hill. The first thing we saw were two soldiers sitting on the ground as guards. The men quickly stood up and did the best they could to straighten themselves up and look like soldiers when they saw Poncho.

What the soldiers had been guarding now came into view. Popeye's head was sticking up from the sand. Ants were crawling around his eyes, ears and mouth. His face was swollen from the ant's bites and the hot sun was already starting to blister his lips. The rest of his body had been buried in the sand.

Poncho knelt next to Popeye's head and looked him over. As he stared at Popeye he said. "Buffole here is my promise to you. I felt it best we bury his body. That way he does not smell so bad. In all my years I do not think I ever met a man who smelled of death and stench as bad as our friend here. It is your choice to do with him as you want."

Poncho got up off the ground and walked over to one of his soldiers. "Henry let me borrow your machete if you will." Henry pulled the machete from his belt and handed it to Poncho. Poncho walked over to Buffole and offered him the machete. "Buffole my friend this would be a quick and easy way to take your revenge. One swift slash and it will be over with. Popeye's body is already buried so we need to dig only a tiny grave to dispose of his head. Or if it pleases you we could put his head on a pole in the camp as a warning to others. What he did to your family and to the many women he raped and murdered will be a good lesson to others not to do the same. What do you say my friend? Would you like to chop off Popeye's Head?"

Buffole took the machete from Poncho and ran his finger along the blades edge. A small drop of blood fell into the sand and quickly disappeared into the heat of the ground. "Poncho your offer is very tempting. I appreciate that you are a man of your word. I am also a man of my word. I told you I wanted a chance to seek my revenge on Popeye. It is to be him against me. I cannot in good conscious kill a man in cold blood. If you will do me a favor have your men dig him up. Then give him some time to get his strength back. If he is better tonight I suggest we give your camp a real show. Popeye and I will have a gunfight man to man. Twenty paces with pistols. If he wins he goes free, if I win. Popeye will be dead."

Poncho laughed out loud and slapped Buffole on the back. "I like you amigo. You are a man of fair play. I think maybe God will be on your side and you will win. If not maybe the Devil will favor Popeye. The priests you know they say God works in mysterious ways. Tonight we find out if God is mischievous. Henry, Poco, you two dig up our friend and get him some food and drink and by the saints give him a bath and clean clothes. If he has to be in our camp at least let him smell good before he dies."

We went back to our tent and found Inez waiting for us. She was full of questions when we arrived. "Buffole I heard gossip in the camp that you are here to kill a man. Just a few moments ago they said the General offered you a machete to put an end to the scoundrel that killed your family and you refused. Now it seems that you want to give this bad man a fair chance to defend himself. Why would you do that?"

"Inez it may seem strange to you but I have a code I live by. Doing what is right and fair are very important to me. I figure if I am in the right I'll win, if I am in the wrong I lose. Giving Popeye a chance is just something I feel I have to do. I've set myself up as judge and jury in this case and if I kill him I figure right was on my side."

"Buffole you have been kind to me and treated me like a lady. I have a favor to ask of you. My fiancé his name is Justin I have told him you are a good man so he is not jealous of our time together. At first when General Villa gave me to you I thought Justin would try to kill you. Now he understands and the two of us are hoping you will do something for us before you leave here. If you should die in your fight with Popeye I promise I will take care of your body and pray for you."

"Just what can I do for you Inez?"

"General Villa I think he likes and respects you. He will take your advice in this matter. Justin and I wish to get married. I am afraid if we ask for permission the General will say yes only if he can spend the first night of our wedding with me. Justin and I are Catholic and this would not be a proper thing to do in the eyes of the church. If you talk to the General he will do what you say."

"Inez I give you my word I will talk with the General. I think I can convince him to let you two marry without his being involved in any way that would be a sin against the church. You best spend some time with your Justin. Sven and I have a few things to do before tonight."

We watched Inez hurry away with a smile on her face. Hopefully Buffole could convince the General to let the lovebirds get married and have a honeymoon away from this war. For now we had decided to spend some time by ourselves to get mentally prepared for our showdown with Popeye.

At the corral we found Shag. He was surrounded by children and they were scratching his ears, giving him rub downs, feeding him and making sure he had fresh water. He had become a celebrity to the young ones in the camp. He rolled his eyes when he saw us. I knew he would deny liking all this attention but it was easy to see he was enjoying it.

"I sure am glad to see you two" he said as we approached. He put his big head down by me and we did a nose to nose touch hello. Buffole told the kids he needed to take Shag for a ride. He explained the big buffalo needed exercise and being cooped up was just not in his nature. The kids were more than eager to help get Shag saddled up and ready. We rode away to the waves of the children. Of course we had to promise we would be back soon.

We rode up into the mountains. It was a beautiful day and Shag was happy to be out in the great open spaces. Trees, rocks, grass and streams all seemed to have a new beauty which we had often taken for granted in our past travels. Once we caught Shag up on the Popeye saga we all rode in silent thought. Each of us had our minds on the outcome of the upcoming showdown between Popeye and Buffole. In our hearts and minds we knew right was on our side. Yet there is always a chance that something could go wrong. If evil has a champion it is the Devil himself and there was always a chance that Satan would make an appearance. We settled for a rest by a mountain stream. The cool clear water tasted like the lips of a sweet maiden or so Buffole told us.

I updated Shag to the developments which had taken place as far as Popeye was concerned. As a leader of buffalo for many years Shag understood that sometimes you need to do what is right in your own mind to have a clear conscious. I felt the same way and I believe that having us all in agreement that Buffole's actions were the right decision to make we all felt whatever happened next would be for the best.

For the next few hours we mostly sat in silence contemplating what a great world we lived in. When you are in the wilderness it is never really silent. The breeze rustling the leaves, the sound of a lizard scurrying across a hot rock, the song of the birds or the creaking of a tree branch are all things we usually take for granted. When you don't talk and just listen all of the sounds of nature are as beautiful a song as any music a man could ever make. These are sounds that make a man relax and appreciate the things around him. Sounds of life carry on no matter what a man does.

Before we knew it we needed to go back to the camp and prepare for our final meeting with Popeye. Shag asked to be picketed near enough to see what was happening. He told me that if he was near and we had to make a quick escape he would be ready.

The ride back to Poncho's camp was uneventful. We took our time and the blazing heat of the sun made us wish for those cool fall days when we lived in Minnesota. When we finished with Popeye our plan would be to head back up north. Maybe a stop at Caldero del Diablo might be part of our plan. At least I was kind of hoping for that as I missed Lena. Whether or not my partner would be in agreement I was not too sure. I figured he had to wonder if Krystal had recovered. Then there was Liza. He loved them both and he might just want to avoid having to make a decision. For now we had more important things to think about. Things like staying alive. If we won our battle would Poncho just let us ride away? Time would tell.

We rode into camp and it must have been siesta time. There was very little activity and a lot of the men were sleeping in the shade. We saw so many men with their sombreros tilted to cover their faces from the sun that it looked like a field of giant mushrooms had sprouted from the ground.

The showdown would be near the same place as the men had run foot races the night before so Buffole picketed Shag within seeing distance. The spot Buffole choose was well shaded by a large tree and plenty of fresh green grass was growing there for Shag to nibble on.

We returned to our tent and it was nice to see that Inez was nowhere in sight. We both felt more relaxed without a woman hanging around taking our attention away from what we needed to concentrate on. Buffole sat on the cot and checked over his LeMat and his Colt .22 caliber guns. He cleaned the barrel and checked the trigger and hammer to make sure everything was in proper working order. A misfire or jammed bullet could mean death during the showdown.

Once my partner was satisfied that his weapons were in top notch working condition he lay on the cot for a nap. I took my position under the cot and lay facing the entrance to the tent. Buffole knew he could rest easy as long as I was on guard.

The sun was setting and I could hear increased activity going on in the camp. I walked over and stuck my head out of the tent flap to see what was happening. Men were lighting torches and the women were setting up a long table for a feast. Poncho was walking towards our tent. "Buffole" I whispered "Time to get up Poncho's coming this way."

Buffole was sitting on the edge of the cot and had just reached for his gun belt as Poncho opened the flap to our tent and invited himself in.

Poncho made no effort to voice his request. "Buffole my friend come it's time for us to have a feast before your showdown with Popeye. My whole army and all their wives and children have gathered to watch. It is to be an entertainment which will live in the stories of my people for generations to come. This will be a real cowboy showdown presented by the one and only General Poncho Villa. Before we go I need you to give me your weapons."

I glanced outside and two of Poncho's men were there with rifles at the ready just in case the issue needed force. Quickly I told my partner to do what he was asked. Buffole un-holstered his gun and handed it to Poncho butt first. Poncho smiled and said. "Buffole my friend I know you have more than just this one gun to hand over to me." Buffole pulled the knife out of its sheath that was behind his back and tucked under his shirt so as to be out of sight. Poncho took the knife and smiling repeated his last statement. Buffole my friend I believe you have at least one more weapon." Buffole pulled his shirt up and handed Poncho the light weight Colt .22 caliber single action revolver that was tucked into the waist band of his pants.

Now it was Buffole's turn to smile and ask. "Poncho you have all my weapons. Tell me my friend why are you disarming me? Did we not have an agreement that you would let me have a fair fight with Popeye?"

Poncho opened the flap of the tent and handed the weapons to his guards for safe keeping. He put his arm around Buffole's shoulder and led him out of the tent as he said. "Amigo it is not so much that I do not trust you but there is no need to tempt fate. I told you in the beginning that Popeye should have a chance to tell his side of the story and as you know I am a man of my word. Popeye has also been disarmed and I thought it would be nice if the three of us sat together at the feast tonight. This way you can hear Popeye's side of the story before the showdown. I really do not care if Popeye is guilty or not as you have said to me in the past 'right' will prevail. So whoever is still alive after the showdown I must figure was the one telling the truth. It is a simple but effective plan don't you agree?"

We walked to the table which had been set up with every type of Mexican food and drink you could imagine. Poncho took his seat at the head of the table. On his left sat two armed guards with Popeye seated between them. Buffole and I were seated on Poncho's right side with an armed guard on each side of us. Popeye glared at us as if he thought he might kill us with his stare. Buffole did his best to stay calm and relaxed. When the showdown came being relaxed and calm could be the deciding factor when it comes to staying alive. I could tell Popeye was nervous as a cat in a tub of water and for my side this was a good thing. Being scared would mean he might make mistakes that could cost him his life.

Poncho grabbed a turkey leg from his plate and took a bite as the grease dribbled down his chin he looked at Popeye and said. "Popeye you've been riding with my army for awhile now. Your reputation for cruelty is somewhat well known but you do get your job done. I feel I owe you a chance to tell your side of the story as to how Buffole's wife and child died. You have also been accused of shooting Buffole's lady friend in the back which is not a very gentlemanly way to shoot someone. What have you got to say in your defense?"

Popeye had sweat beading up on his face as he spoke. "Defense. I need no defense. The man you call Buffole is a greenhorn dairy farmer from Minnesota. My partners Bully, Skinner and I were just keeping his wife company after he went off and left her in Indian country. Her and the boy were left defenseless it was just a good thing me and my partners came along when we did. Ole came riding into camp all hell bent for leather and started accusing me and my friends of all sorts of low down things. Next thing I know he pulled a gun and shot Bully. Then that buffalo of his came charging into camp and crushed Skinner by ramming him into the side of a wagon. His wife and boy was still alive when I high tailed it out of there to save my own skin."

"As for me shooting his lady friend I ain't never even seen her. The whole thing is a pack of lies fabricated by this want a be gunslinger to make a name for himself. General Villa you are a smart man. Who are you going to believe? Me one of your loyal soldiers or some two bit stranger that ain't even smart enough to ride a horse."

Poncho sat back and wiped the grease from his chin with the back of his hand. He picked up a bottle of mescal and took a long swig. "Popeye I know you were in the town where Buffole says the lady was shot in the back. You were with two of my men and they both said you told them that you fired the shot into Buffole's window. Maybe you thought you shot Buffole, maybe not. You might have shot the lady just to punish Buffole for hunting you. Knowing that you lied about shooting the lady I am not so sure you tell the truth about Buffole's wife and boy. I think we let you two have a showdown. That way whoever is alive at the end will be the one who is telling the truth. Let's all drink and eat and have a good time. In one half an hour we will see who tells the truth."

I was standing up with my fur on my back raised and a low growl coming from inside of me as I listened to Popeye tell his lies. Buffole put his hand on my back to calm me down. I heard him whisper to me. "Settle down partner the truth will prevail in the end."

Inez appeared behind Buffole and whispered to him as she filled his glass with beer. "Is there anything I can do to help?"

Buffole whispered back. "Keep Popeye's glass full of mescal. The dunker he gets the better for me."

"No problem. My sister Sandra she is keeping that side of table supplied with food and drink. I will tell her to get Popeye good and liquored up."

Sandra did her job very well. She started flirting with Popeye and telling him what a brave man he was. Luckily his time in the ground when he was buried up to his neck and then a good scrubbing down in a bath had finally alleviated the usual stench that his body always used to have. From where I sat and with my canine sense of smell I could still sense the stench of death coming from every pore in his body. With Sandra building up his ego his nervousness turned to vanity as he started to brag about the many men he had killed and the many women and girls he had raped.

Poncho slowed down his own drinking to listen to Popeye's tales. The smile on the Generals face soon turned to a look of disgust. With Popeye filled with liquor and puffed up with pride Poncho caught him off guard. "Popeye you sound as if you are a great man. Was killing Buffole's wife and child and shooting his lady friend enjoyable for you?"

Popeye smiled at Buffole and then he leaned towards Poncho and in a drunken whisper that was loud enough for Buffole and I to hear him he said. "It was extremely enjoyable." Buffole held his composure but I could see the anger ready to burst from him. As for me my partner quickly gripped a handful of fur behind my neck and held me in place. If it was not for that I would have leapt across the table and tore Popeye's juggler from his neck.

With a serious look in his eye Poncho said to Buffole. "Amigo if you were not here to kill this vermin I would gladly do it for you. Are you sure that you do not want to torture him so that his death is slow and painful?"

I told Buffole to take up Poncho's offer. If anyone deserved a slow painful, agonizing death it was Popeye. "No Sven" he whispered "We'll give these people what they came to see. A real life western showdown. You know what to do when the time comes."

Yes I knew what to do and I would be standing next to Poncho and Inez to do my duty. I also knew the trick we used was only good for one try. If Popeye was not killed by my partner's first shot then Buffole was on his own.

The General's anger at Popeye was getting the best of him. He rose from the table knocking his food and drink over. He pulled a gun from his holster and fired a shot into the air. Everyone stopped talking and looked at the General.

Poncho slowly slipped his gun back into its holster. He looked at everyone to make sure they were paying attention to him. "Guard's take Buffole and Popeye to the showdown area and give them back their weapons."

Sandra followed Popeye over to the table where the weapons had been placed. As Popeye buckled on his gun belt Inez picked up and handed him his skinning knife, a hideaway derringer and she did a quick check of the cylinder of his .45 caliber Remington revolver for him to make sure it was loaded. Filled with the confidence of liquor Popeye hoisted up his pants and made his way to the center of the showdown area.

Buffole strapped on his gun belt and he slipped the LeMat grapeshot revolver into the holster. Then to my surprise he slid the Colt .22 pistol behind his belt and into the front of his pants. He walked slowly but deliberately to the showdown area. If he had any intention of using the Colt it would be akin to taking a peashooter to a gunfight. I could only hope the Colt was there as a backup weapon in case the LeMat might misfire or jam.

Inez, Sandra and I took our places next to the General. We stood off to the side of the showdown area as the guards lined the two contestants up back to back. Popeye's gun hand was fidgeting as the General began the count to twenty paces. Buffole seemed overly calm as if he had made up his mind that he was in no danger. Or maybe he figured this was the end of the trail for him. That .22 caliber Colt was still racing through my mind. This is one time my partner should have told me what his plan of action was going to be.

The General had his two holsters crisscrossed across his chest. He pulled out one of his revolvers and fired it into the air to quiet the crowd of on lookers. I could see Shag in the distance as he stood in the shade of a large tree. He was watching the proceedings and I could tell he was agitated by the way his front hoof was pawing the ground.

Once there was silence the General shouted out the rules of the engagement. "Popeye, Buffole this is to be a fair fight. The rules are simple. Each if you will advance one step as I count to twenty. Once you hear me say twenty you will turn and draw your guns. The survivor will be free to do whatever he wants after the duel is over."

With his guns holstered the General notched his thumbs into his gun belt and puffed himself up to look as important as he possibly could. Then in Spanish the count began "Uno, dos, tres, cuatro, cinco. The count was at diecinueve which was only nineteen in English when Popeye turned and drew his gun. Inez screamed for Buffole to look out. Her scream was just enough to distract Popeye and his first shot at Buffole went wild as my partner turned to defend himself.

Buffole was now facing Popeye but he still had not drawn his gun. Popeye steadied himself and took aim as my partner started walking towards him. I barked and once again Popeye was gullible enough to fall for the distraction that I caused him as his second shot missed its target.

Buffole kept walking forward towards Popeye. With his opponent coming straight at him Popeye lost his composure and his hand was shaking as he squeezed off his third shot. Once again his shot missed the advancing figure of Buffole.

Buffole had covered about ten paces as he kept walking towards Popeye. Finally my partner drew the Colt .22 and he fired from the hip. The bullet hit Popeye in the shoulder just as he squeezed off his fourth shot at Buffole. My partner kept walking forward as his body gave a slight jerk to one side. I could see the side of Buffole's shirt turning a crimson shade of red from a bullet wound.

Using his hand from his good arm Popeye grabbed his gun hand to hold it steady as the blood trickled from his injured shoulder. My partner kept walking straight forward his gun still at his hip as he squeezed off the second shot from his Colt. The Colt's .22 caliber bullet thudded into Popeye's stomach just as he pulled the trigger on his fifth shot. The bullet left his gun but where ever it went it was not into Buffole.

Popeye dropped to his knees as he held his free hand over the gunshot wound in his stomach. The red liquid of life seeping between his fingers. Buffole was now standing only a few feet away from Popeye's wounded body. Popeye still on his knees sat back on his heels as a slow trickle of blood dripped from his mouth. He raised his gun with a shaking hand and aimed it at my partner. Buffole just stood there with his Colt at his side. It seemed as if he was going to let Popeye shoot him dead on the spot and not even try to defend himself. The crowd of onlookers was deadly quiet. Popeye pulled the trigger of his Remington and everyone heard a loud click. The gun had misfired on its last bullet.

Buffole did not even flinch at the sound of the click against a bad cartridge. My partner raised the Colt and pointed it at Popeye's head. Popeye still sitting back on his heels looked defiantly at Buffole as he asked. "A Colt .22 caliber. Why would you use a gun that would most likely not kill on the first shot?

Buffole gave Popeye a serious look and answered. "Popeye I've waited a long time to get my revenge on you. Using this Colt revolver was my way to make you suffer at least a little like you made me suffer. My first shot was just to get your attention. The second shot was to slow you down. The last shot will kill you. Except the last shot will not be from a .22 caliber Colt." Ole slowly lowered the Colt and slid it back into the front of his belt. He reached down and pulled the LeMat from its holster. The click of the LeMat's trigger told my ears that it was primed to shoot of the grapeshot barrel which in all reality was a mini shotgun. Ole pointed the LeMat at Popeye's head. He cited the barrel to put the shot right between Popeye's eyes. "This should do the trick." He said as he pulled the trigger. The blast from the shotgun barrel and the load of buckshot contained there-in exploded Popeye's head into a mass of unrecognizable flesh. When the smoke from the gunpowder cleared we could all see the headless body of Popeye still sitting on his haunches.

The crowd roared with approval and soon they were singing and dancing at the death of a very bad man. Buffole walked over to me and picked me up for a big cowboy hug. I gave him a lick on the cheek to show my love for him. The General slapped Buffole on the back as he congratulated him and said. "Buffole my friend you have done a good job. I think God maybe he was with you when Popeye's gun misfired on his last shot. You should stay here with me and I will make you my second in command. Someday you and me we could rule all of Mexico."

Buffole put me down on the ground and he said to the General. "General you have been a good friend and I appreciate the offer of joining your army but I have places I need to go. I would like to ask a favor of you before I leave."

The General smiled and called for some Mescal as he answered. "Anything you want is yours amigo. You just ask Poncho and I shall grant your wish."

Buffole took Inez by her arm as Inez's fiancé stood next to her. He gave Poncho a serious look as he spoke. "General, Inez and this young men wish to be wed. They seek your blessing. I have heard that you often spend the first night of a couple's marriage with the bride as a gift of yourself to them. I think maybe as a favor to me you might let Inez and her fiancé keep their wedding night and all future nights to themselves like the bible commands them to do. They are good God fearing Catholics and it is their fondest wish to uphold the sacred vows of the church in their marriage. Will you grant me that favor?"

The General stood still for a moment and those around looked worried as if they thought the General might be upset. All of a sudden the General smiled and said. "Buffole you are an honorable man. I think maybe you make a promise to Inez. We will have their wedding tonight and I swear to you that no one will ever disturb their vows to each other." Poncho then gave an order. "Someone go and find a priest for these two so they can get married. Inez you go and get your wedding dress. As for your Fiancé he best get cleaned up and ready to be the groom."

Inez hesitated and asked Buffole about the wound in his side. She pulled up my partner's shirt and the bullet had just made a slight crease on his side. Buffole told her it was just a scratch and it would heal on its own. She took a scarf from around her neck and wrapped it around my partner's waist tying it tight to stop any further bleeding. Buffole kissed her on her cheek and thanked her for doctoring him up. Then he said. "Inez you heard the General now off with you. You've a wedding to attend to."

With the wedding plans in action Poncho took us over to a table for more drinks. He raised his glass in a toast. "To Buffole he has by

God's grace eliminated an evil one from our midst. I know in my heart that God had a hand in this confrontation or else Popeye's gun would not have misfired on his last bullet."

Buffole accepted the toast. Then he said to me. "Sven I doubt that God had a hand in saving a sinner like me, that misfire was just plain old dumb luck. I think I was ready to die for that gut shot I gave Popeye would have let him bleed a slow and agonizing death. I figured my job was done and if it was my time to go well then it was my time."

That statement sort of riled me as I answered him. "Listen here partner you had no right to risk your life like that. I and Shag need you in our lives. If you ever do something so stupid again you'll answer to me."

That little tirade of mine put Buffole in his place. He gently put his hand on my head and said. "You're right Sven I was wrong. Maybe God did step in on this one. You and me and Shag will be riding this land for a long, long time together. I think it might be best we ride on out of here now while the General is in good spirits."

Buffole told the General that we needed to hit the trail. He asked Poncho to have his men tie Popeye's body to a horse and let us take the body with us for disposal as we saw fit. Poncho thought it was a strange request but he gave the order and his men quickly carried it out.

Buffole and Poncho shook hands and then Poncho grabbed my partner and gave him a big bear hug. "Be careful my friend and remember you will always be welcome in Poncho's camp. The General then picked me up and gave me a kiss on the forehead as he said. "Sven you take care of Buffole for Poncho ok?"

We saddled up Shag and one of Poncho's men handed us the reins of the horse that was carrying Popeye's body. The body was wrapped in a blanket and tied securely to the horse's saddle. As we were about to ride away Inez dressed in a beautiful wedding gown came running towards us.

Out of breath she started talking. "Buffole, Sven you don't leave without saying goodbye to me. You should stay for the wedding."

Buffole looked at her with a look that a father might give his daughter. "Inez you look beautiful. You go get married and have many babies. It's best I leave now while the General is in a party mood. I'll think of you often."

As Buffole sat in the saddle Inez reached up and took his hand. She pressed a .45 caliber bullet into his palm and said. "The people they think God blessed you when he made Popeye's gun misfire. I think they are right but God had a little help. Sandra slipped this bullet from Popeye's gun when she helped him get ready for the showdown. God he works in mysterious ways. This time he worked through Sandra to save the life of a good man. God bless the three of you." She kissed Buffole's hand and then ran back to her people.

CHAPTER 20

We rode away from the noise of the wedding party and settled into the lull of Shags body as it swayed us off in to the distance. The quiet and peacefulness of the country devoid of people soon lulled our minds into a security that we enjoyed. The three of us together with no serious worries to cloud our thoughts.

The area we were crossing was dry and only a few cactus and scrub brush dotted the landscape. Occasionally we rode along with a visiting tumble weed. We had packed up a lot of water so thirst would not be an issue. The sun was blazing like a prairie fire by mid day. When night came we made camp amongst some boulders and I scouted the area to make sure no rattlesnakes, lizards, scorpions or gila monsters invited themselves in to our camp. Buffole untied Popeye and let him thud down to the earth. The pack horse whose name was Star was happy to finally have the 'dead' weight released from his back. Popeye was left at the edge of our camp as he was smelling sort of reek. Come to think about it he smelled about the same when he was still alive.

None of us had talked much since we left Poncho's camp. We had left his camp late in the day and made our first nights stay after only a few hours. Now it was our second night out and Shag and I were curious as to just why we were hauling a dead man around with us. Shag was lying down near the campfire and I was close to his side for the extra warmth his big body generated. Our partner was sitting across from us with a cup of hot coffee in his hands trying to keep warm in the chill of the night. I finally asked the question. "Buffole would you care to tell Shag and I why we have Popeye with us and just what do you plan to do with him?"

Buffole took a sip of his coffee and got up to fix his bedroll. He lay down and covered up. Finally he answered my question. "Tomorrow. Yes I think tomorrow I can show you what I have planned for Popeye." Shag slowly shook his mighty head and closed his eyes to sleep. I went over and curled up by my partner and we all called it a night.

The sun was rising in the sky and it pushed the cold air down around us. The fire was dying down so I ran out and gathered some fallen pieces of wood to get us a blaze going. Buffole put on some coffee and fried up some bacon and eggs that he had packed back at Poncho's camp. Shag didn't find much to eat and said he would be fine until we reached some good grass. By Shags estimate we had one more full day across the desert before we reached decent grazing land.

Buffole saddled up Shag and packed up our camp. The last thing he did was to saddle up Star and hoist Popeye's body across the saddle. He tied the two ends of the blanket that held Popeye's body down to the stirrups on Star's saddle so that the body would stay in place. Shag, Star and I hoped that Buffole would get rid of that stinking pile of rotting flesh before the day was out.

It was midday and Popeye was attracting company. Two buzzards had been circling and following us for about an hour. I said "Boys I think we have visitors that want some lunch."

Buffole looked up in the sky and we all stopped to watch the buzzards. Buffole got down off of Shag and he took me from my saddlebag and put me on the ground. He went over and untied the ropes that held Popeye in place on Star's saddle. He pushed the body from the saddle and it fell to the ground with a sickening thud. Buffole then untied the blanket from the body. He picked up the edge of the blanket and pulled hard so that Popeye's stinking body rolled out onto the desert sand. He looked to be a delectable treat for a buzzards feast. Popeye was face up, well he was sort of face up if he would have still had a face. Of course with Ole blowing his head off it was hard to tell. His body was already rotting from the heat so he was cooked warmed and ready for the buzzards to enjoy their meal.

Buffole took Star by the reins and led him over by Shag and me. We all walked about thirty yards away and then Buffole sat down on the ground looking at Popeye. In the sky above us the two buzzards continued to circle slowly making their way towards the ground. Slowly the circle got smaller and smaller as they descended. Finally they landed near Popeye's body. They looked at us and then at the sun cooked meal that was near them. Buffole spoke to the buzzards in a soft tone. "Go ahead and help yourselves I brought Popeye along so that he might at least do one good thing for the world. I figure feeding buzzards was the least he could offer after all the suffering he caused while he was alive."

Those buzzards must have understood because as soon as Buffole stopped talking they made their way over to Popeye. It did not take long before they were peeling huge chunks of Popeye's flesh to satisfy their hunger. Satisfied that Popeye finally served a useful purpose Buffole suggested we mount up and make our way North.

The next two days of riding were uneventful. On the third day we came upon a town built at the base of a mountain. There was a waterfall, well actually it was more of a stream with a six foot cascade of water falling onto the rocks below which then formed a small pool. The water did not exit from the pool so there must be an underground stream draining it off. The town sign seemed fitting for what we had just seen. The town was named Small Falls.

Our first stop was at a water trough so that Shag could get a good drink. Once Shag had his fill of water we walked over to the town livery stable. A young man was outside the stable with a blacksmiths apron on. He was pounding out a horseshoe as we walked up. We watched him for awhile and he was so engrossed in his work that he didn't notice us. Buffole kept shifting around to get his attention. We didn't want to startle him. You just can't be too careful around a man who is working with a red hot horseshoe.

Buffole cleared his throat as loud as he could and finally got the blacksmiths attention. "Howdy, sir my names Buffole and I would like to stable my buffalo here."

The blacksmith looked at Shag and slipped the toothpick in his mouth from one side to the other. "Ain't never had no buffalo in my stable before. That beast does any damage and you'll be responsible to pay for it. How long you staying?"

"Just one night, we'll be on our way early tomorrow morning." Answered my partner.

"My names Shane. It will cost you four bits in advance." He held out his hand and Buffole paid him. Shane then went back to pounding his horseshoe. We went into the barn and found a nice stall filled with hay for Shag. Buffole wiped him down and then he took our saddlebags and we left to find a place to get a drink and bed down for the night.

Shane just kept working when Buffole asked where we could go to get a drink. Not missing a beat on his horseshoe making he said. "Down the street take a left there's a saloon at the far end of the street and a hotel across the way if you need a place to sleep."

The saloon was nothing fancy and it was called the Small Falls Saloon according the faded sign over the door. It looked as if it had never seen a coat of paint and was weather gray with a few loose boards hanging here and there. The entrance had a batwing door. I said door as one was attached and the other one was on the floor leaning against a wall inside the saloon. The front window was fairly large but it was too dirty to see in or out of it. Inside was a player piano coated with dust for musical amusement, which by the looks of it there were no music lovers in this town. Three old men were sitting at one of the rough hewn table's playing cards for what looked to be very low stakes. The bar was a long board supported by two old whisky barrels on each end and one in the middle to keep it from sagging. A picture of a scantily clad woman hung on the wall behind the bar and a few antelope and deer heads hung on the other walls. Behind the bar was a shelf holding bottles of whisky and a barrel of beer was sitting on an old cut off tree stump. The glasses were at least cleaner than the rest of the place. The bartender was old and grizzled looking and he was a perfect match for the rest of the décor. His apron was filthy from spilled liquor and food. It also looked like it doubled as a wash rag and dish towel.

My partner lifted me up and set me down on the top of the bar. No one seemed to notice or care that a dog was on the bar. The Bartender asked what our poison was. Buffole ordered two shots of whisky one in a glass and the other in a bowl for me and two SvenBrew beers. The bartender said. "I've got Rye and warm home brewed beer that's what I got and that's what you get." Had to make you wonder why he asked what our poison was because it didn't seem to matter.

We had our fill of this friendly little establishment and as we turned to leave Buffole dropped a nickel in the old player piano. It started to play something that resembled music in an off key sort of way. The three men playing cards and the bartender stared at the piano as if they had never seen or heard it play before. By the coating of dust that covered it maybe they never had heard play before. My partner just smiled and I wagged my tail as we left the saloon. That little nickel we invested in the player piano sure did liven things up in that old saloon.

Across the street and a half block down stood the Small Falls Hotel. Buffole had our saddlebags over his shoulder and was not paying a lot of attention to our surroundings. He was tired and beat and just wanted a soft bed to sleep in. When he was like this I become the watch dog for any signs of trouble and he knew that so he could relax with me at his side.

We had just reached the entrance of the hotel when a poster that was hanging by the front door of the hotel caught my eye. I stopped dead in my tracks and stood staring at the words I was seeing. Buffole was about to open the hotel door when I stopped him. "Hey partner I think you should stop and read that poster by the door."

Buffole had to take a step back to see the poster. The center had a drawing of a women dressed in western buckskin clothing with two six shooters on her hips and a rifle held in her hands across her chest. The poster read. 'See them in Person, the Mother and Daughter team of Krystal and Jo. Acts of sharp shooter action and prose to warm the hearts of everyone. Coming soon to this location. Presented by the Pierce Players acting Troupe.'

I had to ask. "Well partner maybe we should stay here for a few days and take in the show?"

Buffole turned and entered the hotel and all he said was "I think we best stay the night and then hit the trail bright and early." As we checked in Buffole did ask when the show was coming to town.

The proprietor of the hotel had a surprised look on his face as he said. "Damn is that poster still hanging in front of the door? I plump forgot to take it down. I guess you didn't hear. They were scheduled to be here in two days but that ain't going to happen. I just got word from the telegraph office that Krystal and her daughter Jo were stopped during a stage robbery. They say it was some of the Luther gang that's been terrorizing the area for some time now. What they did to her and her daughter ain't something you would talk about in front of the female sex. When the gang finished having their way with them they shot both Krystal and her daughter in the head and then sent the stage on its way. Seems they wanted to make sure that everyone knew that anyone who messes with the Luther gang will meet up with a horrible death. Whether it's true or not I ain't so sure as there were three stages filled with them acting folk and someone said there were two mother daughter teams coming this way. Maybe I'll just leave that poster hanging up till I'm sure they ain't going to show.

I looked up at Buffole and had him ask about Lena.

Buffole was in shock but he did his best to speak without breaking down and crying. "I knew those two ladies and they was a pair of fine women. They always travelled with a little white dog named Lena. Did you hear if the Luther Gang killed the dog too?"

The proprietor rubbed his chin with his hand as he searched his brain for the answer. "Nope. Can't say I heard nothing about no dog."

That night my partner took out a pen and a paper and wrote a letter. "Dear Liza. I just heard a rumor that Krystal and Jo might have been bushwhacked. If it's true I'm sure the law can handle this one. Hanging is too good for the scoundrels that did this. I guess the Luther gang is still active and trying to take over the country but killing women in the west is way beyond just being robber barons and gunslingers. The man that told me said there were two mother and daughter acting teams traveling the stage route where the murders took place so I can only pray that Krystal and Jo are still safe."

"I finally tracked down Popeye and killed him. I did my best to make him suffer some and after he was dead I fed him to the buzzards. I sort of have a feeling that I should track down Krystal and Jo's killers if the rumor is true but I'm mighty tired of being a man hunter. Anyway it's just a rumor right now. If the law don't handle it I might have to take care of it myself."

"Sven, Shag and I are heading to Deadwood in the Dakota Territory to look up some old friends. Maybe we will do some prospecting for gold. I think of you a lot and Sven in his own way tells me he misses his buddy Einer. If Krystal, Jo and Lena are all right I would be pleased if you would let me know. If you wish to write back you can send a letter to the Deadwood Post Office for general delivery. Sincerely, Buffole."

I was for heading out and finding the Luther gang members that did this but maybe my partner was right. If there was any law worth while they should take care of this problem. Also we were not even sure if the ladies that were killed were Krystal and Jo. After all the man at the hotel didn't hear about a dog and one would think that if Lena was there she would have been mentioned in the holdup. At least I reminded my partner to ask about Lena in his letter to Liza.

When morning came we gathered our things together and Buffole left the letter with the hotel clerk to be mailed. We saddled up Shag and headed north. We told Shag what we had heard might of happened to Krystal, Jo and maybe even Lena. For the next few days none of us said very much. Three guys riding alone in the wilderness does not lend itself to much conversation. This was especially true of me for I had no idea what was on my partners mind as far as women were concerned. As for Shag and me our prospects of finding a female were not good but we were more open minded on the subject then Buffole was. He wanted to be alone with his memories which for now were more alive to him than the women he had left behind.

We rode the trail for a week with no other human contact. A routine had developed between the three of us. We reminisced about the days gone by. Shag with stories of buffalo herds that went on for as far as the eye could see. He told stories that had been passed down to him from generation to generation. Days when the buffalo was the king of all his domain. The buffalo had no real enemies until man came along. Sure there were occasional attacks by wolves and maybe even a hungry grizzly bear but usually they took only the sick or weak from a herd. It was sort of a way to eliminate those the herd could no longer care for. Then the Indians came and killed for food and clothing. The buffalo sort of understood the Indian at the time for he killed only what he needed to survive and the Indians respected the buffalo and even included him in their prayers. When horses came to the Indians the world of the buffalo changed. Now the Indians drove the herds over cliffs killing dozens or maybe even hundreds at a time. If too many buffalo were killed some were left to rot in the sun and be scavenged by predators. This the buffalo did not understand. When the white man came with his guns and killed for meat to feed the railroads the buffalo saw their numbers dwindle. Next the white men killed for hides or for sport. The Indians started to follow the lead of the white man and sold hides to the traders. From this point on the buffalo had an enemy who was vicious and relentless in killing indiscriminately. Shag was afraid that in the future the buffalo would be no more. He and his kind were headed for extinction. It was a sad but true story. Buffole and I told Shag that someday the three of us would settle down and find Shag a wife and he could start his own herd and be forever protected by us and our children and our children's children. I think Shag liked that idea very much.

Buffole told us stories of growing up on a small dairy farm that his grandfather had built from the ground up. The typical American dream. One milk cow that eventually became a herd and then turned into a full scale milking operation that supplied milk, cream and butter to three small surrounding towns. For Shags sake our story of why we came west was also thrown into the mix. It was fun to hear of Buffole's childhood. He was a typical boy playing in the woods and streams near his home. Things had changed a lot since we came west. Now Buffole had a reputation as a hunter of men and maybe even a gunslinger. It was a reputation he would prefer to shake. Until he could bury that reputation he was reluctant to let anyone new into his life. Now I knew why he had walked away from Liza and Krystal.

As for me my life was about as normal as most dogs. Buffole was there when I was born and came to see me every two weeks until I was old enough to come live with him. He's the only parent I really know. Sure I saw some rough times. Watching Buffole's wife and my human brother get killed was traumatic. Now days I watch after Buffole and I am not just his canine son I'm his partner. After all how many dogs get to communicate with their humans. Someday we'll settle down but I figure for now there are a lot of adventures waiting for Shag and us.

The nights were getting cooler and the rolling plains of the Dakota Territory now loomed before us. A few more days and we should reach Deadwood. Mountains and thick stands of trees were slowing us down some but they made for a beautiful sight. We saw smoke from a fire in the distance. Knowing the code of the west we figured anyone who let their smoke from their campsite be seen was either inviting in strangers or very stupid and letting their location be known to Indians or bandits. In the case of the first option that person must be very brave. As per the second option, well that was already covered under the heading of very stupid or maybe just plain ignorant.

We rode up to the camp and a big man dressed in a plaid shirt and jeans was tending the fire. He looked to be a lumberjack. Shag shook his head and snorted as he looked behind the man at what appeared to be his transportation. What we saw startled us all. A huge saddle was on the ground next to the biggest bluest Oxen we had ever seen.

The lumberjack stood up and walked towards us with his hand extended in greeting. He shook hands with Buffole and introduced himself. "Hi my names Paul, Paul Bunyan. That big blue beastie over there is my partner Babe. Welcome to my camp stranger. I'd be pleased if you would share my vittles with me I hate to eat alone. Mighty different ride you got there." He looked at me and his mighty hand sort of made me cower as he reached over and scratched behind my ear as he said. "Nice looking little furry partner you got here what's his name?"

"His name is Sven and they call me Buffole. My ride is also one of my partners his name is Shag. We're mighty glad to make your acquaintance Mister Bunyan and Babe." Buffole unsaddled Shag and we settled down by the campfire with our new friends. Shag went over and hung out with Babe and the two of them seemed to get along real well.

As we sat jawing around the fire I had Buffole ask how it was that Babe happened to be blue in color.

Paul stroked his chin and sat back relaxed as a bear in hibernation and finally he answered our question. "First off you best call me Paul as nobody ever calls me Mister. As for Babe well I found him during the coldest winter any man has ever saw. Why it was so cold the fish all swam south and the snow itself turned blue. I heard a sound and went to investigate. Running around snorting and carrying on was a tiny ox. He was just plumb all upset 'cause the snow was so deep he could not see over it. The poor thing was so cold that he had turned blue as the snow around him. I took him home dried him off and fed him. Named him Babe because that's what he was when I found him just a babe in the woods lost and cold. Ever since then everyone calls him Babe the Blue Ox. He and I are the best logging team in the whole darn northwest. Now it's your turn to tell us about how you come to have a buffalo as a partner?"

Buffole smiled as he finished eating a mouth full of beans. "Well I sure as heck didn't rescue Shag he rescued me from a bunch of scoundrels that killed my family and was about to kill me. Shag and Sven are not only my partners they saved my life. We're heading to Deadwood to see if we can't locate some old acquaintances. Where are you and Babe heading?"

"Babe and me were out in the Northwest territories showing the boys out there how to do some real logging. Now I sort of miss my little gal Lucette so I'm heading to Hackensack Minnesota to see her. How about you Buffole you got a woman in your life? You know it can get mighty lonely traveling around with just your critters as company."

"Sure I got a woman I think about but I've got roaming in my blood for right now. I think Sven and Shag are enough company for a man like me."

The next few hours Paul and Buffole spent swapping tall tales. Paul had some pretty fantastic yarns to weave but my partner was doing pretty well in embellishing our own adventures. I started to feel like we had become western folklore heroes' by the time we all hit the sack for the night.

In the morning we shared breakfast with our new friends. Shag and Babe seemed sad that they had to leave so soon I think they had developed a rather close kinship with each other. After all how many times do you see a blue ox or a buffalo traveling with a human?

Paul and Buffole shook hands and wished each other good fortune in the future. I got a rather rough but lovable ear scratching from Paul before he mounted the saddle on Babes back. It was almost dream like meeting two friends like that. I knew we had not heard the last of Paul Bunyan and Babe the blue ox.

We watched as Babe and Paul rode off into the distance. Buffole and I cleaned up our campsite and prepared to make our way north. Shag told us he liked meeting Babe it was sort of like having a kindred spirit.

The three of us continued on our journey. A lot of wild and hostile country still lay before us. There was also a lot of beautiful country still to be seen. For now we rode along with pleasant thoughts of things we had done well and things we could have done better.

Deadwood would soon see us arrive. Shag, Buffole and me. Hopefully our reputation was unknown there and we could start a fresh new life. Maybe Buffole would have a letter waiting for him from Liza. Something like that could have a profound effect on our future.

THE END